IN THE COLD DARK GROUND

Stuart MacBride is the *Sunday Times* No. 1 bestselling author of the Logan McRae and Ash Henderson novels. His work has won several prizes and in 2015 he was awarded an honorary doctorate by Dundee University.

Stuart lives in the north-east of Scotland with his wife Fiona, cat Grendel, and other assorted animals.

For more information visit StuartMacBride.com
 Facebook.com/stuartmacbridebooks
@stuartmacbride

By Stuart MacBride

The Logan McRae Novels
Cold Granite
Dying Light
Broken Skin
Flesh House
Blind Eye
Dark Blood
Shatter the Bones
Close to the Bone
22 Dead Little Bodies
The Missing and the Dead
In the Cold Dark Ground

The Ash Henderson Novels
Birthdays for the Dead
A Song for the Dying

Other Works
Sawbones (a novella)
12 Days of Winter (short stories)
Partners in Crime (Two Logan and Steel short stories)
The 45% Hangover (a Logan and Steel novella)
The Completely Wholesome Adventures of Skeleton Bob
(a picture book)

Writing as Stuart B. MacBride
Halfhead

STUART MACBRIDE

IN THE COLD DARK GROUND

HARPER

Harper
An imprint of HarperCollins*Publishers*
1 London Bridge Street,
London SE1 9GF

www.harpercollins.co.uk

This paperback edition 2016

5

First published by HarperCollins*Publishers* 2016

Copyright © Stuart MacBride 2016

Stuart MacBride asserts the moral right to
be identified as the author of this work

A catalogue record for this book
is available from the British Library

ISBN: 978-0-00-749467-5

Set in Meridien by Palimpsest Book Production Limited, Falkirk, Stirlingshire

Printed and bound in Great Britain by
Clays Ltd, St Ives plc

MIX
Paper from
responsible sources
FSC™ C007454

www.fsc.org

For Twinkle, Brenda, Dolly Bellfield, and Jean.

Without Whom

As always I've received a lot of help from a lot of people while I was writing this book, so I'd like to take this opportunity to thank: Prof. Sue Black, Dr Roos Eisma, Vivienne McGuire, all at the University of Dundee's Centre for Anatomy and Human Identification and their principal & Vice-Chancellor, Professor Sir Pete Downes; PSD Chief Inspector Allan Ross, and Sergeant Bruce Crawford who answered far more daft questions than anyone should ever have to; Sarah Hodgson, Jane Johnson, Julia Wisdom, Jaime Frost, Louise Swannell, Laura Fletcher, Sarah Collett, Charlie Redmayne, Roger Cazalet, Kate Elton, Sarah Benton, Damon Greeney, Kate Stephenson, the eagle-eyed Anne O'Brien, Marie Goldie, the DC Bishopbriggs Naughty Posse, and everyone at HarperCollins, for doing such a stonking job; Phil Patterson and the team at Marjacq Scripts, for keeping my cat in shoes all these years; and Isla Anderson who helped raise money for a worthy cause to appear as a character in this book.

Of course, there wouldn't be any books without bookshops, booksellers, and book readers – so thank you all, you're stars.

And saving the best for last – as always – Fiona and Grendel.

— Three Days Ago —

He rolls over onto his side, blood pulsing from what's left of his nose. It stains his teeth dark pink. Bubbles at the side of his mouth. Explodes out in a shower of scarlet droplets as the boot slams into his bare stomach again. And again. And again.

He just twitches with the impact. Can't even defend himself – not with both hands tied behind his back. Can't do anything but bleed and groan, naked on the damp forest floor.

His lips move, but the words are broken mushy things forced out between ruined teeth. 'Gnnnnfnnnn … mmmm … nnngh…'

'Do you see?' A boot stamps down on his head. Something crunches. 'Do you see what happens?'

Blood drips onto the mat of rusting pine needles, making it dark and shiny. 'Nnnngh…'

Another voice: quiet, shaking. 'Please. Please, I'll do whatever you want. Please.'

'Damn right you will.'

A black plastic bin-bag crackles out like the wing of a giant bat. It soars above him for a moment, then gets yanked into place, enveloping his head. The scratchy growl of duct tape rips through the air.

And, at last, he finds enough breath to scream.

1

— Wednesday Dayshift —

in loving memory of those
not yet dead

1

Where the hell was Syd?

The song rambled to a halt, and the DJ was back. *'Wasn't that great? We've got JC Williams on in just a minute, talking about her latest book* PC Munroe and the Poisoner's Cat, *but first here's Stacy with all your eleven o'clock news and weather. Stacy?'*

Logan screwed the cap on his Thermos, popped it on the dashboard, then wrapped his hands around the plastic cup. Warmth seeped into his fingers, almost making it as far as the frozen bones. Tendrils of steam mixed with his breath, fogging the windscreen.

'Thanks, Bill. The hunt for missing Fraserburgh businessman, Martin Milne, continues today...'

He wriggled in his seat, pulling himself deeper into the stabproof vest, like a turtle. Knees together, rubbing slightly to get maximum itchiness from the black Police-Scotland-issue trousers. Took a sip from the Thermos lid.

Tea: hot and milky. Manna from heaven. Well, from the station canteen, but close enough.

'...concerned for his safety after his car was found abandoned in a lay-by outside Portsoy...'

Logan wiped a porthole in the passenger window.

Skeletal trees loomed on either side of the dirt track. Gunmetal puddles in ragged-edged potholes. The bare stalks of old nettles poked out of the yellow grass like the spears of a long-dead army. All fading into the dull grey embrace of February drizzle.

Something bright moved in the distance – where the oak and beech gave way to regular ranks of pine – a fluorescent-yellow high-viz smear. Then the woods swallowed it.

'...with any information to call one-zero-one. A teenage driver who crashed through the front window of Poundland in Peterhead was six times over the drink-drive limit...'

Sitting next to the Thermos, his mobile phone dinged, skittering an inch to the right as it vibrated. He grabbed it before it fell off the dashboard. Pressed his thumb on the text message icon.

```
Laz: call me back ASAP!
No screwing about — it's urgent!
Where the hell are you?!?
```

Sodding DCI Sodding Steel. Third time today.

'Leave me alone. I'm *working*, OK? That all right with you?'

He deleted the message. Scowled at the empty screen.

'...*eight pints of cider at a friend's eighteenth birthday party...*'

A pair of headlights sparked in the rear-view mirror: the cavalry had arrived. With any luck they'd brought biscuits with them.

'...*remanded in custody. The body of a young woman, discovered ten days ago in woods outside Inverurie, has been formally identified...*'

Logan took another sip of tea, then popped the door open, climbing out as a battered green Fiat lurched and rolled to a halt, windscreen wipers squealing across the glass.

Everything smelled of dirt and mould and green.

'...*Emily Benton, a nineteen-year-old philosophy student from Aberdeenshire...*'

The Renault's door clunked open and a man climbed out,

dressed in tatty black combat trousers and a quilted black fleece. Big grin on his face. Short grey hair circled a wide strip of shiny pink scalp. His breath steamed out into the drizzly morning. 'Fine day for it.' He pulled a baseball cap from his back pocket: black with 'POLICE' embroidered over a black-and-white checked strip. He put it on, hiding his bald patch from the rain.

Logan toasted him with the Thermos cup. 'Syd. You bring your hairy friends with you?'

'*Emily was last seen leaving the Formartine House Hotel on Saturday night...*'

Syd leaned back into the car and came out with a thick leather lead, draped it around his neck, under his arms, and clipped it behind his back, like DIY braces. 'Thought you and your minions already searched this one.'

'*...anxious to trace the driver of a red Ford Fiesta seen in the vicinity.*'

'Didn't find anything.' A shrug. 'Thanks for coming.'

'Forget about it.' Syd waved a hand. 'Only so many times you can watch *Lord of the Rings*.' He marched around to the back of the car and popped the boot open. A golden retriever scrabbled out onto the track, tail wagging, feet pounding round and round his master, nose up to him, mouth hanging open. 'You ready to put that nose back to work, Lusso? Are you? Yes you are. Yes you are.' He ruffled the dog's ears. 'Do you good to get off your backside and do some work for a change, you fat lump.'

'*...appeal for witnesses. Now, are you ready for Valentine's Day? Well, one enterprising teenager is auctioning his booking for a romantic meal for two at the Silver Darling restaurant in—*'

Logan clicked the radio off and downed the last of his tea. Pulled a padded high-viz jacket on over his stabproof vest, then dipped into the kitbag stuffed down into the rear footwell. Came out with a brown paper evidence bag. 'Here you go.'

'Socks?'

'Better.' Logan opened the bag and came out with a red

T-shirt. The company name was speckled with paint: 'GEIRRØD ~ CONTAINER MANAGEMENT AND LOGISTICS'

'Well, you never know your luck. Since we retired, Lusso's sniffed out nothing more challenging than other dogs' bumholes.' He unrolled a small fluorescent-yellow waistcoat thing and slipped it over the golden retriever's head, clipping the straps together behind its front legs. Then Syd took the T-shirt and wadded it up into a ball. Squatted down and held it under Lusso's shiny black nose. 'Big sniffs.'

Logan pulled on a pair of padded leather gloves. 'We set?'

'As we can be.' Syd stood, then swept his arm out in an arc, hand pointing towards the woods on one side of the track. 'Come on, Lusso: *find*.'

The dog scampered around them a couple of times, then its nose went down and it snuffled away.

They followed Lusso across the damp leaf litter, into the forest gloom, ducking under branches and crunching through brittle beige curls of dead bracken.

Logan nodded at the dog. 'What do you reckon?'

'Long shot, to be honest.' Syd tucked his hands into his pockets. 'If you're after dead bodies, cash, or explosives: Lusso's your dog, but this tracking thing...' He sucked on his teeth. 'Well, you never know.'

The musky brown scent of earth rose from the ground like a blanket, turning sharper and more antiseptic as they crossed the boundary from deciduous to evergreen. At least the *tops* of the trees were evergreen; down here, at ground level, everything was black and grey and jagged.

Through a clearing, tufted with heather and fringed with brambles.

Down a small ravine.

They clambered over a fallen tree, its roots sticking up into the air like a hairy shield.

Up a steep hill, puffing and panting by the time they reached the summit.

But there wasn't much of a view from the top, just more

dark trunks, stretching down and away into the distance. Merging together in the fog and drizzle.

Syd sniffed. 'Of course, trouble is, it's been so long since he's had to actually work, Lusso might think he's out for a walk.'

There was that.

'Well, at least we're—' Logan's mobile blared out its anonymous ringtone. He closed his eyes and sagged for a moment. Then straightened up. Pulled on a smile. 'Sorry. I'll catch up.'

He dug the phone out as Syd worked his way down the hill, following the wagging tail.

'McRae.'

A woman's voice. *'Logan? It's Louise from Sunny Glen.'*

And Logan sagged again.

The crackle and snap of Syd fighting his way through a clump of dead rosebay willowherb faded into silence. Somewhere in the distance a pigeon croooed.

'Logan? Hello?'

Deep breath. 'Louise.'

A sigh came from the earpiece. *'I know this isn't easy, Logan, it's a horrible thing, but there's nothing else we can do for her. If there was, I would. You know that.'*

Of course he did. Didn't make it any easier, though.

'Yeah…' He stared down at his boots. At the tufts of grey-green grass poking out between the dirty pine needles. 'When?'

'That's really up to you. Samantha's… You've been the best friend she could ever have hoped for, but it's time. It's just her time.' Another sigh. *'I'm sorry, Logan. I really am.'*

'Right. Yes. I understand.'

'We have a specialist counsellor you can speak to. She can help.'

Another smear of fluorescent yellow appeared away off to the right, before disappearing into the undergrowth again.

Four beeps sounded underneath his high-viz jacket, followed by a muffled voice. *'Shire Uniform Seven, safe to talk?'*

Logan unzipped the jacket and reached inside, feeling for

9

the Airwave handset. Leaving it on its clip while he pressed the button. 'Give us a minute, Tufty.'

Back to the phone.

Louise was still going: *'…all right? Logan? Hello?'*

'Sorry. I'm kind of in the middle of something.'

'You don't have to decide right away. We're not trying to rush you into anything. Take your time.'

'Yeah, I understand.' The stabproof vest held him tight in its Velcro embrace, keeping everything squeezed inside. 'Friday. We'll do it Friday.'

'Are you sure? Like I said, you don't have to—'

'No. Friday the thirteenth. Samantha would've liked that.'

'I'm sorry, Logan.'

'Yeah, me too.' He hung up and slipped the phone back into an inside pocket. Stared up at the heavy grey sky.

Friday.

When he breathed out, it was as if someone had attached weights to his lungs and stomach, dragging them down.

Another breath.

Then another.

And another.

Come on.

He blinked. Rubbed a hand across his face, wiping away a cold sheen of water. Hauled himself straight.

Then pressed the call button on his Airwave handset again. 'Tufty: safe to talk.'

'Sarge, we've done the loop again. No sign of Milne. You want us to try the burn?'

'Might as well.'

Dripping water made a slow-motion drumroll on the forest floor.

'Sarge?'

'What?'

'Can we go home soon? Only Calamity's gone all blue and purple. Last time I saw someone that colour they were lying on a mortuary slab. Bleeding freezing out here.'

10

'Tell her we'll give it another hour, then back home for tea and biscuits.'

'*Sarge.*'

Logan slithered his way down the hill, picking his way between the trees, following Syd's trail.

Silence blanketed the forest, the needles underfoot and the branches overhead smothering all sounds except the ones he made. Not even midday and it was already getting dark. The clouds overhead had blackened and crept lower. Gearing up for the change from breath-frosting drizzle to a full-on downpour. Maybe an hour was chancing their arm? Might be better to pack it up and try again tomorrow.

And after that it'd be someone else's problem.

A ding and a buzz against his ribcage marked another text message coming into his mobile. No point checking: it'd be Steel. It was *always* Steel.

Wah, wah, wah, why haven't you called me back? What I want is *much* more important than anything you're doing. Wah, wah, wah...

He left his phone in its pocket. Kept going.

It wasn't too hard to follow Syd. His feet had left a scuffed path through the needles, the layer below darker than the ones on the surface. It wound its way between the trees, scratching a zigzag line down and off to the left. Where—

Was that a shout?

Yes. Somewhere off in the distance, but definitely there.

Logan stopped, cupped his hands around his mouth in a makeshift loudhailer. 'SYD?'

Another shout.

Nope, still no idea what he was saying.

Needles slipped beneath Logan's feet as he hurried down the slope and up the other side. 'SYD?'

He froze at the crown of the hill, surrounded by boulders and Scots pine. The ground fell away in front of him: a steep incline punctuated by rocks and gorse between hundreds of circular stumps where the trees had been harvested. A dirt track ran along the bottom of the hill, with another clump of gorse on the other side.

Syd stood in front of it, waving his arms like he was trying to guide a plane in to land. Lusso lay on the ground at his feet, hairy yellow tail sweeping back and forth through the mud.

Logan tried again: 'WHAT IS IT?'

Whatever Syd shouted back, it was swallowed by the wind and rain.

'Sodding hell.' No choice for it then. Logan scrambled down the slope, feet sideways to the drop, skirting the dark-green needles of gorse. Windmilling his arms as a clump of mud shifted beneath him, threatening to send him tumbling.

Keep going...

He clattered onto the track and skidded to a halt before he went over the edge and into a drainage ditch thick with rust-coloured water.

Syd sniffed. 'Took your time.'

'What?'

He raised a finger and pointed at a patch of broom. 'In there.'

Logan smoothed down the front of his high-viz jacket, then stepped over the ditch and onto the bank on the other side. 'Can't see any—'

'Keep going.'

Another couple of steps up the bank and... OK.

There was a dip in the earth: semicircular with a chunk of lichen-covered granite at one end. Stalks of dead weeds poked up through the yellowed grass. And right in the middle, lying flat on its back, was the body of a man. Naked. Hands behind him. One leg crooked out at the knee, the foot resting against his other shin.

His torso was a tie-die pattern of purples, blues, and yellows fringed with green, the bruises spaced randomly across pale-grey skin slick with drizzle.

Syd's voice came from the other side of the bush. 'That him?'

Logan blew out a breath. 'Difficult to tell...'

The head was covered with black plastic – like a bin-bag – fixed around the neck with thick strands of silver duct tape. There was a strange smell too. Maybe bleach?

The pubic hair was a sickly yellowy-white, so it *could* be bleach.

Probably bleach.

Someone covering their tracks, trying to make sure they hadn't left any DNA or trace evidence behind that could be identified. Yeah, good luck with that. Something always survived.

Another smell lay under the bleach, something sweet and meaty and cloying. Like a chunk of mince, forgotten about at the back of the fridge, a couple of days past its sell-by date.

Definitely dead.

Logan unzipped his jacket and pulled out his Airwave handset. Punched in the Duty Inspector's shoulder number. 'Bravo India from Shire Uniform Seven, safe to talk?'

Inspector McGregor's voice crackled out of the speaker, sounding slightly plummy, as if she was eating something. *'Go ahead, Logan.'*

'Guv? I think we might have found Martin Milne...'

2

'Sarge?' Tufty pulled his eyebrows in, made his watery blue eyes all big and puppy-dog. Pouted, sinking his cheeks even further into his bony face. 'Just in case: someone's planning a surprise party Monday, right?'

Droplets pattered off the peak of his cap, hissed through the needles on the trees, rippled the puddles at their feet.

'Monday?' Logan ducked in under a pine, using the canopy of needles to keep the worst of the rain off. Up above, between the branches, the sky was nearly touching the treetops. Heavy and dark.

'Well, Tuesday morning. I know we don't get off nightshift till seven, and most places will be shut, but someone's organizing something, right?'

Logan punched Calamity's shoulder number into his Airwave handset. 'Constable Nicholson, safe to talk?'

A crackle, then her voice came through: *'On my way back now, Sarge. I've taped the road off at the junction.'*

Tufty pulled one shoulder up to his ear. 'Because it's a big thing, isn't it? Not every day you go from being a probationer to a full-blown instrument of justice.'

'You got the tarpaulin, Calamity?'

'What's that supposed to mean? Course I've got the tarpaulin.'

'Well hurry up then. Tufty's going to suffer fatal rectal

14

boot-poisoning if I have to put up with his whingeing much longer.'

There was a little pout, then Tufty inched closer, peering down at the body. 'Funny, isn't it? Soon as you cover a person's face like that, you make them less … human. Like it's not really a person any more.'

'It's still a person.' Logan put his Airwave back on its clip. Cupped his hands to his mouth and blew, filling them with warm fog. 'Wonder how long he's been lying there?'

Tufty ducked, then worked his way through the jagged branches of the tree next to Logan's, until his back was against the trunk. 'First week I was on the job, there was this motorbike crash. Young woman, a girl really, didn't make the corner – straight through a barbed-wire fence. She wasn't wearing a helmet.'

'All this rain. Probably not a lot of trace left on the body. Might get fibres off the bin-bag, though.'

'Head came clean off.'

Then there was the bleach. If whoever did it bleached the body while it was lying here, they might not have turned it over to do its back. Could be DNA there, protected from the rain and the elements.

'Searched for *ages*.' Tufty frowned. 'I found it in a clump of dead nettles. She was staring up at me with this confused look on her face. Surreal…'

The dirt track was the obvious point of entry to the scene. No sign of any tyre marks, though. So, they probably carried the body here from wherever they'd parked. Strange to go to all that effort when you could have just pitched it out of the boot.

Maybe the road was blocked?

Or maybe the victim was still alive when they got here? Maybe the killer made them walk from the car to here? Jesus, how frightened would you be? Naked, hands tied behind your back, picking your way along the forest road, knowing that when you got to where you were going, you'd be dead.

'Anyway, we stuck the two bits back together and: bang, suddenly she was a person again. Never thrown up so much in my life.' He shuddered, then blew out a billow of steamy breath. 'See that? Probably getting frostbite.'

'Feel free to shut up at any point.'

Syd appeared from the woods behind them, hands dug deep into his pockets, golden retriever trotting in lazy circles around him. 'Nothing.'

Logan shrugged. 'Worth a go. Thanks anyway.'

'Been nice to get out and do something for a change. Retirement's not all it's cracked up to be. A lifetime of fixing-up the house and garden, DIY as far as the eye can see...' A shudder. 'Like a wheelbarrow: always in front of you.'

Lusso loped over to Tufty and stuck his nose in the constable's groin.

'Errr...' Tufty flattened himself against the tree. 'Doesn't bite, does he?'

'Anyway, if you don't need me, I'll head off. She Who Must wants a trip to B&Q. Apparently the spare room needs new wallpaper.'

'We'll give you a shout about a statement.'

'*And* that pint you owe me.' Then Syd clapped his hands. 'Come on, Lusso, leave the poor wee loon's winkie alone. We're going home.'

A bark made Tufty flinch, then the golden retriever turned and trotted after its master. Up the slope and away into the forest.

Tufty wiped a hand down the front of his trousers, as if reassuring the contents that the nasty doggie had gone. Then squinted up at the heavy grey sky. 'Think it's cold enough to snow?'

Probably.

The rain fell.

And fell.

And fell.

Sod this. He punched Maggie's number into his handset. 'Maggie, safe to talk? You got an ETA for us yet?'

'*As far as I know they're en route, Sergeant McRae.*'

'Well … if you hear anything, let us know, OK? It's hammering down out here.'

He hooked the Airwave back into place, wrapped his arms around himself and tucked his hands into the armholes of his stabproof vest.

Tufty made a sound like a deflating whoopee cushion. 'First time in my life I'm actually looking forward to a Major Investigation Team waltzing in and taking over. Let *them* stand about in the rain for a change.' He stamped his feet. 'How long's it take to get up here from Aberdeen, anyway? What are they doing, *walking*?'

'You remember what I said about rectal boot-poisoning?'

And the rain fell.

'Up your end a bit…' Logan tugged at the tarpaulin. Then nodded. 'OK, pin it down.'

Calamity lowered a rock onto the edge of the blue plastic. Then another one. And another. Her black bob stuck to the sides of her face in rain-twisted strands, making her look a bit like a damp crow. She sniffed, then wiped a gloved hand under her pointy nose. Every time she bent over, water poured out from the brim of her bowler hat, spattering down her high-viz jacket. 'Can't feel my fingers.'

'Just in case: we're having a celebration after work on Tuesday morning, aren't we? For Tufty's coming out party?'

Calamity thunked another rock into place. 'Thought Isla was organizing something.'

'Do me a favour and check, OK?' He tugged on the tarpaulin, securing the last corner with a big lump of quartz. 'He'll sulk for months if we don't.'

She stood and stretched, hands in the small of her back, staring down at their makeshift crime-scene marquee. 'What do you think: is this Martin Milne?'

'Hope so.'

'What if it's not?'

Logan ducked under the tree again. Waved Calamity over and dug out his phone.

She squeezed in under the branches next to him as he scrolled through the photos of a naked man, lying on his back on a forest floor, with a black plastic bag duct-taped over his head. 'Got one distinguishing feature.' He zoomed in on the left shoulder – a tattoo was just visible through the multicolour rainbow of bruises – held the phone out. 'That look like a dolphin to you?'

She squinted, tilted her head to one side. 'Could be a whale…? No, look, it's got a unicorn horn: narwhal.'

'Is it?' He took the phone back and frowned at it. 'Could be. Did Martin Milne have a tattoo?'

'You know what I think?' Calamity pointed a toe at the tarpaulin. 'Serial killer.'

Logan put his phone away. 'That's not funny.'

'Isn't meant to be. Look at it: middle of nowhere, dead body, dumped with a bag over its head.'

'Calamity—'

'And it's not the first one, either. What about that student, Emily Something, turned up dead in woods near Inverurie a week and a half ago?' Calamity nodded to herself. 'Could be *dozens* of dead bodies out there, dumped in woodland all over the northeast.'

'You been watching Scandinavian crime dramas again?'

'Five quid says the post mortem turns up sexual activity, before and after death. That's what the bag's for: he's dehumanized the victim by hiding the face. Doesn't want to be looked at while he does his thing.'

'Don't you start as well. Had enough of the "doesn't look like a person" thing from Tufty.'

'Exactly my point. There's a murder victim lying right there.' She pointed. 'Someone's brother, father, son, husband. Someone with hopes and dreams, like you and me. And we're standing here chatting about Tufty's party. Been dehumanized.'

Ah…

Logan put his phone away. 'Fair enough.'

'Another fiver says we find the next body before the fortnight's out.'

'Get on to Isla: see if we've got any missing persons with a narwhal tattoo on their left shoulder.' A frown. 'Actually, don't. Tell her *any* sort of tattoo will do. Don't care if it's a dolphin, elephant, narwhal, or Sandi Toksvig riding a unicycle, if there's a misper with a tattoo on their arm I want to know about it.'

'Sarge.'

'With any luck we'll solve this before the MIT turn up and trample over everything.'

Calamity got on the Airwave. 'Constable Nicholson for Constable Anderson, safe to talk?'

A tiny voice crackled out of the speaker, sounding as if it belonged to a wee girl. *'Go for it, Calamity.'*

'Isla, I need you to search the misper database for us...'

Then a piercing whistle crackled from the brow of the hill and there was Tufty, waving. A man in an overcoat struggled up next to him, then another, and a third. All with mud clarted up to the knees of their suit trousers.

Speak of the devils and they shall appear.

They struggled their way down the hill, holding on to each other in an admirably stupid display of team spirit. Meaning if one of them went down he'd take the other two with him.

At least Tufty had the common sense to steer clear of them. He picked his own path through the gorse and tree stumps, until he stood in front of Logan. Then jerked a thumb at the suits. 'Found this lot wandering in the woods, Sarge. Can we keep them?'

The tallest of the three picked spiny green bristles out of his navy overcoat. 'We were *not* wandering.' Water dripped from the brim of his trilby hat, something else dripping from the end of his little pink nose. A sniff. Then he raised his hat, showing off a spiky mop of gelled blond hair. 'Logan.'

'Well, well, well. Defective Sergeant Simon Rennie, as I live and breathe.' Logan smiled, then lowered his eyes to Rennie's dirt-spattered trousers. 'Were we playing in the puddles?'

'Bloody place is like a swamp. With trees. And mud. A muddy foresty swamp.' He stuck his hat back on. 'Steel's on her way. Till she gets here, this is DC Owen…'

Owen – a broad-shouldered lump of a man with greying curls plastered to his head by the rain. A nod. 'Sarge.' His teeth looked as if they'd been designed for a mouth three times bigger than his, poking out at all angles.

'…and this is DC Anthony "Spaver" Fraser.'

Fraser's nose had been destined for the same oversized face as Owen's teeth. 'Sergeant.' He jerked it in the direction of the tarpaulin. 'That our body?'

'Not yet it isn't.' Logan held his hand out towards Tufty. 'Constable Quirrel, pass me the Sacred Wooden Stick of Crime-Scene Dominion.'

There was a pause as Tufty blinked at him. Then realization must have dawned, because two seconds later a branch was pressed into Logan's grasp. It wasn't big – about two foot long, with a forked bit at the top. 'Here you go.'

Logan offered it to Rennie. 'Do you accept the Sacred Stick?'

A lopsided grin. Then he took the little branch and held it aloft as if he'd just pulled Excalibur from the stone. Posing. 'I hereby claim this crime scene for Detective Chief Inspector Roberta Tiberius Steel and the glory of the Sontaran Empire!'

'Good for you.' Logan wiped bits of bark from his palm. 'Body's an IC-one male: tattoo on the upper left arm. Heavy bruising to the torso, bin-bag over the head. Duty doctor, Procurator Fiscal, pathologist, and Scenes Examination Branch have been informed.' He turned. 'Tufty, Calamity: pack up, we're out of here.'

She shifted the Airwave handset to her other ear and nodded.

Rennie frowned. 'But what about guarding the scene? Aren't you going to—'

'Not our scene any more. You've got the Sacred Stick, remember?'

His eyebrows went up, making a short row of wrinkles between them. 'But—'

'Body was probably dumped using the logging road. Get someone to search for tyre tracks. And don't stand there with your gob hanging open, you look like a goldfish.'

A click, as Rennie closed his mouth. 'Can't we just—'

'Probably not. But make sure you get your common approach path sorted before the PF and the Pathologist get here, or they'll make you eat your hat.' Logan patted him on the shoulder. 'Oh, and I want my tarpaulin back when you've finished with it.'

The hill was a lot steeper on the way up than the way down, and by the time they reached the top sweat was trickling down between Logan's shoulder blades and into his pants. He paused at the crest, looking back towards the makeshift SOC tent, breath fogging the air in thick white puffs.

Calamity's face had gone all flushed and shiny. She gave him a lopsided grimace. 'Got a bad feeling about this.'

'They've investigated murders before.'

'Only two types of people wear trilby hats, Sarge: auld mannies and tossers.'

'Really?' Tufty unzipped his high-viz jacket and flapped the sides. Steam rose from his stabproof vest. 'I think they're kinda cool.'

'Which proves my point.' She took off her bowler hat and fanned herself with it. 'And why's he holding that stick?'

'He thinks it makes him in charge. How did you get on with Maggie?'

'Strange stick obsession and a trilby hat.' Calamity did a bit more grimacing. 'He's a tosser, isn't he?'

'Detective Sergeant Rennie isn't a tosser.'

Down at the base of the slope, Rennie was directing his constables as they did a preliminary sweep of the scene

21

– standing on a tree stump and using the Sacred Stick like a conductor's baton. He was getting into it, swinging his arms about, wheeching the stick back and forth.

Logan bared his teeth. 'OK, he's a bit of a tosser. But…'

Rennie slipped and went flat on his backside in the middle of the track.

'Actually, I'm going to leave it there.'

'And they made *that* a detective sergeant.' Calamity sighed. 'Isla says we've got half a dozen mispers on the books with tattoos. That's going back three years, including the unsolveds.'

'Half a dozen?' Tufty stopped flapping. 'How many without tattoos?'

'Hundred and twelve.' She shrugged. 'Half the time no one bothers to tell us Uncle Stinky's come home. Other half…' Another shrug.

One of the DCs – Owen, was it? – hauled Rennie to his feet. Then picked up the stick and handed it back to him.

Yeah, because *that* was a good idea.

Probably end up putting someone's eye out with it.

'Don't suppose it matters now. Not our case. It's theirs.' Logan stuck his hands in his pockets. Still, it wouldn't hurt to take an interest, would it? Just in case. He cleared his throat. 'Don't suppose any of our tattooed half-dozen have a narwhal on their upper left arm?'

'Nope. Or if they do it's not in the database.' She folded her arms, staring down at the three-man advance unit from Steel's MIT. 'Look at them. Here we are, serial killer on the loose, and our only hope for catching him is Tweedle-Dee, Tweedle-Dum, and their boss: Tweedle-Dumber.'

Couldn't really argue with that.

'Come on, we've got a division to police.'

Logan turned his back and headed for the car.

3

'COME BACK HERE, YOU WEE SOD!'

But Lumpy Patrick was off, bone-thin arms and legs pumping for all he was worth. Long greasy strands of hair flapping about like damp string as he sprinted. Pilfered packs of bacon and cheese cascading from the pocket of his stained brown hoodie.

Logan grabbed hold of his peaked cap and gave chase through the rain.

They hammered down High Street with its strange collection of old stone buildings and harled monstrosities.

A lunge to the left and Lumpy sprinted across the road by the wee hidden library. A rusty Vauxhall Nova slammed on its brakes, the horn screeching out like an angry badger. Logan nipped across the back of it, picking up a bit of speed on the downhill run.

More tiny Scottish houses, their dark stone walls and slate roofs slick with rain.

A soggy woman at the bus stop watched them wheech past. Cigarette in one hand, can of energy drink in the other, screaming toddler kicking off in a pushchair.

Lumpy got to the corner and skidded round onto Skene Street, heading downhill back towards the centre of Macduff. Two packs of streaky and a chunk of cheddar went flying out into the road, where they were flattened by a Transit van.

Logan followed, pulse thumping in his ears – past rows of old grey buildings, past the chip shop, across the road, past the Plough Inn where a couple of damp smokers, sheltering in the doorway, stopped mid-fag to cheer Lumpy on.

He almost collided with an auld mannie coming out of Buttons & Bobs, skittered around him instead with some fancy footwork in his stained trainers, dropped another pack of smoked streaky, and kept on going. Ignoring the OAP's torrent of abuse and rude gestures hurled at his back.

The gap was narrowing. Logan lengthened his stride, kept his mouth open. Long slow breaths, free arm swinging, the other keeping his hat in place.

Sploshed through a puddle.

Where the hell was Calamity?

Then a gap opened up between the buildings on the right – at street level, the house on this side looked single storey, but the ground dropped away sharply on the other side of a wall, had to be at least twenty feet.

Lumpy didn't even pause: he vaulted up onto the wall and jumped, arms windmilling.

Sod that.

Logan screeched to a halt, grabbed the wall.

A line of garages stretched away from him, about twelve feet down: parking for the four-storey block of flats on the other side of the gap. Lumpy was back on his feet, limping along the line of corrugated roofs.

Gah.

Deep breath. Then up. Logan scrambled onto the wall and over the other side. Dropping like a breezeblock. The garage roof rushed up to meet him, then *BANG* he was through it, clattering into the empty garage in a hail of broken grey slabs and dust.

The concrete floor was a lot less forgiving.

Ow…

He lay there, flat on his back, staring up at the drizzle.

Dragged in a ragged breath.

Everything hurt. Arms, legs, back, head. Even his teeth hurt.

Probably did himself a serious injury.

Probably broke something, other than the roof, in the fall.

Probably going to die of a punctured lung, right here on the garage floor, and no one would know till the owner of whatever flat it belonged to came home and discovered his body.

Ow...

And then his Airwave bleeped at him. Calamity's voice came through, sounding out of breath. *'Shire Uniform ... Seven, ... safe to talk?'*

Come on. Up.

He raised his head off the floor an inch. The garage was a mess, littered with bits of broken roof. Lined with stacks of cardboard boxes all bound up with parcel tape.

Up!

Nope.

Let his head thunk back down again.

Here lie the mortal remains of Logan Balmoral McRae, between the old copies of *National Geographic* and that fondue set we got from Aunty Christine and never used. Decorated police officer. Absent son. Dutiful boyfriend. Sperm-donor father of two little monsters. He is survived by a girlfriend in a coma, a small fuzzy cat called Cthulhu, and a huge credit card bill.

His Airwave bleeped again. *'Shire Uniform Seven? Sarge? Are you OK?'*

No.

He struggled onto his side. Then to his knees.

Ow...

Pressed the talk button. 'Where *were* you?'

'Got him, Sarge. Lumpy was pelting full tilt down Low Shore – pulled out right in front of him.' A laugh. *'You should've seen*

it, went sprawling across the bonnet, all arms and legs and packets of Edam.'

Logan hauled himself upright, wobbled a little. Leaned on the wall. 'Come get me.'

The coast slid by the window, grey and dreich, robbed of colour by the driving rain. The Big Car's wipers squeaked and squonked across the glass, thumping at the end of each smeared arc. The noise fought against the roaring blowers – on full, and losing the battle against Lumpy Patrick's truly *unique* odour.

Rancid onions and garlic and off cheese, underpinned by something warm, diseased, and peppery.

'God's sake…' Calamity buzzed her window down an inch, letting in the roar of the road and the hiss of the rain. 'Did you go swimming in a septic tank, Lumpy?'

He was hunched in the back seat, with his hands cuffed behind his back, unwashed hair covering his face, hiding him from the rear-view mirror. 'Said I was sorry.'

Logan turned away and stared out of the passenger window. The North Sea pounded against the cliffs, slate grey against dirty brown. Or was it the Moray Firth here? Either way it wasn't happy.

Calamity shuddered. 'You sure we can't put the blues and twos on, Sarge?'

'Sharing an enclosed space with Lumpy Patrick isn't an emergency. Police Scotland frowns on that kind of thing.'

A sniff from the back seat. 'Not my fault. It's my glands.'

'It's being allergic to soap and water.'

More rain. More cliffs.

Then the road twisted away inland.

Another sniff. 'This shoplifting thing. Any chance, you know: slap on the wrists and that? Learned my lesson. Promise to be a good boy in the future?'

Calamity laughed. 'You're kidding, right? How many times is this now? Sheriff's probably going to make an example of you, Lumpy. Can't have druggies nicking all the bacon and cheese in Banff and Macduff.'

'Didn't nick it. I was... It... Hold on. I found it. Yeah. Found it.'

'Course you did.' Logan shifted his legs in the footwell. Grimaced as little shards of ice gouged through his left ankle. Bloody garage roof. What was the point of building a garage if the roof wasn't sturdy enough for someone to land on it without going straight through?

'You know what, Lumpy?' She threw a scowl at the rear-view mirror. 'I tried to get some smoked streaky for butties yesterday and there wasn't a single pack in Tesco *or* the Copey. You and your druggy mates had the lot on five-finger discount.'

More shards of ice when he rotated the ankle left and right. Should've strapped it up and stuck some frozen peas on it. Probably be the size of a melon by the time they reached Fraserburgh station.

'What do you think, Sarge? Four months? Out in two with good behaviour?'

Not to mention all the paperwork needed to compensate the garage's owner.

'You're screwed, Lumpy.' Calamity grinned. 'But look on the bright side: at least you'll get regular showers in the nick. It'll do your social life a world of good, not smelling like a dead sheep.'

She slowed down for the limits at New Aberdour. Then put her foot down again a minute later when they'd passed through the matching set on the way out. Then buzzed her window down a little further. 'Can't believe we've got to suffer this all the way to Fraserburgh.'

The kettle rattled and pinged its way to a boil. A dirty-cauliflowery smell pervaded the canteen, giving it the unwelcome ambience of a hospital waiting room. The place was at least four times bigger than the one back at Banff station, with not one but *two* vending machines, an open-plan kitchen area, a picture window, a row of recycling bins, comfy sofas, big flatscreen TV, and enough space to hold a reasonably intimate ceilidh if you moved the four tables up against the walls.

A faint buzzing oozed out of vending machine number two – which was out of chocolate – competing with the mindless drone of some Cash-in-the-Bargain-Hunt-Cheap-and-Nasty-Antiques-Car-Boot-Sale rubbish coming from the TV.

Logan retrieved the remote and switched the TV off, killing a permatanned idiot mid-ramble, leaving nothing but buzzing and rattling in the large yellow room that smelled like hospitals.

He put the remote control down.

A voice, behind him. 'What's with the face?'

Logan didn't look around. 'Just thinking.'

'Sounds dangerous.'

He turned back to the kettle as it clicked itself off. Dumped a teabag in a dayglow pink mug with 'WORLD'S GREATEST DUTY SERGEANT' printed around the outside. Poured boiled water in on top. 'You want a tea?'

'Can't. Persistent vegetative state, remember?'

'Yeah…' He stirred the bag, turning the water brown. 'Do you think you'll feel anything? When they switch you off?'

Her hand was warm on his shoulder. 'When *they* switch me off?'

Logan dug the bag out of the mug with the spoon. Squeezed it against the side to make it bleed. 'Will it hurt?'

'What's this "they" business? After all we've been through, you're wimping out on me?'

Milk.

'Don't make me…'

'Logan.' A pause. Then the hand on his shoulder squeezed. 'Logan, look at me.'

He puffed out a breath. Put the semi-skimmed down on the countertop. Turned.

Her hair glowed scarlet in the canteen lights. Tribal tattoos poked out from the sleeves of her skull-and-crossbones T-shirt, their spikes mixing with skulls and hearts and swirls. But the ink wasn't bright and vibrant any more, it was faded and grey, as if she'd been photocopied one time too many. A gold ring looped through the edge of one nostril, semi-precious stones glittering in lines up the outside edge of her ears. She smiled at him and the small stainless-steel ball bearing that stuck out below her bottom lip turned into a dimple. 'I'm not going to feel anything, OK?' Samantha draped her arms over his shoulders, stepping in close. 'I died five years ago. This is just housekeeping.'

'That why I don't... I don't really *feel* anything?'

'Hmmm.' She sighed. 'Speaking of which: this morning, the body in the woods. You used to care, Logan. You used to feel for them. You used to empathize. What happened?'

Outside the picture window, rain lashed the streets of Fraserburgh, drummed on the roof of parked cars. Sent an old man with an umbrella hurrying across the road.

Logan frowned. Shrugged. 'I was just doing my job. You heard what Calamity said: covering the face dehumanized the body. Made it less of a person. Doesn't mean I don't care.'

'Maybe it's not the victim who's been dehumanized.'

The old man lost hold of his umbrella and it went dancing away in the wind, pirouetting and whirling into the distance as its owner stumped after it.

To add insult to injury, a small red hatchback wheeched past on the road, right through a puddle that sent a wall of water crashing over the stumpy man. He stood there, arms out, dripping, staring after the disappearing car.

'Logan?' Samantha pulled his face back to hers. 'I'm worried about you.'

'If that auld mannie's any sort of proper Brocher, he's going to hunt them down and shove that umbrella up their backsides. Then open it.'

'Logan, I'm serious.'

He closed his eyes and rested his forehead against hers. 'I'm doing my best.'

'I know you are. But if you leave it to someone else to switch me off on Friday, I swear on God's Holy Banjo I'll rise from the grave and kick your pasty—'

'Sarge?'

Logan blinked. Cleared his throat. 'Calamity.'

'That's Lumpy Patrick been processed. Says he doesn't want a lawyer, which is a first. With any luck we can burst him and get back to Banff before half three.' She looked left, then right, checking no one was eavesdropping. 'Or, if you're still strapped for cash, we could spin it out a bit for the overtime?'

A deep breath hissed its way out. 'Right. Yes. No. Let's get home.'

'You OK, Sarge?'

He forced a smile. 'Vending machine's out of chocolate.'

Little creases appeared between her eyebrows. 'You *sure* you're OK? Was one hell of a fall. We could get the duty doctor in?'

'It's fine. Never better. Now, did—' His phone launched into 'The Imperial March' from *Star Wars*, dark and ominous. He closed his eyes. Scrunched his face up. 'Great.' Then sighed and pulled his mobile out. Nodded at Calamity. 'Stick Lumpy in Interview Two – and make sure the window's open. I'll be with you in a minute.' As soon as she left the room, he pressed the button. 'What?'

A pause. Then Steel's voice grated out of the earpiece, like smoked gravel. *'That any way to talk to a Detective Chief Inspector, you cheeky wee sod?'* She snorted. *'And what the hell were you thinking, turning up a body in the middle of nowhere, in the mud and the rain? Shoes are like squelchy buckets of yuck now.'*

'Is there a point to this call, or did you just ring up to moan? Only I'm off shift in ten, and I've got a suspect to interview. So…?'

'Oh aye? And what's your suspect saying to it? You got a line on my victim you're no' sharing with me?'

'OK, I'm hanging up now.'

'*Oh don't be such a girl, Laz.*' There was a sooking noise. Then a sigh. '*Called to do you a favour. Our beloved Chief Superintendent Napier – the Ginger Ninja, the Nosy Nosferatu, the Copper-Top Catastrophe, the Duracell Devil himself – is on the prowl. So watch your back... Hold on.*' A muffled conversation happened in the background, the words too far away to hear properly.

Samantha raised her eyebrows. Pointed at the phone. Made the universal hand gesture for onanism. 'Oh, and I want a *proper* send off. Black coffin, red silk lining, all my bits and bobs, OK? Full battle-paint. And that leather corset. Not going to meet the worms dressed like someone's mum.'

'Anything else, your ladyship?'

'Yes. Cheer up, for God's sake. You've got a face like a skelped backside.'

And Steel was back. '*Swear I'm going to swing for that idiot Rennie before the day's out.*' She made a little growling noise, then sniffed. '*Right, where were we? Yes: Napier. Slimy git retires in a couple of months, and he wants to go out with a bang. That means stitching some poor sod up. And you* know *he's always had a hard-on for you and me. Let's not hand him a threesome, eh?*'

Now there was an image. 'Don't care. Let him dig, I'm clean.'

Well, kind of...

Ish...

If you didn't count the whole flat-selling fiasco. Which Napier most certainly would if he ever found out about it. Logan ran a hand across his face. He wouldn't find out. Never.

There was no way he could.

Could he?

'*Laz, you still there?*'

Logan cleared his throat. 'It'll be fine.' Or it would all go horribly wrong. 'Right, got to go: suspect waiting. Give Jasmine and Naomi my love, OK?' He hung up before she could answer.

Then switched his phone off, just in case.

31

4

Even with the window open, Interview Room Two *stank*. The cause sat on the low bench on the other side of the small white table. Fidgeting.

Lumpy Patrick's arms stuck out from the sleeves of his T-shirt like dirty pipe cleaners. They were little more than bone, the muscles knotted bungee cords, stretched taut and thrumming. Skin peppered with dark pocked scars where the needles had tracked time and time again. His hands had taken on a brown-grey tinge, a mixture of dirt and ... more dirt. Ragged black crescents for fingernails. Sunken cheeks and eyes the colour of Tabasco – fringed with clumps of yellow. And when he spoke, the smell of a thousand backed-up toilets spewed into the room. 'I want you to let us off on the shoplifting.'

Logan pulled as far back into his seat as possible. Breathing through the side of his mouth. 'And why would we do something silly like that?'

''Cos it's just bacon and cheese, yeah? Not like it's anything major.'

He picked up a clear evidence bag and held it in front of Lumpy's face. 'For the tape, I am now showing Mr Hay the two wrappers of heroin found in his pocket when he was arrested.' Logan put them back down again. 'And before you deny it: we know they're heroin, because we tested them.'

'Ah...' A nod sent greasy wisps of hair rocking. 'Well, *supposing* I told you where you could, like, get a whole lot more of that stuff? Yeah, right?' His pale tongue crawled out between his chapped lips, glistening. Then Lumpy leaned forward, enveloping Logan in his stench. 'Way I hear it, Ma Campbell's got herself a shipment coming up from Weegietown. Yeah?' He held his filthy hands up, about two feet apart. 'Big shipment. You like that?'

Calamity leaned back against the wall by the open window. 'Who's the delivery for?'

'Oh no. We do us a deal first, yeah? I tell you stuff, we forget all about the shoplifting and that. Deal?'

'Depends on whether you're telling us the truth or not.' Logan pulled out his pen and pointed it across the table. 'Who's it for?'

The smile that bloomed on Lumpy's face was like watching something rot, it exposed a set of grey gums almost devoid of teeth. 'You know Ricky Welsh?'

That got him a groan from Calamity. 'Oh God. Not Ricky and Laura...'

'Yeah. Big shipment coming in from Glasgow. All them Weegie drugs.'

Logan tapped his pen against his notebook. 'Not meaning to be funny, Lumpy, but are you seriously sitting there clyping on Ricky and Laura Welsh? After what happened to Abby Ritchie?'

When Lumpy shrugged, his whole body slumped to the side, until the ends of his hair made little oily marks on the table. 'Me civic duty, isn't it? Can't have Weegie imports ruining it for local businessmen. Not right.'

Yeah, because Lumpy Patrick was a fine upstanding member of the Banff and Macduff Chamber of Commerce.

Logan clicked his pen out. 'When and where?'

'Noooo. First we gotta talk my reward for being civic. I

get...' He tilted his head, coiling more hair on the tabletop. 'Three thousand quid *and* you get me off on the shoplifting and possession. Yeah?'

Outside, a car grumbled past.

The rain hissed down on the world outside, the sound clear through the open window as the vertical blinds swayed in the breeze.

A phone rang somewhere in the depths of the station.

Calamity was the first one to crack, spluttering out a snigger that exploded into a full-on laugh.

Logan wasn't far behind, rocking back in his chair, hooting. Letting it ring out.

Lumpy just stared at them.

Eventually the laughter rattled to a halt.

Logan sighed. Wiped his eyes. 'Priceless.'

'Three grand, Lumpy?' Calamity shook her head, still grinning. 'You'll be lucky if we don't bang you up for wasting police time. Remember the last red-hot tip of yours?'

He shifted on his bench. Lowered his voice and his gaze. 'Wasn't my fault.'

'Any idea how many crimes we could've been solving, instead of traipsing round the countryside trying to find your non-existent dealer from Newcastle?'

'Wasn't my *fault*.'

'And now you're giving us this rubbish about Ma Campbell and the Welshes?'

Logan tapped the pad again. 'Who do you owe three grand to?'

No answer.

'Come on, Lumpy. You didn't come up with that figure out of the blue, you owe someone, don't you? Let me guess...' Logan bit down on his bottom lip for a moment. 'It wouldn't be *Ricky Welsh*, by any chance, would it? That'd be a coincidence. You owe him a big chunk of cash, and here you are dobbing him in.'

Calamity sucked a breath through her teeth. 'Lumpy,

Lumpy, Lumpy. Clyping on someone you owe money to, just so we'll bang them up and you won't have to pay them back. Should be ashamed of yourself.'

'No!' Lumpy's bottom lip wobbled for a bit. Then he shrugged his way down to the tabletop, so his cheek was resting against the chipped white surface. 'Civic duty...'

'OK. Well, we're done here.' Logan stood. 'Good luck sorting things out with the Welshes. I'm sure Laura will be very understanding when she finds out you tried to weasel out of paying by informing on the pair of them. She'll probably bake you a cake. She can send it to you, care of HMP Grampian, where you'll be spending the next four to six months.'

'Noooo...' The thin arms came up over his head.

'Officer Nicholson will show you back to your cell.'

She snapped her fingers. 'Come on, Lumpy, on your feet. Maybe we can ask the Custody Sergeant to hose you down before beddy-byes?'

'All right! All right, I'll tell you.'

'What do you think?' Logan sat back in the visitor's chair.

The room's dark-blue carpet was getting a bit scuffed near the door. Large corkboards covered the two walls either side of the desk, one with a street map of Fraserburgh covered in little red, green, and yellow pins; the other with a map of B Division, surrounded with memos and official leaflets. And a poster of a kitten peeking out of an old boot.

'And you're sure it's Ma Campbell?' Inspector McGregor swivelled from side to side in her seat, chewing on one leg of her glasses. 'Hmm...' Her heart-shaped face creased itself into a frown, pulling wrinkles around her eyes. A thick streak of grey hair reached back above each ear, disappearing into a no-nonsense bun that matched the two no-nonsense silver pips on each epaulette fixed to her black Police Scotland T-shirt. She stopped swivelling and pointed her glasses at the only other person in the room. 'What do *you* think, Hugo?'

'What do I think?' Inspector Fettes shrugged. Standing

beneath the overhead strip light, his hair was a spectacular mop of fiery curls. As if Little Orphan Annie had a sex change and joined the rozzers. He folded his arms, hiding a pair of huge hands covered in freckles, like the ones that spattered across his nose and cheeks. 'Honestly?' He screwed one side of his face up. 'I think Logan needs to go on a diet. Crashing through a garage roof? That's too many pies, that is.'

Logan reached down and rubbed at his swollen ankle. 'I am *not* fat.'

A smile twitched at the corner of McGregor's mouth. 'I meant, what about Patrick Hay?'

Fettes checked the clock mounted on the desk. 'You're still Duty Inspector. Not my problem for five more minutes.'

'Thanks a heap.'

'Hey, what happens on dayshift stays on dayshift. When it's Backshift's turn to worry about it, I'll worry about it.'

'Hmm...' She went back to swivelling. Picked up a sheet of paper from her desk on the way past. 'Ma Campbell, real name Jessica Kirkpatrick Campbell. Runs all the drugs, prostitution, and protection rackets from Paisley to East Kilbride.' McGregor dumped the paper back on her desk. 'I could do without this woman taking an interest in Banff and Macduff. Assuming Lumpy Patrick isn't talking out of his crenulated bumhole again.'

Logan just shrugged.

'It'll take a lot of money and manpower to dunt in the Welshes' door, and the budget's tight enough as it is. If we don't get a result...'

Inspector Fettes settled on the edge of the desk. 'Well, if you want my opinion: anything that gets Ricky Welsh and his homicidal wife off the streets has *got* to be a good thing. It's worth a punt.'

'Agreed.' She checked her watch. 'Two minutes. Logan, anything else I need to know?'

'Canteen vending machine's out of chocolate.'

Fettes's eyes widened. 'OK, *that* I'm going to get right on.'

'Wise choice.' Inspector McGregor pulled the keyboard of her computer over and poked at it. 'And when you're done, be a darling and get some spare bodies and the Operational Support Unit organized so we can pay Ricky Welsh a visit, OK? Logan, do you have a date in mind?'

'No way we'll get it all sorted for tomorrow, not with the MIT barging about all over the place hoovering up resources, and we're off Friday–Saturday, so ... Sunday nightshift? We go in about half ten, eleven, something like that? Give ourselves plenty of time to ransack the place.'

McGregor nodded. 'Agreed.' Another glance at her watch. 'And we're done for the day. Bravo India is off to do the shopping, long live Bravo India.' She stood and shuffled out from behind the desk. Picked up a framed photo of two boys, a girl, and a Jack Russell terrier, and slid it into a rucksack as Inspector Fettes settled into the vacated seat.

'Mmm, still warm.' He raised his eyebrows at Logan. 'Right, Sergeant McRae, off you sod. I've got important police business to attend to.' He grabbed the phone and pressed a button. 'Sophie? Get me the number for those vending machine people...'

Rain pattered against the back door, making streaks on the glass, blurring the view of the car park behind the station. The doorway sat at the bottom of the back stairs, next to the tradesman's entrance to the cellblock. A pile of Method of Entry equipment was heaped in the space under the stairs – mini battering rams, hoolie bars, arm, shin, elbow, and kneepads, those horribly uncomfortable helmets with the neck guard that always smelled like someone had peed in them. All sitting behind a sign proclaiming, 'DO NOT PUT ANYTHING IN THIS AREA!!!'

Inspector McGregor pulled on her gloves. 'I don't like it, Logan. I don't like it one little bit.'

A shrug. 'I know. But what are we supposed to do, ignore it?'

She turned and frowned. 'Ignore what?'

'Lumpy Patrick's info.'

'No, not Lumpy. The body in the woods.'

Ah. Logan jerked a thumb up the stairs. 'Calamity thinks it's a serial killer.'

'That's *all* we need. We'll never get rid of the MIT if it is.' A shudder. 'I don't like Major Investigation Teams stomping all over my division, causing trouble. They're like locusts.'

OK...

'She might have a point, though. What about the young woman found outside Inverurie ten days ago?'

'Nothing like it.' Inspector McGregor shook her head. 'Emily Benton was beaten to death with an adjustable wrench. She didn't have a bag over her head. And she wasn't naked. So unless the Northeast's answer to John Wayne Gacy is a bit confused about his MO, it's not exactly likely, is it?'

'Probably not.' Logan checked his watch. *Still* no sign of Calamity. 'We were a bit surprised to see you here.'

'Think I'm welded to my desk back at Banff, do you? Office-bound? There's more to my job than counting paper-clips, *Sergeant*, thank you very much.'

'OK, OK...' Logan backed off, hands up. 'Only making conversation, Guv. Didn't mean anything by it.'

She sighed. 'I was here for a MAPPA meeting, if you must know. Multi Agency Public Protection Arrangements my shiny backside. More like Morons And Police Pricking About.' McGregor dug out her car keys. 'Four agencies represented, and do you know what startling insight we came to? *Apparently* Charles Richardson still represents a very real danger to little old ladies who don't like being raped. Two hours it took us to come up with that.'

Footsteps rattled on the stairs above. Then Calamity appeared, zipping up her high-viz jacket. 'Sorry, Sarge.'

'Thought you'd fallen in.'

The Inspector pulled her peaked cap on and pushed the door open, letting in the shhhhhhhhhhhh of rain on tarmac.

'Do we have any idea who the victim is? The one with the bag over his head?'

'Nope.' Logan followed her out into the downpour. 'PF won't let them take the bag off till the post mortem. Steel was all for ripping it off then and there, but you know what the Fiscal's like.'

McGregor stopped beside a shiny grey BMW with mud spattered up around the wheel arches. 'Suppose it's just as well. No point compromising any trace evidence left inside the bag.' She pointed her keyfob and the car's lights flashed. 'Don't suppose there's any chance we could solve the whole thing on our own tomorrow, is there? I don't want to get back to work on Sunday night and find the MIT have moved in permanently. Like ticks on a dog.'

'First they're locusts, now they're ticks?'

'And leeches, and cockroaches, and fleas.' She popped open her door then slid into the driver's seat. 'I don't like my station being infested, Logan. I don't like it at all.' Then *clunk*, the door shut and she drove off.

Calamity hunched her shoulders up around her ears, rain bouncing off the brim of her bowler and the shoulders of her high-viz. 'Is it just me, or is the guvnor getting weirder?'

'Probably.' Logan limped towards the Big Car. 'Come on then: hometime.'

'Night, Maggie. Night, Hector.' Logan zipped up his fleece and stepped out into the rain. Pulled the blue door shut behind him. Squeezed between the two patrol cars that sat outside the tradesman's entrance – one with a flat tyre, the other with a cracked windscreen – and onto the road.

Banff Police Station loomed in the orange sodium glow: three storeys of rain-slicked stone, with fancy gables, cornicing, twiddly bits over the windows, and urns on the roof. A small tree had sprouted in the thin fake balcony that jutted out over the main door. Water dripped from its leaves, ticking down onto the illuminated police sign. Making little sapphire splashes.

Lights shone from the bottom-left windows, but the rest of the place was in darkness. Much like the street. Four in the afternoon, and the whole town had been swallowed by gloom.

From here, Banff Bay gleamed like a slab of pewter, hissing and spitting against the beach. Nothing between him and the North Sea but a small car park, a stretch of tarmac, and a chest-high wall of speckled concrete.

He hunched his shoulders, turned, and limped along the road, heading past the ancient buildings, their pastel-coloured walls slick with rain. Every step sent needles jabbing into his ankle. Stupid garage roofs...

There weren't many people on the streets, just an old woman fighting with the umbrella in her left hand and the Doberman attached to her right. Both of which seemed determined to go in opposite directions.

Left at the discount store with its racks of high-viz jackets sitting out the front, dripping. Up the road and out into what passed for a town square at the end of Low Street, where the squat sandstone lump of the Biggar Fountain looked like an evil gothic cupcake, complete with buttresses and crowned cap.

Someone had wedged three traffic cones into the structure, adding to the general pointiness.

Logan's phone launched into 'The Imperial March' again. Brilliant. Should never have turned the damn thing back on.

He ducked into the doorway of the takeaway and pulled his mobile out. Hit the button. 'For God's sake, what now?'

'Been calling you for ages. Where the hell have you been?'

'Doing my job. Try it sometime.'

'You think your job's tough? Try leading a Major Investigation Team in a sodding murder case, when the sodding pathologist and *sodding SEB won't let you take the sodding bag off your sodding victim's sodding head.'* Her voice went up in volume, as if she was playing to an audience. *'How am I supposed to ID someone when I can't see their face? What use is that?'*

'Are you finished?'

'Don't suppose you've had anyone reported missing with a bag over their head, have you? Because that's the only way I'm going to get an ID.' A sniff. *'I'm cold, I'm wet, and I need a drink. Or six. Better call it a bottle.'*

'Tough.'

The old lady made it around the corner, still struggling with dog and brolly.

'Lazy sod's no' doing the post mortem till ten tomorrow.'

'At least you can get fingerprints.' He shifted the phone to his other ear. 'Look, I'm kind of busy here, so if you don't mind...?'

'Fat lot of good fingerprints did us. Put them through our fancy new handheld scanner and do you know what came up? Sod all.' There was a sigh, then Steel's voice took on a bit of a whine. *'Don't suppose you fancy joining the team, do you? If I have to put up with Rennie much longer he'll be singing soprano for the rest of his life. And Becky's no' much better: woman looks like someone's jammed a traffic cone up her backside.'*

'No chance.' Logan hung up and slid his phone back into his pocket. Took a breath, then lumbered out into the rain, round the corner and up the steep narrow brae – wincing with every needle-filled step – past the grey row of little shops on one side, and the bland slab of buildings on the other. Popping out onto Castle Street.

His phone went again. He yanked it out as he limped across the road. 'No, I am not joining your bloody MIT. Leave me alone!'

There was a pause. Just long enough for Logan to pass the solicitor's and the butcher's.

Then: *'Mr McRae. Long time, no speak.'* A man's voice, with more than a hint of Aberdonian burr to it.

Logan slowed to a trot as he reached the building next to the Co-op. Stopped with one hand on the door. 'Can I help you?'

'It's me: John.'

Nope, no idea.

'John Urquhart? I bought your flat?'

Logan flinched. Snatched his hand back as if the door had burnt it. Licked his lips. 'How did you get this number, Mr Urquhart?'

'Call me John, yeah? Known each other for what, six, seven years, right? John.'

'Is there something wrong with the flat?' Because if there was he could take a flying leap. No way Logan was paying to fix anything. Things were bad enough as it was.

'I'm calling on behalf of Mr Mowat. He wants to see you.'

And now, they were *worse*.

5

Logan closed his eyes and leaned against the door. 'I can't—'

'*He* really *wants to see you, Mr McRae.*' Urquhart puffed out a breath. '*He's an old man. And he's dying.*'

'He's not dying. No way a little cancer is getting the better of Wee Hamish Mowat: it wouldn't dare. He's—'

'*Oncologist says maybe a week, week and a half if he's lucky.*'

Oh. 'I see.'

'*Please?*'

Logan pushed through the door into a warm, small-ish room with a couple of leather settees arranged on two sides of a glass coffee table. Tasteful flower arrangements. Framed testimonials on the walls. An understated desk with a brass carriage clock on it – no computer, no brochures, no paperwork. And no sign of anyone. 'I'm a police officer, I can't... If they find out I'm sitting vigil with Wee Hamish—'

'*He's dying and he wants to see you. It matters to him.*'

'I...' Logan's shoulders slumped, dragged down by the weight of all the knives stabbed between them. 'I can't promise anything. But I'll try, OK? If I can.'

'*Thanks. He's looking forward to it.*' And Urquhart was gone.

Logan stood there, frowning down at his phone till the screen went dark.

Wee Hamish Mowat.

Oh, Chief Superintendent Napier would *love* that. Gah... Why did the Ginger Whinger have to be sniffing about now? Why couldn't he have waited a month or two till it was all over?

By then, with Hamish dead, Reuben would've taken over. And after he'd finished killing everyone, Logan would probably be facedown dead in a ditch somewhere and wouldn't have to worry about getting hauled up in front of Professional Standards and done for corruption.

Yeah, that was it: look on the bright side.

Logan put his phone away. Scrubbed a hand across his face.

Oh God...

And when he lowered them, a thin man in a black suit was standing in front of him, head lowered, hands clasped together. 'Can I help you, sir?' Then an eyebrow went up. 'Sergeant McRae? Well, this is a pleasant surprise.' He stuck his hand out for shaking. 'I'm not used to *you* coming to *us*.'

Logan shook. 'Andy.'

'Come, come.' He turned, beckoning Logan to follow him as he stalked towards a curtain behind the desk. Pulled it back to expose a plain wooden door. 'Tea? Or we have a rather nice coffee machine. It's new. I think there may even be biscuits.'

Logan followed him through into a bare breezeblock room, with a small metal table in the corner, a kettle, fridge, microwave, sink, and a huge shiny chrome coffee maker. Posters lined the walls – displaying different brands of coffin with all the associated added extras.

'Sit, sit.' Andy pointed at the plastic chairs tucked under the table. 'Now, tea or coffee?'

Logan sat. A heady whiff of pine air freshener pervaded the room, along with something much darker seeping under a door through to the rear of the building. 'I need to arrange a funeral.'

'I see. In that case, I think a cappuccino.' He poked and

fiddled with the chrome monster. 'May I ask the name of the deceased and when they passed?'

'Samantha Mackie. And it'll be the day after tomorrow. She's not dead yet.'

The eyebrow climbed higher up Andy's forehead. 'Sergeant McRae, we here at Beaton and Macbeth consider ourselves to be a *very* progressive firm, but we do draw the line at interring the living.'

'It's my girlfriend. Well, partner. Sort of. She's been in a coma for years, they're … *we're* withdrawing life support on Friday. She can't breathe on her own. So… Yeah. Friday.'

'I'm sorry.' Andy's fingers twitched and clicked off one another. 'And I took you back *here*. I'm so sorry, Sergeant McRae, please, let's repair to the chapel of rest and I can—'

'No. It's OK. Here's fine.' Logan took a deep breath. 'I need a black coffin with a red silk lining. And do you have anything with skulls-and-crossbones on it?'

The Sergeant's Hoose sulked on the corner, diagonally opposite Banff station and a lot less impressive. Large patches of rough stonework poked through the crumbling render on the gable wall, one of the windows there still boarded up. Have to do something about that. The front was a bit better. Kind of. If you ignored the entire right-hand side with its sealed off doors and windows.

Logan switched the carrier bags to his other hand and dug his keys out. Let himself in. Dumped the carrier bags.

'Cthulhu? Daddy's home.' He clicked the hall light on, took his soggy fleece off, and went to the bottom of the stairs. 'Where's Daddy's little kittenfish?'

No reply. No thump of fuzzy paws battering down the stairs. No prooping or meeping.

'Cthulhu?'

Nope.

Lazy wee sod was probably still asleep.

Logan picked up the mail from the mat, flicking through

it on his way to the kitchen. Bill. Bill. Bill. You May Already Have Won!!! Donate To Charity Now! Buy A Hearing Aid. Do You Need New Windows And Doors?

He dumped the lot on the table and stuck the kettle on, then limped through to the living room while it groaned and pinged towards a boil.

The answering machine glowered at him with its angry red eye. He jabbed the button and a flat electronic voice growled from the speaker. '*MESSAGE ONE:*' Then Helen's replaced it, every word carving out a jagged chunk from his chest. '*Hello? … Logan, are you there? … Please pick up if you're there. … I'm sorry. I didn't mean for it to end like that. I…*' A sigh. '*Look, this was a mistake. I just… I wanted to hear your voice again.*'

Bleeeeeep.

His finger hovered over the delete button a moment too long.

'*MESSAGE TWO:*' A harsh, smoky voice gravelled out into the room. Steel. '*Laz? Where the hell are you? Why've you no' called me—*'

Delete.

'*MESSAGE THREE: Mr McRae? It's Sheila here from Deveronside Family Glazing Solutions…*'

A soft *meyowp* came from the doorway behind him, then a small fuzzy body leaned into his leg with a thump – brown and grey and black stripes leaving hairy trace fibres on his damp 'Police-Scotland-issue' trousers. She wrapped her big fluffy tail around his leg, adding yet another layer of hair.

'Where have you been then?'

'*…let you know that your new windows have come in.*'

'About time, been waiting six weeks.'

He bent down and picked Cthulhu up, turned her over so she was lying on her back, white fuzzy tummy on display as she stretched out her arms and curled her big white feet. He rubbed her belly, getting a thick rumbling purr in return.

'*So if you want to come in any time in the next week or so, we can get the invoice sorted out.*'

Bleeeeeep.

'You wouldn't believe how much money Daddy spent on a custom coffin today.'

'*MESSAGE FOUR: Logan, it's your mother. You know I don't like talking to this infernal machine. Why on earth you can't simply—*'

Delete.

'Going to have to live on lentil soup and the cheap cat food for a couple of years. Sorry about that.'

'*MESSAGE FIVE: Hello, my name's Debora McLintock, Louise at Sunny Glen gave me your number. It's my role to help families when the decision has been taken to end—*'

Delete.

'*YOU HAVE NO MORE MESSAGES.*'

He played Helen's message again. Then deleted the lot.

Samantha lay back on the couch with her legs across Logan's lap. 'Any good?'

He frowned up from the book. 'Put it this way: JC Williams is no MC Beaton. *PC Munro and the Poisoner's Cat*? Nothing but a half-baked Hamish Macbeth rip-off.' Logan sniffed. 'She's only getting media attention because she's a local author. If this wasn't set in Banff, no one would touch it with a sharny stick.'

'So don't read it then.' She dragged her fingers through her hair, working a chunk of it into a scarlet plait. 'Or at least stop moaning about it.'

'I mean, listen to this: "Och, hud your weesht," said PC Robbie Munro dismissively, "the lad's clearly been poisoned. His tongue's all black and that always happens when someone's given arsenic."' Logan lowered the book. 'Which is utter bollocks. The only way you can tell someone's taken arsenic is with a blood toxicology screen.'

His left foot rested on a pillow on the coffee table, a bag of not-so-frozen peas balanced on the ankle. He stretched the joint out, flaring his toes. Ankle was a bit numb from the cold, but it was better than the throbbing ache. And at least the swelling was going down.

Samantha wriggled her legs. 'You know, you don't *have* to live on lentil soup. Soon as I'm gone there'll be no more care-home bills to pay.'

'And who the hell poisons people with arsenic? It's not the eighteen nineties: do you have any idea how difficult it is to get hold of arsenic these days?'

'Rat poison.'

'Thought that was warfarin?'

'Not all of it. Maybe you could go on holiday or something? Head over to Spain and see Helen.'

Yeah, because the last time worked out *so* well.

He went back to his book. 'I'm not talking about this again.'

'And ant poison. Why not?'

'Can we just leave it, please?'

'And weed killer. What are you scared of?'

He poked the book. 'I've read this sentence three times now.'

'Come on, Logan, it's not as if you don't get urges. I've seen your internet browser history and—'

'You're not dead, OK? *That's* why not.' He thumped the book down on the coffee table. 'You're... I don't know what you are. I don't know what *we* are any more. You're lying on your back, hooked up to all those machines in the care home, and I'm sitting here arguing with a bloody hallucination!'

'Logan—'

'No wonder Helen...' He picked up the book and slammed it down again. 'Five years since the fire. *Five years* of you lying there. We only went out for two. I've known coma you nearly three times as long as the real thing.'

She pulled her legs from his lap and stood. Then knelt in front of the couch, holding his elevated knee. 'Do you want me to go?'

'If you'd died five years ago, I could've mourned and moved on. But this...'

'I'll go if you want me to.'

The doorbell launched into its flat, two-tone, *bing-bong*.

Samantha sighed. Hung her head. 'Saved by the bell.'

'I don't know what I want.' He stood. 'But this isn't helping.'

Bing-bong.

'All right, all right, I'm coming.' Logan headed into the hall, unlatched the Yale, and opened the door.

The man on the pavement smiled, making the pockmarks on his cheeks dimple. He had a black umbrella, black overcoat, black suit, and black shoes. The only concession to colour was the green silk shirt. He stuck his hand out. 'Mr McRae. You ready?'

Logan frowned at him. Why did he look familiar? ...

Oh.

Damn.

Something curdled deep inside Logan's stomach.

'You're John Urquhart.'

'Guilty as charged.' Urquhart shrugged, then he turned his offered handshake into a hitchhiker's thumb and jiggled it at a black Audi TT. 'Thought it might be best if I gave you a lift, like. Mr Mowat's really looking forward to seeing you. Been ages.'

Logan pulled his shoulders back. 'This a request, or an order?'

'Nah, don't...' A grin. 'It's not an *order*. God, no. If it was an order it wouldn't be me, it'd be three huge guys with a sawn-off, some duct tape, and a Transit van. Nah, this is just in case you and Mr Mowat have a wee dram or something. Don't want you getting pulled over for drink-driving, right? That'd be embarrassing.' The thumb came around and Urquhart poked himself in the chest with it. 'Designated driver.'

So it was go with Urquhart and have a drink with a dying gangster, or wait at home for the three guys and an unmarked van.

Not much of a choice.

And Napier would twist either into a sign of guilt, even the duct-tape-and-van option. Tell me, Sergeant McRae, don't you think it's *suspicious* that Wee Hamish Mowat's boys picked *you* to abduct? Why would they pick you? What makes *you* so special to the man who runs Aberdeen's underbelly?

Still, at least this way he'd get to keep all his teeth.

'OK.' Logan let his shoulders droop. 'Let me get some shoes on.'

The Audi purred through Oldmeldrum. Past the knots of newbuilds lurking beneath the streetlights, the old church, the garage, bungalows, old-fashioned Scottish houses, and out into the fields again. The purr turned to a growl as they hit the limits.

Logan turned in his seat, looking out through the rear window as the town receded into the darkness.

Urquhart raised his eyebrows. 'You OK?'

He faced front again. 'Used to know someone who lives there.'

'Right.'

The Audi's windscreen wipers swished and thunked back and forth across the glass. Swish, *thunk*. Swish, *thunk*.

Urquhart tapped his fingers against the steering wheel in time with the wipers. 'No offence, but your house is a bit... Let's call it a development opportunity, yeah? Fix up the outside: some render, bit of pointing, coat of paint. Get those boarded-up windows ripped out and replaced with a bit of decent UPVC.' He frowned, bit at his bottom lip for a bit. 'What's the inside like? Bit manky?'

'Work in progress.'

'Cool. Cool. So spend a couple of grand – ten, fifteen tops – and you could probably flip it for a pretty decent profit. I could help, if you like?' He reached into his jacket pocket and came out with a business card. 'Got a couple of boys I use. Did three places for me last year. Good finish too, none of your cowboy rubbish. They'll do it at cost, you know, as you and me go way back.'

Logan turned the card over. Then over again. 'The house belongs to Police Scotland. I just live there.'

'Ah. Not quite so cool.'

And let's face it – their last transaction didn't exactly help.

Trees and fields swept past in the gloom. A handful of cars coming the other way, stuck behind a big green tractor with its orange light flashing. The windscreen wipers played their mournful tune.

Urquhart tapped his fingers along the steering wheel again. Then, 'You want I should put the radio on?'

It was going to be a long night.

6

On the other side of the glass, Aberdeen twinkled in the distance and darkness like a loch of stars.

Logan leaned against the windowsill.

The red, white, and green flashing lights of an airplane tracked across the sky, making for Dyce airport.

Muffled voices came through the door behind him – it sounded like an argument, but the words were too faint to tell what it was about.

And then the door opened and John Urquhart stepped out into the corridor. Closed the door behind him. 'Sorry about that.'

Logan nodded at it. 'Reuben?'

'Nah. Doctor's kicking up a fuss. Says Mr Mowat's too weak to see people, he needs to sleep. So Mr Mowat tells him to pick which kneecap he'd like removed with a jigsaw, and suddenly Dr Kildare decides that visitors are fine.'

'Funny how that works.'

'Yup.' Urquhart joined him at the window, frowning out into the darkness. 'Reuben's...' A hissing sound, as Urquhart sucked at his teeth. 'Yeah. Going to be interesting times ahead.'

Logan turned his back on the darkness. 'Is he planning something?'

'The Reubster? The Reubenator? Ruby-Ruby-Reuben?' A

little laugh. 'Anyway, you can go in now.' He opened the door and held it for Logan.

Picture windows made up two walls, the view hidden away behind louvre blinds. It was dark in here, with a wooden floor, a couple of leather armchairs by the French doors, a settee and a coffee table opposite them in the gloom. And right in the middle, lit by a single standard lamp: a hospital bed – set up where its occupant would have an uninterrupted view out over the garden and the city beyond. A sweet earthy scent filled the room, presumably coming from the pair of joss sticks on a low table, their twin ribbons of smoke coiling around each other like ghosts.

The bed was grey and huge, bracketed by banks of equipment and drip stands, all hooked up to the paper skeleton lying there.

Wee Hamish Mowat's skin was milk-bottle pale, his veins making dark green-and-blue road maps under the surface. Beneath the liver spots and bruises. Wisps of grey clung to his scalp in demoralized clumps. Cheekbones like knives, his nose large and hooked – getting bigger as the rest of him shrank. Watery grey eyes blinked out above the plastic lip of an oxygen mask.

Had to admit that the doctor was right: Wee Hamish didn't look up to visitors. He didn't look up to anything at all.

Logan pulled on a smile and walked over, trainers squeaking on the wooden floor. 'Hamish, you're looking well.'

A trembling hand reached up and pulled the oxygen mask away. 'Logan...' Voice so thin and dry it was barely there. 'You came.'

'Of course I came.' Logan stood at the foot of the bed.

A shape lumbered out of the gloom: a bear of a man; tall and broad, with a massive gut on him. His face was a landscape of scar tissue, knitted together by a patchy grey beard. Dark sunken eyes. A nose that was little more than a knot of squint cartilage. All done up in a sharp suit, tie, and shiny shoes.

When he smiled, it was like small children screaming. 'Well, well, well.' The words were thick and flat, dampened by that broken nose. 'If it isn't Sergeant McRae.'

Logan didn't move. 'Reuben.'

A bone-pale hand trembled into the air above the sheets. 'Boys...'

Reuben turned to Wee Hamish and his smile softened. 'Don't worry, Mr Mowat, the sergeant and me have come to an accord, like. Haven't we, Sergeant?'

The machines beeped and hissed and pinged.

Then Logan nodded. 'Yes.'

'Good.' Wee Hamish took a hit on the oxygen, closing his eyes as he breathed. Then sank deeper into his pillows. 'John ... can you get ... Logan a seat? ... And ... bring the Glenfiddich. ... Three glasses.' More oxygen.

'Yes, Mr Mowat.' Urquhart hurried off to the corner and came back with a wooden chair. He placed it beside the bed, level with Wee Hamish's elbow.

Logan sat. Scraped the chair around by thirty degrees to keep Reuben in sight. 'How are you feeling, Hamish?'

A long, rattling sigh. 'I'm ... dying.'

'No, you're—'

'Please, Logan.' He placed a hand on Logan's – bones wrapped in cold parchment. 'Just ... shut up ... and listen.' He buried his face in the oxygen mask again. Three long damp breaths. 'You have ... power of attorney. ... If I ... slip into anything, ... you tell them ... to let me ... die. ... Understood?' The hand tightened. 'I don't ... want these hacks ... keeping a sack ... of gristle and mush ... breathing for ... the hell of it.' A smile twitched at the edge of his lips. 'Promise me.'

Logan stared at the liver-spotted claw covering his own hand, then up at Wee Hamish. The hollow cheeks and sunken eyes. Why not? It wasn't as if he'd never had to make *that* decision before. 'Promise.' Twice in one day.

Urquhart came back to the bed, carrying a tray with three crystal tumblers, a bottle of whisky, and three glasses of water. He lowered it onto the foot of the bed, then backed away out of sight.

Wee Hamish trembled a finger at the tray. 'Do the … honours, … would you?'

The foil cap was still on, so Logan slit it open with a fingernail. The cork squeaked out of the neck, then came away with a pop.

Logan poured a finger of mahogany-coloured whisky into each tumbler. A rich leather-and-wood scent coiled up from the crystal as he placed one into Wee Hamish's hand.

It wobbled, grasped in knotted fingers as it was raised in toast. 'Here's … tae us.'

'Fa's like us?'

Reuben picked his glass from the tray, intoning the final words like a death sentence. 'Gey few, and they're a' deid.'

They drank.

One line of whisky dribbled down the side of Wee Hamish's chin. He didn't wipe it away. Picked up the oxygen mask instead and dragged in a dozen rattling breaths.

Reuben just stood there. Looming.

Over in the corner, someone cleared their throat.

The machines bleeped.

Finally, Wee Hamish surfaced. 'Tired…'

A man appeared at his shoulder, glasses flaring in the room's only light. He'd rolled his sleeves up to the elbow and tucked his tie into his shirt, between the buttons. He fiddled with one of the machines, then licked his lips. Stared off into the gloom, not making eye contact with Reuben. Probably thinking about that threatened jigsaw. 'I'm sorry, but Mr Mowat really needs to *rest*.'

Reuben grunted, then jerked his chin up, setting the folds of flesh wobbling.

Wee Hamish reached beneath the sheets and produced an envelope. Held it out to Logan. It fluttered like a wounded bird. 'Take the … bottle … with you. … Drink it … for me.'

Logan swallowed, then reached out and took the envelope.

Slipped it into his jacket pocket. Stood. Patted Wee Hamish on the arm. 'I'm sorry.'

'Goodbye … Logan.'

Stars glared down from the cold dark sky. Aberdeen's street-light glow hid them from view on one side, but on the other they stretched across the baleful darkness like angry gods.

The house lights reflected back from Urquhart's shiny black Audi.

Reuben closed the front door and stepped down onto the gravel driveway beside Logan. 'He's dying.'

Really? What gave it away? The machines? The smell? The terrified doctor?

Logan nodded. Kept his mouth shut.

'Soon as he does, that's it. I'm the man, you got me? I say jump, you don't ask "why", you ask "how high".'

'It's a different world, Reuben. I've not been CID for years.' He shifted Wee Hamish's bottle from one hand to the other. 'I'm a uniform sergeant way up on the coast.'

'Don't care if you're a pantomime dame in Pitlochry, you'll do what you're told.'

Logan did his best not to sigh, he really did. 'It doesn't have to be like this.'

'Oh aye, it does. Cause I *say* it does.' The big man stepped in close. 'Your protection dies with Mr Mowat. You either get with the team, or you and me are going to have *words*.'

The whisky bottle was cold and solid in Logan's hand. It'd make a pretty decent weapon.

Reuben grinned, then dropped his voice to a growling whisper. 'Well, I'll have the words, you'll be too busy screaming.'

Could batter Reuben's brains in right here and now. Probably. As long as he got the first blow in. And kept on going till the huge sod stopped breathing.

Logan stared back at him. 'Grow up.'

Reuben lunged, grabbed Logan by the throat and shoved him back against the car, held his big scarred face close. The words came out on a wave of bitter garlic. 'Listen up and listen good, you wee shite, I will skin you alive, do you hear me? And I'm not being metaphoric, I will take a knife and slit the skin from your pasty wee body!'

The whisky bottle came up, ready to hammer down.

Then Urquhart's voice boomed out from the door. 'STOP IT RIGHT THERE!'

No one moved.

'Mr Mowat was very clear about this, Reuben. What did he say?'

Reuben hissed another sour breath out through gritted teeth. Then he shoved Logan and stepped back at the same time. Shot his cuffs. Glowered.

Urquhart took out his keys and plipped the Audi's locks. 'OK then.'

A huge paw came up, one finger prodding at Logan's chest. 'Enjoy your whisky, *Sergeant*. I'll be in touch.' Then he turned on his heel and lumbered back into the house.

Logan sagged a little. Opened the car door and settled into the passenger seat. Clutched the bottle against his chest where Reuben had poked him.

The front light went out, plunging the driveway into darkness.

'So...' Urquhart put the car in gear and drove down the drive towards the gates. 'You and the Reubster, then.'

'Who does he think he is? Threatening *police* officers?' Logan hauled on his seatbelt. Kept his face forward. 'Moron.'

'Yeah, Rubey Doobie Doo. Hmm.' The gates buzzed open and Urquhart took them out onto a narrow country road. 'You know he's moved into Mr Mowat's other house? Set himself up like lord of the manor over there in Grandholm. You ever meet his fiancée?'

Logan stared across the car. 'Someone's *marrying* that?'

'Big Tam Slessor's daughter.'

Ah. A marriage made in the Hammer House of Horror studios.

'Yeah, Mr Mowat gave them the Grandholm place for an early wedding present. I got them a dozen towels and a fondue set from John Lewis. Very classy.' He turned right at the junction, heading for Aberdeen along the dark winding road. The Audi's headlights reflected back at them from the rain-slicked tarmac. 'You getting them anything?'

How about a shallow grave?

Trees whipped past the windows.

Logan shifted in his seat. 'When I asked you if Reuben was planning anything, you laughed.'

'Well, you know Reuben. These days he's all about the strategic planning.' Urquhart cleared his throat. 'Mr McRae?'

The headlights caught a stiff bundle of feathers in the middle of the road – a pheasant, with its bottom half flattened and stuck to the road.

'See, I was wondering... When Mr Mowat's gone, he wants you to take over, right?'

'I'm a police officer.'

'Yeah, but he wants *you*, right? He doesn't want Reuben. Doesn't think the Reubmeister's up to running the show. Thinks it'll all just collapse into anarchy and war: all these guys coming up to carve Aberdeen into bite-sized chunks.' A hand came off the steering wheel, ticking them off one finger at a time. 'Malk the Knife from Edinburgh, the Hussain Brothers from Birmingham, the Liverpool Junkyard Massive, Ma Campbell from Glasgow, and Black Angus MacDonald with the Dornoch Mafia.' A frown. 'I know for a fact the Hussains are already sniffing about.'

They weren't the only ones. Not if Lumpy Patrick was telling the truth. Which would be a first.

Drizzle misted the windscreen, and Urquhart put the wipers on. 'Anyway, point is: they're lining up to take their chunks. And soon as Mr Mowat's gone, they'll be here. And it'll be war.'

'And Reuben can't stop it?'

Urquhart bared his teeth. 'Tell the truth? I think he's looking forward to it.'

Logan waited for the Audi's tail-lights to disappear around the corner before letting himself into the Sergeant's Hoose. Closed and locked the door. Put the snib on, just in case. Probably wouldn't hurt to get a chain fitted. Maybe one of those metal bar things as well...

Not that it'd stop Reuben or his minions from coming in the window.

Still, that didn't mean he had to make it easy for them.

He clicked the switch, setting the hall's bare bulb glowing. 'Cthulhu?'

Samantha poked her head out from the lounge. 'You're still alive, then. No trip to the pig farm for you?'

'Not tonight. Not till Hamish Mowat dies.'

'You want a tea?'

'Nope.' Logan held up the bottle. 'Present.' Through to the kitchen for a tumbler, which got a good splash of the Glenfiddich.

Samantha's hand on his shoulder. 'You need a plan, you know that don't you?'

He rolled a sip of warm leathery whisky around his mouth. 'Thought I'd give Beaton and Macbeth your photo from Rennie's engagement party. You always liked that one. Get them to match your make-up.'

'This is serious, Logan. Reuben's dangerous, you *know* that. If you don't do what he wants, he'll kill you. Slowly.'

'Can't decide what to do about all the piercings, though. I mean, he's a nice enough guy, but I don't fancy Andy fiddling about getting your nipple ring back in. Never mind the more intimate ones. Maybe he could get George to do it?'

'You need a plan!'

'I know George has got huge hands, but she's not as rough as she looks. Did I tell you she breeds chinchillas?'

'God's sake, Logan, *listen* to me. Reuben will grab you, torture you, kill you, then feed you to Wee Hamish's pigs. Is that what you want? Are you *happy* with that?'

Another sip of whisky. It seeped through his innards, spreading across his chest. He lowered his head. 'I'm a police officer.'

'And I don't care.' She stepped in front of him. 'You have to kill Reuben, or you have to get the hell out of Narnia. If you don't, you're pig food.'

'Maybe not.' Logan swirled the tumbler, leaving smears of whisky around the glass. 'Maybe he'll go to Professional Standards and tell them I sold my flat to one of Hamish Mowat's minions for twenty grand over the asking price?'

'Yes, but you didn't *know* you were selling to someone dodgy.'

'Think that'll matter to Napier?' A grimace. 'I could fit Reuben up? Get him sent down for something. Keep him out of the way for eight to twelve years.'

'And all he has to do is make one phone call to the outside world and have some of his minions pop up to Banff and do the job for him.' A sigh. 'Oh, Logan...' She stepped in, her body warm against his chest. Reached up and kissed him. 'I'm sorry, but you're going to have to kill Reuben.'

— Thursday Dayshift —

when the elder gods die

7

'Of course they're no' connected, you idiot.' Steel had a pull on her e-cigarette, then let the steam trickle out of her nose. It found its way down the wrinkles either side of her mouth. Then the ones around her eyes deepened. 'Now, does anyone *else* have a stupid question?' Her grey suit looked as if someone much larger than her had slept in it. Whoever it was had done something unmentionable to her hair as well. Possibly involving an electric whisk, a Van de Graaff generator, and a bucket of wallpaper paste.

The DC lowered his hand and mumbled something. Pink flushed the back of his neck, darkening the skin above his suit jacket.

Steel had a dig at her underwire and settled on the edge of a table parked beneath the whiteboard. The board took up nearly the whole wall of the station's Major Incident Room.

The conference table in the middle of the room was packed with uniformed and plain-clothed officers. They'd commandeered every chair in the place, set up in a long line facing the board. More Uniform stood around the walls, arms folded across their black police-issue T-shirts.

'Moving on.' Steel stopped fiddling with her upholstery for long enough to point her fake cigarette at the whiteboard. An array of photographs – much like the ones Logan had on his phone – were Blu-Tacked across the shiny white surface, along with an OS map of the woods. 'Post mortem is at ten. Till then, the powers that be are no' letting us unwrap our present.'

The e-cigarette clicked against a close-up of the bin-bag taped over the body's head.

Another hand went up. 'Guv: how come?'

She didn't look at the questioner. 'What did I say about stupid questions?'

The hand went down again. 'Sorry, Guv.'

'Soon as they break the seal and invalidate the warranty, DS Dawson will be taking an ID photo and emailing it straight up. If we're lucky, one of the local bunnets will recognize our victim. But just in case: I want posters. Becky? You're on that. Blanket coverage.'

A large woman in a black suit nodded, sending her frizzy brown hair wobbling. 'Guv.'

'Next.' She tossed a pile of printouts to the person sitting nearest – a thin bloke in a cheap fighting suit and seven-quid haircut.

He took one, then passed the rest on.

She waited for the printouts to get halfway around the room. 'We got an MO hit on the database. Naked body, battered, bag over the head, dumped in woods. Last one belonged to a Lithuanian pimp operating on Leith Walk, Edinburgh, six months ago.'

The stack had made its way as far as Logan. Steel's handout had half a dozen photos on it: different views of a body like the one from yesterday, only this victim was lying on a mortuary slab instead of the forest floor and the bag over his head had been slit open, revealing a gaunt face with a hooked nose and crooked teeth. More bruising. Both eyes swollen shut.

'Allegedly, Artūras Kazlauskas didn't bother asking Malk the Knife's permission before hooring women out in his city, so Malky sent someone round to teach him some manners. Details are the same, right down to the body getting a dose of bleach after death to mask DNA and trace evidence.' She took a sheet of paper from a folder and stuck it to the whiteboard with some fridge magnets. It was blown-up from a magazine, part of the text running down one side of the image. A man with a short haircut, baggy eyes, cheery cheeks, and a tuxedo. It was the kind of face that belonged on a Rotary Club steering committee, that always bought the first round, that invited friends from work over for a barbecue, and never forgot the receptionist's birthday.

Steel poked it in the forehead with her fake fag. 'Malcolm McLennan, AKA: Malk the Knife. Edinburgh's Mr Huge. You run drugs, guns, illegal immigrants, or prostitutes in the city, he gets a cut or you wind up missing important bits. *If* you're lucky.'

Logan turned his sheet over. There were another three bodies pictured on the back. All naked, all male, all battered, all with bin-bags duct-taped over their heads.

Steel sniffed. 'And before some smart aleck asks the obvious question: no, we don't know who killed this lot. Don't even know if it's the same person each time. And the Organised Crime and Counter Terrorism Unit can't prove Malky ordered the killings either. So they're about as much use as Rennie in a knocking shop.'

'Hey!'

'Shut up.'

Logan turned the paper back over again. Jessica Campbell was bringing drugs into Aberdeenshire from Glasgow. And now Malcolm McLennan was killing people in Banff. John Urquhart was right: Wee Hamish Mowat might not be dead yet, but the big boys were already muscling in.

Which meant that sooner or later, Reuben was going to kick back. Hard.

The post-briefing rush for the canteen and the toilets thundered through the station as Steel lounged by the Major Incident Room window, smoking her fake cigarette and exploring her armpit with one hand while the other pinned a mobile phone to her ear. 'Yeah... Nah... Did he? ... Yeah...'

Logan folded the printout with its dead bodies into four and stuck it on the table.

Rennie slouched over. 'You run B Division, right?'

'Why?'

'The guvnor wants a couple of bunnets to go door-to-door when pics of the victim's face come in. You can spare me two or three, can't you?'

Logan stared at him. 'First: you don't get to call my divisional officers, "Bunnets".'

Rennie pursed his lips. 'Someone's touchy the day.'

'Second: my *divisional officers* will be busy policing B Division. They will *not* have time to go running about doing your legwork for you.' Logan took a couple of steps, then poked Rennie in the chest. 'Third: most of them have been in the job a lot longer than you, and they deserve a bit of respect. Are we clear?'

Rennie's bottom lip popped out. 'Only asking.'

He stepped closer, till they were nearly nose-to-nose. 'Well don't.'

There was a snort from the corner, then Steel's gravelly tones burst across the room. 'For God's sake, will you two just kiss and get it over with? Could cut the sexual tension in here with a spoon.'

Logan stayed where he was. 'Detective Sergeant Rennie and I were discussing resource allocation.'

'Nah, you pair were about to whip out your truncheons and give each other a good seeing to. But far be it from me to stand in the way of young love: if you promise no' to give Rennie back with his arse all covered in lovebites, you can "discuss resource allocations" to your heart's content.'

'What?' There was a shudder, then Rennie backed away wearing his spanked child expression. 'I only wanted a couple of bodies to help with the ID. You didn't have to get all threatening about it. Was only—'

Steel rapped her knuckles on the tabletop. 'Rennie: coffee. Two and a coo.'

'But, Guv, I wasn't doing any—'

'You heard: milk and two sugars. And I hear rumours someone's got a malt loaf planked somewhere. I'll have a slice of that too.'

'But, *Gu-uv...*'

'*Now*, Detective Sergeant.'

His bottom lip got poutier. Then he turned and shuffled out of the room. Closed the door behind him.

Steel crossed her arms and frowned at Logan. 'Who crapped in your porridge then?'

'I don't have to—'

'Having a go at poor wee Rennie. Police Scotland doesn't approve of workplace bullying, you grumpy old sack of—'

'Oh come off it, you say worse to him all the time! And—'

'You were being a dick, Laz. Spoiling for a fight.' Steel shook her head. 'With *Rennie*. Be like kicking a puppy, then sticking it in a tumble dryer with a bucket of broken glass. Then setting fire to the tumble dryer.'

Yeah.

Logan sighed. Screwed his face up into a knot.

She was right: picking on Rennie wasn't fair. Steel's DS might be an idiot, but it wasn't *his* fault Logan had barely slept. Wasn't his fault Reuben loomed over everything like a massive rabid dog.

'Sorry.' Logan ran a hand across the stubble on top of his head. 'Been a tough week. I'll apologize.'

'Don't care how rough it is, you don't ruin a perfectly good tumble dryer.' She took a puff on her e-cigarette. 'Going to be a total nightmare to live with now. He'll be slumping about with a face like a cat's bum, all martyred and woe-is-me.'

'I'll talk to him.' Logan looked away. Outside, the violet sky was fringed with pre-dawn blue and pink. The lights of Macduff twinkled on the other side of the bay. 'We're switching Samantha off tomorrow. Life support.'

A sigh. Then Steel took hold of his arm and squeezed. 'You going to be OK?'

'Yeah. Course.' He frowned. 'Don't know.' Then let out a long, slow breath. 'Anyway, suppose I'd better...' He nodded at the door. 'Got to go brief the team.'

'...so make sure you keep your eyes open, OK?' Logan settled back against the windowsill and rested his mug of tea on a stack of case files.

The Constables' Office wasn't a large room. Old-fashioned with worktop desks on two walls, covered in paperwork and four ancient grey computers. Four office chairs, most of which looked on the verge of collapse – the foam rubber stuck out of one as if it had prolapsed. Three uniformed officers in Police Scotland ninja black stared at him.

Calamity clicked the point of her pen in and out and in and out. *Click, click, click.* 'What about a national appeal? Maybe we're not getting any sightings because Tracy's left the area?'

A wee soft voice piped up. 'Can't really blame her, can you?' Isla pulled her auburn hair back into a thick ponytail and tied it off. Didn't matter if she was in her thirties or not, she still looked like a teenager – heart-shaped face, red lipstick, with more eyeshadow and mascara than was strictly necessary for arresting people. Her little legs barely reached the ground as she swivelled back and forth in her chair, the toe of her boots barely scraping the carpet. 'If I had Big Donald Brown for a dad? I'd do a runner too.' Hair done, she took a sip of coffee. 'Good luck to her.'

Logan frowned up at the rogues' gallery above the radiator – a double row of local drug dealers and thieves scowled back at him from their photocopied pictures. Big Donald Brown was second row, three in from the right. A slab of flesh with a broad forehead, prominent ears, and the kind of eyebrows that wouldn't have looked out of place on a Border terrier. 'Anyone know if she's run away from home before?'

Tufty checked his notes, the pink tip of his tongue poking

68

out between his lips as he skimmed them. The strip light glowed in his ginger crewcut, giving him a fiery halo. Which was probably as close as he was ever going to get. 'She's nineteen, Sarge. It's not really running away from home, is it?'

'Still…' Logan chewed on his bottom lip for a moment. 'Doesn't matter how much of a scumbag her dad is, he's worried about her.' He pointed. 'Isla, get onto the media office and tell them we're after a spot on the news and all the social media they can throw at it. If they give you any grief you have my permission to do the little-girl-lost routine you think none of us know about.'

A nod. 'Sarge.'

'Next: Constable Quirrel, I believe you have an announcement for us.'

A grin ripped across Tufty's thin face. He swept his arms out, as if introducing a magic trick. 'And on the second-last shift of his indented servitude, verily didst the Probationer say, "Let there be jaffa cakes!"'

Calamity and Isla gave him a round of applause.

Logan couldn't help smiling. 'Well done, young Tufty. You shall go to the top of the class.'

The grin got bigger. 'Thanks, Sarge.' He dipped into his desk and came out with the promised packet of cakey biscuits.

Logan helped himself. 'And as a reward, you can lead the rest of the briefing.'

Tufty swivelled his chair around and wiggled his mouse, bringing up the next slide on the daily PowerPoint presentation. Martin Milne stared out at them. A strong face with high cheekbones and a dimple right in the middle of his chin. Straight brown hair with a Hugh Grant fringe. 'I checked distinguishing features on the misper form, and there's no mention of Milne having a tattoo. So that means whoever we found yesterday, it's not him. Might be worth checking signs of activity on his bank or credit cards?'

Isla rolled her eyes. 'You got any idea how long it'll take his bank to authorize that?'

'Ah, but no, my dearest Constable Anderson, because I has a *clever*.' Tufty leaned forward. 'We don't need to hang about and wait for his bank to approve access if he's on internet banking: we can ask his wife to log on and check. Could ask her about the tattoo while we're there – make sure that whatever muppet filled in the misper form got it right.'

'Is that *cynicism* I hear?' A smile pulled Isla's cheeks into shiny pink apples. 'Ah, Tufty, we'll make a police officer of you yet.'

'Next.' A click of the mouse and a man's face filled the screen: jowls, one solid eyebrow, hair shaved at the sides to match the bald spot at the top. 'Mark Connolly violated his parole, Friday...'

Sitting in the driver's seat, Tufty doo-de-doo-de-dooed along with the old Oasis track jangling out of the speakers. He slowed down as the beige outskirts of Whitehills appeared, then took a left, heading towards the slate-grey sea.

Wind buffeted the Big Car, rocking it on its springs. Rain crackled against the windscreen, blurring the world for a moment, before the wipers squeaked it away. Only for more rain to replace it moments later.

Logan shifted in his seat. The limb restraints made a hard lump in the small of his back, right where the stabproof vest ended. And would they shift? Of course they wouldn't.

The road narrowed – lined on both sides by billowing green clouds of jagged gorse. Writhing beneath a raven sky.

Why did Samantha think he could just kill Reuben? That he was even capable of killing another human being. OK, maybe 'human being' was stretching things a bit where Reuben was concerned, but still. To actually *murder* someone. Cold. Premeditated.

Logan's stomach lurched, sour and gurgling.

Oasis faded a bit and the DJ teuchtered all over them. *'Wisn't that a flash fae the past? You're listening till "Gid Mornin'*

Doogie!" and it's bang on eight, so here's oor Ashley with a' the news and weather.'

'Thanks Dougie. A family of four died in a three-car pile-up on the A90, just north of Portlethen last night…'

Tufty kept on drumming. 'Sarge? You know *time*, right?'

Logan let his head thunk against the passenger window. 'Here we go.'

'No, listen. Quantum mechanics and the theory of general relativity have these, like, completely different ideas about how time works.'

'…Mrs Garden, sixty-nine, was remanded in custody following a road-rage incident outside the Strichen Post Office…'

'Einstein says time's relative, depending on where you are and how fast you're going, yeah? Faster you go, the slower time is.'

Logan turned and faced the passenger window. 'He's right. When I'm in the car with you it slows to a sodding *crawl*.'

Brown and dull-green fields stretched away on either side of the road. A flock of sheep huddled in the lee of a drystane dyke.

'…man's body discovered in woods south of Macduff yesterday. Police Scotland aren't releasing any details until the next of kin have been informed…'

'Quantum mechanics, on the other hand, says time's absolute and external to the universe: keeping track of the wave function in quantum systems.'

Maybe getting killed by Reuben wouldn't be so bad? At least he wouldn't have to sit here listening to Tufty any more.

'…were angry scenes outside BP's offices in Dyce yesterday, as protesters gathered to picket the oil giant over redundancies and proposed cuts to service companies' rates…'

Skinned alive and fed to the pigs.

Logan closed his eyes. Swallowed down the bitter taste of tarnished copper.

How was he supposed to kill Reuben? How?

What switch was he supposed to flip to make that possible?

A hand squeezed his shoulder, delicate, the nails painted a shiny black.

Samantha leaned forward from the back of the car. 'Maybe you could sneak a gun out of the firearms store? There was that hunting rifle you confiscated last week – the one with the telescopic sight and silencer. That'd do it. Get a bit of distance, find somewhere with a good vantage point, and put a bullet straight through Reuben's head.'

'Never going to work.'

Tufty nodded. 'Exactly: they can't both be right, can they? Time's either fixed or it isn't. And some scientists say it doesn't really exist at all.'

'All you've got to do is squeeze the trigger.'

'I'm not talking about this.'

'Yeah, I know it's a bit complicated, but stick with me, Sarge.'

Pull the trigger? Simple as that? Point a gun at someone's head and kill them?

Logan's stomach lurched again.

'*…further protests organized for tomorrow. Weather now…*'

'According to the thermal time hypothesis, time's a statistical artefact—'

'For God's sake, Tufty. Can we … five minutes… *Please.*'

'*…afraid this cold snap looks set to continue for the rest of the week. The Met Office have issued a yellow warning…*'

Tufty pursed his lips. Shrugged one shoulder. 'Thought you'd be interested.'

Half a dozen bungalows appeared on the right, clustered in the corner of a field. They looked like the advance guard of a much bigger army, posted on the clifftop to keep a lookout over the waves. An eight-foot-high chain-link fence wrapped around the chunk of field next to them, already scarred with a rough arc of gravel and concrete. Pipes and cables jutted up from concrete foundations like thick plastic weeds. Reinforcements on their way.

Samantha squeezed his shoulder again. 'Just think about it, OK? That's all I'm asking.'

'*...back with more at nine.*'

'*Thanks Ashley. Noo, let's kick off the hour with a wee bittie Proclaimers and "Sunshine on Leith", cos looks like we're gettin' neen o' that fir weeks up here.*'

Tufty slowed, then indicated, and turned into the scheme as the singing started.

Kept his eyes forward.

Not speaking.

It was like working with a small child.

Logan let his head fall back against the rest. 'Sorry.'

Another shrug. Then Tufty pointed through the windscreen at the furthest bungalow in the development. It was huge – had to be at least five bedrooms – with a blockwork drive, double garage, conservatory, and landscaped front garden that looked a lot more bedded in than any of the other houses. 'That's it.'

A couple of manky hatchbacks lurked at the kerb to either side, engines idling. Windows rolled down a crack so the warty individuals inside could smoke while they waited for something to happen.

Tufty pulled onto the drive, parking in front of a white Range Rover Sport. Switched off the engine. And sat there, still not saying anything.

'I said I was sorry.'

'No problem.' Then Tufty climbed into the rain, jamming his hat on his head. Clunked the door shut and marched up the drive to the front door. Rang the bell.

A very small, very annoying child.

Logan grabbed his high-viz jacket from the back seat and got out of the Big Car.

The occupants of the hatchbacks scrambled out, shoulders and hoods pulled up, fiddling with big digital cameras. 'Hoy! Over here! Sergeant? Did you find Martin Milne's body yesterday? Is it him?'

Wind snatched at the fluorescent-yellow material of the jacket as Logan fought his way into it. Rain hammered and pattered off the surface. Off his hat. Off his stabproof vest. Stinging his face and hands like a thousand frozen wasps. While the two lumpy middle-aged men snapped photos.

'How did Martin Milne die? Did he commit suicide?'

Logan hauled the zip up and turned his back on the wind. 'How long have you two been out here?'

'It's Martin Milne, isn't it?'

He pointed at the hatchbacks. 'Police Scotland aren't issuing any statements at this time. Now, please return to your vehicles and respect the Milne family's privacy.'

The garden sloped away to the East, where the sea surged and pounded against the curling line of the headland. Probably really impressive in summer, when the sun was shining, but on a dreich Thursday in February? Sod that.

The shorter of the two curled his top lip. 'Come on, Sergeant, throw us a bone, eh? Been freezing my nuts off out here since six. Is it Martin Milne?'

'We're not issuing any—'

'"Statements", yeah, I got that the first time.' He tucked his camera into his coat. 'Off the record?'

The other one sidled up beside him. A nose like a sand-blasted golf ball, wrapped round with broken spider veins. 'Promise we'll sod off if you let us have something.'

Logan stared at the ground for a moment. 'I can't right now, but...' He glanced over his shoulder at the house and dropped his voice to a whisper. 'Look, give me your business cards, and I'll let you know what's going on soon as I can. You get first dibs.'

Frozen Nuts sniffed. 'What, *both* of us?'

'But you have to promise not to tell anyone else I tipped you off, OK?'

'Deal.' Golf-Ball Nose dug into his pocket and came out with a card. 'Bob Finnegan, *Aberdeen Examiner*. That's got my mobile number and my email.'

His opposite number produced a card of his own. 'Noel McGuinness, *Scottish Independent Tribune*. You promise?'

'If *you* promise to back off and leave the family alone till I give you the nod.'

The two of them shared a look, then nodded.

A quick shaking of hands and they retreated to their cars. Got in. And drove away.

Soon as they were gone, Logan marched up the drive to the front door. Gave Tufty's arm a thump with the back of his hand. 'Are you planning on sulking all day?'

Tufty poked the bell again, setting something buzzing inside the house. 'I'm not sulking. I'm disappointed.'

'*You're* disappointed?'

'Calamity or Isla: I could understand them not getting it, but I thought you were interested in the...'

The door clunked then swung open.

A woman glared out at them from behind a pair of large square glasses. Long dark hair pulled back in a ponytail with a sprinkling of grey at the roots. Teeth bared. Already going at full volume: 'IF YOU VULTURES DON'T GO AWAY, I'M CALLING THE POLICE!'

Tufty raised his eyebrows. 'Hello, Katie.'

'Ah.' She closed her mouth. Grimaced. 'Officer Quirrel. Sorry. I thought you were that pair of...' Then she stared at them, eyes widening. Bit her bottom lip. Wiped her hands down the front of her green-and-white striped apron. 'Oh God, they were right. It *is* him isn't it? The body they found in the woods? It's Martin.'

She staggered back a step, blinking at the wood laminate flooring. Holding onto the doorframe.

Tufty held out a hand. 'Katie, does Martin have a tattoo on his left shoulder? Maybe a dolphin or a whale or something?'

8

'What?' Mrs Milne pulled her chin in, wrinkling her neck. 'No. No he doesn't. He doesn't have any tattoos. Why would he have tattoos?'

Logan stepped forward. 'Then it's not Martin, Mrs Milne: the man we found yesterday had a tattoo.'

She sagged where she stood, letting out a long breath. 'Oh thank God.' Another breath, one hand against her chest. 'Look at me. Sorry. Come in. Please.'

The hallway was light, airy, with framed photos and scrawled crayon drawings lining the walls.

Mrs Milne led them through into the kitchen, where a little boy sat at a rustic table, both hands wrapped around a tumbler of orange juice. Blond hair, red sweatshirt, white shirt, black trousers. Plaster cast on his right arm. The smell of frying butter filled the air.

'Would you like a tea, or coffee, or something? Or pancakes? I'm making for Ethan.'

The little boy stared back at them through glasses like his mother's.

Logan slipped out of his jacket and hung it over the back of a chair. It dripped onto the slate floor. 'Tea would be lovely. But don't worry, Constable Quirrel can make it. Can't you, Constable?'

A nod. 'Don't want to stand in the way of Ethan's pancakes.'

'Oh. That's very kind.' She went back to the hob while Tufty poked about in the cupboard above the kettle.

The place must have cost a fortune. It was big enough for a full-sized dining table, a central island with hob and sink, fitted units around the outside in what was probably oak, granite work surfaces, slate tiles on the floor, a massive American-style fridge freezer. One of those fancy taps that did boiling water. Bit of a difference from Logan's – cobbled together out of whatever was cheapest at B&Q and Argos.

There were about a dozen more crayon scribbles in here, most of them featuring what looked like potatoes with arms and legs, but instead of being stuck to the fridge door like in a normal house, they were displayed in elaborate wood-and-glass frames.

Logan settled into a seat and nodded at the little boy. 'That's some cast you've got there, Ethan, what happened to your arm?'

He stared back in silence.

OK...

Mrs Milne shook her head. 'I love him to bits, but he can be a clumsy wee soul sometimes. Can't you, Ethan?'

A shrug, then Ethan went back to his orange juice.

'He's a bit shy.' She ladled batter into the frying pan and pulled on a gleaming smile. 'So, who's for pancakes?'

Logan wandered over to the window, rolling up a pancake – smeared with butter and raspberry jam – as if it were a fine cigar. Bit off the end and chewed.

Outside, Ethan slouched through the rain, good hand held in his mother's. The cast on his other arm pressed against his chest. A scarlet people-carrier idled at the kerb, and as they reached it the driver's window slid down, revealing a large woman with a Lego-bob haircut who smiled at them.

Mrs Milne bent down and kissed Ethan on the cheek, wiped

the lipstick away, and saw him into the back of the car. Made sure he was belted in. Then stood there, in the rain, waving as the car wound its way out of the small development, onto the road, and away. Stood there a moment or two longer. And finally turned and trudged towards the house again.

Tufty appeared at Logan's elbow. Had a sip of tea from a mug with Winnie the Pooh on it. 'Doesn't seem like a very happy kid.'

'His dad's vanished.'

'True.'

Another bite. 'And then there's the broken arm.'

'I was forever falling out of trees when I was five.'

'Let me guess: you landed on your head a *lot*.' Logan frowned out at the rain. 'Get onto Social and see if anyone's raised any flags about Ethan. Doctors, hospitals, teachers. Exactly how "clumsy" is he?'

'Sarge.'

A clunk, then a rattle, and Mrs Milne was back looking as if she'd just been for a swim. She grimaced at them. 'Poor wee soul's having a hard time at school. Some of the kids think it's fun to wind him up, because Martin's missing. Can you imagine anything so *cruel*?' She dabbed at her long black hair with a tea towel. 'Yesterday, someone told him Martin's run off with a younger woman. That Martin doesn't love him any more.' She shuddered. 'Well, you know what kids are like. Horrible little monsters.'

Tufty beamed at her. 'Sorry to be a pain, but could I use your loo? Too much tea.'

'Out into the hallway, second on the right.'

'Thanks.' And he was off, unclipping his Airwave handset as he went. Not exactly subtle.

Idiot.

Logan polished off the pancake. Sooked his fingers clean. 'Do you know if your husband has online banking? And if he does, can you get access to it?'

'Martin hasn't run off with some tart. He wouldn't do

that to us.' She looked away, lowered her voice. 'He loves us.'

'Mrs Milne? The banking?'

'Of course – we've got joint accounts.' She went over to the Welsh dresser and opened a drawer. Pulled out a small laptop. 'Oh, you should have heard them when we got married: "He's *far* too young for her", "He's a toy boy", "She's *such* a dirty old lady", "Must be like he's shagging his mum".'

The laptop went on the kitchen table. Then whirred and beeped into life.

'Kids aren't the only monsters.' She logged in. 'Suppose that's where they get it from.'

Logan took the seat next to her. 'You said Ethan was clumsy sometimes?'

'Hold on, it wants to install updates…' Mrs Milne hunched over the keyboard, fingers clattering across the plastic. 'Do you mean his arm? He says he fell over in the playground, but I don't know. Why didn't the teachers see anything? Surely if a wee boy falls over and breaks his arm, they'd see *something*.' Then she sat back again. 'Here we go. What do you need?'

Logan pointed at the bank's summary page of accounts. 'Can you call up all recent transactions? We want to see if Martin's used his credit or debit card.'

She hesitated. 'You think he's run away.'

'We're only looking for some clue to where he is. If he's taking money out in Dundee, we know to get the police there looking for him.'

She bit her bottom lip again, then fiddled with the trackpad, bringing up a list of the last ten credit card transactions. Pointed. 'These are mostly me: Tesco, Tesco, shoes for Ethan, Tesco, Tesco again, heating oil. That one's Martin's: the petrol station in Peterhead on Friday. Then it's just Tesco, Tesco, Tesco.'

'What about the current account?'

'Erm…' She clicked again. 'Nothing since Monday. I got fifty pounds out to pay the window cleaner.'

So Milne had been missing since Sunday night and not bought a single meal on his credit card, or taken a penny out of the bank. If he really had been on the run for three days and four nights, surely he'd have to spend something. 'And he doesn't have any other accounts? Maybe from before you were married?'

'Martin and I don't keep secrets from one another.' Her chin came up. 'If he had another account I'd *know* about it.'

Yeah, you keep telling yourself that. Everyone had secrets.

Logan nodded at the screen. 'Any chance you can print off everything for the last three months or so?'

She rested her fingers against the keys, staring at her bitten nails. 'What if something's happened to him? What if he…' Mrs Milne cleared her throat. 'What if they're right? What if he thinks we don't matter, and he can do better somewhere else with someone his own age? What if he's dead?'

He probably was, but there was no point telling her that.

Logan placed a hand on her shoulder. The jumper was damp and cool. 'We're going to do everything we can.'

She nodded. Then sniffed. Then wiped a hand across her eyes. 'Yes. Right. I'll download those statements.'

Logan settled back against the work surface, a fresh cup of tea steaming away in his hand.

The back garden was a shivering mass of bushes and low trees, slapped about by the wind. A shed sat in the bottom corner, surrounded by terracotta pots, their contents covered with white fleecy material. What looked like a vegetable plot lay along the far end of the garden. All very bucolic and genteel. Perched on the edge of the world.

He checked his watch. Half eight and there was still no sign of Tufty. Knowing Logan's luck, Mrs Milne had probably left the front door open and Tufty had got out. He'd be climbing trees, chasing cars, and pooping on people's lawns.

The room was quiet, just Logan and the *hummmm-swoosh-hummmm-swoosh* of the dishwasher.

He dug into his pocket and came out with the two business cards. Well, a promise was a promise... He ripped both up and dumped them in the pedal bin.

A newspaper lay on the worktop next to it, open at the crossword. Half the grid was filled in, a blue biro sitting next to the paper. Logan peered at the clues.

She'd got four down wrong.

And that wasn't how you spelled 'DISCONTENT' either. Or 'INCALCULABLE'.

Then Mrs Milne's voice cut across the dishwasher. 'Sorry. I had to change the cartridge in the printer.'

Logan turned. 'You're a crossword person.'

Pink flushed her cheeks. Then she held out a small stack of paper. 'Bank statements for the last twelve weeks.'

'Thanks.' He flicked through them.

Regular entries for petrol and food. A pub in Peterhead every Wednesday. A few entries for Amazon. Some for Waterstones in Elgin... Nothing jumped out.

Mrs Milne picked the newspaper up and ruffled it back into shape. 'Martin was always the puzzle solver. Into his Miss Marples and his crime drama on the TV.' She closed the paper, shutting away the crossword. Smoothed it down. 'Don't know why I bother really, I'm always terrible at it.'

There, spread across the *Aberdeen Examiner*'s front page, was a photo of the entrance to the woods, all cordoned off with blue-and-white 'POLICE' tape. A uniformed constable stood behind the line, in the pouring rain, while behind him a patrol car sat with all its lights on. 'GRISLY DISCOVERY IN MACDUFF WOODS' with the sub-headline 'IS BODY IN WOODS MISSING BUSINESSMAN?'

No wonder she'd thought the worst when they'd turned up on her doorstep.

Logan reached out and took the newspaper from her. 'You shouldn't be reading this kind of stuff. They don't know anything, they're just speculating. Making things up to sell more copies.'

'Keep it.' Mrs Milne turned away. 'I never liked doing the crossword anyway.'

Her back was broad beneath the damp jumper, but rounded, as if she spent a lot of time trying to make herself look smaller. Maybe her husband was a short man and he didn't like being towered over? Little man syndrome.

The dishwasher whispered and moaned.

Rain spattered across the kitchen window.

Logan folded the newspaper and tucked it under his arm. 'We're going to do everything we can, I promise.'

She didn't turn around. 'Thank you.'

Then the kitchen door thumped open and Tufty poked his head in. About time.

He pulled on a big grin. 'Katie? Can I ask a...' He nodded back towards the front of the house. 'It's a quickie.'

She followed him down the hall, Logan bringing up the rear.

'Any idea who this is?' Tufty pointed at one of the framed photos. A close-up group of eight men, standing around a barbecue in T-shirts. Baseball caps and sunglasses. Sunburn and grins. A couple had their drinks raised in salute. 'On the left, with the corn-on-the-cob.'

Mrs Milne blinked, frowned. 'It's Pete. Peter Shepherd. He's Martin's business partner. Him, Martin, and Brian set up GCML together nine years ago. Why?'

'Cool, cool.' Tufty tapped the frame. 'And he lives...?'

'Pennan. He's got one of those sideyways houses. Look, why do you want to know?'

Tufty shrugged. 'Just interested. Any chance I can borrow the photo?'

Logan fastened his seatbelt. 'Well?'

Tufty waved through the windscreen at Mrs Milne. Then turned the wheel and took them out of the little development. Soon as he got to the junction with the main road, he reached back into the footwell and pulled out the framed photo of the barbecue. Passed it over. 'Notice anything?'

'They've burnt the sausages?'

'Guy on the left, Peter Shepherd. Check the arm.'

Martin's business partner had a green T-shirt with a sort of Viking logo on the front. He'd ripped the sleeves off, exposing the swollen biceps of someone who spent far too much time down the gym. And there, on his left arm, was a narwhal tattoo.

9

Banff sulked beneath the heavy lid of stone sky, the buildings crouched together in the rain. Tufty took them in through the limits and down the hill. 'Station?'

'Pennan.' Logan pressed the talk button on his Airwave. 'Maggie, I need you to look someone up for me. Peter Shepherd, lives in Pennan.'

'Give me a minute, Sergeant McRae, the MIT are hogging all the bandwidth so everything's running like a slug.'

Tufty took a right, onto Castle Street – its rows of old-fashioned buildings giving way to the same buildings but with shops occupying the ground floor. 'Sarge, should we not… You know, tell DCI Steel that Shepherd's her corpse?'

'No guarantee it's him, Tufty. We're just doing a bit of legwork. Making sure we don't waste anyone's time.'

'Yeah, but—'

'When Mrs Milne reported her husband missing, did you go talk to everyone at his company?'

'No one had seen him since Friday. He bunked off early, about half three, which was par for the course.'

'What about Shepherd?'

He shrugged. 'Didn't ask. We were looking for Milne, didn't even know Shepherd existed.'

Which was fair enough.

A handful of bodies tramped through the rain, bent nearly double under its relentless assault. All the cars had their headlights on, edging along not much faster than the people on the pavement.

'What about this Brian person, the other partner?'

Something crawled across Tufty's face, wrinkling bits of it, before fading away, leaving him smooth as a baby's backside. 'Got him: Brian Chapman. Financial Director. Big sticky-out mole on his forehead.'

'That it?'

'Didn't know where Milne was, and seemed genuinely worried when I told him we'd found Milne's car abandoned, Sunday night.'

'Sergeant McRae? I've got three speeding tickets over the last six years and that's it.'

'Vehicles?'

'Two registered at his property: a Mitsubishi Warrior and a Porsche Nine-Eleven.'

That explained the speeding tickets. Mind you, you'd have to be an optimist to own a Porsche in Pennan. A rear-wheel-drive sports car? And that hill? In winter? Be lucky if you got it out of the garage half the year.

'Do you want me to check if he made any complaints?'

'Please. And the phone number.'

The sandstone spire of Banff Parish Church went by the passenger window. A group of OAPs, dressed like carrion crows, shuffled in through the door, single file. A couple of floral tributes sat either side of the entrance as the minister shook hands with each and every one of them. Probably holding a sweepy in his head as to who he'd have to bury next.

Tufty chewed on his lip. 'Sarge, are you *sure* DCI Steel isn't going to blow a hairy when she finds out we didn't come clean about Shepherd?'

The road swept around to the left, then past the football pitch and the golf course.

'Sarge?'

'Tell me about Martin Milne.'

He blew out a breath. Screwed up his face for a moment. Then, 'OK. Martin Carter Milne, thirty, BA in business from Robert Gordons University, married to Katie Milne, one child: Ethan, six. Drives a dark-blue Aston Martin DB9. Very swish. Really wanted a go in it, but Traffic pulled rank.'

'Impounded?'

'Secure parking in Mintlaw. Mrs Milne can pick it up anytime she likes.' The Big Car bumped over the bridge. The River Deveron was a swollen grey snake, rasping at its banks below, surging out into the bay. 'Milne got a caution for aggravated assault three years ago. Fiscal didn't take it to court because he was wading in to break up a fight at a Bloo Toon, Elgin City match. Left a guy with a fractured cheekbone and a broken arm.'

'Bit of a bruiser then.' Logan scanned the barbecue photograph for Milne.

He was in the middle, overseeing the ritual burning of the sausages. Red T-shirt with the same Viking logo as Peter Shepherd, only he'd left his sleeves on. Big arms. Not over-muscled like Shepherd's, but thick enough to do some damage.

'Sergeant McRae? I've got records of Peter Shepherd's house being burgled last year. The thief got away with an antique gramophone and a set of three regency candlesticks. All recovered. He's made four complaints in the last six months about vandalism. And there's two ongoing investigations about his business premises being broken into in Peterhead.'

'Ongoing since when?'

'Three years.'

So for 'ongoing' read, 'no one has a clue'.

'Just in case, better give me his work number too.' Logan turned to Tufty. 'What are they called?'

'GCML: Geirrød Container Management and Logistics, Peterhead.'

'You get that, Maggie?'

'Do you want me to text them through to your phone?'

'Thanks.'

'And are you coming back to the station anytime soon, Sergeant McRae? Only the MIT are being ... difficult.'

'Sorry. It's oot-and-aboot for me and the loon. If anyone asks, we're chasing up a misper.'

And with any luck, Steel would believe it.

'And you've not seen Mr Shepherd since Friday?' Logan pinned his phone between his ear and his shoulder as he wrote the details down in his notebook. Leaning into the corners as the Big Car wheeched along the winding road.

'Yup, he's off seeing a supplier in Chesterfield.'

Oh no he wasn't. He was dead.

'But you haven't heard from him?'

'Nah. Don't usually when he's off on his travels. Likes to keep a low profile does our Pete, so it's all text messages and emails.'

'OK, well, if you hear from him, tell him we'd like a word.'

'Will do.'

Logan hit the button and ended the call. 'GCML say Shepherd's off down south, buying them some new containers.'

Tufty overtook a tractor with mud-spattering tyres. 'So *maybe* it isn't him we found. Maybe it's someone else. Maybe he'll turn up tomorrow with a bunch of containers and a confused look on his face.'

'Maybe.' But it wasn't likely.

Logan tried the other number again. Got the answering machine again.

'Hello, you've reached Pete Shepherd. I'm sorry I can't come to the phone right now, but leave a message and I'll get back to you. Thanks.' Then a pause. *Bleeeeeeeep.*

He hung up.

'Shepherd's still not answering his mobile.'

A nod from the driver's seat. 'Well, he can't, can he? Not

if he's dead. Roaming charges are probably extortionate from the afterlife.'

'...but that's nonsense, isn't it? Of course time exists. And do you know what I think?'

Logan ruffled the copy of the *Aberdeen Examiner* he'd taken from Mrs Milne. 'Nope.' Wasn't interested either, but there was no point telling Tufty that, he'd only sulk again.

So instead, Logan skimmed an article on the new development going into the gap where Aberdeen's Saint Nicholas House used to be. Not exactly riveting, but it was better than listening to Tufty rambling on about physics. '"We'll Never Stop Protesting Against The Evil Concrete Rubik's Cube!" Says Local Campaigner.' Who bore an uncanny resemblance to a scrotum in a shirt and tie.

Outside the car windows, rain lashed the fields and bushes and trees, making the tarmac shine in the Big Car's headlights as they wound their way along the Fraserburgh road.

'I think time's an emergent property of an entropic field. You know, like the Higgs boson is caused by vibrational ripples in the Higgs field?'

'Hmm...' Then there was an article about a project to get big, painted, fibreglass sheep installed across the city. Because all the dolphins weren't enough.

'And just as the Higgs field gives particles their physical mass, the entropic field gives particles their *chronological* mass.'

Next up, a long piece on Emily Benton's death. Quotes from her parents and friends about how lovely she was and how everyone liked her and she didn't have any enemies. Which obviously wasn't true, because someone battered her to death. The *Examiner* had gone out and done a vox pop in Inverurie – little photos of cold-looking shoppers above banal statements about how that kind of thing shouldn't happen and their prayers were with her family.

'So time is actually a boson. You see?'

'Hmm...'

Then there was a half-page on Banff Academy raising money for Macduff lifeboat station after one of the pupils nearly drowned on a fishing trip.

'And that's why the faster you move, the slower time gets. The entropic field is like cornflour – go slow and you pass through it without noticing, go fast and it seizes up.'

Logan turned the page, where there was an opinion piece on the number of bodies being found in woods about Aberdeenshire. 'Of course, you know what this means, don't you?'

'Exactly. Time is the physical manifestation of a non-Newtonian-fluid-like field.'

Logan looked at him over the top of the paper. 'No, it means we're going to have to release details of the bodies, or the papers will start screaming, "Serial Killer!" Surprised they haven't already.'

'Oh. Right. Well, anyway, so the entropic field only allows travel in one direction or it violates the second law of thermodynamics, right? And—'

'The chronology's interesting, isn't it?'

Tufty beamed. 'That's what I think. Entropy, thermodynamics, the time boson—'

'Emily Benton's body is discovered in woods ten days ago. Then Martin Milne disappears a week after Emily was found. And Peter Shepherd turns up battered to death with a bag over his head, in different woods, three days after that, when he's meant to be in Chesterfield buying containers.'

The sign for Gardenstown flashed by on the left, and the sea was back – a thin line of charcoal on the horizon.

'So...' That thinky frown worked its way across Tufty's face again. 'Milne killed Emily, *and* his business partner? Thought the MO was meant to be different?'

'Her skull was bashed in with an adjustable wrench. We've got no idea what happened to Shepherd's head: there's a bag over it.' Logan went back to the paper, frowning at an article about childcare services getting cut in Ellon. 'Maybe that's why they're different? Emily was killed in situ. Imagine you've just gone berserk on someone's skull with a wrench, and now you've got to dump the body. That head's going to leak blood and fluid and bits of brain all over your boot. So you stick a bin-bag over it and duct-tape it tight around the neck so nothing oozes out.'

'Ooh. That has a sensible…'

'Then you get the hell out of Dodge, before the police come looking for you.'

The windscreen wipers droned across the glass, clearing a path that immediately vanished to be cleared again.

Tufty coughed. 'Mind you. Bit of a coincidence, isn't it? Shepherd's death just happens to be exactly the same MO as this Edinburgh gangster?'

'Hmm…' There was that.

'And why kill Emily Benton?'

There was that as well.

A big four-by-four rattled past in the opposite direction, its driver oblivious on her mobile phone, big Dulux dog in the back seat.

More fields drenched with rain.

'How long till Pennan?'

Tufty peered at the dashboard clock. 'Five minutes?'

Trees swallowed the road, thumping heavy droplets from their sagging branches. Then out the other side.

Next: an article on diesel thefts around Turriff.

OK, so the evidence was circumstantial at the moment, but Milne's disappearance made him look guilty. If he had nothing to do with Shepherd's death, why did he run? Innocent people didn't vanish three days before their business partners turned up dead in the woods.

And then there was Milne's obsession with crime fiction and TV shows. All those stories telling him how not to leave forensic evidence behind.

Couldn't deny that it fit.

Martin Milne killed Peter Shepherd, dumped the body, covered his tracks, then did a runner.

Logan wriggled in his seat, getting comfortable. Steel had a team of what, twenty officers? Maybe thirty? And she didn't have a clue. Here he was, with nothing but Tufty for backup, and he'd already solved the murder. *Two* murders, if Milne killed Emily Benton as well.

Tufty was right: Steel wasn't going to be very happy. But you know what? Tough.

He flipped the page.

Sometimes the gods smiled upon...

Oh.

No.

The breath curdled in his lungs. His fillings itched. A wave of electricity riffled the hairs on the back of his arms and neck, finally settling in his bowels.

There, sandwiched between something on house prices in Strichen and a bit about a new music festival in Fraserburgh, was a photo of Wee Hamish Mowat.

All the moisture disappeared from Logan's mouth as his throat closed up.

'Local Businessman's Charity Legacy'

The newspaper trembled in his hands.

Under the photo, the caption was: 'Philanthropist Hamish Alexander Selkirk Mowat Passed Away In His Sleep Last Night.'

How the hell did the *Aberdeen Examiner* get the news out so fast? What did Reuben do, hire a publicist?

There was a quote from the Lord Provost about what a great man he'd been. There were quotes from three different charities about how *generous* his contributions were. But there was nothing about him running the biggest criminal empire in the Northeast of Scotland. Nothing about the punishment beatings. Nothing about the pig farm where people disappeared.

Nothing about the fact that Reuben would be coming for Logan now.

Oh God...

'Sarge?'

The funeral was set for Friday. Tomorrow.

But then Wee Hamish Mowat was never one for hanging about.

And neither would Reuben.

'Sarge? You OK? You look like you've swallowed a bee.'

Logan lowered the paper. Blinked out at the hostile world. 'Yeah.' He nodded. 'Fine.'

Liar.

10

The road wound around and down the cliff face, steep enough for Tufty to change into second gear. Pennan appeared as a cluster of rooftops, all huddled together for protection against the North Sea as it hurled itself against the little harbour's walls, the cliffs, and the stony beach.

Of course, it wasn't really all *that* surprising the *Aberdeen Examiner* had been ready to go with the story of Hamish Mowat's death. They'd probably had the whole thing filed and ready for months. Just waiting. Freshening up the quotes from time to time.

The BBC had the same kind of thing all ready to go for when the Queen popped her royal slippers, didn't they? Testimonials, photos, documentaries. Why should Aberdeen's biggest crime lord be any different?

Especially with Reuben waiting in the wings: the king is dead, long live the king.

They slowed to a crawl, squeezing the Big Car between a slab-like greying lump of a building and the whitewashed Pennan Inn. Out onto the tiny village's only street. Houses on one side, the angry swell of the sea on the other.

Tufty took a left. Rain pelted the windscreen, clattered off the roof, sparked on the bonnet. 'Bit bleak, isn't it?'

Waves boomed against the seawall, sending up arcs of

spray that hovered for a moment like heavy clouds, before smashing down across the tarmac.

Some of the houses faced front, but most of them stood sideways, with their gable ends pointing out at the storm. Narrow alleys separated the buildings, the front doors sheltering from the wind.

Tufty pulled the car over and pointed at a one-and-a-half storey, traditional Scottish house, with whitewashed walls and a Porsche parked out front. 'That's us.' Another wave smashed into the seawall – the spray completely engulfed the sports car. He grimaced. 'What do you think, wait for it to ease up a bit?'

'Be here all week.' Logan unclipped his seatbelt, pulled on his peaked cap, then struggled into his high-viz. Doing his best not to bash Tufty in the face with an elbow. 'Come on then.'

It was like being pelted with frozen nails.

He slammed the car door and hurried across the road, slipping into the alley between the front of Peter Shepherd's house and the back of the next one in the row as another wave crashed down.

'Aaaaaagh! God … sodding … bloody…' Tufty shuffled into the alley with his arms held out from his body, dripping, mouth hanging open. 'Gagh…'

Logan tried the bell.

A trilling ring sounded inside, but no one answered.

One more go.

And again.

Tufty raised one leg and shook the foot. 'I'm *drenched*.'

OK, so there was no one home. But then, given that Shepherd was lying on his back in a refrigerated drawer in the mortuary, waiting for his turn to be dissected, that wasn't too surprising.

Logan tried the door handle.

Locked.

'Could've jumped in the sea and I'd be drier…'

He turned. The house with its back to Shepherd's had a couple of windows on this side. Light shone out from one of them, the glass all steamed up, what sounded like Led Zeppelin belting out in there. Logan knocked on the window.

A shadowy figure loomed, then wiped a hole in the fog revealing a lined face, with lots of dark eye make-up and a grey quiff. She frowned for a moment, then opened the window. Rock music pounded out into the rain, accompanied by the sweet buttery scent of baking. 'HELLO?'

'We're trying to—'

'YOU'LL HAVE TO SPEAK UP!'

Logan huddled closer. 'WE'RE TRYING TO TRACE YOUR NEIGHBOUR. PETER SHEPHERD?'

'PETE? NO, HE'S NOT HERE. HE… HOLD ON,' she held up an arthritis-twisted finger, as Robert Plant's wailing gave way to a guitar solo, 'I LOVE THIS BIT.' Nodding along with her eyes closed, thrashing away on a clawed-hand air guitar.

'DO YOU KNOW WHEN HE'LL BE BACK?'

'WHO?'

'YOUR NEIGHBOUR.'

'OH. HAS HE DONE SOMETHING?' Still rocking along.

'NO. WE'RE WORRIED ABOUT HIS SAFETY. WE… LOOK, CAN YOU TURN THAT DOWN A BIT?'

She shrugged, then turned and padded back into the room. The music clicked off, leaving nothing behind but the booming waves, clattering rain, and howling wind. 'There we go.'

'Do you have a key to Mr Shepherd's house, Mrs…?'

'Call me Aggie. Give me a minute to grab my coat: I've got to go round and feed his cat anyway.' Then she thunked the window shut and disappeared.

'Here we go.' Aggie swung the door open and stepped inside. 'Onion? Unnnnn-yun, where's kitten?'

Logan followed her inside. Shepherd had obviously had a bit of work done to the place. It might look all traditional and Scottish vernacular on the outside, but inside – the living room and kitchen were one big open-plan space full of gleaming surfaces, leather, and abstract oil paintings.

Shepherd and Milne's container business must be making a fortune.

Tufty closed the front door behind him, and stood there, dripping on the hall tiles. 'Gah...'

Aggie hobbled up the stairs. 'Onion? Come on, time for nom-noms.'

Soon as she was gone, Logan poked Tufty on the shoulder. 'You try Shepherd's mobile again, and try not to get everything soggy. If he's not dead, I don't want him suing the force because you ruined his carpet.'

A dining room sat on the other side of the stairs, with a long oak table and matching chairs. The only other room on the ground floor was a study. Bookshelves lined the walls, all crammed to overflowing with textbooks, folders, lever-arch files, boxes, and hardback books. A proper office-style desk with a docking station for a laptop and a pair of flatscreen monitors on armatures. Swanky office chair with more buttons and levers than most family saloons. A pair of oak filing cabinets.

No diary or appointments calendar. But then everyone was all electronic these days, weren't they? Whatever happened to the good old days, when people actually wrote things down, then left them lying around for police officers to find?

He scanned the bookshelves. The textbooks all had titles like *Optimisation For Hydrocarbon Support Industries* and *Logistic Management in the Norwegian Sector – Regulations and Compliance Volume VII.* The folders were just as bad. And the books all seemed to be true crime. Biographies of murderers and case studies on serial killers. A collection of gangster memoirs. All neatly ordered, alphabetically, by author and title.

So Milne wasn't the only crime freak.

Logan tried upstairs.

A big bathroom, all done out in dark slate tiles and

spotlights, with a freestanding enamel bath big enough for three. A box room, full of boxes. A small bedroom with a lot of lace and flowers in it, completely out of keeping with the rest of the place. And last, but not least, the master bedroom.

Aggie was on her knees at the side of the bed, bum in the air, one arm wiggling about in the space underneath. 'Come on, Onion Pickle Pie, it's only policemen, they're not really that scary.'

A king-size bed dominated the room, with a maroon velvet headboard. Huge telly on the facing wall. Thick, smoke-coloured carpet. One wall a deep claret, the others stark white. Normal people didn't have houses like this. This was what happened when you hired a decorator who specialized in boutique hotels.

Aggie sat back on her heels and bared her top teeth at Logan. 'He's not normally this shy.'

Logan wandered over to the window, looking down on the narrow alley that separated the two houses. 'Do you look after his cat a lot?'

'Only if he's going to be away for more than one night. Onion doesn't really like change. Likes to know his Aunty Aggie's looking after him.' Then she leaned forwards, bum up in the air again. 'Come on, sweetie. I've got lovely tuna for you. Your favourite. Yum, yum!'

The room wasn't just swanky-hotel designed, it was swanky-hotel clean as well. No personal knick-knacks, bits, or bobs. No deodorant, hairdryer, or combs on show. No clothes dumped over the chair in the corner. The only thing out of place was the book on the bedside cabinet. And even that was perfectly lined up with the edges.

The Blood-Red Line. Subtitled, *How Malcolm McLennan Founded Edinburgh's Biggest Criminal Empire.* The author's name was picked out in white, 'L. P. Malloy', over a montage of towerblocks, Edinburgh Castle, somewhere dark in the Old Town, and a line of crime-scene tape. With a few tasteful blood spatters thrown in for good measure.

L. P. Malloy had to be a pseudonym. No one would be thick enough to write an exposé about Malcolm McLennan and use their real name. Not if they wanted to keep all their fingers. Surprised anyone was brave enough to publish it.

'Oh come on, Onion, be a *good* cat for Aunty Aggie.'

Logan flicked through the pages. A biro inscription was scrawled on the title page, 'To Peter, You're a Sick Bastard For Reading This Stuff, But I Love You Anyway. Martin XXX!' Bit gushing, but there you go.

There was a wodge of printed photos in the middle of the book – most in black-and-white and copied from newspaper reports. But a couple were clearly crime-scene pics, reproduced in vivid gory colour. One of a young man in a Seventies suit with his throat slashed, lying crumpled in a toilet stall. One of a burned-out car with blackened human remains in the driver's seat. A woman lying twisted beneath a railway bridge. And one of a naked man, lying on his back in some woods, with a bag over his head.

Logan stood at the window, looking down into the little alley. The paving slabs glittered with water, the puddles rippled in the battering rain. He pressed the talk button on his Airwave handset. 'OK, that's great news. We'll get it set up soon as I've handed over to the MIT.'

Inspector McGregor's voice crackled from the speaker. *'Glad to hear you're being so grown-up about it.'*

Aunty Aggie bustled out of the front door, hauling the jacket hood up over her quiff. She disappeared into the downpour.

'No point fighting the system, is there? Besides, I've got a dunt to organize.' And maybe this way Steel would be too busy running around trying to find Martin Milne to be a pain in Logan's backside.

'Make sure you keep me up to date then.' And McGregor was gone.

'SARGE?'

Logan stuck his head out of the bedroom door. 'WHAT?'

'YOU WANT A TEA?'

'HAVE YOU FOUND ME A NEXT OF KIN YET?'

'WAITING TO HEAR BACK. SO: TEA?'

Shouldn't really be helping themselves to the contents of a murder victim's cupboards... But it wasn't as if Peter Shepherd would have grudged them a cuppa. 'THANKS.'

He went back to the bedroom and opened the bedside cabinet. Handkerchiefs, a watch, various flavours of chapstick, pens, mixed with bits-and-bobs that would never come in handy again. Next drawer down was all socks. The one below that, pants and boxers. All neatly folded.

The cabinet on the other side had a huge remote control in it, along with a box of tissues and some lubricant in the top drawer. So no prizes for guessing what normally played on the huge wall-mounted TV opposite the bed. Next drawer down: more socks and some aftershave. Bottom drawer: more underwear.

Logan settled onto the edge of the duvet and picked up the remote. It was about three times bigger than it had any right being, with a corresponding number of extra buttons. He pressed the one with the power icon on it. There was a pause, then the TV played a three-note tune and displayed the manufacturer's logo.

Instead of defaulting to BBC One, the screen displayed a series of folders and icons under the title 'MEDIA HUB'. He picked a folder marked 'CHILE 13' and a slideshow popped into life: photos of alpaca and mountains and two men backpacking through stunning scenery, accompanied by a soundtrack of something bland played on the panpipes. Lots of photos of Peter Shepherd grinning and posing for the camera.

Logan tried another one. 'SHETLAND 09': a much younger Shepherd, tootling about in an open-top sports car with a woman in rock-chick chic. This time it had some sort of Jimmy Shand accordion soundtrack.

'DUBAI 14': Shepherd and two men in denim shirts and chinos, wheeching about through sand dunes in a four-by-four, riding camels, buying things in a souk, drinking cocktails on a rooftop terrace with a dirty big skyscraper in the background. Middle Eastern music.

'STUFF&THANGS': ...

OK, that was ... *different*.

Tufty appeared in the doorway with a mug. Then froze, staring at the TV. 'Oh.'

On the screen, three people were caught in a *very* intimate tableau – a middle-aged woman with long blonde hair, Peter Shepherd, and Martin Milne. She was on all fours, on the bed in this very room, with Milne at the back – doggy style – and Shepherd in her mouth. A classic spit roast. All done to a backing track of classical music. The image was high-res, not taken on a phone, or a webcam. Probably an expensive SLR digital camera, on a tripod going by the shadows on the bedroom carpet.

Tufty cleared his throat. 'Don't think we should be watching porn in a dead guy's house, Sarge.'

The next image was the same three people, only this time Milne was in the middle.

'Ooh...' Tufty flinched. 'Yeah, definitely shouldn't be watching it.'

This time it was just the two gents. Which explained the dedication in the book.

Pink rushed up Tufty's face. 'I'll be downstairs.'

'Bloody hammering it down.' Steel barged past Logan into the hallway, with Becky hot on her heels. Steel gave a little shake, like a terrier, and ran both hands through her wet hair, smoothing it down to her head. Then flicked the water off onto the tiles. 'This better no' be a wild goose chase, Laz, or I'm going to forget I'm a lady and do things to your bumhole that'd make Genghis Khan blush.'

Becky closed the door on the downpour, brown curls

plastered to her forehead. 'Urgh... Need water wings just to walk here from the car. Don't you teuchters *do* proper weather, or are you too busy shagging sheep?'

'DS McKenzie: stop mocking the afflicted. It's no' their fault they're all inbred.' Steel shoogled out of her coat and handed it to her sidekick, then turned and thumped Logan on the chest. 'Come on then, Mr Mysterious, make with the ID.'

He took a sip of tea. 'Have they taken the bag off your victim's head yet?'

Steel checked her watch. 'PM's no' till ten. You've got five minutes to astound me.'

'Peter Shepherd.' Then he turned and marched up the stairs. 'Who the hell is Peter Shepherd when he's at home?'

'He was Martin Milne's partner.'

Steel hurried after him, boots clunking on the steps. 'Business or sex?'

'Bit of both. And he's got a narwhal tattoo on his upper left arm.'

In the bedroom, Logan pointed the remote at the TV and got the slideshow rolling again. This time, the classical soundtrack was accompanied by Milne and Shepherd having a threesome with a redhead in stripy holdups and a Zorro mask.

'Kinky.' Steel pursed her lips. 'Course, she's a bit chunky for me, but I'd no' mind with the lights off. Just gives you more to hold onto.' She grinned over her shoulder at Becky. 'How about you?'

DS McKenzie shuddered. 'No thanks.'

'Suit yourself.'

Logan hit pause and peered at the remote. Then pressed the button marked 'Zoom', fiddling with the direction arrows until Shepherd's tattoo filled the screen. It was a detailed illustration of a horned whale's head emerging from the sea, contained in a ring of rope, with scallop shells around the outside, and the motto 'Corneum Cete Sunt Optimus' underneath. 'You know what this means, don't you?'

'Don't speak Latin.' Steel dug into her jacket pocket and came out with an e-cigarette. Popped it in her mouth. 'There more porn on this thing?'

'It means Peter Shepherd disappeared at some point over the weekend, only no one notices because he's supposed to be away down to Chesterfield to speak to a supplier this week. Martin Milne goes missing Sunday night. Shepherd's body turns up three days later.'

She snatched the remote from Logan's hand and pressed play, setting the slideshow rolling again. Sank onto the edge of the bed, e-cigarette sticking out of her mouth as if it was on Viagra. 'Aye, very good, Miss Marple. Only problem is, if it's Shepherd who's dead – and I'm no' saying it is – but *if* it is, then how come it looks like he got bumped off by an Edinburgh gangster?'

On the screen, Milne, Shepherd, and their anonymous friend switched one contorted position for another one. As if they were going for some sort of record.

Logan picked up the book and dumped it in Steel's lap. 'Page one-fifty-two.'

'Ooh...' She didn't look at the book. She tilted her head to one side and gaped at the TV instead. 'How did he get his leg all the way over there? Surely that's no' physically possible.'

'God's sake.' Logan grabbed the book back and flicked through to the right page, then held it out, poking the photo with a finger. 'Look. There's a complete description there too. Milne and Shepherd get into some sort of fight. It gets out of hand. Milne panics, he has to ditch the body. And right *there*, sitting on the bedside cabinet, he's got a blueprint of how to do it and make the whole thing look like a mob hit.'

Steel stared, open-mouthed at the screen.

Becky sighed. 'Lot of trouble to go to if you're only wanting rid of your humpbuddy, isn't it?'

'Phwoar... Look at the size of that strap-on! Could beat a horse to death with that. Surely she's not going to stick that up his... Ooooh yes she is. That's *gotta*—'

102

'Give me that.' Logan took the remote back and switched off the TV.

'Hoy! I was watching—'

'Milne killed Shepherd and staged the body so we'd think it was Malcolm McLennan. You're supposed to be running the investigation, so stop watching porn and go investigate.'

'I'm no' "watching porn", I'm reviewing evidence.' Steel reclined on the bed, resting on her elbows. Nodded at her sidekick. 'Becky, let's imagine for a wee moment that our body was Mr Flexible up there.' She pointed at the blank screen. 'Does that mean Martin Miller is our killer.'

'No, Guv.'

'It's Milne. Martin *Milne*. And he's disappeared. Vanished. Run away. Skipped out on his family, Sunday night.'

'Yeah...' Steel bared her teeth. 'Still. Looks more like a gangland killing than a lovers' tiff.'

He shook *The Blood-Red Line* at her. 'Because of the book! It's right there – a how-to guide. Milne set it up.' Logan chucked it down on the bed. 'It's obvious.'

'It's a wild stab in the dark is what it is.' She picked up the remote and set the slideshow playing again. 'Seconds out, round two.'

He stepped between her and the TV, blocking her view. 'What is *wrong* with you?'

Becky sighed. 'Come on, McRae, even you've got to see this is a stretch. We still don't know if our body's Peter Shepherd. Could be anyone.'

'Of course it's Shepherd!'

Steel stared at him for a bit. Then took another puff on her fake cigarette. Hissed out a thin line of steam. 'You used to be a lot more fun.' A sniff. 'Actually, scratch that, you've always been a misery-guts.'

'Yeah? Well this misery-guts has had enough of your—' His phone blared out its anonymous ringtone. 'God's sake.' He yanked it out. 'What?'

There was a brief pause, then a thick dark voice oozed

into his ear like evil treacle. *'Good morning, Sergeant McRae. "Long time, no speak", as I believe the expression goes. Which isn't normal for you and I, is it?'*

Logan ran a hand over his eyes. Gritted his teeth. Then forced a smile as he turned and walked from the room. 'Chief Superintendent Napier.'

'Have you been behaving yourself, Sergeant? Or have you just been very good at getting away with it?'

Through into the floral-print bedroom with its kitsch pillows and crocheted bedspread. 'I hear you're retiring soon.'

'Ah yes, but not to worry: there's still time for a final hurrah. And speaking of rumours, a little birdie tells me that you're working with DCI Steel again.'

Then silence from the other end of the phone.

Rain hammered the window.

More silence.

Fine, two could play at that. If Napier thought Logan was going to leap in and fill the gap with something incriminating he could wait till his ears dropped off.

Classical music seeped through from the other room.

'And tell me, Sergeant McRae, how are you getting on with the Detective Chief Inspector?'

Like an orphanage on fire.

Logan raised his chin. 'We're making progress.'

'I see, I see.' Another pause. *'You two have a good working relationship, don't you, Sergeant? She confides in you. She* trusts *you.'*

Here we go.

'Tell me, has she ever mentioned a Mr Jack Wallace to you? Possibly in connection with a case she investigated last year?'

'Never heard of him.'

'Really... Hmm. Interesting. Well, if she does mention him, do think of me and our little chat. Till then, take care.' Napier ended the call.

What the hell was that about?

Logan put his phone away and stepped out onto the landing. Stood there, listening to the violins and cellos.

Then there was a dinging, buzzing sound. Followed by, 'You wee beauty!'

Whatever had happened on Shepherd's porn slideshow, she could keep it to herself. He was out of here. Had better things to do.

He'd got halfway down the stairs when the music died and Steel charged out of the bedroom, phone held high like the Olympic torch.

She pointed at him. 'Hoy, where do you think you're going?'

'Banff. Got a dunt to organize.'

'Time for that later. Look.' She shoved her phone at him. On the screen was a photo of a bruised face, ringed with black plastic. The features were swollen, and the skin between the blue and purple stains was the colour of rancid butter, but it was definitely Peter Shepherd. 'After careful consideration, I have decided to give you, your grumpy man-panties, and your half-baked theory a second chance. Get in the car: we're off to see this Martin Milne's wife. If the wee sod's done a runner, I want to know where.'

'Told you: I'm *busy*.' Logan started back down the stairs, then stopped. Frowned up at her. 'Who's Jack Wallace?'

Steel's eyes narrowed, deepening the wrinkles. 'On second thoughts, you can sod off back to Banff.' She took a deep breath. 'BECKY! ARSE IN GEAR, WE'RE LEAVING.'

11

Calamity handed the mug to Logan, then nudged the door shut. 'Sorry, Sarge, MIT's had all the milk.'

Logan peered into the depths of his dark-brown tea. Still, it was better than nothing. Then he had a sip... Actually, no it wasn't. A tiny shudder, and he put the mug down on the windowsill. 'It's the thought that counts.'

Even with the door closed, the sounds of a busy station seeped into the Constables' Office. Banging doors. Heavy booted feet. Ringing telephones. Shouting.

Calamity settled into her chair. 'It's like a football match out there. Never seen so many people in the station at one time. And the *stench*!'

Isla bared her teeth. 'Locker room smells like a tramp's sock dipped in Lynx deodorant. It's seeping along the landing like sarin gas.' She thumped a can of diet Irn-Bru down on the worktop, setting loose a curl of ginger froth. 'But do you know what really grips my shit? Someone's done kippers in the canteen microwave. *Kippers!*'

'Ooh, watch out,' Calamity pulled her chin in, 'the Ginger Mist is rising.'

'Damn right it is.' She jabbed a finger at the closed door. 'What kind of antisocial, thoughtless—'

'All right, that's enough whingeing about the Moronic Idiot Team. Tufty?'

No reply. The wee sod was sitting with his back to the room, hunched over doodling something on a notepad.

'Constable Quirrel!'

He swivelled around and grimaced, mobile phone clamped to his ear. 'Right. Thanks, Lizzy, I owe you one.' He hung up. 'Social Services, Sarge. Apparently Ethan Milne's had a fair number of bruises and scrapes. The broken arm's the worst of it, but he's been to the doctors and A-and-E so many times he's got a frequent flier card. Lizzy says the kid's probably eighty percent TCP by now.'

Logan picked up his mug again. 'Suspicious?'

'Don't know. According to the teachers he's about the clumsiest thing they've ever seen. Forever falling over in the playground and walking into doors and things.'

'Right. Well, you can get on with the briefing then.'

'Sarge.' Tufty clicked the mouse and a pair of ID photos appeared on his computer monitor: Ricky Welsh with his shoulder-length hair, bloody nose, and split lip. He'd grown an elaborate Vandyke with twiddly handlebars on the moustache. What looked like a chunk of the Declaration of Arbroath wrapped around his throat in dark-blue tattooed letters. Laura Welsh was bigger; tougher; thickset; one green eye, one black; and an off-blonde perm. Bruises swelled across her left cheek like a tropical storm. Because, 'It's a fair cop, I'll come quietly' just wasn't in Laura or Ricky's vocabulary. They were more of a, 'You'll never take me alive, copper!' kind of family.

Tufty checked his notes. 'Inspector Fettes has got us the Operational Support Unit, a dog unit, and four bodies from Elgin to help dunt in the Welshes' door. Watch yourselves, though: one of the Elgin lot's a Chief Inspector doing his "in touch with the common folk" thing.'

Isla groaned. 'Not *again*.'

Calamity covered her eyes with her hands. 'Why us?'

'You know fine well, why.' Logan risked another sip of tea. Nope: still horrible. 'Keep going, Tufty.'

'ETD – that's Estimated Time of Dunt – will be twenty-three hundred hours. Though with assorted dicking about, probably closer to midnight. I've called Fraserburgh and asked them to reserve two of their finest en suite rooms for Mr and Mrs Welsh. Something with a view and a roll-top bath.'

'Hmm...' Calamity dug into her fleece and came out with a tartan wallet. 'Anyone want a fiver on how many people end up in hospital?'

Isla sucked her teeth. 'Just our lot, or all in?'

'Ours. I'll kick off with two.'

A five-pound note was produced. 'Three. Tufty?'

'Fiver on ...' he squinted one eye, 'four. Sarge?'

'Can we get on with the briefing, please? Some of us have jobs to do.'

Calamity collected the bets. 'Let us know if you change your mind.'

Tufty went back to the PowerPoint presentation, bringing up an aerial shot of Macduff ripped off Google Earth. A crude red arrow with 'RAID HERE!!!' sat on top of the image, pointing at Ricky and Laura Welsh's place.

Click, and it was replaced with a front-view of the house: a whitewashed cottage, sandwiched a third of the way down a terrace of identikit Scottish homes. The slate roof boasted a pair of dormer windows, which – along with the two downstairs windows and red-painted door – gave the place a slightly startled appearance. As if it didn't approve of the things going on inside it.

Isla scanned the briefing notes, a wee crease forming between her eyebrows. 'If Jessica "Ma" Campbell is the one supplying the drugs, are we expecting her or one of her minions to be there protecting their investment? If we are, I want to up my hospital number.'

'It's possible, but I'd be more worried about the Welshes'

dog.' *Click*. A massive Saint Bernard replaced the house photo. 'Looks cuddly, but we're talking full-on Cujo here.'

'Exactly.' Logan pointed at the three of them. 'So anyone not carrying Bite Back deserves all they get. Are we—'

A knock at the door, and Inspector McGregor peered into the room. 'Ah, there you are.' She pulled on a smile. It didn't look very convincing. 'Logan, have you got a minute? We need to chat.'

OK, well that didn't sound ominous at all.

'Guv.' He gave Tufty a nod. 'Finish up the briefing, then I want the Method of Entry paperwork sorted. And *no* spelling mistakes this time. Let's be ready to rock first thing Sunday night.' Then Logan followed the Inspector out into the corridor.

The smell of smoked fish hung in the air like a manky perfume.

Voices boomed out of the open canteen door – someone telling a joke about two nuns, a druggy, and a greengrocer.

This bit of the corridor was lined with street maps of Banff and Macduff, with all the sketchy houses marked in red. Then there was the tiny alcove lined with high-viz jackets on one side and a little sink on the other. The door to the gents lurked beyond the coats, the sounds of whistling coming from within. Past the alcove was the canteen, where, apparently, one of the nuns was doing something sacrilegious with a cucumber. Then the door through to the main office.

A plainclothes officer peered out of it into the corridor. She frowned at them. 'Sorry, but has anyone seen DS Robertson? Anyone? No?'

Laughter burst from the canteen as whatever the punch-line was arrived.

She rolled her eyes. 'Never mind.' Then marched across the hall into the canteen, where all hilarity immediately ceased.

'My station is *infested*.' Inspector McGregor glowered at the open door for a moment, then smoothed down her black police-issue T-shirt. 'Logan, DCI Steel tells me you identified her murder victim *and* a possible suspect.'

'She did?' He pulled his chin in, backing away from the subject. 'That's a bit out of character. Normally you can't prise credit out of her with laxatives and a crowbar.'

Especially given how they'd left things: him ditching her to come back here, her storming off to Whitehills with Rennie. And Steel was giving him credit?

'Apparently your assistance has been invaluable in progressing her investigation.'

'OK, now you're scaring me.'

There was a thump and a rattle. Then the door to the tiny gents loo opened and a large bearded man in a baggy suit appeared, hauling his trousers up around his armpits. He pulled the door shut. 'Sergeant. Ma'am.' He turned the taps on above the little sink and washed his hands. 'I'd give it five minutes if I were you.'

McGregor narrowed her eyes. '*Infested*.' Then she turned and marched down the corridor. 'Logan: heel.'

Logan followed her through the main office with its collection of new people – all bashing away at the phones and laptops – out and round into the stairwell – where a lumpy man in a lumpier suit was blethering away into his mobile – and up the winding wooden steps to the first floor. Where they had to squeeze past two officers womanhandling a desk along the landing.

McGregor led the way through a blue door that had 'BANFF & BUCHAN INSPECTOR' printed out on a laminated sheet of paper on it, mounted beneath a removable brass nameplate: 'WENDY McGREGOR ~ INSPECTOR'.

As soon as Logan was inside, she slammed it shut.

Just like the Fraserburgh Inspectors' Office, there were a pair of corkboards mounted on opposite walls. One with a map of B Division, the other a street map of Banff and Macduff. But where Fraserburgh was all beech units and sleek modern lines, this one had the same high ceilings as the rest of the station, fancy cornices, and a moulded ceiling rose. Two windows sat in the corner of the room, the left-hand one giving a rain-streaked view of the street, the one straight ahead overlooking the car park and the bay.

She stamped across the blue carpet and hurled herself into the seat behind her desk. 'They're like ... bloody ... *vermin*! They've eaten all the Maltesers from the vending machine, we can't keep milk in the fridge,' she leaned forwards and jabbed a finger against her mouse mat, 'and I had a whole malt loaf here yesterday. Now there's nothing left but the wrapper. There's not even crumbs; they licked it clean!'

Logan stood to attention. Kept his mouth shut.

Probably safest. Just in case she felt like lashing out at someone. Best not to give her an excuse.

'I want them gone, Logan.' She swivelled left and right in her chair. 'I want them *gone*.'

Waves surged along the darkened beach.

She hissed out a breath, then spread her hands along the desk. 'DCI Steel has put in a formal request to the Area Commander. She wants you seconded to her Major Investigation Team for the duration.'

The crafty, conniving, manipulative, old bag. So *that's* why Steel was so keen to share the credit for identifying Peter Shepherd and Martin Milne. She wanted Logan running around after her again, solving her cases, doing her job for her. Just like the bad old days.

That or she wanted to keep him close, so she could torture him.

'Yeah... Erm... About that, Guv, I mean, I've got a division to run.' He held up a hand. 'I'm not saying Peterhead, Fraserburgh, and Mintlaw can't look after themselves, but we both know they need a grown-up in charge to make sure they're not all off eating Plasticine and sticking marbles up their noses.'

'Steel says you've proven yourself a valuable resource in progressing the case.'

'And then there's the dunt.' He shifted his feet on the

standard-issue blue carpet tiles. 'We need to get set for bashing in Ricky Welsh's door and—'

'She says your experience and local knowledge is an invaluable asset.'

'It's simply not possible. I need to be here so we can—'

'I want them gone, Logan.'

'But—'

McGregor leaned forward. 'I – want – them – gone!' Jabbing the desk with every word. 'As I see it, letting the DCI borrow you means her bunch of noisy, messy, smelly, *sticky* vermin get out of my station that much sooner.'

'But the division...?'

McGregor sat back in her seat. 'Sergeant Stubbs will fill in for you as Duty Sergeant. She's been moaning about getting more responsibility: let's see how she likes having to supervise every station from Portsoy to Cruden Bay. That should shut her up for a bit.'

'Great. So my job's a punishment now?'

'Hopefully. And someone needs to run your team here.'

Sod standing to attention. Logan slumped into one of the visitors' chairs. 'What about Laura and Ricky Welsh?'

'I was thinking Nicholson could act up while you're away. She's done her sergeant's exam, it'll be a good development opportunity for her.'

He let his head fall back. There was a dirty big spider, wandering across the ceiling rose. 'But it was *my* dunt.'

'A major drugs raid is probably a bit much for Nicholson's first full day in the role. You'd better hand everything over to Sergeant Ashton when she gets on at three. She can green-shift it.'

'Gagh...' Logan's arms dangled at his sides, fingertips brushing the carpet. '*Please?*'

'Oh don't be such a baby. Get out there, find Martin Milne, and get him banged up. The sooner you do, the sooner my station gets fumigated.'

*   *   *

Calamity's eyes widened as she settled into Logan's seat. She ran her hands along the desk. 'Really?'

'Don't get too comfy, it's only till I can wriggle out of the MIT.' Logan leaned back against the firearms store door. 'Sergeant Stubbs is your new Duty Sergeant, she'll keep you right. And Sergeant Ashton will run the dunt on Sunday night. Other than that: it's all yours.'

A nod. 'Stubby and Beaky, got you.' Then she curled her lip and sniffed. 'Has something died in here?'

Logan narrowed his eyes. 'Not yet, but it can be arranged.'

She was right, though: the place did have a whiff of mouldy sausages about it. To be honest, the Sergeants' Office wasn't the nicest room in the station. It needed a coat of paint for a start: the magnolia was peeling off around the skirting boards and cornices, and the high ceiling had a suspicious coffee-coloured stain spreading out from one corner. Hopefully *not* from the male toilets on the floor above.

Two desks were jammed in, back to back, each with its own manky old computer, in-tray, and phone. A line of body-worn video units blinked away in the holder, lined up like dominos. The station's only CCTV monitor lurked on its mount in the corner, with views of the empty cellblocks and public areas in ten little windows.

Not exactly homey.

'If anything happens you can give me a ring. But as of now, you're acting up.'

She stroked the desk again and lowered her voice to a hissing whisper, 'My *preciousssssssssssss…*'

'And make sure you keep an eye on Tufty. He's not had a complaint against him in four months, let's keep it that way. And if he starts banging on about time and entropy, you have my permission to kick his—' Logan's phone rang and he pulled it out. 'Hold on.' Then pressed the button. 'McRae.'

'*Yeah, hi, Mr McRae. It's John?*'

Took a moment, but then it clicked. John Urquhart. Wee

113

Hamish's designated driver. 'Give me a minute.' He held his hand over the microphone and grimaced at Calamity. 'Got to take this.' Then slipped out of the door, through the bedlam of the main office, past the stairwell, down the corridor, and into the old cellblock.

Pale-blue walls, grey-blue floor, an ancient wooden desk/unit thing, and two cells.

No sign of Steel's sticky minions.

Better safe than sorry, though. Logan pulled open the door to cell number two and slipped inside. It was a small magnolia box of a room, with a glass-brick window and grey-painted concrete floor. The blue plastic mattress had been propped up against the wall, one end resting on the ankle-high concrete sleeping platform.

He closed the cell door and took his hand off the microphone. 'Mr Urquhart.'

'You heard the news, right? Mr Mowat passed away last night.' His voice sounded thick and forced, as if someone was choking him. *'Doctor says it was pretty painless.'* A sniff. *'He would say that, though. We find out it was anything but, and he's going home without legs.'*

'Yes. I heard. I'm sorry.' For more than one reason.

'Yeah. Thanks.' Urquhart cleared his throat. *'Anyway, funeral's at half twelve, Friday, Old Ardoe Kirk. No flowers. Be good to see you there.'*

Logan let the silence grow.

Urquhart puffed out a breath. *'And Reuben wants me to pass on a message. He says you've got one last chance to get with the team. Which is kinda unique, normally he goes from nought to wrath-of-God like that.'* A clicking noise.

'I'm a police officer.'

'There's a guy called Stevie Fowler going to be in your neck of the woods next week. You collect a package from him and keep it somewhere safe till Reuben tells you who to hand it over to and where.'

Even though there'd been no one banged up in the cells

for over a decade, the power was still on. There was a radiator hidden inside the ceiling – behind the render – and it belted out heat, making the tips of his ears glow. 'What's in the package?'

'Don't tell anyone you've got it, and squirrel it really out of the way. OK?'

'What – is – it?'

'No idea.'

Logan raised his chin. 'And if I don't?'

Urquhart sighed. *'Then Reuben sends round the three guys in the Transit van, and you get to feed the pigs.'*

Not much of a choice, was it?

Become a crooked cop or die.

Samantha's voice was warm and soft in his other ear. 'Or you could kill Reuben. You won't have to do favours for him if he's dead.'

Logan licked his lips. 'I can't.'

'Mr McRae, you can… Look, it doesn't have to be like this.' A deep breath sounded in the speaker. *'You can still take over from Mr Mowat, like he wanted.'*

'Kill him.' She wrapped her arms around his neck. 'Get that rifle from the firearms store and blow his big fat head off.'

'If you took over, you could get the guys in the van to go pick Reuben up instead. Turn him into pig food.'

From Duty Sergeant in B Division to head of Aberdeen's biggest criminal empire in one easy step.

Yeah.

Right.

Samantha's lips brushed his ear. 'One way or the other, he has to die.'

Logan closed his eyes and leaned forward until his forehead thunked against the cell wall. 'Steve Fowler. When and where?'

12

Rain lashed the window, rattling the glass in its peeling wooden frame. 'Well I hope you're happy.'

The little room was a bit of a hole. Wedged in at the top of the stairs, the walls were close enough to reach out and touch with both hands. And yet, somehow, Steel's minions had managed to cram a desk and two chairs in, amongst the filing cabinet, a filing cupboard, and the two lockers that usually lived there.

On the other end of the phone, Steel's voice was all tinny and echoey – as if she was calling from inside a porta potty. *'Aye, I'm dancing a jig here, can you no' hear the band?'* She blew a wet raspberry.

Whoever had shifted the desk in had piled all the existing boxes of files into the corner, where it made a wobbly tower of grey cardboard and archived crimes.

'Wifie Milne swears blind her husband's no' run off. He's a model husband and father.'

Logan sat on the edge of the desk. 'You didn't show her the photos then?'

'No, but it's going to come out eventually, Laz. Can't protect her forever.'

'What about holiday homes, or family and friends?'

'If you were her, would you want the first time you hear about

your hubby having threeways and hot man-on-man action with his business partner to be right there, in open court? When the defence try to make out he'd never kill Shepherd because he loved him? Several times a week. Oh, and here's the photographic evidence.'

She had a point.

'We need to get posters up at all the ports and stations. Set up a Scotland-wide lookout request.'

'Do we? Wow. I'd no' have thought of that all by my little old self. Good job we've got a big strong man like you on the team to keep us right.'

Logan scowled at the carpet tiles. Someone had tried to fix a couple of them with duct tape. 'Are you finished?'

'Becky's already done it. Now get rid of the PC Plod outfit: I want your scarred backside in a fighting suit and ready to go in ten. You, me, and the boy Rennie are off on a family outing to Peterhead.' The grin was obvious in her voice. *'Be just like old times.'*

'That's what I'm afraid of.'

Rennie peered out of the car windscreen. 'How do you think you pronounce it? Gayrod? Geeirod? Jerryod?'

Rain dripped off the big green sign: *'GEIRRØD ~ CONTAINER MANAGEMENT AND LOGISTICS'* with the same Viking logo Milne and Shepherd had been wearing in the photo. An angry bearded man, in a winged helmet, with a double-headed axe in his hands.

The sign sat in front of a bland two-storey office block of brick and glass, with a handful of cars parked out front on a stretch of potholed tarmac. A security hut sat to one side, where a fat old man watched the metal barrier that controlled entrance to the container yard. The whole place was wrapped around with chain-link fence, punctuated with warning notices about razor wire and guard dogs patrolling this area.

Steel reached across from the passenger seat and whacked Rennie on the arm. 'Yes, because they set up a company, and called it "Gay-Rod".'

117

'Ow.'

'Well, don't be so homophobic. What, two blokes are shagging each other so they're going to call their company "Gay-Rod"?'

Sitting in the back, Logan kept his mouth shut.

She gave Rennie another thump. 'That's a "slashed O", you ignorant spud. It's pronounced "*eau*".' Steel made a noise like a dying sheep. 'Now park.'

He lumped the pool car through the holes and into the spot marked 'Visitors' by the front door. Then sat there, rubbing his arm. 'Why have you got to be so horrible?'

'I'll be horrible to your backside with my boot in a minute.'

Yeah, just like old times.

Logan unclipped his seatbelt and climbed out of the car.

Heavy grey clouds covered most of the sky, but at least it had stopped raining. There was even a patch of blue big enough to let shafts of golden light shine through. They set off a glowing rainbow above the power station in the distance.

GCML's office and yard sat on the southernmost corner of a small industrial estate. Lots of chunks of machinery and pipes, locked away behind high fences. A place that specialized in refrigerated lorries sat across the road, the sound of shrieking metal coming from a large open-fronted garage.

Steel slammed her door shut, then had a dig at her bra – jiggling its contents. 'Right, listen up, children. You will be on your best behaviour. You will do what you're told. You,' she pointed at Rennie as he locked the car, 'will no' embarrass me. Are we clear?'

He stuck his nose in the air. 'Not going to dignify that with an answer.'

'Right, here's the plan: I want... Hoy, Laz, where do you think you're going?'

'To do your job for you.' Logan marched up the steps and into the building. 'As usual.'

Reception was a small room with a row of plastic seats along one wall and a closed hatch in the other. A doorbell sat on the counter, with 'RING FOR ATTENTION' on a small plastic plaque.

He did.

Steel bustled in behind him. 'Cheeky sod.' She peered at the sign next to the bell. Then mashed her thumb down on the button. Holding it there as the sound of ringing droned out somewhere inside the building. 'SHOP! ANYONE IN? COME OUT WITH YOUR HANDS UP! HELLO? SHOP!'

Logan slapped her hand away and the ringing stopped. 'OK, I *think* they heard you.'

She raised an eyebrow and stared at him. 'Where'd you get that suit, Tramps-R-Us?'

'We kick off with the third partner – the financial director. Assuming he's not disappeared as well.'

'Looks more like a sleeping bag than a suit.'

'Then we split the staff in three, take one third each.'

'Trousers are hanging off you.'

'Anyone seems a bit sketchy, we double up on them.'

'And that's possibly the ugliest tie I've ever seen.'

He glanced down at it: blue with tiny red dots. 'Jasmine gave me this for Christmas.'

'She did?' A frown. 'For a seven-year-old, she's got horrible fashion sense.'

'Maybe Martin Milne has an accomplice?'

'She gets that from *your* side of the family.' Steel banged her open palm down on the desk. *Bang. Bang. Bang.* 'SHOP! HELLO? GET A SHIFT ON!'

'We should get Rennie to run a quick PNC check on all the employees before we start.'

'They never warn you about that when you get your wife up the stick with a turkey baster, do they? Warning: donor sperm may cause your child to buy ugly ties.'

Logan stared at her. 'Are you finished?'

A grin. 'Any other skeletons lurking in your family cupboard I should know about? Any history of mental abnormality?' Steel went back to hoiking at her underwear. 'Mind

119

you, I've met your mum, she's about as normal as morris dancing. What about your dad, was he a nutter too? Suppose he must've been to marry your mum.'

'Can we get back to the case, please?'

The hatch rattled open, revealing an orange-skinned bottle-blonde in a polo shirt and fleece – both of which had the Geirrød logo on them. She smiled and fluttered her eyelashes, playing the coy young thing. Which, given the fact that she had to be pushing fifty, was a bit of a stretch.

Steel sniffed. 'Beginning to think you didn't exist.'

The smile slipped a little, leaving its wrinkles behind. 'Can I help you?'

'Aye: your financial director about?'

'I'm afraid Mr Chapman is *very* busy. Do you have an appointment?'

Steel pulled out her warrant card. Held it under the woman's nose. 'And while you're at it, I'll have a coffee. Milk and two.'

'I don't know, all right? I don't know.' Brian Chapman paced back and forth, in front of his office window. The room sat on the first floor, looking down on the rows of containers laid out in the yard. Chapman ran a hand through what was left of his hair, pausing to tweak the big brown mole growing just above his right eyebrow. As if he were trying to tune his head in. Dark stains lurked in the armpit of his denim shirt. A smudge of dirt on the backside of his tan chinos. He got to the line of filing cabinets and started back again. 'If I knew where he was, I'd tell you. *Believe* me.' His other hand clenched into a fist, then spread out, then clenched, then spread. Like a throbbing pulse.

Steel slouched in her seat, dunking a chocolate biscuit in a mug of coffee. 'What about Shepherd, you been in touch with him?'

Chapman stopped pacing and glared at the mound of paper-work on his desk. 'Oh, I've tried. If I get my hands on him, he's dead. I'll bloody kill him.' Then Chapman must have remembered who he was talking to, because he licked his lips, then went back to pacing again. 'You know what I mean.'

Logan tilted his head to one side. 'Why don't you explain it to us?'

'Do you know what I got yesterday? Do you know what came in the post?' He dug into the pile and pulled out a letter. Waved it at them. 'What the hell were they thinking?'

Steel clicked her fingers and Chapman handed the letter over. She squinted at it for a bit, then held it out to Logan. 'Do the honours.'

The Royal Bank of Scotland logo sat in the top corner. 'It's from the bank. A final demand on a loan of a hundred and fifty thousand pounds, plus interest.'

'First I'd heard of it was when it landed on my desk. I'm supposed to be the financial director. How can I financially direct if I haven't got a clue what's going on?'

A shrug from Steel. 'So pay it off.'

'How? What with?' He held his arms out, exposing the stains again. 'Magic fairy-dust and wishes? We're skint!'

'Oh.'

'I've managed to keep us afloat this long, but the down-turn in the oil price is killing us. No one wants to pay for anything any more. I had to lay three people off last week. Do you have any idea what that *feels* like?' He reached across the desk and snatched the letter from Logan. 'So I phoned the bank and told them it had to be a mistake. We hadn't borrowed any money. And do you know what I found out?' Chapman scrunched the letter into a ball and hurled it at the wall. 'I found out that this isn't the only loan. There's another one for seventy-five thousand that's due in three weeks.' Spittle flew from his lips. 'THREE WEEKS!'

His face had taken on an unhealthy redness, his whole body trembled. 'I'll bloody kill the pair of them.'

'Aye, well, we can save you the trouble there, Brian.' Steel licked the melted chocolate off her bit of biscuit then dunked it again. 'We found Peter Shepherd's body, dumped in the woods, yesterday morning.'

Chapman froze. 'Peter's *dead*?' He sank into his office chair and blinked at them, mouth hanging open. 'I can't... He's really dead?'

Logan pointed at the letter, lying crumpled on the floor. 'Who took the loans out?'

'Peter and Martin. They countersigned for each other, with the business as guarantee. Two hundred and twenty-five thousand pounds we don't have.' His hand crept up and twiddled the mole again. 'I'm going to have to call in the liquidators.'

'What did they use the money for?'

'I'll lose everything. We put our houses up as collateral when we started the business. Oh God...'

'Did they buy equipment, or supplies?'

'It never even touched the company bank account.' His eyes shone, the tip of his nose reddened. 'They had the money paid into a different account then emptied it. What am I supposed to tell Linda?'

Steel polished off the last of her biscuit. 'How come you didn't call us soon as you got the letter, Brian? You know we're looking for Martin Milne.'

'Why didn't...? I've been trying to save the company, *that's* why!' The tears broke free, dribbling down his flushed cheeks. 'I've been trying to save everyone's jobs. I've been too busy finding out how screwed I am.' He scrubbed a hand across his face. 'They took the money, they lumbered me with the debt, and then they disappeared. Martin and Peter can burn in hell for all I care.'

Steel blew a lopsided cloud of steam into the drizzle. 'Any luck?'

'Nope.' Rennie checked his phone. 'Most we've got is a couple of outstanding parking tickets, and one guy not allowed within two hundred yards of his ex-wife.'

'Can't say we haven't got a motive now.' Logan stuffed

his hands deep into his pockets and hunched his shoulders. Say what you like about Police-Scotland-issue itchy-trousers-stabproof-vest-and-high-viz-jacket combination, at least it kept you warm.

The container yard was full of large metal boxes, all painted blue with a big angry-Viking logo on the side. Some were just about big enough to park Logan's Fiat Punto in, others could've fitted a full-sized minibus. Some with external refrigeration units, others with fancy sliding doors. Like the one they were standing in, sheltering from the thin misty rain.

'What about the death message? Those lazy Weegie sods delivered it yet?'

Rennie nodded. 'Becky says Greater Glasgow Division tracked down Shepherd's next of kin half an hour ago.'

'Cool. Tell the Media Office I want a slot on the evening news. Appeal for witnesses, heinous crime, blah, blah, blah.' Logan checked his watch. 'Better head back to Banff. Shift ends in forty minutes.'

'You're no' in the Bunnet Brigade today, Laz, you're in the Magnificent Intellectual Team. We don't do shifts. Shifts are for the weak, remember?'

He closed his eyes and thunked the back of his head off the container's metal wall, getting a ringing *bonggggg* in return.

'Rennie, how many of these GCML monkeys we got left?'

'Erm… Just the receptionist.'

'Right, you trot off like a good wee boy and have a word with her. And try no' to fall for her wrinkly sunbed charm, we all know how you like an older woman. Pervert.'

Rennie sloped off into the rain.

Steel waited till he'd disappeared back into the office building. Then took a long drag on her e-cigarette. 'Who told you about Jack Wallace?'

'Who is he?'

She shrugged. 'A paedo. Caught him with a big wodge of kiddy porn on his laptop.' Another drag. 'It was Napier, wasn't it?'

'Wanted me to keep an eye on you. See if you mentioned Wallace.'

'Gah.' She worked a finger down into her cleavage and had a rummage. 'Told you, didn't I? Napier's hit his thirty years and they're chucking him out to pasture. Slimy wee sod's been holding on by his fingernails since the re-org.' Dig, rummage, fiddle. 'How do you think it plays back home when we've got one Chief Superintendent in charge of the whole division, and there's Napier, same rank, spodding about in Professional Standards? Big Tony Campbell's been trying to get shot of him for ages.'

'So why's he interested in Wallace?'

'He's just on the sniff. Doesn't want to slump off into obscurity without first screwing over one more poor sod.'

Logan stepped in front of her. 'So there's *nothing* dodgy going on?'

'Sod, and indeed, all. Forget about it.' More rummaging. 'You know what I think?'

Logan waited.

Dig. Fiddle. Hoik. 'I think this is Susan's bra.'

13

Steel put the cap back on her marker pen. 'Any questions?'

There weren't as many people in the Major Incident Room as there had been for the morning meeting – about half of them were away doing things – but that still left a dozen plainclothes officers. They sat around the conference table, chairs all turned towards the whiteboard. Behind them, Logan leaned back against the wall, stifling a yawn.

Should've been home by now.

DS McKenzie put her hand up. 'So are we treating this as a crime of passion, Guv? Or is it all about the cash?'

'Crime of passion?'

'Yeah, maybe Milne finds out Shepherd isn't as faithful as he thought? Maybe he's shagging someone else behind his back? Or maybe the bag over his head's a kind of auto-erotic asphyxiation thing?'

Steel stared at her. 'Bit extreme for a stranglewank, isn't it, Becky? Don't know about *your* love life, but when I'm doing your mum I tend to draw the line at duct-taping a bin-bag over her head.'

Becky folded her arms across her chest, chin in the air. 'So it's money.'

'Two hundred and twenty-five *thousand* pounds of it.' She turned and underlined the figure on the board. It sat between a photo of Shepherd and one of Milne. One titled 'VICTIM' the other, 'SUSPECT #1'.

A huge DC in an ill-fitting suit stopped doodling penguins on his notepad. It was Rennie's friend from yesterday, the one with the awful teeth. 'What about this gangland angle? We ignoring that now?'

Steel stuck her nose in the air. '*We* are ignoring nothing, Owen. We're focusing our resources. And just for that, you're searching Shepherd's place again. You, Donna, and Spaver. Fine-toothed comb this time.'

His shoulders slumped. 'Guv.'

'Robertson?'

A whippet-thin man with horrible sideburns nodded. 'Guv?'

She chucked a flash drive across the table to him. 'Homemade porn from Shepherd's house. Between wanks, I want you IDing everyone on there. Background checks and interviews.'

'Guv.'

Then Steel held her arms out, as if she was about to bless everyone in the room. 'Now get your sharny backsides out there and find me Martin Milne.'

Chairs were scraped back, and, one by one, the team shuffled out of the room.

Logan didn't bother to hide the yawn this time as Steel shut the door behind them.

'No' boring you, are we?' She dug out her phone and poked at the screen for a moment, then put it against her ear. 'Make yourself useful and grab us a coffee will you? And some cake. Or biscuits. Crisps will do at a—' She held up a hand and turned away from him. 'Super? Yeah, it's Roberta. Just wanted you to know we've got a suspect *and* a motive for the Shepherd murder. I've got a slot booked on the news, so if— ... No. ... Yeah, I know they think it's the same MO, but listen, we— ... No, sir. ... Yes, sir. But we—' Steel marched over to one of the room's two windows and stood there, glaring out at the rain. 'I *understand* that, sir, but we're making progress here. *I'm* making progress. And— ... No. OK. ... Bye.'

Steel lowered her phone. Then swore at it.

'Good news?'

She turned and glared at him instead. 'Sodding Superintendent Sodding Young says we're getting a sodding babysitter.' Steel jammed her e-cigarette in her mouth and chewed on the end. 'Some arsebag Central-Belt bumwarden from Forth Valley Division. Apparently, she's an expert on Malk the Knife. *Apparently* she's very efficient and good at her job. *Apparently* she's already on her way.'

Logan tried not to smile, he really did. 'Not nice when someone waltzes in and takes over your case, is it?'

'Oh ha, ha.' Steel thumped herself down on the window-sill, rattling the blinds. 'Any chance we can catch Milne and beat a confession out of him in the next,' she checked her watch, 'hour?'

'Probably not.'

'Well, look at you, all booted and suited.' Sergeant Ashton leaned back in her chair and gave him the once-over. She'd had her hair done again, blonde highlights and brown lowlights giving her head the look of a humbug that'd fallen down the back of the sofa and got all fuzzy. 'To what do I owe the honour?'

Piles of boxes littered the Sergeants' Office, all of them tagged and sealed. Some used to contain crisps, some frozen peas. Some had willies drawn on the outside.

Logan settled into the seat opposite. 'Aye, aye, Beaky. Foos yer doos, the day then?'

'You're getting better. But for maximum teuchterness it should be "*i'* day", not "*the* day".'

He nodded at the boxes. 'Has Mum been to Iceland?'

'Confiscated them from a van in Macduff. Counterfeit handbags.' She pointed. 'Might have something that'll go with your outfit, but you'll need nicer shoes.'

'Did Inspector McGregor speak to you about my dunt?'

She grinned. 'It's *my* dunt now, Laz. I'll be getting all the credit.'

'You remembering it's Ricky and Laura Welsh?'

'There is that.' Beaky pulled her lips in and chewed on them for a bit. 'I've got a fiver on no one gets hospitalized, which is about as likely as Scotland winning the next World Cup. But what can you do? Got to at least pretend it'll all go to plan.'

'Keep me in the loop though, eh?'

'Anything else I should know about?'

'Tufty's got one shift to go till he's a proper police officer. Try and keep him out of trouble on Sunday night.'

'They grow up so fast, don't they?'

'Oh, and can you and your hired thugs do me a favour? Keep an eye on Portsoy tonight. Some wee sod's been setting fire to people's wheelie bins. Be nice to catch him before he graduates to houses.'

'Think I can manage that. We've got—'

A knock on the door, then it opened. One of Beaky's PCs loomed on the threshold, his shoulders hunched and his face in need of a shave. 'Sorry, Sarge, but Sergeant McRae's got a visitor.'

Beaky wafted a hand at him. 'Tell whoever it is to park their bum. We're doing important handovery stuff here.'

'Yeah…' He grimaced. 'No offence, but Sergeant McRae's visitor is *way* above my pay grade.' The constable held a hand six inches over his own head. 'Like *way* above.'

Logan raised an eyebrow. That would be Steel's babysitter, the Superintendent, arrived from C Division ahead of schedule and itching to take over. Probably wanted to debrief him in person, after all, he was the one who ID'd the victim *and* the killer. 'Ah well.' He stood, stretched.

Sergeant Ashton tucked her hands into her fleece pockets. 'Don't worry, I'll take good care of your team while you're off playing cops and robbers.'

'Thanks, Beaky, yir a fine quine.'

'You're a knapdarloch yourself, Laz.'

Whatever that meant.

The PC flattened himself against the doorframe, and pointed past the photocopier, at the corridor. 'He's in the canteen.'

He? Didn't Steel say it was a she?

Still, it wouldn't be the first time she'd got that wrong.

Logan crossed the corridor and into the canteen.

A table stuck into the middle of the room like a breakfast bar, with three chairs on either side and what looked like an empty box from the baker's on top. Doughnuts, going by the crime-scene trail of blood-red jam on the black tabletop and the trails of castor sugar.

His visitor was in the corner, with his back to the room, pouring boiling water into a mug. Full Police Scotland black outfit – the shoes, the trousers, the fleece – but instead of the expected three pips on the epaulettes, there was one pip and a crown. His red hair was swept back, not quite covering the expanding bald patch at the back.

Not Steel's babysitter after all. Something far worse.

Sod.

He was humming a wee tune to himself, away in his own happy little world.

It wasn't too late. Could back away right now and sneak off. Get in a car and...

Chief Superintendent Napier turned around and raised his mug. 'Ah, Sergeant McRae, the very man I wanted to see.' His long thin nose twitched. 'Do you have any milk?'

Logan cleared his throat. 'Milk. Right.' He crossed to the fridge, opened it, and pulled out the big four-litre plastic container of semi-skimmed. Gave it a shoogle. Empty. 'Sorry, sir, the MIT must have drunk it.'

'Oh now, that *is* disappointing.' He poured the contents of the mug down the sink. 'I think, in that case, we should go for a walk, don't you? That might lift our spirits on a

129

cold February afternoon. We could buy the station some more milk.'

'Milk. Right.'

Napier's smile wouldn't have been out of place on a serial killer. 'You said that already.'

'Yes.'

Oh bloody hell.

He pointed a long thin finger at the windowsill, where a piggybank sat next to a white concrete gnome. Someone had painted angry black eyebrows on the gnome and stuck a little paper dagger in his hand. 'Shall I put thirty pence in the bank, or do you think buying the milk will cover it?'

Logan licked his lips. 'I'll get my coat.'

Wind growled along Banff Bay, whipping the water into lines of white peaks. Bringing with it the smell of seaweed and death.

The tide was out, and Napier's thin feet left bullet-shaped marks in the wet sand. 'Bracing, isn't it?' He'd pulled on a peaked cap – complete with waterproof shower-cap-style cover – and a high-viz jacket. Rain pattered against the fluorescent yellow material.

Logan trudged along beside him, suit trousers rippling against his legs, water dripping from his own high-viz gear. No condom on *his* hat though, thank you very much. Might have been practical, but it made you look a complete tit. 'No offence, sir, but you didn't come all the way up here to walk about in the freezing rain.'

'Perceptive as ever, Sergeant.' A sigh. 'I've spent most of my thirty years in Professional Standards, Logan. Oh, I did my stint in CID, the GED, on the beat, in the control room, even a short period seconded to the Home Office. But when I joined Professional Standards, I knew *this* was what I wanted to do with my career.'

A young woman in a stripy top went by the other way, long curly dark hair streaming out behind her like a flag, a wee Scottie dog bounding along at her side – its black fur clarty with wet sand and mud.

'It was my first case that did it: investigating a sergeant who'd taken money from a local businessman to look the other way in a rape investigation. The businessman had broken a poor woman's jaw and nose, cracked three of her ribs, and dislocated her shoulder. Then he raped her three times. She was nineteen.'

Out in the distance, the lights of a supply vessel winked, probably tying up to ride out the storm.

'Imagine that. There you are, supposedly investigating a serious sexual assault, and you know who did it, but instead of building a case, arresting, and prosecuting the criminal, you stick your hand out and demand three thousand pounds. And three thousand pounds was a lot of money in those days.'

Napier stopped, and stared out to sea. 'That's what I've spent my career doing, Logan. Tracking down the bribe-takers, the constables that steal from crime scenes, the officers who think it's perfectly acceptable to beat a confession out of someone, or to demand sexual favours in return for facilitating prostitution. Money. Drugs. Violence. Privilege.'

Logan turned his back on the wind, hunching his shoulders. The young woman was a faint figure in the distance, the dirty wee Scottie dog nearly invisible.

A smile twitched at Napier's lips. 'We police the police. We make sure the force can hold its head up high and say to the people, "Believe in us. Trust us. Because *no one* is above the law, not even us."' He shrugged. 'And instead of being grateful that we weed out the rot in their midst, our fellow officers call us Rubber Heelers, and sinister bastards, and all sorts of pejorative nicknames. Make the sign of the cross when they think we're not looking.'

There had to be a reason for this strange little heart-to-heart.

Logan's stomach clenched.

Oh God. What if he'd found out about the trip to Wee Hamish's deathbed? What if Reuben had decided to screw him over after all? What if Napier knew all about Urquhart buying Logan's flat for twenty thousand pounds over the asking price? Or that he'd agreed to pick up Steve Fowler's mystery package?

Napier turned and walked on. 'Other officers look at us the way that junkies and thieves look at you, Logan. Waiting for the long arm of the law to fall upon their shoulders.'

And why here? Why do this out in the freezing cold not-so-great outdoors? Why not back at the station with a witnessing officer and a video camera?

Maybe he was going to cut Logan a deal? Something not quite legal: that was why he needed seclusion to do it.

The beach curled around to the right, where the bay became the River Deveron. But before they got that far, Napier stopped again. 'Tell me, Logan, what do you know about Jack Wallace?'

Logan blinked. OK, wasn't expecting that. 'Not much. He's a paedophile?'

'Jack Wallace, thirty-two, currently serving six years for possession of indecent images of children.'

'Good.'

'Is it?' Napier turned and marched up the beach, leaving the sand behind for a line of grass. 'What if Jack Wallace isn't a paedophile after all? What if evidence has emerged that suggests his conviction is unsafe? What if the images found on his laptop were planted there?'

Past a low wall topped with a brown picket fence, and out onto the pavement.

Logan grabbed his arm. 'Why?'

'The evidence used to convict Wallace all came from DCI Steel. No corroboration, no paper trail, just a laptop with images of child abuse on it.' He peered over Logan's shoulder, across the road. 'Ah, look: a Co-op. We can get milk there.'

'Are you saying Steel fitted him up?'

'Jack Wallace had no history of child abuse. No hints. No

warnings. No suspicions. And then, one day, all of a sudden his laptop is full of kiddy porn. Does that not strike you as suspicious?'

'Not really. He was good at covering his tracks. Some of them get away with it their whole lives.'

'That's true.' Napier wandered across the road, past the boarded-up garage. 'Tell me, Logan, do you think DCI Steel is the kind of officer who would fabricate evidence? Who'd bend the rules to get a result? Even if she had to bend them so far they shattered?'

'No.' Of course she would, but there was no way in hell he was telling Napier that.

'I see.'

They passed the bus shelter, where a young man in a sodden hoodie slouched with a pushchair. Fag in his mouth as he texted away.

'These are serious allegations, Logan. There has to be an investigation: a thorough one. If Detective Chief Inspector Steel's done nothing wrong, then we'll exonerate her. But if I find out that she's perverted the course of justice, she'll find herself on the receiving end of an eight-year stretch in Glenochil.'

Napier pulled a packet of fruit pastilles from his pocket, helped himself to one, then held them out to Logan. 'This isn't the 1970s, it's not *The Sweeney* or *Life on Mars*. The modern police force has to be squeaky clean, or we're no better than the thugs and politicians.'

The pastilles hovered between them.

'What's it got to do with me?'

'You know DCI Steel. You've worked for her. You know her methods. You have her confidence. The people working for her now – the MIT – they can't be relied upon, they're in her thrall. But you've been all the way up here in B Division for over a year, beyond her grasp.'

'How do you know I won't go right back there and tell her everything you've just told me?'

'Do you have any idea how many times I've investigated you over the last decade? Many, many, many times. And each time it's turned out that you were in the right all along. No one's *that* good at covering their tracks. You're an honest man, Logan McRae.'

Logan's fingers twitched, then drifted up towards the packet.

'Of course, I could force the issue: get you formally seconded to Professional Standards, but I don't want that. I want you to help because this is what's best for DCI Steel *and* Police Scotland. A thorough investigation to either clear her name, or... Well, let's hope it doesn't come to that.'

'I see.' The investigation was going to happen whether he helped out or not. And if he didn't, it would simply give Napier an excuse to start grubbing about in Logan's business too.

Yeah, that really, *really* wouldn't turn out well.

And maybe Napier was right? Maybe this was for Steel's own good? An investigation would clear her name and that would be that. And if Logan was involved he could make sure no one jumped to the wrong conclusions. Napier could retire and everyone else could get on with their disaster-ridden lives.

So why not?

Logan took the top pastille and popped it in his mouth. Lime. 'Suppose I said yes, and I'm not, I'm only asking. But *if* I said yes, what would you want me to do?'

14

'Ooh, here we go.' Steel settled into one of the canteen chairs. 'Turn it up, turn it up.'

Logan picked the remote off the table and pointed it at the TV mounted on a shelf above the recycling bins. Cranked up the volume. Then grimaced. The remote was all gritty and sticky. 'For God's sake...' The thing was smeared with blobs of doughnut jam and a dusting of castor sugar.

'Shhh!'

On the screen, a newsreader in a serious suit frowned for the camera. Behind them, Banff station lurked in the rain, water dripping from the curlicues and semi-balconies. *'Thank you, Stacy. Police Scotland have named the man found in woods outside of Macduff, Aberdeenshire, yesterday as Peter Shepherd. Mr Shepherd, a director at a support services company...'*

Logan dumped the remote on the draining board and washed the sticky off his hands. 'Inspector McGregor's right, it's like sharing a station with vermin.'

'Will you shut your yap, Laz? Trying to watch this.'

'...following statement.'

The shot cut to the station front door, where Steel stood beneath an umbrella held by someone out of shot. *'We are anxious to trace the whereabouts of Martin Milne, a partner at Geirrød Container Management and Logistics.'* Milne's photo filled the screen – the one of him at the barbecue. *'We are very concerned for Mr Milne's safety. If you have any information, you've seen him or spoken to him, we need you to get in touch.'* Then she was back on the screen again. *'Mr Milne was last seen on Sunday night, wearing a green waxed Barbour jacket, red fleece shirt, blue jeans, and tan-coloured boots.'*

Out here, in real life, Steel pointed at the screen. 'Do my boobs look perkier than usual?' She stuck a hand down her shirt and fiddled with the contents. 'Maybe I should wear Susan's bra more often?'

A microphone popped into shot, clutched in a gloved hand. *'Chief Inspector, can you comment on rumours that Peter Shepherd's death resembles a gangland execution?'*

'I'm no' playing the speculation game, here, Sunshine, I'm appealing for witnesses.'

Logan drew a breath in through his teeth. 'Did you really just call the BBC News guy "Sunshine"?'

'Martin, if you're watching this, it is extremely important you get in touch with us. Your family are worried about you.'

'I wonder if they do it in a balconette?' Fiddle, fiddle, fiddle. 'That's always good for a bit of jiggly-wobbliness. Susan would like that.'

He shuddered. 'Can we please not discuss your breasts?'

There was a knock on the doorframe, followed by, 'I'd ask if I'm interrupting anything, but I think we all know the answer.' A woman stood with her arms folded. Black suit. Black boots. Black shirt. Long blonde hair tucked behind one fairly large ear and cascading over the other. A strong jaw. The smile she pulled didn't go anywhere near her eyes, or the bags underneath them. 'Would someone care to tell me why we put out an appeal on national television?'

Steel gave up on her cleavage. 'Because, Little Miss Undertaker, I'm trying to catch a murderer. That OK with you?'

The smile got colder. 'That's Little Miss *Superintendent* to you.'

Oh great. Their babysitter from C Division.

'Superintendent, eh? Well, well, well. And you no' long out of gymslips too.' Steel held up a finger. 'And before you go all feral on me: that's a compliment. Empowered women, glass ceilings, role model to all the wee girls, blah, blah, blah.'

On screen, the reporter handed back to the studio.

Logan picked up the sticky remote and turned the TV off. Stood up straight. 'Super.'

She didn't even look at him. 'Let me guess, you must be Detective Chief Inspector Steel.'

'Guilty as charged.'

'And probably a lot more besides.' The Superintendent leaned against the doorframe. 'Let's be clear, DCI Steel, there will be no more maverick behaviour on this case. Your Major Investigation Team works for me now, it does what I tell it to do, and that includes you.'

Steel pursed her lips. 'Oh aye?'

'You will not release anything to the media without my authorization. Are we crystal?'

Outside in the corridor, someone coughed.

A phone rang.

The fridge and vending machines hummed.

Then Steel nodded. 'Guess we are.'

A short man in a double-breasted suit appeared at her elbow. He was all hairy and fidgety, with a full wiry black beard and a Royal Stewart tartan turban. 'Super? We've got the victim's car. SEB are on their way.'

Logan put the remote down. 'We've got Martin Milne's car in lockup at Mintlaw, so if—'

The Superintendent pointed at him. 'Did anyone ask for your opinion, Sergeant McRae?'

OK… How did she know his name?

'I'm just trying to—'

'And you're out of uniform. That suit looks ridiculous. Change.' She turned to her hairy friend. 'Narveer, this whole operation smacks of ineptitude and indolence. Gather the senior officers in the incident room. Time to deliver a kick up the jacksie.'

'Ma'am.'

Then she turned and stormed off, shouting instructions into her mobile phone.

Narveer puffed out a breath. Shook his head. 'Sorry about that, she's not usually like this. Don't know what's rattled her cage.' Then he stuck his hand out. 'DI Singh, I'm Detective Superintendent Harper's minder, sidekick, and general dogsbody.'

Logan shook it. 'Logan McRae. This is DCI Steel.'

She waved. 'Like the turban, Narveer. Very sexy.'

A blush darkened the skin at his cheeks. 'Right. I'd better … get on with it. Major Incident Room in, about fifteen minutes? That sound OK?'

At least it would give Logan time to change.

Rennie looked Logan up then down again. 'Thought you were plainclothes now?'

The Major Incident Room bustled with muffled conversations as they waited for Detective Superintendent Harper to appear. Steel had taken the seat at the middle of the table, facing the whiteboard, flanked by two DIs in much better-fitting suits than Logan's. Two DSs sat on one side, Becky on the other – not talking to anyone, poking away at her phone instead.

Logan straightened the epaulettes on the shoulders of his black Police-Scotland-issue fleece. 'Our new Central-Belt overlord's idea of making friends.'

'Eeek.' He bared his teeth. 'Let me guess: bit of a ball-breaker? Tough woman in a man's world, having to try harder than anyone else to get the same amount of respect?'

'Or she was just being a dick.'

'Point.' He straightened up and dropped his voice to a whisper as the door opened. 'Talk of the dick and she shall appear.'

Narveer was first in, carrying a stack of paper bags from

the Tesco at the end of the road. He dumped them on the table as DSup Harper swept into the room.

She took up position directly behind Steel. 'Ladies, gentlemen, glad you could join us.' A bright smile. 'Can someone get the lights please?'

Rennie scurried off to oblige, plunging the room into semi-darkness. Lit only by the glow of the streetlights outside.

'Now, do help yourself to cakes while I get this set up.'

There was a rustling of bags and the occasional 'Oooh!' as the MIT dug into doughnuts, yumyums, raisin whirls, and custard slices. How to win friends and influence police officers, lesson one: bring cakes.

A roller screen hung on the wall opposite the whiteboard. Harper pulled it down to full size, then pointed a remote at the projector mounted to the ceiling. It hummed and whirred, then a PowerPoint slide appeared on the screen.

Motes of dust drifted in the beam.

Logan dipped into the last bag and came out with an Eccles cake. The rotten sods had taken all the good stuff.

'OPERATION HOURGLASS ~ BRIEFING SLIDES' blurred across the screen, until Narveer stood on a chair and fiddled with the focus.

Harper clicked the button, and a photo of her appeared. 'In case you don't know by now, my name is Detective Superintendent Niamh Harper. I work for the Serious Organised Crime Task Force, bridging the gap between Police Scotland and various local and governmental support agencies. I specialize in putting kingpin figures behind bars.' That smile again. 'Which is why you've been lumbered with me.'

It wasn't exactly *Billy Connolly's Greatest Hits*, but it actually got a chuckle or two from the assembled team.

Click.

A man's face filled the screen, taken with a long lens probably from a concealed location.

'Allow me to introduce you to Malcolm McLennan, AKA: Malk the Knife.'

It was a much more candid photo than the one Steel had used at the morning briefing. Middle-aged, receding hairline cropped short. A strange, youthful look to his skin and cheeks, but his eyes peered out from hooded lids. As if he were someone much older wearing a mask.

'Born twenty-third of April 1960, in a little mining village in Fife. Got into trouble as a kid – low-level stuff, nothing serious – then graduated to the armed robbery of a security van in Edinburgh when he was eighteen. He did four years, and when he came out he was a different man.'

Click.

It was one of the crime-scene photos from the book in Shepherd's bedroom. The one where a man slumped in a bathroom stall with his throat sliced open. Blood soaked the front of his frilly shirt.

'Antony Thornton, one-time business associate of McLennan. Word on the street was that Thornton wanted to cut a deal with Lothian and Borders CID, McLennan slashed his throat so deeply the head nearly came off. Nothing could be proved.'

Click.

Another man, this one floating facedown in the harbour, arms and legs spread as if he were playing at being a starfish. 'David Innes. Drug dealer. Allegedly he was skimming off the top. McLennan gutted him. Again, no evidence, no prosecution.'

Click.

A young man, sprawled across the back seat of a car, eyes wide open, hands curled in his lap. Everything from his chin to his lap was soaked in blood. 'Edward Tucker—'

'Aye, no offence,' Steel brushed pastry crumbs from her cleavage, 'but fascinating as the history lesson is, Super, when do we get to the bit that's got anything to do with Peter Shepherd?'

Harper laughed. 'A very good point, Roberta.'

Roberta? So she'd gone from 'Do what you're told' to first-name terms in fifteen minutes?

She raised the remote. 'Let's fast forward a bit.'

Click. Blood. *Click.* Death. *Click.* Blood. *Click.* Bodies. *Click.* Blood. *Click.* Death. *Click.* More bodies.

'And then we arrive at Michael Webb.'

Click.

Another young man, this one lying on his back, naked, with his arms behind him. Black plastic bag taped over his head. His torso was a mass of green and purple bruises, then porcelain skin, then a line of red where the blood had pooled nearest to the ground after death. Settling through the tissues.

'Low-level drug dealer. His hands were tied behind his back, then he was beaten around the head, neck, and torso. Then they duct-taped a bin-bag over his head and watched him suffocate to death. The remains were dumped in woodland just south of the Forth Bridge and drenched in bleach to destroy any trace on the body.'

Click.

Different body, different woods, but the MO was the same.

'Daniel Crombie – used to smuggle cigarettes and alcohol in from the Continent.'

Click.

And again.

'Alex Ward – pimp.'

Click.

'Walter Gibson – retired police officer turned loan shark.' Harper dumped the remote on the table. 'I've got another dozen of these, spread over a space of twenty-six years. All our victims were rivals or inconveniences to Malcolm McLennan, but there's nothing but rumour connecting him to the killings.'

She picked up one of the empty cake bags and scrunched it into a ball. 'We're pretty certain he doesn't kill them personally, but he does order it. The actual murders are carried out by multiple, unknown, persons. No one has ever been arrested for these crimes, never mind prosecuted.'

Harper lobbed the bag into the bin from a distance of about eight feet. 'Any comments?'

Rennie put his hand up. 'What about trace *inside* the bin-bags? The bleach can't get in there, if the seal's reasonably tight. And black plastic bags are like static electricity hoovers for dust and fibres.'

'Good question ...' she checked a sheet of paper, 'Simon. No viable DNA from anyone other than the victim – which isn't surprising, given the warm moist environment inside the suffocating hood. No fingerprints on the bags either. And there hasn't been any correlation between fibres found on the various bodies. So no two of them were killed in the same place. And none of the fibres match anything at Malcolm McLennan's home or place of work.'

Another hand.

Harper checked her paper again. 'Yes, Becky, isn't it?'

'It's all very flashy and unnecessary – leaving the bodies lying about when you could make them disappear. It's sending out a message: this is what happens when you mess with Malk the Knife.'

'Of course.'

'So,' Becky sat forward, 'what we need to do is figure out who this is a message *for*. There's no point killing Shepherd like this if the intended recipient doesn't find out about it.'

'Good idea.' Harper gave her a smile. 'I want you to produce a list of all the local villains running more than a one-man operation. Let's see if we can rattle their tree a bit. Anyone else?'

Logan had a go. 'What about our prime suspect, Martin Milne, ma'am? We've got him tied to Shepherd sexually *and* financially. They embezzled nearly quarter of a million pounds from their company. And Milne did a runner three days before we found Shepherd's body.'

She stared at him.

The radiators creaked and pinged.

One of Steel's DIs cleared their throat.

'Firstly, *Sergeant*, I do not appreciate your casual sexism. You will address me as "Sir", "Superintendent", or "Super". Are we clear?'

Warmth bloomed in Logan's ears, spreading down the back of his neck. 'Yes, Super.'

'Secondly, Martin Milne is no longer a suspect, he's a potential victim. It's much more likely he's on the run because Malk the Knife's boys are after him. Assuming he isn't dead already.'

'But—'

'Milne didn't kill Shepherd, you idiot.' She pointed at the DS sitting on the far end. 'Donna, tell Sergeant McRae what you found in Shepherd's house, please.'

She turned in her seat to face him. Brushed the lank greying fringe from her eyes. 'We turned up two residency visas and work permits for Dubai, one lot in Peter Shepherd's name, the other in Martin Milne's. They've been hired to run logistics for one of the contractors building infrastructure for the World Expo there in 2020. You wouldn't *believe* how much they were getting paid, and dirty-big bonuses every quarter too.' She held up an evidence wallet. 'Visa's valid from the end of the week. They were running away together.'

Probably with two hundred and twenty-five thousand pounds of GCML's money.

'That doesn't mean Milne didn't kill him.'

She sighed. 'And it doesn't mean he did.'

'But if Milne—'

'Enough.' Harper thumped her hand down on the table. 'If you've quite finished wasting everyone's time, Sergeant McRae, perhaps you'd like to sod off and make the tea? Don't worry if it's too complicated for you, Narveer will supervise.' She nodded towards the door. 'Off you go.'

143

15

Logan slammed the milk down on the work surface, next to the line of mugs. Yanked the drawer open and jammed his hand in, ripped out a spoon. Clattered that next to the milk.

Leaning back against the canteen table, DI Singh sighed. Shook his head. 'I don't understand it. I have *never* seen her take against someone like this.'

Teabags were hurled into five of the mugs. Coffee granules got thrown into the other four.

'And I'm including the tosser who set fire to that block of flats in Arbroath last year, because the residents dobbed him in for selling drugs to kids.'

Logan snatched the kettle off its stand and filled it, before thumping it back on its charger.

Narveer sucked his teeth. 'Are you sure the pair of you haven't met before? Maybe you ran over her dog, or her grandma, or something?'

The kettle growled and hissed.

'I don't get it, this *really* isn't like her. I swear.'

Logan rammed the sugar back in the cupboard and slammed the door shut. 'What the hell is her problem?'

A shrug. 'Genuinely, if I knew I'd tell you. Giving me heartburn, all this tension.' Then he puffed out a breath. 'Her dad died a couple of months ago, maybe that's it?'

'All she's done is bitch and whine and moan and act like a complete and total—'

'Now, Sergeant, let's not forget ourselves. There is such a thing as chain of command.'

He put a hand on the kettle. Took a deep breath as it grumbled. 'Sorry, *sir*.'

'Hmm…' Narveer turned and picked the concrete gnome off the canteen windowsill. 'Heavy little fellow, isn't he?'

'And what was with the "casual sexism" remark? You called her "ma'am" earlier and it was fine, but when I do it?'

'Don't know. That's a new one on me too.' He frowned down at the white lump in his hands. 'Why *do* you have a lawn ornament in here?'

'I don't even want to be on the bloody MIT. I've got a division to run, a drugs raid to organize, and what am I doing? Making the *tea*.' The kettle rattled to a halt and Logan drowned the teabags and coffee granules. Glowered at them. Then mashed the teabags against the side of the mugs and hurled their remains in the bin. 'You're here to make sure I don't spit in Harper's tea, aren't you?'

'Couldn't possibly comment.' There was a clunk. 'Sergeant… Logan. I don't know why the Superintendent has it in for you, but if I find out I'll let you know. Meantime, till we figure it out, it's probably best you keep out of her way.'

With pleasure.

'Where do you think you're going?' Steel's voice grated down the corridor as Logan's hand hit the doorknob.

'Home.' He hauled open the door. 'My shift ended at three. It's nearly quarter past six.'

'How many times do I have to tell you, Laz? Shifts are for the weak.'

Outside, the rain had given up. Or at least called a truce. The road was slick and shiny in the orange streetlight glow.

He turned. 'Detective Superintendent Harper has made it *perfectly* clear I'm not wanted. And that's fine with me.'

'Come on, Laz, don't be like that.'

'Oh, and thanks for the support, by the way. When she was tearing me off a strip and calling me an idiot. Thanks. I really appreciate it. Hope you liked your coffee.' He stepped out into the night and thumped the door closed behind him.

It opened a moment later. 'What did you do to my coffee? Did you put bogies in it? You did, didn't you? You filthy wee—'

'You told Inspector McGregor you wanted me for local knowledge and experience.' Getting louder and louder. 'So why am I in there playing SODDING TEABOY?'

Steel took out her e-cigarette and stuck it in her gob. Sucked on it, setting the LED in the tip glowing blue. 'Are we finished having our whiney little strop?'

'Get stuffed.' He stuck his hands in his pockets and marched off.

Her voice rang out behind him. 'So you'll no' care that Martin Milne's just turned up.'

Logan froze. 'Is he alive?'

'Get in the car.'

The car screeched to a halt on the kerb, outside Milne's house. Logan yanked the keys out of the ignition and scrambled out into the darkness. Wind slammed into the garden, making the bushes writhe, snatching the breath from his throat as he jammed the peaked cap on his head and followed Steel up the drive to the front door.

Only when they got there she slapped him on the arm. 'Round the back, you great lump. What if he does another runner? Count of ten.'

Logan ducked and ran, keeping low past the front of the house and around the side. The wail of a siren grew louder in the distance. Backup on its way.

Nine. Eight.

Around the side of the house. He vaulted the gate, set into a knee-high drystane dyke. Stumbled in the darkness beyond. Kicked something plastic. Swore at it. Then hobbled around the back.

Five. Four.

The lights were on in the kitchen, spilling out into the garden.

A paved patio stretched almost the length of the house, with built-in barbecue and raised beds around the outside. A shovel, a trowel, a fork and a hoe were stacked against a water butt, their wooden handles faded and cracked by the winter. The set of rattan garden furniture hadn't fared much better.

Three. Two.

Logan eased himself along the wall and peered in through the kitchen window.

Katie Milne stood by the sink, glass of wine in one hand, the other massaging her forehead. Black streaks on her cheeks where the mascara had run. So where was... There. Martin Milne sat at the kitchen table, slumped over a very large tumbler of whisky. His face was either dirty or bruised, difficult to tell from the garden.

One. Zero.

Then Steel must have rung the bell, because they both jerked upright and turned to face the front door.

Katie said something, but Milne shook his head and stood. His whole body trembled.

Outside, the siren got louder. Couldn't be far away now.

Then Katie shook herself. Pulled her chin up, and headed for the kitchen door. As soon as she closed it behind her, Milne was up, running for the French doors.

He flung one of the doors open and leapt out onto the paving slabs.

Logan stepped out of the shadows. 'Leaving so soon, Mr Milne?'

Milne's mouth fell open, eyes wide. One of those high cheekbones of his was coloured purple and blue, another bruise on his dimpled chin. Another on his forehead. Crusts of dried blood made dark rings around both nostrils.

He tensed, legs bent. One hand reached for the shovel.

'You'll get four, maybe six, feet tops.' Logan pointed. 'And if you pick that up, I'll be doing you for resisting arrest and assaulting a police officer as well.' He unclipped his extendable baton and clacked it out to its full length. 'Want to risk it?'

The siren's wail died away, followed by the slamming of car doors.

'Come on, Martin. It's over.'

Milne sank down to the patio floor, curled his arms around his head and sobbed.

The convoy of police vehicles threaded their way through the damp and the dark – a glowing caterpillar of crisp white headlights and scarlet tail-lights, following the flashing blue-and-whites of the lead car.

Last in line, Logan followed them down the hill, then up again.

Steel shoogled back and forth in the passenger seat. 'Does this thing no' go any faster?'

'We could've taken *your* car.'

'You're no' man enough to drive *my* car. That's why you own a manky old Fiat Punto. I've seen BBC costume dramas that move faster than this.'

'Feel free to get out and walk.'

She folded her arms and scowled out of the window. 'All the way to bloody Fraserburgh. We should be interviewing the murdering wee sod, no' driving halfway across the country!'

God, it was like sharing a car with a sulky teenager.

He gritted his teeth, squeezing the words out between them: 'It's *not* halfway across the country, it's twenty-five miles. And we're going there because it's the nearest station with a custody sergeant and up-to-date interview rooms. OK? This is how it works now.'

'Waste of time, that's what it is.'

'Then why don't you wave your magic wand and give me another dozen full-time officers? Go on. It'll make my life a hell of a lot easier.'

Steel shook her head. 'You're such a moan.' She dug out her phone and poked at the screen. Listened to it for a bit. Then, 'Detective Superintendent Young, you're sounding very sexy this evening. ... No. ... Oh, she told you. Yeah, we caught Martin Milne. And when I say "we" I mean *me* and grumpy old Sergeant McRae. ... That's right. We're wheeching him off to Fraserburgh now.'

They roared through New Aberdour without slowing down.

'Uh-huh. ... Uh-huh. ... No, Superintendent Harper turned up and called dibs. He's riding with her. ... Yeah, well I wasn't quite so polite about it. ... Yup.' Then Steel threw back her head and laughed, setting her cleavage wobbling in the dashboard light. The laughter faded, replaced by a frown instead. 'She did? Seriously? ... Hold on.'

Steel stuck the phone against her chest. 'You'll no' believe it, but Madame Bipolar Panties told the Boss that catching Milne was all down to me. If it wasn't for my magnificent performance on the news, the neighbour would no' have known to give us a shout when he turned up. Apparently, my initiative is to be lauded, admired, and rewarded with cake and nipples.'

Logan tightened his grip on the wheel, ground his teeth together. 'Course it is. Because all those interviews *my* team did with the neighbours and the posters *we* put up had *nothing* to do with it.'

'Blah, blah, blah.' Back to the phone. 'You still there? ... Good. Looks like someone's given Milne a bit of a hiding, but nothing a night in the cells won't sort out. ... Not sure. If Laz had let Milne take a swing at him we could've done him for assault. But *no*, he had to be all peaceful resolutiony about it.'

A gap in the clouds opened up just long enough for a

half-moon to glare down. Pale grey light turned the countryside into a washed-out monochrome as it rushed by the
Punto's windows.

'Yeah, I will. ... What? ... No, we got a tip-off from one
of the neighbours. She saw Milne rock up and gave us a call
so we wouldn't worry about him any more. ... Yeah, OK.
Will do. ... Bye.'

Steel hung up, then squinted out through the windscreen
with a pinched face. 'No idea what we're going to charge
Milne with. Knowing our luck he'll clam up, call his lawyer,
and walk right out again.'

The silhouetted bones of a forest scratched by on the left,
before the clouds swallowed the moon again – returning
everything to darkness.

Steel had another go at a smoke ring. Failed. 'Are we
having a sulk?'

'You know what? Fine. I'm off tomorrow and Saturday.
You can all stand round in a circle patting each other's backsides till they fall off. This is nothing to do with me.'

'Oh no you don't: you work for me now, remember? All
leave is cancelled till— AAAAGH!'

He kept his foot hard on the brake as the Punto slithered
on the wet tarmac. It jerked to a halt, sideways across the
road, nose inches from a deep ditch.

Steel was frozen in the passenger seat, both hands gripping
the dashboard like talons. Eyes wide. Breath coming in tiny
gasps. Then she turned her head and stared at him. 'What
the goat-buggering hell do you think you're—'

'No.' The words came out smooth, slow, and level. 'I'm
switching Samantha off tomorrow. Then I'm going into town
to clean out the caravan. Then I'm going to get very, *very*
drunk. And if you've got a problem with that, my resignation
will be on the Inspector's desk two minutes after we get to
Fraserburgh.'

She unpeeled her fingertips from the dust-paled dashboard. 'Don't be so melodramatic. It's—'

'I don't care if I have to write it on the back of a fag packet, I'm done.'

Steel held up her hands. 'OK, OK. Two days off.' She pointed. 'Now get this bucket of sharny rust turned the right way round, before someone comes round the corner and squishes us.'

Logan swallowed the knots in his throat. Deep breath. Then turned the key in the ignition, doing a four-point turn to get the Punto pointing towards Fraserburgh again. 'I mean it.'

Reuben, Napier, Harper: they could all tie rocks around their necks and jump in a septic tank. Let them sink in the filth while he disappeared off somewhere warm to start a new life.

Steel reached across the car, took hold of Logan's leg and squeezed. 'I know. Sorry.' She gave him a pained little smile. 'Force of habit.'

He nodded.

Fields and fences slipped by in the darkness.

She let go of his leg and had a rummage down the front of her shirt instead. 'Still don't know what we're going to charge Milne with.'

'How about embezzling two hundred and twenty-five thousand pounds?'

She raised her eyebrows and nodded. 'That might do it.'

'Then we can figure out how to charge him with Peter Shepherd's murder.'

'For the record, I'm showing Mr Milne exhibit G. Mr Milne, do you recognize this?'

On the little screen, DSup Harper placed a clear plastic evidence bag on the interview room table. The camera was mounted high in the corner, looking down over Harper's shoulder at Martin Milne. Even from here it was obvious what was inside: a hardback book. That would be the copy of *The Blood-Red Line* they'd found in Shepherd's bedroom.

Milne's solicitor sat next to him, a saggy man in a dark-blue shirt and tan sports coat, looking more like a disappointed father than a legal firebrand. Narveer was next to Harper, scribbling things down in an A4 notebook.

Harper pushed the evidence bag closer to Milne. *'Would you like me to repeat the question?'*

Steel dug into her trousers and came out with a ten-pence piece. Clicked it down on the worktop next to Logan's notepad. 'No comment.'

A rancid curry smell pervaded the Downstream Observation Suite, as if someone's rogan josh had died in here and not been given a decent burial.

Logan dug ten pence from his own pocket and clicked it beside Steel's.

The room wasn't much more than a cupboard, with a worktop down one side and a couple of creaky plastic chairs. A cluster of pixels were dead on the flatscreen monitor, darkening the top-right corner of the picture like a station ident. A couple of microphones were wired into the wall, on bendy stalks, the 'TALK' buttons dark and lifeless.

On screen, Martin Milne reached for the evidence bag. Picked it up and blinked at the contents. *'It's a book?'*

Steel slumped. 'Sod.'

Logan scooped both ten-pence pieces off the surface and stuck them in his pocket.

She folded her arms. 'What kind of solicitor doesn't tell their murdering scumbag client to "no comment" everything?'

'Still, have to admire the guy's speed. Got up here quick enough.'

'Very good, Mr Milne, it's a book. Do you recognize it?'

Steel dug out another ten. 'No.'

Logan clicked one next to it. 'Yes.'

The little version of Martin Milne lowered his head. *'It's Peter's. He's reading it. He likes true crime.'*

'Gah! Are you kidding me?'

Logan scooped them into his pocket too.

'*Have you read this book, Mr Milne?*'

Mr Disappointed knocked on the interview room table. '*I don't see what my client's reading habits have to do with anything, Superintendent.*'

'*Mr Milne knows. Don't you, Martin?*'

'*My client has had a traumatic ordeal. He's just learned that his business partner and long-time friend has died. He's cooperated with your inquiry, and now it's time to let him get back to his family.*'

'Aye, good luck with that.'

'*We appear to have different definitions of the word "cooperated", Mr Nelson.*' Harper counted off the interview on her fingers: '*Your client "can't remember" where he's been for the last five days. He "doesn't know" when he last saw Peter Shepherd. He has "no recollection" of applying for a loan of one hundred and fifty thousand pounds and countersigning another for seventy-five thousand. He "can't remember" where—*'

'*All right, that's enough. You're badgering my client. If Mr Milne says he can't remember, then he can't remember.*'

Steel stretched out in her seat, arms behind her head. It made her shirt ride up, exposing a gash of pasty skin. 'This is a complete and utter waste of time.'

'*Tell me, Mr Milne, is there anything you* can *remember?*'

Logan jingled the stack of change in his pocket. 'I had a visit from Napier today.'

'Oh aye?'

Milne wiped a hand across his eyes. '*I can't believe Pete's dead…*'

'Wanted to talk about Jack Wallace.'

'Did he now?'

'*I mean, Pete… He and I…*' A sniff.

Harper leaned forwards. '*You were lovers.*'

'He did.'

'*What?*' Milne shook his head. Wiped at his eyes again. '*No. Of course we weren't. I'm married.*'

Steel stretched further, exposing more stomach. 'He's got

it into his silly little ginger head that I fitted Wallace up on the paedo charge. And do you know why? Because Wallace is a nonce, stuck in HMP Grampian for the next five and a half years, who thinks crying "stitch-up" will get his sentence reduced.' A hand reached down to scratch at the fishbelly flesh. 'As if I'd ever do something like that.'

'Mr Milne, you are aware that Peter Shepherd photographed your sex sessions, aren't you? He had them all set up as a slideshow on the TV in his bedroom. Or have you forgotten that as well?'

Milne stared at her.

'I can have prints made, if you think that might jog your memory?'

Steel narrowed her eyes. 'That reminds me.' She pulled out her phone and poked at the screen. Held it to her ear. 'Robertson? Where's my big list of everyone in Shepherd and Milne's home porno pics? ... No, I *don't* think you can give it a miss now we've got Milne in custody. Finger out, you sideburn-wearing seventies-throwback waste of skin. ... No, I want that on my desk tomorrow. ... You heard.' She hung up. Stuffed her phone away. 'Anyway, I didn't need to fit Wallace up, the dirty wee sod did it all himself. Didn't even try to hide it either, like he was *proud* of his collection.'

'Nothing to say, Mr Milne?' Harper tilted her head to one side. *'Did Peter Shepherd tell you he loved you? Did he promise the photos were just for him?'*

'All right, that's enough.' The solicitor knocked on the inter-view room table again. *'Martin, I have to advise you to answer these intrusive and insulting questions with "no comment" from now on.'*

'Oh for goodness' sake.' Steel sat up straight. *'Now* he tells him!'

16

'Anyone?' Detective Superintendent Harper sat back against the desk, arms folded, as Logan eased in through the door.

Fraserburgh's Major Incident Room had fancy interactive whiteboards on the walls and a long conference table down the middle – lined on either side with the MIT's senior officers. AKA: everyone from the rank of sergeant up, dragged over here from Banff. They all had their notebooks out, serious expressions on their face.

Logan lowered his tray onto the table. Ten mugs clinked against one another, beige contents sloshing from side to side.

Join the police, see the world. Make it coffee.

Harper helped herself without so much as a thank you. 'Come on, someone must have *some* idea. How are Milne and Shepherd connected to Malk the Knife?' She took a sip, then grimaced. Spat it back into the mug. 'This is revolting.' Harper held the mug out towards Logan. 'Do it again, *properly* this time.'

Don't rise to it.

Count to ten.

One. Two. Three. Four. Five. Six. Seven. Eight. Nine. Ten.

'*Now*, Sergeant.'

Logan took a deep breath, then the mug. 'Yes, *sir.*'

'Try and get *something* right, Sergeant.'

A spit and bogie special coming right up.

He slipped out into the corridor and closed the door behind him. Then stuck two fingers up at it, before turning and stamping away down towards the canteen. The floorboards creaked and rocked beneath him, like an ill-fitting coffin lid.

The sound of laughter came from the other side of the canteen door. It died as soon as Logan entered. Two uniforms sat on the sofa in front of the telly with Martin Milne's solicitor. At least they had the good sense to blush.

One of them – the lanky one with the side parting and pointy chin – stood. 'Sarge.'

His partner nodded at the solicitor. She was a proper farmer's daughter, with a ruddy complexion and arms that could probably bench-press a tractor. 'We were just discussing a case with Mr Nelson. Dog fighting in Peterhead. Someone lost a leg.'

Logan marched over to the kitchen area. 'Well, at least that explains the hilarity.'

'Right.' PC Lanky shuffled sideways. 'Suppose we'd better get back to it.'

'Yeah. No rest for the wicked.'

They bustled out of the room.

Milne's solicitor – Nelson, wasn't it? – took a pair of glasses from his pocket and polished them. 'It's not their fault. I was gasping for a cuppa and I forced them to make me one. At gunpoint.'

'And where is this firearm now, sir?' Logan tipped Harper's coffee down the sink.

Nelson made a gun out of the fingers of his right hand, holding it up as if he was about to fire a warning shot into the ceiling. 'I'll come quietly.'

Logan turned his back and let a gobbet of spittle splash into the bottom of the mug. Then buried it with a teaspoon of coffee granules. 'How's Martin?'

'Confused, frightened, grieving. Take your pick.' Nelson

slipped his glasses on. 'I've been Martin's solicitor for ten years. I held his hand when he was executor for his father's estate. I helped him buy his house. I did the contracts when he and his friends set up GCML. I *know* him.'

Logan turned away again, slipped a finger up his nose, had a quick rummage, then wiped the results on the mug's insides, below the high-tide mark.

'There's no way he killed Peter, it simply isn't possible. He's not that kind of person.'

The mug went under the boiling-water tap, steaming liquid going instantly brown as it hit the granules. Hiding all manner of sins.

'And I'm not saying that because I'm his solicitor, I'm his friend too. He doesn't even fiddle his taxes, for God's sake.'

A dollop of semi-skimmed added to the lies. 'You know he's not doing himself any favours, don't you? All this "I can't remember" nonsense just makes him look guilty.'

'Sergeant, he got me to draw up divorce papers last week. Martin wouldn't kill Peter. He *loved* him.'

'That's what they all say.'

'Are you coming home tonight or not?' There was an edge to Samantha's voice. Disapproval, mixed with resignation.

Logan stopped at the bottom of the stairs, one hand on the balustrade, phone pressed against his ear. 'Still waiting on Steel.'

The car park behind Fraserburgh station was full – Steel's MIT convoy taking up the usually empty spaces. That thin drizzle was back, casting halos of yellow around the rear lights.

'How much life have you wasted waiting on that woman? She takes advantage of you, Logan, always has.'

'What am I supposed to do, abandon her?'

'She can get a lift back with the rest of the team. Why does it have to be you? Let someone else suffer for a change.'

He let his head slip forward, until it rested against the cool glass door. 'I know.'

'You don't want to come home, do you? You want to string this out as long as possible.'

A patrol car pulled into the car park, ignoring the only free space and stopping right outside the rear entrance to the cells instead.

'Of course I want to come home, it's not—'

'You don't want to come home, because the sooner you do, the sooner you go to sleep, and then you wake up, it's tomorrow, and you have to kill me.'

The passenger door opened and the lanky PC who'd been watching TV with Milne's solicitor scrambled out.

'I'm not killing you. I'm...' A sigh. Yes he was. Calling it a 'decision to withdraw medical treatment' didn't change the facts.

'So you work through. Put off going to bed. It just means you're knackered tomorrow.' Her voice softened. *'Think that'll make it any easier?'*

Officer Lanky opened the back door and reached inside.

'Probably not.'

A bellow from inside the patrol car was followed by a thud and swearing – then a pair of feet lashed out of the patrol car and *bang*, PC Lanky was lying on his back, peaked cap bouncing off into a puddle. A huge man erupted out of the car, shirt ripped on one side, spattered with blood on the other, hands cuffed behind his back. He wobbled. One leg still, while the other walked itself around in a little circle. Then he lurched forwards and slammed his boot into Lanky's leg.

'Got to go.'

Logan burst out through the door, into the rain. Reached for his extendable baton... Only his hand closed on thin air. Wonderful. Why did he have to take off his stabproof vest and equipment belt?

Because it was heavy and uncomfortable, and he was only

meant to be lurking around the station, making cups of booby-trapped coffee.

Gah.

Mr Drunk-And-Huge landed another kick on Lanky's thigh. 'C'mn ... hvago... Fnnnmgh ... ME!'

'You: on the ground now!' Logan charged across six feet of rain-slicked tarmac and leapt. Curled his shoulder and slammed into the blood-spattered chest, sending the pair of them clattering backwards.

Crunch, the guy slammed into the patrol car. 'Aaagh... Fgnnn kll ye!'

A knee cracked up into Logan's ribs, hard enough to shove him sideways, crushing the breath from his lungs.

The big sod whipped his head back, then forward again. *Fast.*

Logan flinched out of the way ... almost. *THUNK*. The world whipped right, riding on a wave of hot yellow noise and the taste of AA batteries. He staggered. Lurched. His legs weren't working properly, they wouldn't hold him up. The left one folded, thumping him down on his knee.

Towering over him, the big lump spat. It splattered against the shoulder of Logan's fleece.

'Killlnnn fgnnn plsssssss bsssstrds...' He lurched sideways a couple of paces and back again. Grinned a gap-toothed grin, the bitter-sharp stench of vomit leaking out. 'Ha!' Drew back his foot for a kick.

Logan blinked. Made a fist of his own. Then rammed it up into the guy's groin, twisting, putting his weight behind it.

Bloodshot eyes bugged. The mouth fell open. 'Nnnnnngh...'

Then he lurched forward and Logan scrambled sideways, out of the spatter zone as the big sod puked all down himself. Then folded over. Thumped onto the vomit-flecked tarmac, and curled around his battered testicles. Moaning.

'Gnnn...' Lanky's partner wobbled out of the patrol car, one hand clutched over her nose, blood dripping from between her fingers. She tilted her head back. 'Thags, Sarge.'

Logan pulled himself up the side of the car. Bracing himself against the bodywork as the car park jostled and whistled at him. He pointed at PC Lanky as he struggled upright. 'You: get this vomity lump on his feet and processed.'

Lanky scooped up his fallen hat, and fondled the back of his own head. 'Ow...'

'Now would be good, Constable.'

A nod. A wince. Then he hauled the big guy to an almost-standing position, hissed through gritted teeth, and dropped him. 'Nope.'

For goodness' sake.

Logan grabbed the other arm and together they frog-marched the reeking lump through the customer entrance and into the cellblock. The grey terrazzo floor squeaked under the big guy's trainers as they half-carried half-dragged him to the processing area.

The short desk, covered in posters, with a glass partition above it, made the place look more like the reception of a student hostel. And going by all the warning leaflets about rights, blood-borne diseases, drugs, and rape, a really manky one.

Voices came from somewhere within the cellblock, muffled by thick metal doors and concrete walls. Barely gone nine and it sounded as if they already had a lot of overnight guests.

Logan knocked on the processing desk. 'Anyone in?'

A thickset woman with thinning hair and a squinty eye appeared from a side room and peered out at them. She sniffed. 'What is *that*?'

Lanky heaved Captain Vomity forward. 'Nicholas Fife. Breach of the peace. Assault. Urinating in a public place. Assaulting a police officer—'

'Three police officers.' Logan shoved Mr Fife against the desk. The man's shirt left a little smear of what might have been pre-chewed doner kebab on a 'COMBATTING RELIGIOUS EXTREMISM' poster.

'Sorry, *three* police officers. Oh, and I think he may have crapped himself too.'

The Police Custody and Security Officer had another sniff. 'Well you're not leaving it here.'

Lanky jerked his chin up. 'We're not taking him home to live with us, he's not a puppy!'

She slapped a clipboard down on the countertop. 'Care and Welfare of Persons in Police Custody, Standard Operating Procedure. Part five, subsection three is perfectly clear: any suspect in need of immediate or urgent medical care *must* be taken directly to hospital until such time as they are no longer deemed at risk. And that includes head injuries, overdoses, and anyone who's completely and utterly pished out of their...' The PCSO scowled as a line of pale-yellow spittle fell from Mr Fife's lips and sploshed against the regulations. 'Urgh.' She snatched her clipboard back, then grabbed a leaflet about fly-tipping and scrubbed at the dribble. 'He is *not* choking on his own vomit in my cells. Get him up the hospital.'

'Come on, Denise, don't be a—'

'I've never had a death in custody and I'm not starting now.' Her arm jabbed out, pointing at the door. 'Hospital.'

Lanky's shoulders dipped. 'Fine. We know when we're not wanted.' He turned. 'Claire!'

His partner appeared. Thick tufts of green hand-towel poked out of each nostril, the paper darkened and browned with blood. 'Whad?'

'Grab an arm, we're leaving.'

'Soddig hell. *Towd* you we should've god straid to the hosbidal.'

They took hold of Mr Fife and steered him towards the exit. His testicles seemed to have recovered a bit, because he was able to limp along without having to be dragged.

Logan stayed where he was as the door clunked shut behind them.

'The same argument, every Thursday night.' The PCSO

shook her head. Then frowned at him. 'You all right, Sergeant? Only if you aren't: would you mind buggering off and not bleeding on my nice clean floor?'

'What?'

She pointed. 'There's a sink in the back if you want to wash up.'

Logan hunched over the sink in the tiny galley kitchen off the side of the custody processing area – barely enough room for a grown man to stand sideways without brushing the units on one side and the wall on the other. He splashed water on his face. Tiny pink droplets fell onto the stainless steel.

He prodded his left cheek – the skin was already tightening as it swelled, red flushing across the growing lump. A gash ran sideways across it, not far below his eye. Going to be a decent bruise. Nicholas Fife had a *really* hard head.

The water eased the stinging throb for a couple of breaths, then it was back again, digging its claws through Logan's face and into his skull.

Sod this. Samantha was right: Steel could find her own way back to Banff.

He patted his face dry with paper towels. Then applied a sticking plaster from the first-aid kit. Little red dots showed through the beige plastic.

A thump behind him, and the PCSO was back. Denise looked him up and down. 'You still here?'

'Nope.'

'Cupboard at your knees – dig in there and find us a red, a brown, and a blue.'

Logan bent down and something large and burny throbbed through his brain. He opened the cupboard, revealing stacks of microwave meals in coloured boxes. Red, brown, blue: shepherd's pie, chicken and vegetable madras with rice, and an all-day breakfast. He turned the blue box over. '"Beans in a rich tomato sauce, with potatoes and two succulent pork

162

sausages."' He handed it to Denise. 'This lot eat better than I do.'

'He doesn't usually.' She pulled the black plastic trays from the cardboard boxes, stabbed the film lids with a fork, and slid the lot into a battered grey microwave. 'Don't think the poor sod's seen solid food since last time he was in here.' Denise beeped the buttons. 'How's the head?'

'Sore.'

'As long as it doesn't make a mess, I don't care.' She curled a lip. 'Been mopping up sick all evening. Why you lot have to arrest people with dodgy stomachs I'll never know.'

The microwave dinners buzzed and hummed around in a circle.

'Thought you didn't allow drunks.'

'Oh, he was very apologetic about it, but it didn't stop him barfing everywhere.'

Buzz and hum.

She shuddered. 'We had a cat once, soon as its shoulders started going you knew what was coming.' Denise hunched her shoulders up and down a couple of times, then made *'ack'*ing noises. 'All over the place. Couldn't just stand still and throw up: much more fun to back away and make sure there was a big long line of the stuff.'

Buzzzzzzzzz...

'Worst was when he got into the knicker drawer. Urgh... All over my thongs.'

Now there was an image to put you off your chicken curry ready-meal.

Hummmmm...

It'd be really nice to go now, but there wasn't any room to squeeze past Denise and her pukey pants.

She produced a polystyrene cup and made some milky tea in it.

Buzzzzzzzzz...

Ding.

Denise picked up the tea then pointed at the microwave. 'Grab those for me, will you? There's a tray over there.'

He tweezed them out of the microwave with sizzling fingers, dumping them on a round brown tray that looked as if it'd been half-inched from a pub.

She turned and marched from the room, leaving him to follow.

What was it with women? Why did they all expect him to run around after them? Did he have 'DOORMAT' printed across his forehead in two-inch-high letters only they could see?

Logan picked up the tray and followed her.

Denise produced a bunch of keys, flipping through them as they walked past the entry corridor and right, past the female cells, and through into the new bit where two rows of big blue doors stretched away in front of them. They each had a slide-down hatch, safety notice, intercom, and a little whiteboard mounted on the metal surface. Someone had scrawled prisoner warnings on those, like: 'BEWARE!!! HE BITES!', 'DIABETIC', 'SPITS', and 'ALLERGIC TO WHEAT'.

She stopped outside one marked, 'NEEDS FEEDING UP' and slid down the hatch. Peered through the plastic viewport. Then unlocked the door. 'Felix? How you feeling?'

A stench of mouldering garlic and dead mice oozed out into the cellblock.

'You hungry? Bet you are. Got you a lovely cup of tea too.'

What looked like a mound of dirty laundry stirred on the blue plastic mattress. Then Felix rolled over.

His skin was a mottled grey brown, the wrinkles darkened with dirt. There wasn't much hair on his liver-spotted head, but what he had was yellow and straggly. He blinked at them with rheumy eyes. 'Hmmm?'

'Come on, Felix, see what we've got for you? All your favourite foods.'

Thin trembling fingers reached for Logan's tray, a smile cracking the skeletal face.

Logan put it on the blue plastic mattress next to him. 'Watch, they're hot.'

He dug into the chicken curry with a plastic spoon. Shovelling it into his ragged mouth.

Denise smiled. 'There you go.'

Logan leaned against the blue strip, painted halfway up the wall. 'Anyone exciting in tonight?'

'Usual collection of Thursday-night drinkers. Couple of druggies in for possession. A lovely young lady, in the other block, stabbed her granny in the leg because she wouldn't buy her a new iPhone.' A sniff. '"Stinky Sammy" Wilson's back again. Thinking of giving that boy a season pass.'

Felix polished off the last chunk of curry, licked the plastic tray clean, then started in on the all-day breakfast. Getting bean juice all over his stubbly chin.

'What did he do this time?'

'Cheese and bacon, same as every other druggy.' She shook her head. 'Doesn't even make any sense, does it? Shoplifting cheese and bacon. Who's going to buy a slab of Gouda and a pack of smoked-streaky from a smackhead in a pub? You'd have to be mental.'

Beans and sausages and potatoes disappeared.

Logan glanced out into the corridor, with its rows of heavy blue doors. 'What about Martin Milne?'

'Ah yes. *Mr* Milne.'

Felix slurped the last of the breakfast from the tray and polished it with his tongue. Only the shepherd's pie to go.

'Giving you trouble?'

'I can understand why someone gave him a spanking, put it that way.' She turned back to their resident garbage disposal unit. 'There we go, is that nice?'

Felix kept on shovelling.

'Which one's he in?'

'Course it is. You eat up.' Then up to Logan. 'Number five. If you want to fall him down the stairs a couple of times, let me know and I'll nip out for a fag.'

Logan raised an eyebrow.

'Joking.' A shrug. 'Kind of.'

He stepped out into the corridor and wandered across the hall to the cell door marked 'M5'. The whiteboard had 'PAIN IN THE HOOP' scrawled on it. Logan slid the hatch down halfway – until it clicked into the viewing position.

Martin Milne sat on the edge of his thin blue mattress, with his elbows on his knees and his head in his hands. A shudder rippled across the shoulders, setting them quivering. He wiped a hand across his nose and stared at the silvery pink line it left on his forearm.

Then he looked up and round. Stared right back at Logan. Wiped his eyes dry.

Logan slid the hatch back up again.

Turned to go.

There was a knock on the other side of the door – three light bangs, muffled by all that metal. *'Hello?'*

Logan clicked the hatch into the viewing position.

Martin Milne stood on the other side of the little Perspex window, blinking at him with swollen bloodshot eyes. 'Hello. You were there. At the house.' He sniffed. Wiped away the tears. 'Can I see him?'

'See who?'

Milne turned his face away. 'Peter. Can I see him?'

'Don't you think you've done enough, Mr Milne?'

'I *need* to. They wouldn't let me say goodbye.' He leaned his bruised forehead against the window. 'I just want to say goodbye.'

'You want me to ask Detective Superintendent Harper if you can see the body of the man you killed? I can ask, but I know what she'll say.'

'I didn't kill him. I…' Deep breath. 'I loved him.' Milne cleared his throat. 'About those photographs, at Pete's place. My wife doesn't need to find out about them, does she?'

'They'll probably be used in evidence.'

'But…' Milne looked up, straight into Logan's eyes.

'They're not important. Pete liked to watch the slideshow while we... It's not *illegal*. Everything was consensual. Everyone was over eighteen. If someone didn't want their face on camera they could wear a mask.' He bit his bottom lip. 'It'd break Katie's heart. *Please?*'

Should have thought of that in the first place.

Logan shook his head. 'It's out of my hands. You'll have to...' Wait a minute. 'Who? Who wouldn't let you say goodbye?'

'Please. I'm begging you.'

'No, you said someone wouldn't let you say goodbye. You weren't talking about Detective Superintendent Harper, were you? Who wouldn't?'

'It doesn't matter.' Milne turned around and slid down the inside of the door – still visible in the convex mirror mounted on the cell's ceiling. 'None of it matters any more.'

OK...

Logan went back to the other cell, where Denise was collecting up all the licked-clean ready-meal containers and humming 'Twinkle, Twinkle, Little Star'. Felix was curled up on his mattress with his back to the cell, looking like a pile of dirty laundry again.

'Denise, have you—'

'Shhh!' She stuck a finger to her lips, then put the Styrofoam cup on the tray and crept out of the room. Eased the door shut behind her. 'Only just got him off.'

'Are you two...?' Logan pulled his chin in and pointed at the cell.

'The poor sod's got dementia. He hates his care home, so he disappears for a couple of weeks at a time.' She slid the hatch up, hiding the sleeping Felix away. 'But he gets confused and too hot and takes all his clothes off – which is when we get a phone call from some distraught mother of two, because he's done a strip in the local Post Office, or Asda. And he ends up in here for the night.'

'Can you open up number five?'

'Least we can do is feed him up. He's skin and bones under them rags.' She dug out her keys. 'Why do you want into five? Seriously, I was only joking about the "falling down stairs" thing.'

'Need to ask Mr Milne a couple of questions.'

There was a pause, then a shrug. 'Don't see why not. Long as you sign for him.'

17

'No.' Martin Milne hunched into himself on the other side of the interview room table. His fingers twitched themselves into knots and out again. 'No recordings.'

Logan pressed the button on the machine, setting the digital camera running. 'It's for your own protection, Martin. This way everyone knows it's all above board and no one tried to make you say anything.' The unit gave a bleep. 'Interview with Martin Carter Milne, of number six, Greystone View, Near Whitehills. Present, Martin Milne and Sergeant Logan McRae. It's ...' he checked his watch, 'twenty-one forty, Thursday the twelfth of February—'

'No comment.'

Great.

Try not to sigh. 'Martin, if you don't want to talk to me, why are we—'

'No comment.'

Well, it was pretty obvious why they'd written 'PAIN IN THE HOOP' on his cell whiteboard.

'Martin, can we—'

'I said, "no comment". I have no comment to make.'

Complete waste of time.

'Interview suspended at twenty-one forty-two.' He pressed

the button and switched it all off. 'Let's get you back to your cell.'

The lines around Milne's eyes deepened. He spread his hands out on the tabletop. 'They'll kill me if they find out.'

Here we go.

'Who'll kill you, Martin?'

'They made me *watch*.' His eyes glistened. 'They wouldn't let me say goodbye, but they made me watch.' Tears sparkled on his eyelashes. 'They said if I told anyone about it, they'd do the same to me and my family. To Ethan. They're going to kill my wee boy.'

Logan sat back in his seat. Slipped his hands into the pockets of his trousers. Felt for his mobile. 'It's OK, Martin, you're safe here. Why don't you— Damn it.' He hauled his phone out and poked at the screen. 'Sorry about that: got it on vibrate.' Then placed the thing facedown on the table. 'Should have switched it off earlier.'

Outside the room, the floorboards groaned like a dying dog, the noise fading as whoever it was passed down the corridor.

'Why don't you start at the beginning? Tell me what happened and we'll try to sort it out together, OK?'

Milne nodded. Wiped a hand across his eyes. 'It was just meant to be a meeting. We turn up and hand over the cash and everything's done.' He swallowed. 'Only, when we got there, they started screaming about more money. They said two hundred and twenty-five thousand wasn't enough. They wanted an extra hundred grand.'

'The money you borrowed from the bank.'

A nod. Then a sniff. 'We told them we didn't have it. It'd take some time. And this big guy, he starts hitting Peter and screaming at him: "We want our money, Bitch. We want our money." And I tried to stop him, but they jumped me and they're kicking and punching…'

Milne hauled in a deep, rattling breath. Stared down at his twitching fingers. 'Then this other guy comes in and he

170

says that if we want to get out of this alive, we're going to have to sign GCML over to them. We're going to have to start doing *favours*.'

Sounded familiar.

'Course Peter says, "No way. Deal was for a loan, not this." And they start in on him again. They're stamping on his chest and his head and he's crying and...' Milne ground tears from his eyes with the heel of his hand. 'They tied his hands behind his back and stuck a bin-bag over his head. I promised them. I promised them anything they wanted, but they ... they...' He bit his bottom lip. 'They taped it tight around his neck. And he's thrashing against the floor, and he can't breathe, and I can't breathe, and they're laughing, and...'

Milne folded forwards, until his forehead rested on the tabletop. He put his hands over his head, pressing down, as if he could force it through the scarred Formica. Muscles bunching in his thick arms. Shoulders trembling. Then the sobbing started.

Logan sat back and watched.

Somewhere outside, a patrol car's siren burst into life. Then faded off into the distance.

He reached across the table and put a hand on Milne's lurching shoulder. 'Shh... You're safe here. You're safe.'

Milne didn't look up, the words coming out jagged and torn. 'If I ... if I don't do what ... what they want, ... th ... they'll *kill* me and my ... my wife and my little boy.' A wail grew from somewhere deep inside his torso. 'Like ... like they ... they killed Peter.'

Detective Superintendent Harper scowled up from her desk. 'This better be important, *Sergeant*, some of us have work to do.' She pulled back in her chair. 'What happened to your face?'

The office had the same bland, flat-pack elegance as the rest of the station. Two desks along one wall, one in the middle of the room. Harper had commandeered that one, while Narveer had the one nearest the door. Both of them poking away at fancy laptop computers, rather than the usual hamster-wheel-powered lumps of ancient plastic everyone else had to fight with.

Logan folded his arms, shoulders back. 'Martin Milne claims he was present when Peter Shepherd was killed.'

'Does he now?'

'Their container business was failing, they needed new contracts. Peter Shepherd came up with the idea of bribing officials in Nigeria to let them bid for a bunch of oilfield logistic projects off the coast there. Only they needed the money in a hurry. So they went to one of Malcolm McLennan's goons.'

'Hmmm...' Harper closed her laptop. 'Narveer?'

Her sidekick swivelled his seat around to face them. 'It's a connection.'

'Apparently Shepherd wasn't just into true-crime books, he liked to kid-on he was connected. A little bit dangerous. When he bumped into someone he recognized from *The Blood-Red Line* at a fundraiser, he let it slip they needed two hundred thousand for something dodgy.'

'I see.' She picked up a pen and wrote something in her notebook. 'And we should believe you, because?'

Logan held up his phone. Pressed his thumb against the button marked 'PLAY'.

Martin Milne's voice burst out of the speaker, slightly distorted and tinny. '*...from the bank, but he said we couldn't get the money fast enough. We had to get these guys bribed by Wednesday or—*'

He pressed 'PAUSE'.

'I *accidentally* set my phone on voice-memo mode and left it on the interview room table. Might not be admissible in court, but that doesn't mean we can't act on the information till he agrees to make a formal statement.'

She tilted her head to one side and stared at him in silence.

Narveer adjusted his tartan turban. 'So that's why they needed those loans from the bank. They had to pay off Malk the Knife.'

'Two hundred thousand, plus twenty-five grand interest. Only when they tried, the price went up another hundred thousand and they had to hand over the company. Shepherd refused and they killed him.'

Harper narrowed her eyes. 'Hmm...'

Logan put the phone back in his pocket. 'And now Milne has to use his containers and ships to shift stuff in and out of the country for Malcolm McLennan – lose them among the other manifests – or the same happens to him and his family.'

She pushed her chair back and stood. 'Send the audio file to Narveer, Sergeant. We'll take it from here.' Harper waved at the door. 'You can go now.'

You're sodding welcome.

Steel spread her mouth wide, showing off rows of grey fillings in a jaw-cracking yawn. Then slumped and shuddered. 'Where the hell have you been? Dropping off the spar, here.'

Logan grabbed his stabproof vest from the corner of the Sergeants' Office and dragged it on, scritching the Velcro flaps together so the whole thing was tight. 'I'm leaving now. You're either in the car, or you're walking.' Equipment belt next, complete with the truncheon he could've done with when Nicholas Fife was on the rampage.

She stretched. Let him see her fillings again. 'Pfff... I fancy some chips. Anywhere open for chips?'

'It's after ten. No. Now are you coming or not?'

'All-night bakery?'

He snatched his high-viz jacket from the rack by the door – checked to make sure it actually *was* his, hauled it on and stormed out. 'Stay here then.'

'All right, all right.' Steel hurried along behind, pulling

on her coat. 'Who poked a burning ferret up your bumhole today?'

Across the corridor and through the door at the top of the stairs. 'I'll tell you who – Detective Superintendent Holier-Than-Thou Harper, that's who.' Logan's boots hammered down the steps. 'Doesn't matter what I do, that bloody woman treats me like something to be scooped up in a plastic bag and dumped in a park bin. Well, you know what? She can—'

'Sergeant?' Narveer appeared at the top of the stairs, mouth stretched out and down as if he was doing a sad frog impersonation. 'Glad I caught you.'

Logan stopped. 'Detective Inspector Singh: I'm off duty. And I'm going home.'

A sigh. Then Narveer closed the door and leaned his elbows on the handrail, looking down the stairs at them. 'I wanted to say, good job. You did well. Milne wouldn't talk to any of us, and you got him to open up.'

Was that *credit*?

Dear Lord, wonders would never cease.

He pulled his chin up. 'Thank you, sir.'

'We're going to offer Milne a deal. See if we can't intercept one of Malk the Knife's shipments.' A smile widened Narveer's face. 'This is the closest we've come in *years* to pinning anything on McLennan.'

Tell that to Detective Superintendent Harper.

Narveer looked away, picking at the handrail with a fingernail. 'Erm, Sergeant McRae? How did you get him to talk to you?'

No idea. But it wouldn't do to let DI Singh know that.

Make something up.

'Harper battered away at him, tried to grind him down. I treated him like a human being.'

'Right. Good cop to her bad cop. Cool.' The DI pulled on that big smile again. 'Anyway, like I said: good job.' He slipped back through the door, leaving Logan and Steel alone in the stairwell.

174

She sucked on her teeth, making squeaking noises. 'Think he fancies you.'

'Oh shut up.' Logan turned and marched down the stairs.

'Ooh, Sergeant McRae, you're so *sexy*. Kiss me, Sergeant, kiss me like I've never been kissed before. Make a woman of me!'

He hauled the door open and stuck his hat on. Stepped out into the rain.

'Oh come on, Laz, stop being such a Pouting Percy. You just got a pat on the bum from our new overlord's sidekick.' She followed him across the car park to where the Punto sagged under the weight of the drumming rain. 'Which, on balance, maybe doesn't sound all that impressive, but it's better than nothing. And Narveer's a nice boy: he'd probably take you to dinner before humpity-humpity.'

Logan unlocked the car and slid in behind the wheel. Chucked his cap in the back. 'Are you coming or not?'

'Still, going to be a longshot. Hanging about, hoping Malk the Knife will turn up and...' A frown settled onto her face. 'What?'

'Shhh. Thinking.' She dumped herself into the passenger seat. Then a smile bloomed across her face and she thumped a hand on the dashboard. 'Of course! Why'd I no' see it before? It's *obvious*!'

'You know how to get Malcolm McLennan?'

'That big Asda we passed on the way in – we can get something to eat there!'

Moonlight speared down through the clouds, raking the fields as they slid by the Punto's windows. Off to the right, the North Sea was a slab of polished granite. The world black-and-white beyond the car's headlights.

'Mmmnnnghph mnnnphh?' Small beige flecks of pastry shone in the dashboard lights as they spiralled out from Steel's mouth.

'God, you're disgusting.'

She swallowed. 'Oh don't be such a Jessie.' Then took another bite of her pasty. Chewing with her mouth open. 'I said, "Do you want the chicken curry or the steak-and-onion?", you grumpy old sod.'

Oh.

'Steak-and-onion.'

The road wound along the coast, then headed inland, hiding the sea as Steel struggled with the packaging. 'Ha!' She handed it over. She'd even rolled the first inch of plastic down, so he could bite straight into it.

Logan did. Chewing on chilled soft pastry and cold meaty filling. It coated the roof of his mouth with a thin layer of waxy grease. Not exactly three Michelin stars, but better than nothing.

Steel polished her pasty off. Sucked the crumbs from her fingers. 'When you doing it?'

He talked around a second mouthful. 'Doing what?'

'Tomorrow. With Samantha.'

Oh. That.

'Don't know. In the morning, probably.' He puffed out a breath as stones and boulders gathered in his stomach, pulling it down. He cleared his throat. 'Did you hear about Wee Hamish Mowat?'

She reached across the car and squeezed his leg. Second time that day. 'You want me to come with you?'

The stones grew heavier. 'Now he's dead, we've got criminals from all over descending on Aberdeenshire. Looking for a chunk of the pasty.' He took another bite, but it curdled in his mouth.

'Give me a call, OK? You phone me when you're heading over and I'll dump everything and come sit with you.' Another squeeze. 'I mean it.'

He forced the greasy mouthful down. Blinked. Nodded. Then let out a long shuddery breath. 'Thanks.'

'Don't worry about it.' She pointed at the pasty in his hand. 'Now are you done with that, cos I'm still starving.'

18

Logan pulled up outside a little B-and-B on the northern fringe of Banff. A dozen feet of patchy grass separated the road from the cliffs. A pebbled beach hissed at the base of them, turned into a lunar landscape by the bleaching moonlight. The North Sea a solid slab of clay – glistening and grey.

Steel brushed pastry crumbs off her front and into the footwell. 'Right. You call me tomorrow. Promise?'

'Promise.'

'Good boy.' She climbed out into the night and stood there, peering back into the car while all the heat escaped. 'I mean it, Laz: no trying to do it on your own. You've got family now.'

'OK, OK, I get it.'

'Don't forget.' She thumped the door shut, then turned and huddled her way over to the B-and-B and let herself in. Paused on the threshold to wave at him.

Logan waved back.

Soon as the door closed, shutting off the light, he bent forward and boinked his head off the steering wheel. 'Great...'

Why was it, sympathy just made things hurt so much more? Indifference, even animosity was fine – could turn that into anger and cope – but sympathy?

He boinked his head off the wheel again. 'Ungrateful tosser.'

Yeah.

Logan turned the car around and headed back towards the station. Past the silent darkened houses and empty streets.

How was he supposed to investigate her for Napier? If she sat there, holding his hand while he switched Samantha off, what was he supposed to do? Thanks for the support at this difficult time, now do you mind if I screw you over and work for the Ginger Whinger behind your back?

The harbour was full of yachts, berthed up for the winter. A handful of tiny fishing boats tied up closer to the harbour entrance.

But if he *didn't* investigate her, Napier would only get someone else in to do the job. And maybe that someone wouldn't be quite as understanding of Steel's little foibles. Or her bloody huge character flaws.

Gah.

Maybe it was all just a misunderstanding? A quick poke about in the facts of the case, and bingo: Steel's exonerated. She'd be delighted that he'd cleared her name... Or she'd kill him for being a disloyal wee sod and investigating her in the first place.

Great. So the whole thing was a lose-lose for him.

He parked outside the Sergeant's Hoose. Sat there staring out at the bay. All cold and still and dark. The lights of Macduff glimmered on the other side of the water.

And then there was Samantha...

The stones were back, clumping in his stomach.

Come on. Out.

A long, black, sigh huffed out of him. Then he got out and locked the car. Crossed the road.

A couple of women stood outside the Ship Inn, smoking cigarettes and shivering. One looked up and stared at him as he let himself into the Sergeant's Hoose. Like he was something strange to be studied, in his bright-yellow high-viz jacket – the stripes fluorescing in the streetlight.

Logan thunked the door behind him and locked it.

Sagged.

Tomorrow was going to be … just … *terrific*.

God.

A soft furry body thumped into his leg, followed by a tiny prooping noise.

Logan let his breath out. 'Cthulhu. How's Daddy's bestest girl?' He unclipped his equipment belt and hung it on the end of the banister, then stuck his hat on top. Peeled off his stab-proof vest and leaned it in the corner. Bent down and ruffled the fur between Cthulhu's ears. 'At least you still love me.'

She purred, little white paws treadling on the laminate floor.

A handful of post lay on the mat and he picked it up, flicking through it. Yet another election leaflet from the Lib Dems, one from the SNP, and a brochure about free hearing aids for the over fifties. And last an envelope with no stamp, no postmark, and a black border around the edge. Hand delivered.

Logan turned it over and paused, one finger poised to rip through the flap. Maybe not the best of ideas. Use a knife instead. He marched into the kitchen and dumped everything else on the table. Took a butter knife from the draining board and slit the flap open. Poured the contents out onto the countertop.

Mr Logan McRae

is respectfully invited to attend

the memorial service for

Hamish Alexander Selkirk Mowat

At 12.30 on Friday the 13th of February at
Old Ardoe Kirk, South Deeside.

No flowers, by request of the deceased, but a donation
to Cancer Research would be welcomed.

No razor blades or needles were taped under the flap, lying in wait for an unwary finger. Instead the envelope contained a gilt-edged rectangle of cardboard engraved in flowery script.

Right. Well there wasn't much chance of him turning up for Hamish's funeral, was there?

When he'd just switched Samantha off?

And besides, it probably wasn't a good idea to be in the same postcode as Reuben, never mind graveyard. No telling what would happen. But it probably wouldn't be anything good.

He propped the invitation on the windowsill, next to the dying herbs.

Then dug out a squat glass tumbler and poured in a slug of the whisky Hamish Mowat had given him. Toasted the rectangle of card. 'Sorry, Hamish. But I can't.'

Took a sip. Warm and fiery and leathery and smooth.

Wait a minute.

He frowned at the tumbler, and the lines of amber crawling down the inside of the glass. There had been a letter, hadn't there? Wee Hamish had handed it over, then the doctor threw them out and Reuben started throwing his weight around.

Back through to the hall and the collection of coats, jackets, and fleeces.

It was in yesterday's coat pocket.

The word 'LOGAN' was scratched across the front in smudged trembling fountain-pen letters.

He sat at the kitchen table and opened it, while Cthulhu wound herself back and forth between his ankles.

Probably another appeal for him to take over Hamish's criminal empire, because nothing said 'Career Police Officer' like running a stable of drug dealers, prostitutes, and protection rackets. Still, had to admire the man's tenacity – even when he was dying he didn't give up.

The contents were almost illegible, written in the same pained hand as the envelope. It must've taken Wee Hamish hours to do, given how weak he was at the end.

Dear Logan,

I'm afraid we have come to the end of our journey together, but I want to thank you for all your kindnesses over the years, I do appreciate them.

But I'm dying, so please forgive me if I seem blunt ~ I need you to kill Reuben.

He will kill you, if you don't kill him. Perhaps not today, or tomorrow, but it will come soon, in the dark, when no one is watching. And it will take a long, long time. You pose too much of a threat to his ambitions for it to be otherwise.

I know I could order someone to kill him for you, but that would cost you the respect of the employees. And if you don't have their respect, you can't lead them.

So please grant a dying man one final kindness and kill Reuben before he kills you.

With love, your old friend,

Hamish

Wow.

Logan read the letter through again. Put it down on the table.

Took a mouthful of whisky.

Gave it one more read. Then picked Cthulhu up, carried her out into the hall, and closed the kitchen door, shutting her out. He cracked the window open, dug the kitchen matches out of the cupboard, held the letter over the sink, and set fire to it. Turning it back and forth until the flames took hold.

Heat seared the tips of his fingers and he dropped the burning letter into the sink. The gritty cloying smell of burnt paper filled the room.

The letter blackened around the words, then a line of vivid orange washed across it, leaving the sheet white and powdery, but still bearing Wee Hamish's instructions. He jabbed the ashes with a wooden spoon, beating them into dust. No point taking any risks: the envelope suffered the same fate.

Gah...

Samantha lowered herself down on the couch next to him. 'What we watching?'

'Hmm?' Logan looked up from the tumbler in his hands.

Some vacuous pap cop show lumped its way across the TV screen, about as divorced from the reality of actual policing as Henry the Eighth was from his wives.

Samantha poked him in the shoulder. 'He didn't divorce any of them. They were either annulled or beheaded. Well, except for the last one. And the one that died of natural causes. Don't you ever watch *QI*?'

Logan had a sip of the whisky. 'Don't do that.'

'Don't do what?'

'Don't jump in when I haven't said something out loud. Makes me look like a lunatic.'

She turned to the TV, nose in the air.

Onscreen, a man in an SOC suit wandered about a crime scene without wearing goggles or a facemask. Because, on television, no one ever got ripped apart in court for not following proper procedures. No, *they* could contaminate the scene to their hearts' content, as long as the halfwit viewing public could see their pretty actory faces.

'Look at these muppets. Bet none of them would last two minutes in the witness stand against Hissing Sid.'

'It's not my fault.'

Another sip. Then he put on a posh Scottish accent, 'Tell me, Detective Inspector McActor, while you were parading all over the scene of the alleged crime, did you remain on the common approach walkway? No? Did you have the hood of your Tyvek suit up? No? You felt it was more important to show off your magnificent head of flowing hair? I see...'

'This thing between you and Reuben has been brewing for years.'

'And were you wearing your goggles and mask, or did you ponce about spewing your own DNA over everything? And did...' Logan jabbed a hand at the TV, dropping back to his own voice. 'Oh for God's sake. Look at it: you don't pick up a murder weapon with the pen from your pocket! What are you, a *moron*? How did this idiot get admitted to a crime scene?'

'You broke his nose. He was never going to forgive you for that.'

'Who wrote this garbage?'

'Logan!' She turned and grabbed his face in both hands. 'Listen to me: I'm right, *Wee Hamish* is right – you have to kill Reuben. Have you even got a plan?'

On the TV, DI McActor was snogging one of the Scenes Examination Branch, in the middle of the crime scene, with the body lying at their feet.

Deep breath. Logan lowered his eyes and ran a fingernail along a chip in the rim of his glass. 'I'm trying not to think about it, OK? I don't want to kill Reuben. I don't want to kill anybody.'

'You have to start planning for it, you *know* that. Fitting him up isn't going to do it.' She let go of Logan's face and poked him in the chest. 'Come on: how, when, where, and what do you do with the body afterwards?'

183

He let his head fall back and stared up at the stippled white ceiling for a moment. 'Gun. Has to be a gun. And it has to be soon. Somewhere out of the way with no witnesses. And there's no point burying him, it'd take forever to dig a hole big enough.' Logan swirled the dregs of his Glenfiddich around the glass, leaving trails up the side of the glass. 'Fire. Stick the body in a car and set fire to it. Burn off any trace evidence and DNA. When they find the body they'll think it was one of the rival gangs trying to muscle in.'

She smiled. 'There you go. I'm proud of you.'

Wonderful.

Assuming he could lure Reuben to somewhere out of the way without anyone else showing up. Assuming he could actually pull the trigger. Assuming Reuben didn't kill *him* instead.

And then all he'd have to do was pray that Reuben hadn't lodged an insurance policy with a solicitor somewhere. In the event of my untimely death, the following letters are to be sent to the media and Professional Standards for the purpose of screwing Sergeant McRae to the wall by his testicles.

Speaking of which.

He pulled out his phone and turned it on again. Scrolled through the call history. And selected a number. Then listened to it ring.

Click. 'You've reached the desk of Chief Superintendent Napier, I'm unavailable at the moment, but you can leave a message after the tone.'

Of course he wasn't there – it was nearly midnight.

Beeeeep.

'It's Logan. McRae. I've been thinking about your investigation.'

Samantha stared at him, both eyebrows raised.

'I'm in.'

— Friday Rest Day —

this ship is sinking

19

'…*neighbour killed himself, because his business went bust. There's fat cats whooping it up in London and his wife's got to bury him in a council grave. Where's the social justice in that?*'

Logan groaned beneath the duvet.

'*Well, that's a good point. OK, next up we've got Marjory from Cullen. Go ahead, Marjory.*'

There was a proop-meep noise and something heavy landed on his bladder. 'Argh…' Then walked up his torso and sat on his chest.

'*It's this oil price downturn. We all know these oil companies make billions of profits, so why are they squeezing the supply companies? How's the industry supposed to survive if shareholders are wringing every penny out of the North Sea?*'

He peered out at the clock radio. Half eight.

'*And let's not forget, eighty percent of a gallon of petrol goes straight into the government's pocket! That's Scotland's money.*'

'Go away.' He reached out and thumped the snooze button. Slumped back on the pillow.

A little fuzzy head appeared above the edge of the duvet and biffed its cheek against his nose. Purring like a tumble dryer full of gravel.

A yawn.

The phone went, ringing downstairs in the living room.

Then fell silent. Followed by the distorted sound of his own recorded voice telling whoever it was to leave a message.

Cthulhu biffed into his face again.

'Yes, I know you want sweeties, you wee monster.' He picked up the pack of cat treats from the bedside cabinet as the machine downstairs bleeped and a dark voice replaced his own.

Who the hell was that?

Another biff.

'OK, OK.' He dug a treat out and held it in front of her pink nose.

Crunch, crunch, crunch.

Samantha settled on the end of the bed, running a brush through her bright-red hair – making it shine. 'You're actually awake? Thought you were going to sleep till noon.'

Another treat.

'It's half eight, give me a break.'

Crunch, crunch, crunch.

She took hold of his foot through the duvet. 'Big day, today.'

'I know.'

Crunch, crunch, crunch.

'Come on then: up and showered. You're not switching me off looking like someone dragged you backwards through a combine harvester. Sunday best, Mr McRae.' She smiled. 'After all, it's not every day you get to kill your girlfriend.'

Logan wandered back through to the bedroom, scrubbing at his head with a towel. The cool air made the hair on his arms stand up and pimpled the flesh beneath. He paused in the doorway, sniffing.

Was that bacon?

How could he smell frying bacon?

Maybe he was having a stroke?

...

Wait, were those *voices*?

188

He wrapped the towel around his middle, tying it off.

There were definitely voices coming from downstairs.

Maybe it was Reuben, come up to finish the job himself. Well he was out of luck, because... Oh for God's sake. The equipment belt wasn't where it should have been – on the chair in the corner of the bedroom. It was still hanging over the end of the banister.

Argh.

Improvise.

He hauled on a pair of jeans and tiptoed out onto the landing. Opened the cupboard and lifted the toolbox out. Selected an adjustable spanner from the pile of tools. Big and heavy.

Logan smacked the business end into the palm of his other hand.

Not quite an extendable baton, but if it got him to the bottom of the stairs where the equipment belt was, it'd do.

He crept down the stairs. No sign of anyone.

The voices coming from the living room sounded more like the TV than real life.

'*...news and weather where you are, but first we've got the singing sensation taking* Britain's Next Big Star *by storm on the* Breakfast *sofa...*'

Logan unclipped the CS gas canister from its holster, fiddling with it until the bungee cord holding it to the belt let go. Then slipped the extendable baton from its...

Someone was singing in the kitchen. A sweet, but smoky, growl of a voice, belting it out.

> '*Adventure Cat, Adventure Cat,*
> *The cosmic kitten with a magic hat,*
> *Fighting evil, doing good,*
> *Having naps and eating food,*'
> It wasn't Reuben, it was Steel.
> '*With her sidekick Lumpy Bear,*
> *Catching villains unaware,*'

Logan lowered his armoury and stuck it through the balus-trades onto the stairs, then pushed through into the kitchen.

She was standing at the cooker, shoogling a frying pan that hissed and sputtered. Singing away, oblivious:

'Making friends and having fun,

Doing stuff for everyone.'

He leaned against the work surface. 'What are you doing?'

Steel froze for a second, then went back to her shoogling. 'Making breakfast.' Then she looked around and raised an eyebrow. 'Laz, how many times? I'm flattered, but I'm no' shagging you. Now get dressed.' She waved a spatula at him. 'Sight of all them scars is putting me off my grub.'

He folded his arms across his chest. Then lowered them to cover the shining puckered lines that snaked across his stomach. 'How did you get in here?'

'No point being a keyholder if you don't use your key, is there?' She went back to poking at the pan. 'Five minutes. And stop picturing me naked! We had words about that.'

Gah…

Logan turned and headed back into the hall. Maybe if he poured bleach in his ears it'd get rid of that particular mental image.

He stopped with one hand on the newel post at the foot of the stairs. 'Who was on the phone?'

But she was off again.

'Adventure Cat, Adventure Cat,

Foiling evil Dr Rat,

And his schemes most dastardly,

To save the world for you and meeeee!'

Why did he bother?

Through in the lounge, the red light on the answering machine blinked at him.

On the TV, two newsreaders tried to be chatty with a permatanned couple who had big hair and unnaturally shiny teeth.

'…amazing. And did you ever think you'd be this popular?'

'*We have to say the fans have been absolutely fabulous, haven't they, Jacinta?*'

'*Oh yeah,* totally *fabulous. I mean,* completely. *Me and Benjamin been—*'

Mute.

He pressed the button on the answering machine.

'*MESSAGE ONE:*' That same dark voice that had been barely audible through the floorboards oozed out of the speaker. '*Sergeant McRae? It's Chief Superintendent Napier, I got your message about the … project we discussed.*'

Oh crap.

Logan lunged across the carpet and thumped the living room door shut.

'*I think it would be prudent for you to come in and discuss it in person. That way you can review the evidence.*'

Well, Napier would have to wait. He had more important things to do than undermine and manipulate a Professional Standards investigation into Steel today. And tomorrow was blocked out for the hangover that came afterwards.

'*I think it's important we get this underway as soon as possible, don't you? After all, the longer it exists in limbo, the more chance there is of the papers getting hold of it. I think we can all agree that a trial by media would be regrettable for all concerned. If you'd like to call me back, we can set up a mutually convenient appointment. Thank you.*'

Bleeeeeep.

Logan glanced at the wall separating the room from the kitchen. No way she could have heard any of that. Not still singing her lump-filled head off.

Unless, of course, she'd turned up when the call came through in the first place.

'*Message Two:*' Steel's voice came from the machine. '*Laz? You there? … Laz? … Pick up if you're there.*'

On the TV, they cut from the permatanned talentless toothmerchants to the ident for local news.

'*You better no' still be in your scratcher, you lazy wee sod.*'

Probably lying there, playing with yourself, aren't you? Well stop it, you'll go—'

Delete.

The Scottish newsreader was replaced by a mob outside one of the oil company headquarters in Dyce. The words, '...SCENES OF UNREST AS PROTEST ENTERS THIRD DAY...' scrolled along the bottom of the screen.

'*YOU HAVE NO MORE MESSAGES.*'

Logan held down the delete button until the message count went back to zero, blanking Napier's incriminating call.

The protests at Dyce gave way to woodland and a line of blue-and-white 'POLICE' tape.

'...HUMAN REMAINS IDENTIFIED AS LOCAL BUSINESSMAN, PETER SHEPHERD...'

He switched the TV off. Time to get dressed.

Steel put one foot up on the dashboard, scratching at her ankle, mobile phone pinned between her ear and shoulder. 'Yeah. ... Did he? ... Nah...'

Logan drove them along the winding road, west out of Banff. Taking his time.

White lines scratched along the sea's blue face. Pounding against the cliffs. Sending up walls of spray. It glowed in the warm golden light that ramped up the colour of everything.

'When was that? ... Oh aye? ... I'm no' happy about that, Becky. I put *you* in charge of babysitting the wee scumbag, no' Spaver: so sort it. ... Yeah.'

Samantha leaned forward from the back seat. 'Still don't see why *she's* got to come with us.'

'She's worried about me.'

A huge puddle spread across the tarmac and he slowed for it. The tyres growled through, making their own walls of spray. Only grey and gritty instead of shining white.

'She's a pain in the backside. Always has been.'

'That's true.'

Steel put her phone away, then swore as it blared into

life again. Dragged it back out. 'Yes? ... Superintendent Harper— Yes, yes I know. ... Me?' She cast a glance across the car at Logan. 'Yeah, I'm following up a couple of things at the moment. ... Definitely. Be back in the office in a couple of hours? Ish? ... What?' Steel had another scratch. 'Oh for God's sake. How'd he get away with that? ... The greasy goat-molesting scumbag — What?'

'Thought it was going to be you and me today. My final morning on earth. Who invited the Wrinkled Witch of the West?'

'Can you two not fight today? Please? Just for once?'

'...No. Of course. We'll get a cordon up. Malk the Knife'll no' make contact if Milne's got half the world's media camped outside his front door. ... Uh-huh. Will do.'

A sign loomed into view. 'SUNNY GLEN 1 ➜'

Samantha put a hand on his shoulder. 'Not long now.'

'Am I the only one who feels sick?'

'Uh-huh. ... Uh-huh. ... OK. Thanks.' Steel hung up, took her foot off the dashboard, and put her phone away. 'What you chuntering on about, Laz?'

He shrugged. Indicated. Took the road to the right, heading closer to the cliffs.

Steel had a wee burp, then rubbed at her stomach. 'Where'd you buy your tomato sauce, Halfords? Stuff's like battery acid.'

'Or it could be the three bacon butties you wolfed.'

'*No*, it was your cheap-and-nasty own-brand bargain-basement sauce.' She had another burp. 'Apparently the media's been camped outside Martin Milne's house since we released Shepherd's name. It's like a rugby scrum.'

'Not to mention the four cups of coffee.'

'They caught some tabloid tosser shinnying over the back fence, having first pumped the neighbour and the wifie that does the school run for everything they had.'

'So get Milne to make a statement. They won't go away until he does.'

Sunny Glen appeared around the next bend: single storey for most of its length, with a balcony overhanging a large patio area where the ground fell away towards the cliffs. A couple of wheelchairs were out, their occupants positioned in the February sunshine.

Logan let out a long slow breath. 'Here we go.'

Steel squeezed his leg. Again.

'Hoy!' Samantha banged on the seat. 'Hands off, you old bag.'

'She's only being nice.'

There was a frown from the passenger seat. 'What? Who's being nice?'

The Punto slotted into a parking space outside the admin wing. 'Milne's wife, Katie. She's trying to be nice to everyone. Can't be easy after everything.'

Steel took out her e-cigarette and had a puff. 'With her husband shagging a dead bloke? Probably no'.' She climbed out into the sunshine and had a scratch at her belly.

'Gah, it's like sharing a car with a Labrador.' Samantha thumped back into her seat and folded her arms. 'Scratching and fidgeting and fiddling with her boobs.'

'You coming?' He grabbed his jacket.

Steel bent down and peered into the car. 'Course I am.'

'Right. Yes. Good.' He led the way to reception: a glass-fronted room with pot plants, watercolours, and a big beech desk.

The young man sitting behind it looked up as Logan entered and smiled. 'Mr McRae, how are you today?'

'I'm not sure yet, Danny.'

'Ah, of course.' He stood. 'Please, take a seat and I'll get Louise. Would you like a cup of coffee, or...?'

'No. Thanks.'

'OK then.' He picked up the phone and had a muttered conversation while Steel stalked around the room, squinting at the paintings, hands behind her back, like a badly creased crow.

Samantha wound her hand into Logan's. 'It's going to be OK.'

He just breathed.

Steel took his other hand. 'How you holding up?'

'I appreciate the gesture, but I'm fine.' He shuffled his feet. 'You don't have to be here. You've got a murder to solve.'

'Well Harper can rant and rave all she wants, some things are more important.' She gave his hand a squeeze. 'Couldn't leave you to go through this alone.'

He squeezed back. 'Thanks.'

'You're still not allowed to think about me naked, though.'

'Urgh.' He took his hand back and wiped it on the front of his jacket. 'OK, now I'm going to be—'

'Logan, hello.' A woman marched into the room. Her bleached pixie cut curled across her forehead, cowboy boots clicking on the wooden floor. She held her arms out and the sunlight caught the linen sleeves of her shirt, making her glow like an angel. She wrapped him up in a hug. Then stepped back. 'How are you?'

Why did *everyone* have to ask that? How the hell did they think he was?

'Fine. I'm fine, Louise.' It sounded better than: dead inside.

Samantha leaned in, her voice a warm soft whisper in his ear. 'Liar.'

'Now you're sure you want to go through with this? Remember, there's no rush.'

'I know.'

'OK.' Louise stroked his arm. 'If there's anything that's unclear, or you want to stop at any time, let me know. It's not a problem.' Then she turned to Steel. 'You must be Logan's mother. He's told me so much about you.'

The wrinkles deepened across Steel's forehead. 'No! I'm no' his *mum*, I'm his moral support. Nowhere near old enough, for a *start*!'

Louise's smile slipped for a moment. 'Right. Sorry. My

mistake.' Then she turned and gestured towards the door leading deeper into the building. 'Shall we?'

The corridors were alive with the wub-wub-wub of a floor polisher and the noise of music coming from the rooms – each one playing something different. It blended into an atonal mush of sound, like a radio picking up multiple stations at once.

Men and women lay on their beds, some connected to machines, some breathing on their own. A couple propped up and strapped into armchairs, heads on one side, dribble soaking into their bibs.

'Here we go.' Louise held the door to number eighteen open and ushered them inside.

Samantha lay beneath the covers, an oxygen mask over her pale face. Her hair was almost all brown roots now, slipping into a faded scarlet only at the tips. A little dot marked her nose and another her bottom lip, more up both sides of her ears where the piercings had healed over. The tattoos stood out against her almost translucent skin, coiling up and down both bare arms – skulls and hearts, wound round with brambles and tribal spines. They looked so much blacker than they used to. As if they'd been leeching the life out of her all these years and were now ready to break free from the flesh.

Her cheekbones were sharp and pronounced, riding high on her sunken face. But the thing that really didn't look like her was the big dip in her head, above the left ear, as if someone had taken a big ice-cream scoop out of her.

Louise placed a hand on Logan's arm, turning him away from the bed towards the room's other occupant. 'Logan, this is Dr Wilson, he'll be in charge of withdrawing Samantha's medical treatment.'

A dapper man with no hair stuck a hand out. His chinos had creases down the leg you could shave with, denim shirt rolled up to the elbows with a pink tie tucked in between the buttons. 'We'll take good care of her, Logan. She won't feel a thing.'

'How does this work?'

'We give Samantha a dose of morphine, wait for it to take hold, then switch off the respirator.'

'So she suffocates.'

'I know it sounds distressing, but she won't be in any pain.'

At least that was something.

Dr Wilson folded his hands together, as if he were about to say a prayer. 'Are there any questions you'd like to ask?'

Samantha's chest rose and fell beneath the blankets, marking time with the hissing respirator.

'Logan?'

Someone nudged him in the ribs. And when he looked around, Steel was frowning at him.

Her voice was soft. 'You OK? 'Cos we can sod off home and do this some other day, if you want.'

Deep breath. 'No.' He reached out and took Samantha's hand in his. The skin was dry and papery, cool to the touch. 'It's time.'

'I understand.' Dr Wilson nodded. 'The procedure should—'

'You're not doing it.'

He pulled his chin in. 'I know this is difficult, but I can assure you I've done this many times—'

'You didn't know her.' Logan brushed a lock of hair forward on Samantha's head, covering the dent. 'It should be me.'

'Ah...' The doctor looked at Louise. 'I'm not sure that's such a good—'

'She deserves that much. Not to be switched off by a stranger.'

Steel's frown deepened. 'Laz, you sure you want to do this?'

'Doesn't matter what I want: I owe her.'

'Mr McRae, please. I think you should reconsider, it's—'

'You heard the man, Doctor.' Steel stepped between them and held her arms out, as if she were breaking up a fight in a pub. 'Show him how to do it, then off you trot for a nice cuppa tea and a chocolate Hobnob.'

20

The machines pinged and hissed.

Logan pulled the visitor's chair from the corner of the room and positioned it alongside the bed. Sat in it. Hissed out a long breath.

It was a lot less crowded in here without Steel, Louise, and Dr Wilson. Just Logan and the two Samanthas – the one in the bed and the one in his head.

'You sure you know what you're doing?' She settled onto the bed next to him, one hand on the dying Samantha's leg. 'Don't want you screwing this up. I could end up with brain damage, and then where would you be?'

Another breath.

'Don't I look pale?' She leaned forward and ran a finger around the dent in the body's forehead. 'And that was never flattering, was it? Oh yes, let's hack a big chunk out of her skull to relieve the swelling on her brain. That's a good look.'

'Don't.'

'What? I'm keeping your spirits up. Don't be ungrateful.' Samantha swung her legs back and forth. 'And look on the bright side: think of all the cash you're going to save, me not being here. This place costs a fortune. You should sell the caravan too.'

'I never grudged it.'

'Take the money and go on holiday for a change. How about Spain? You could go see Helen. I always thought—'

'No.' He looked away. 'We're not talking about this again.'

'I'm lying there on my deathbed, I'll talk about anything I like.'

'It *didn't* work, it's not *going* to work. So can we please—' Logan's phone blared out its ringtone. Cocking hell. He denied the call, then switched the thing off. 'I'm sorry.'

'It's OK.'

'If it wasn't for me, you wouldn't have fallen. They set fire to the place because of me. You're here because of me.'

She placed her hand over his where it held the dying Samantha's. 'You're right. You're a horrible human being and you never deserve another day's happiness in your life.'

A little smile tugged at his mouth. 'I liked it better before you started answering back.'

'You ready?'

'Yeah.' Something large sat on his chest, squeezing out the air. Logan pressed the button and the morphine pump whirred.

Samantha blinked. Wobbled a bit. 'Whoa, that's a head rush.'

The her in the bed didn't even twitch.

'Logan? What's going to happen to me?'

'I don't know.'

'If I'm dead, will you forget about me?'

'Of course not.'

'Maybe you should.' She checked her watch. 'It's time.'

He reached out and clicked the switch on the respirator. The hissing died away. Samantha's chest sank beneath the blankets and didn't rise again.

'Logan, I'm scared.'

A knife slipped into his throat, blocking it, then twisted. The words would barely come. 'It'll be OK.'

He swallowed, but the blade stayed where it was.

He squeezed her hand.

Hauled in a harsh jagged breath.

'I'm sorry.'

The room blurred.

Everything tasted of broken glass.

Oh God.

'I'm so sorry.'

Steel lowered the mug of tea onto the coffee table. 'Milk and two sugars. And before you say anything, I know you don't take sugar. Hot sweet tea's traditional.'

'Thanks.'

She sat on the arm of the settee, placed a hand on his back. 'Feeling any better?'

'I keep telling you: I'm *fine*.'

''Cos you don't look fine, you look sodding awful.'

'Yeah, well.' He took a sip of tea. 'I'm having a bit of a day.'

Sunlight streamed into the living room, catching motes of dust and making them glow. Cthulhu lay on her back, on the rug, arms stretched out, feet curled into fuzzy quote marks, white belly absorbing as much solar radiation as possible.

Logan stood and picked her up. Buried his face in her fur, breathing in the scent of biscuits and sunshine. Shuddered it out again. 'Just you and me now, kiddo.'

'Maybe you should put in for compassionate leave? Could come down to Aberdeen and stay with me and Susan for a bit. Hang out with the kids.'

He flipped Cthulhu over, rubbing her tummy as she stretched and purred. 'And who'd look after Little Miss Monster with her stretchy arms and curly feets?'

More purring.

Steel frowned at him. 'You been drinking already?'

'Basic cat anatomy: arms at the front, legs at the back. Paws at the front, feets at the back.'

'Yeah…' She pulled her chin in, multiplying the wrinkles. 'You've been living on your own for far too long, Laz. We need to— In the name of the scrabbling bumhole.' She yanked out her ringing phone. '*What*?' Then stood. 'Uh-huh. … Yeah.

... OK, OK. Well it's no' like I can trust *you* to do it, is it?'
Steel mouthed the word 'Rennie' at him, then wandered
across to the window, blocking Cthulhu's light. 'Yeah. ... I'll
be there in fifteen. Don't let him out of your sight till then.'
She hung up. 'Sorry.'

'I know. Everyone's sorry.'

'We're taking your suggestion and getting Milne to make
a statement. With any luck the baying hordes will sod off
and leave him alone long enough for Malk the Knife's goons
to get in touch.'

'Good for you.'

She hauled up her trousers. 'You want me to get Susan
up here? She could keep you company. Shoulder to cry on.
Make loads of hot sweet tea and the occasional sandwich?'

'Thanks, but I'm fine.'

Steel folded her arms. 'You're going to get blootered, aren't
you?'

He toasted her with the mug.

'Aye, well, probably for the best. Soon as I get off shift
I'll join you. Till then, I'd better shoot.'

She cleared her throat. Fiddled with the sleeves of her
jacket. Then bent down and kissed him on the cheek. Before
harrumphing a couple of times, and letting herself out.

The front door slammed shut, leaving him alone in the
quiet.

Reunited with her sunbeam, Cthulhu purred.

Logan topped up the whisky in his tumbler. Took a sip of
Glenfiddich. Let his head fall back and stared up at the living
room ceiling as the whisky spread its warm tentacles through
his body. 'You there?'

No reply.

Of course she wasn't there. She was dead. And all he had
left was a big aching hollow, right in the middle of his chest,
wrapped around with whisky.

Of course, it was obvious what she'd say if she was here.

He cleared his throat. 'Get off your backside, Logan. Stop wallowing in it. Find yourself a gun and figure out how to get Reuben somewhere killable.'

As if that was ever going to happen.

But then, she was always the practical one.

So, if it was quite all right with everyone else, he was going to sit here and wallow.

The doorbell gave its long mournful *drrrrrrrrrrrrrrrrrrrrrr-rrring.*

'Go away.'

Cthulhu stopped washing her pantaloons and stared at the living room door.

Drrrrrrrrrrrrrrrrrrrrrrrrrrring.

'God's sake.' He levered himself out of the couch and slouched out of the room, taking his whisky with him. Why couldn't everyone sod off and let him wallow in peace. Was it really too much to ask for?

Drrrrrrrrrrrrrrrrrrrrrrrrrring.

'All right, all right.' Logan unlocked the door and yanked it open. '*What?*'

A wall of muscle filled the threshold. It was dressed in a black suit, white shirt and black tie. Which didn't really go with the words 'KILL' and 'MUM' tattooed on the knuckles of two big fists. The face wasn't much better, topped off with a haircut even shorter than Logan's.

The creature that evolution forgot smiled. It didn't help. 'Can Sergeant McRae come out to play?'

A Transit van was loomed at the kerb behind him. It might have been white once, but the paintwork had aged to a dirty yellow, covered in a timpani of dents. Two other thugs stood on either side – one of whom seemed to be carrying a body bag.

Screw that.

Logan slammed the door, but it was too late: Smiler had his foot in the way.

He put one tattooed hand against the wood and pushed

his way into the house. The other hand reached into his jacket and came out with a short-barrelled revolver. 'Easy way, or hard way?'

The two outside didn't move.

A taxi droned past.

Somewhere in the distance, a seagull screamed.

So this was it. Reuben hadn't even waited till after the funeral. Pig time.

Should be fighting back. Should be kicking off and struggling and biting and... But what was the point? After this morning, what did it matter?

Logan took a sip of whisky. 'I've got a choice?'

Smiler snapped his fingers and one of his mates stepped forwards – a wee bloke with big blond sideburns and a ratty ponytail – holding out the body bag. Only up close it looked a lot more like a suit carrier.

The gun twitched towards the stairs. 'Better get changed, Sergeant. You've got an appointment.'

Bench seats ran down both sides of the Transit's load bay. Logan sat on the driver's side, with Smiler at the other end, blocking the door. One of his mates, a thin man with bad teeth and a lazy eye, sat opposite, playing on a hand-held games console. Tongue poking out the side of his mouth as the thing bleeped and binged.

The van lurched around a corner, then accelerated.

That would be them leaving Banff.

Difficult to tell. There were no windows back here – the walls lined with big rectangles of chipboard covered in metal hooks and the vacant outlines of tools.

Goon Number Three had the radio on in the cab section, singing along to ABBA's 'Dancing Queen' at the top of his voice. The noise rattled through the bulkhead wall, clashing with the plinkity music from Mr Teeth's game machine.

Logan loosened his tie: black, like his suit and shoes. It wasn't a bad fit, but it wasn't exactly classy. The kind of outfit you could pick up for a few quid at one of the larger super-markets. All three of them dressed up like something out of *Reservoir Dogs*.

He jerked a thumb at the bulkhead. 'So, what, we're on our way to a Blues Brothers revival?'

Smiler didn't smile. 'Shut up.'

Thick plastic sheeting covered the load-bay floor. Just right for preventing all those nasty, hard-to-clean bloodstains.

Not too hard to see how today was going to end.

Should have listened to Samantha. Should have listened to Wee Hamish Mowat. Should have killed Reuben instead of sitting on his backside waiting for the murderous bastard to make the first move. Well, it was too late now.

But then again, it was always going to end this way, wasn't it? In a kill-or-be-killed world, the normal people always ended up dead.

Logan let his head thunk back against the chipboard.

Yup, this was turning into a really top-notch Friday the thirteenth.

The engine noise dropped to a low growl, then the Transit swung to the left. Crunching came from the wheel arches. They'd turned onto gravel. Either a track or someone's drive-way. Which meant the magical mystery tour was about to come to its unpleasant conclusion.

More crunching.

The van rocked and lurched a bit, then slowed to a halt.

Through in the cab, the seventies musicfest died.

Then came the clunk of the driver's door and the *scrunch, scrunch, scrunch* of his footsteps.

Here we go.

The back door opened, letting in a flood of sunlight.

Smiler turned and hoiked a thumb at the view. 'Out.'

Logan clambered down from the tailgate onto a gravel driveway at the side of a rough stone building surrounded by trees. A door hung open, its red paint flaking like leprous skin.

A large finger pointed at the dark hole of the doorway. 'In.'

Something twisted deep inside Logan's chest.

Maybe there was a way out of this? Slam his elbow back and up into Smiler's face. Ram the arm forward and break Mr Teeth's nose. Kick Captain ABBA in the balls. Then run for it before any of them got themselves together.

Deep breath.

It wasn't going to work.

But it wasn't as if he had anything to lose, was it? Probably wind up dead either way.

OK. In three, two—

A cold hard lump pressed against the back of his neck. 'Don't even think about it.'

Logan turned, just far enough to see Smiler out of the corner of his eye. That cold hard lump was the snub-nosed revolver's barrel.

Yeah... Maybe not.

Logan straightened his tie instead. Took a breath. Then marched in through the door.

Inside, it was one big gloomy room, the only light coming from the doorway behind him and a couple of dirty skylights. There was barely enough to make out the bare rafters and the closed garage doors.

And the big sheet of heavy-duty plastic spread out in the middle of the concrete floor. Like the one in the van, only much bigger and with stitches of duct tape holding it down.

A big hand in the small of his back propelled him forward, until he was standing right in the middle of the crinkly sheet.

'Stay.'

The thing in Logan's chest twisted again, turning his heartbeat up to a deafening thump. Thump. Thump. Sweat prickled across the back of his neck.

He was going to die here. Slowly. Then be dragged away for pig food.

Smiler retreated to the shadows while Mr Teeth took up

position by the door. He was bent over his Gameboy/DS thing again, pinging and dinging away to repetitive doodly music.

No sign of Captain ABBA.

Slow calm breaths.

And then Reuben appeared in the doorway. He'd stripped off to the waist. The patchwork of scar tissue and fur that marked his face continued down his barrel chest and across his gut in a foot-wide strip of twisted skin. His bottom half was covered in a pair of overalls, the arms tied in a knot beneath his stomach. Big rig boots on his feet – nice and heavy with steel toecaps. Perfect for kicking someone to death. ''Bout time.'

Reuben rolled his head to one side, then the other. Flexed his shoulders. Puffing himself up. 'Some of the guys think you can't be trusted, McRae.' The hands were next, coiling into huge fists. 'Think you're going to stitch me up.'

Logan swallowed. Forced his chin up.

Don't tremble. Don't let the bastard see you fall apart.

Fight back. Make him pay for it.

'See, I can't have that, McRae. Can't have that at all. Got to have a hundred and ten percent loyalty from my team. You get that, don't you?'

He'd come fast and he'd come hard. Use that bulk of his to pin Logan down and then batter the living crap out of him.

Logan shifted his weight to the balls of his feet, knees slightly bent.

OK. Go for the eyes. Gouge them out of his fat ugly head.

At least then he'd have something to remember him by.

The lump in Logan's chest wound itself into a knot.

'Take this wee prick...' Reuben stepped aside and Captain ABBA was back, hauling a shivering man with him.

The newcomer wore nothing but a stained pair of pants, the elastic going at the waist. Bruises made angry patterns across his skin, wrapping around his legs, torso, and face. He clutched one arm to his chest, the elbow swollen like a grapefruit and the wrist flopping in a way nature never intended, fingers poking out in all sorts of horrible directions. 'Plsss…'

The word barely managed to squeeze its way out of his swollen lips.

Reuben pointed, and Captain ABBA dragged the man onto the plastic sheet and dumped him at Logan's feet.

'This is Tony. Say hello, Tony.'

He coiled up on the floor, tears and snot ribboning his face. 'Plsss… Plsss dnt kgggh mmmi…'

'Tony thought it would be fun to help himself to the merchandise and the profits. Didn't you, Tony?'

'Plsss…'

'Well, Tony, *was* it fun?'

'Mmmm ssssrree…'

'Too late to be sorry, Tony. That ship sank long ago.'

'Plsss dnt kgggh mmmi…'

Reuben snapped his fingers.

Mr Teeth put the Gameboy away and pulled out a claw hammer. Captain ABBA produced a semiautomatic.

All the moisture vanished from Logan's mouth, tightening his throat. He held his hands up. 'Come on, Reuben, you don't have to prove—'

'I'm not an unreasonable man, Tony, I'm going to give you a choice.' Reuben reached out and took the claw hammer. 'You want this or the gun?'

'Plsss…'

'Going to be one or the other. What's it to be, quick and shooty, or slow and thumpy?'

Lying at Logan's feet, Tony sobbed.

'Or, if you like, you could go to the pigs as you are? All thrashing and screaming as they eat you alive. Might be more fun for them. Bit of sport.'

'Plsss…'

'Going to have to hurry you, Tony: gun or hammer?'

'Gnnn… Gnnn.'

'Good boy.' Reuben pointed with the hammer and Captain ABBA stepped onto the plastic, hauling back the semiautomatic's slide. *Chick-clack.* All primed and ready to fire.

Logan hauled in a breath.

Do something.

Now.

Do it *now*.

Because otherwise it'd be too late and...

He frowned as Captain ABBA held the gun out to him.

The guy stood there, with the primed semiautomatic held at arm's length by the barrel. 'Here you go, chief.'

'You're kidding, right?'

'Nope.' Reuben shook his head. 'See, I've been telling the doubters, McRae isn't going to screw us over. McRae can be trusted. And right now I'm trusting you to put Tony out of his misery.' A shrug. 'And in case you're wondering, he's dead either way. Question is: are you on the team or not?'

OK...

Logan reached out and took the gun. Heavy. Cold. No idea what make it was, but there were Cyrillic letters above the trigger guard. He pulled the slide back a fraction, far enough to see a sliver of brass in there. Loaded. Thumbed the magazine release and let it fall into his palm. It was nearly full – had to be nine or ten shots in there.

Captain ABBA smiled. Then backed away until he was on the concrete floor again.

Really?

Logan clicked the magazine back into place, then pointed the barrel right between Tony's eyes. Poor sod probably couldn't see much – they were a mass of broken blood vessels set in swollen bags of dark purple. They'd broken his nose, probably his jaw too.

'Plsss dnnnt...'

'Come on, McRae, chop-chop. Some of us got a funeral to go to.'

'Plsss...'

Kill Tony, or be killed. Same bloody dilemma he'd been facing for days, only with the names changed. Murder or be murdered. Round and round and on and on.

Well, enough. Time to take a stand. Go out with bang.

He was dead anyway.

Logan snapped the semiautomatic up, two-handed, and aimed right at the middle of Reuben's chest.

'Tsk.' The big man shook his head. 'Dear, oh dear, oh dear.'

'I won't kill for you.'

Smiler stayed where he was, hands in his trouser pockets – nowhere near his revolver. Mr Teeth remained by the door, noodling away at his game. Captain ABBA just sighed.

There was a scenario like this on the firearms training course. Only *there* the bad guys were printed on bits of paper stuck to chipboard. They didn't bleed and scream and die.

Logan slowed his breathing and clicked off the safety catch.

Samantha had been right all along. This was the only way. Didn't matter if he liked it or not, he didn't have any choice.

'See, McRae, that doesn't look too trusting, does it? You're not being a team player, there.'

Do it.

Right now.

Pull the damn trigger.

So he did.

Click.

Oh no.

21

No, no, no, no, no.

Bloody gun wasn't working.

He racked the slide back – *chick-clack* – sending the unfired cartridge flipping end-over-end out onto the plastic sheet, and pulled the trigger again.

Click.

Reuben grinned. 'Do you really think I'm that stupid?'

One last go.

Chick-clack. Another cartridge went flying.

Click.

'That's the funny thing about guns, McRae: don't work without a firing pin.'

Logan lowered the semiautomatic.

Idiot.

Of *course* they wouldn't give him a working gun.

'See, this whole thing's been a test, hasn't it, Tony?'

Lying on the floor, Tony cried.

'A wee test to see how big your balls are, McRae.' Reuben held out a hand and Captain ABBA handed him a white bath towel. 'We weren't going to *shoot* Tony. Nah.' He wandered onto the plastic sheet. It scrunched beneath his rig boots. 'Wouldn't do that.'

Tony struggled to his knees. 'Thhnkkk yyyy...' His swollen

lips trembled, a mixture of drool and blood spilling down his chest.

Reuben hunkered down beside him. Dabbed the towel against Tony's face, turning the white tufts pink and red. 'There we go. That's better, isn't it?' He passed him the towel.

'Thhhnnnk yyyy...' Tears and snot and trembling. He held the towel over his face; blood soaked into the fabric.

'Shhh, it's OK.'

Logan backed away. 'You weren't going to kill him?'

'Tony's learned his lesson, haven't you, Tony?'

'Pllsssss...' He placed a grimy hand against his own chest, fingers splayed. 'Immm srrrryyyy...'

Reuben stood. Stepped behind the snivelling figure and put a hand on his shoulder. 'So, Tony, what are we going to do with Sergeant McRae? What do you think?'

The whole thing was one big set-up.

'Shall we give him a second chance?' Reuben's voice chilled. 'Or shall we show him what happens to disloyal wee shites?' He snatched both ends of the towel and hauled, snapping Tony's head back so his face pointed to the ceiling, covered in blood-flecked white fabric. Reuben wrapped the ends into one fist. Then battered the hammer down into Tony's upturned towel-covered face. Once. Twice. Three times. Fast. Putting his weight behind it. The sound of cracking bone gave way to wet sucking noises as the white fabric became saturated with scarlet.

Logan stepped forward. 'NO!' But Smiler's revolver appeared again, pointing right at his head. He froze.

Four. Five. Six.

Tony's right foot twitched in time with the blows, but the rest of him sagged in place – only held upright by Reuben's grip on the towel.

Seven. Eight. Nine. Ten.

Reuben let go of the dark-red fabric and Tony's body slumped sideways onto the plastic sheet. No movement. No breathing. A puddle of blood oozed out onto the surface.

The whole thing had taken less than eight seconds.

Logan swallowed.

Smiler kept his gun levelled at him.

'Oh yeah.' Reuben stood there, grinning, puffing for breath. 'That's what we do to them.' He passed the hammer back to Mr Teeth, who dropped it into a plastic freezer bag and ziplocked it tight.

A shadow filled the doorway behind him, then John Urquhart stepped into the garage all dressed up in funeral black-and-white. He glanced at the body on the floor, then up at Reuben. 'Going to have to go or we'll miss the start.'

'They'll wait.' Reuben crossed to the far side of the plastic sheet. Picked what looked like another suit carrier from the shadows and pulled out a packet of baby wipes. Rubbed a couple across his face, clearing away the tiny spatter of red dots. He kicked off his boots. 'You screwed up, McRae. Was going to let you do the job, prove you're trustable, but now? Nah.'

Oh he was *so* screwed.

Logan tightened his grip on the semiautomatic. It might be no good as a gun, but it would still work as a cudgel.

Reuben untied the arms of his boilersuit and the whole thing fell to the floor, exposing a pair of hairy legs and red pants. 'I'm going to go bury Mr Mowat, and then I'm going to have a chat with a chief inspector friend of mine.' A pair of black trousers came out of the carrier, and he pulled them on. 'Tell him how you took a bribe.'

'I didn't take any bribe!'

A white shirt was next, buttoned up by thick brutal fingers. 'Twenty grand over the asking price, wasn't it? Twenty grand of Wee Hamish Mowat's money.'

John Urquhart stepped closer. 'Yeah, about that. Kinda not the best idea.'

Reuben tucked in his shirt. 'You're going down, McRae.'

'I didn't *know* it was Hamish Mowat's money.'

'Erm...' Urquhart held up a finger. 'See, the only way

you can dob McRae in, is if you dob *me* in at the same time, isn't it? I bought the flat. And if I bought it with Mr Mowat's cash, then that makes me dodgy too.'

A black tie was subjected to a schoolboy knot. 'And?'

'Look at it: far as Police Scotland's concerned, I'm a small-time property developer and I'd kinda like to keep it that way. How am I gonna be your right-hand guy if the cops are digging away and following me everywhere?'

Creases formed between Reuben's eyebrows. Then he slipped his feet into a pair of shiny black shoes. Grunted.

'Come on, Reubster, you know it makes sense.'

He pulled on a black jacket to go with the trousers. Scowled at Logan. 'You got kids, don't you, McRae? With that bull-dyke lesbian boss of yours. You just mortgaged them against your debt.'

Logan took a step forwards. 'Don't even think about it.'

'And *you*.' He turned and poked a finger at Urquhart. 'From now on you're responsible for him, understand? He does what he's told, when he's told, or the pair of you are up to your ears in the piggery.'

Urquhart's eyes widened. 'Let's ... not get all hasty and that. We... Reuben?'

But the big man had turned on his heel, walking along the edge of the plastic sheeting, and out through the open door. 'Funeral time.'

'Damn it.' Urquhart ran a hand across his face. Looked down at what was left of Tony, lying there with his head bashed in. 'You three, tidy this up. Sergeant McRae and me have to go bury an old friend.'

It was one of those old-fashioned Scottish churches: a rectangle of granite with a tiny bell-spire and a slate roof, surrounded by ancient tottering headstones and fields. A long line of cars stretched along the road, parked half on the grass, leaving barely enough space for the next vehicle to squeeze past.

John Urquhart eased the Audi's passenger-side wheels up onto the verge and killed the engine. Then groaned and curled into himself. 'Why me?'

Logan undid the seatbelt. 'I thought the gun worked.'

'He's going to feed me to the pigs.'

'If it worked he'd be dead by now.' And Tony would still be alive... He closed his eyes, but there was the image of Reuben battering the claw hammer down again and again. If the gun had worked, it wouldn't have been murder. It'd be justifiable homicide. Saving another person's life.

Bloody hell.

Worse: now Jasmine and Naomi were at risk.

'Oh God...' Urquhart covered his head with his hands. 'We're doomed.'

'Welcome to my world.'

'I should have stayed outside, I should have—' His phone burst into song. He dug it out. Flinched. Then dragged on a smile. 'Hi, Reuben. How's it going, big man? ... Uh-huh. ... Uh-huh. .... OK, we'll be there soon as. ... Yeah. ... OK, bye.' He hung up and slipped the phone back in his pocket.

Outside, the sunshine streamed through the bare branches of a tree, casting ragged shadows across the road. A swarm of midges glowed in a patch of light. Second week of February and there were midges. Welcome to Scotland.

Urquhart sagged back in his seat. 'Guess who's showed up to "pay their respects"? Malcolm McLennan, Angus MacDonald, Stevie Hussain, and Jessy Campbell.'

'Jessica "Ma" Campbell?'

'Told you we were doomed.' He stared at the car's ceiling. 'Man, the French Revolution's got nothing on the terror about to fall on Aberdeen. These scumbags respected Mr Mowat, but Reuben? No chance.'

Logan opened his door and climbed out into the sun. 'You coming?'

He locked the car. 'They'll turn Aberdeen into a warzone. Mr Mowat would *hate* this.'

They walked past the line of parked cars and in through a rusting iron gate. Headstones stretched off into the distance, along with a couple of mort safes and a big granite mausoleum topped with weeping cherubs.

Urquhart stopped. 'Mr McRae? You're going to do what Reuben says, aren't you? I mean, *exactly* what he says and when he says it?'

'Don't know.'

'I stuck my neck out for you! And I mean *way* out...' His head drooped until his chin rested against his chest. 'This is what it's going to be like from now on, isn't it? Everyone running scared. No stability. War.'

Logan turned, scanning the ranks of the dead. Just because *he* couldn't do it, didn't mean everyone else had the same problem. There wasn't a single living soul in sight, but he dropped his voice anyway. 'Then kill him.'

'Reuben?' Urquhart backed off a couple of paces, eyebrows up. 'Me? Kill Reuben?'

'You said it yourself: Hamish didn't think Reuben is up to running the business. He's going to make everything worse and get a lot of people hurt.' Logan stepped closer. 'So maybe *you* could do a better job? Maybe *you* could take Hamish's place instead of him? Prevent everything falling apart; stop the war before it starts.'

'But...' Urquhart licked his lips. 'I mean Reuben...' He cleared his throat. Looked back towards the car. 'OK, so he's totally *not* suited to being in charge. He's a great enforcer, but strategy? Planning? Keeping everything low-key and efficient?'

'All the things Hamish Mowat was good at. Keeping Aberdeen stable. You saw what he did in that garage; Reuben's unhinged. You could step in.'

'I know, but—'

'Who was he?'

Urquhart pulled his chin in. 'Who was who?'

'You *know* who.'

'Oh. Tony?' A shrug. 'Tony Evans. Low-level distributor

216

and three-strike loser. You'd think he'd have learned the first two times. Suppose some people can't take a hint, not even when it's, like, getting both your arms broken.'

The church bell pealed out three mournful chimes.

'I mean it: Reuben's going to get everyone killed. He has to go.' Logan had another quick look around. Still no witnesses. 'For the good of the city.'

Urquhart blinked at him for a moment, then took a deep breath. 'Anyway.' He pulled his shoulders back and marched away along the path, head held high.

Logan gave it a beat, then followed.

It wasn't even one o'clock yet, and already he'd killed his girlfriend, witnessed someone getting beaten to death, and embarked on conspiracy to commit murder. Friday the thirteenth just kept on getting *better*.

The path led down the side of the church and around to the back. Which turned out to be the front. A set of large wooden doors lay open, with a minister standing before them all dressed up in his long red dress with black scarf/shawl thing over the top. He shifted from foot to foot, clutching a handful of small booklets. Worked a finger into the neck of his white collar, pulling it away from his throat. Jerked upright when he saw them. 'Hello.' His voice wasn't exactly steady as he held out one of the booklets to Logan. 'Order of Service. We can start as soon as you're ready.' Beads of sweat glistened on his top lip.

Poor sod probably wasn't used to having his church full, never mind full of gangsters.

Urquhart took an order of service and patted the minister on the arm. 'Soon as you're ready.'

'Yes. Yes, of course. Right away.' He turned and bustled off, red skirts billowing out behind him.

Inside, Old Ardoe Kirk was packed. Every pew in the place was rammed with men and women – all dressed in black, all talking in low voices. No wonder the minister had been bricking it outside on the doorstep: there were a *lot* of big blokes with close-cropped hair, scars, and tattoos. Hard-faced women with bleached hair and fists as cruel as the men's. The kind of people who would have no problem beating someone to death with a claw hammer.

A coffin lay on a set of trestles, at the top of the apse, in front of the altar. A small arrangement of white lilies sat on the lid, their petals turned multicoloured by the light streaming in through a stained-glass window.

'This way.' Urquhart led the way down the middle of the church to the second row of pews from the front. He bent and picked two laminated A4 sheets with 'RESERVED' printed on them from the wooden surface, then sat and tucked them under the bench.

Logan looked around. Set off a bomb in here and you could probably halve Scotland's organized crime problem. It was a Who's Who of Aberdonian thuggery too. The McLeod brothers were there, the Flintoffs, Benny the Snake and his sister, and about a dozen others whose faces weren't so familiar. All sitting there in their Sunday best, waiting for Hamish Mowat's final outing.

Wait a minute, was that...? Of course it was. Because today wasn't bad enough already.

A tartan turban bobbed about somewhere near the back row of pews, visible through the heads of the crowd. And if Narveer was here, that meant Detective Superintendent Harper wasn't far behind.

Great – that made everything *so* much better.

Why the hell were *they* here? They couldn't have followed him, not when he made the trip bundled in the back of a Transit van. And if they had, they'd have intervened and stopped Reuben killing Tony.

Wouldn't they?

Reuben's huge rounded bulk loomed in the front row, next to his bride-to-be – a short round lump of hate and gristle, with a peroxide bob so severe it wouldn't have looked out of place on a Lego figure. And Reuben sat there. Calm as you like. No indication that he'd beaten someone to death with a claw hammer less than twenty minutes ago. Not so much as a spatter of blood on his ugly scarred head.

Raining the hammer down, again and again. The towel keeping the bloody spray to a minimum. The sound of thunking and crunching...

Logan's hand trembled. He put it in his pocket.

The murmuring died down as Minister Nervous stepped up into the pulpit. Coughed. Then leaned into the microphone. His amplified voice echoed around the granite walls. 'Lord Provost, ladies and gentlemen, I'd like to start by thanking you all for attending this afternoon. We're here to give thanks for the life of Hamish Alexander Selkirk Mowat, a pillar of the Aberdeen business community, a philanthropist, and a keen gardener...'

'Thank you for coming.' The minister shook Logan's hand, then moved onto the next person shuffling away from the graveside. 'Thank you for coming.'

The Mowat family plot was marked by a statue of a weeping angel on a large polished granite plinth. The headstone was still missing Hamish's name, but at least now he'd be reunited with his wife and son. His grave lay open, the coffin at the bottom spattered with handfuls of cold claggy dirt as one by one the mourners paid their final respects.

From here the ground sloped down towards a high stone wall, with nothing on the other side but grey-green fields fading into the haar. It blanked out the horizon, oozing in from the North Sea, reaching its grey arms towards the graveyard.

A knot of large men with short hair stood over by a mausoleum, smoking. Another knot of women passed around a hipflask. Lots of murmured conversations and backslapping going on.

Must be strange being a gangster. There wasn't much opportunity to network in a social setting. Unless they had conferences and festivals no one had told Logan about. Four nights in an anonymous hotel in the Midlands, watching presentations on the latest way to break someone's kneecaps, body disposal 101, kidnapping for fun and profit.

That tartan turban appeared again, weaving its way between the headstones, bringing DI Singh with it. He stopped right in front of Logan. 'Well, well. If it isn't Sergeant McRae.'

'Detective Inspector Singh.'

'Didn't think we'd see you here, Sergeant. And sitting down the front too.'

The other mourners made a bubble around them, as if going out of their way not to get contaminated by the stench of police.

'Tell me, Sergeant, were you a close friend of the deceased?' Narveer's face was impassive, voice clipped. So much for Mr Nice Inspector.

Harper emerged from the church and stopped next to him. 'Well, well, if it isn't—'

'Your sidekick's already done that bit.' Logan crossed his arms. 'And for your information, yes: I knew Hamish Mowat. I was in Aberdeen CID for ten years, I've investigated a lot of the people here. The local ones anyway. Even managed to put a few of them away.'

Harper jerked her thumb at a tree standing guard in the corner of the graveyard. 'Let's take a walk.'

She picked her way between the tombstones, with Narveer close behind her. Logan dawdled along at the rear.

He could tell her to mind her own business. Tell her it was his day off and he could do whatever he bloody well liked with it. Tell her to take a running jump into a skip full of broken bottles and rusty nails. Tell her to take Police Scotland and shove it so far up—

He bumped to a halt, as someone walked into him. 'Sorry.'

It was a short man, with close-cropped hair trying to draw attention away from the spreading swathe of shiny scalp.

Hooded eyes looked Logan up and down. Then a smile spread across his face. When he spoke, the accent was pure Morningside: 'No, my fault. Wasn't watching where I was going.' He nodded back towards the church. 'Lovely service, wasn't it? Hamish would have been proud, don't you think, Sergeant McRae?'

Logan pulled his chin in. 'I'm sorry, have we...?'

The wee man stuck out his hand. 'Malcolm McLennan. I've heard a lot about you.'

Malcolm McLennan, AKA: Malk the Knife.

Oh Christ. Harper would *love* that.

22

Malcolm McLennan's smile positively sparkled. 'I understand you're looking into the death of that unfortunate gentleman in Macduff, Sergeant. What was his name ... Peter Shepherd?' A sigh. 'Ah, it's a terrible thing. The grapevine tells me he was beaten, bagged, and bleached.'

Of course it did.

'Well, Sergeant, I know imitation is meant to be the sincerest form of flattery, but it's not so flattering when it brings with it the unwarranted scrutiny of the police. Don't you think?'

'Are you saying your people didn't kill him?'

'Well, of course they didn't. My people don't kill *anyone*, Sergeant, we build affordable housing for hardworking families. We undertake public construction works. We raise money for Alzheimer's research.' A shrug raised the shoulders of what was probably a very expensive suit. 'We try to do our bit.'

Logan returned the smile. 'So all that stuff about prostitution, protection rackets, illegal firearms, people trafficking, drugs – that's, what, a misunderstanding?'

'Exactly.' McLennan winked. 'But if it *were* true I can assure you we'd have no interest in someone like Peter Shepherd. You're following a trail of breadcrumbs, through the woods, to the wrong cottage. This one doesn't lead home.'

No it led to Granny's cottage, and the wolf was in residence.

'So the fact that you lent him two hundred thousand pounds was just a coincidence?'

'Two hundred…?' Wrinkles appeared between his eyebrows. 'Who told you that? Why would I lend him money?'

'Because his company was going bankrupt.'

McLennan leaned in closer. 'Trust me, Sergeant McRae, I don't invest in failing businesses. If I'm interested in them I wait for them to fail, then I scoop up the assets once they've gone into receivership. I don't throw money away.'

Had to admit he had a point. Why give Shepherd a loan he couldn't pay back, just to get your hands on a container logistics company that'd be bankrupt by the end of the month anyway?

'So if it wasn't your people, who was it? Hypothetically.'

'Ah, if I knew that, Sergeant McRae, I'd tell you. And if I find out, don't worry: I'll be doing my civic duty.' The smile fell from his voice. 'I don't take kindly to people trying to fit me up.'

A couple walked by, glaring at each other and muttering in low voices.

Someone laughed in the distance.

The sound of car engines starting filtered through from the other side of the graveyard wall, as people departed the land of the dead.

Malcolm McLennan patted Logan on the arm. 'Glad we cleared that up.' He turned and walked off towards the road, joining a couple of massive goons in identical black suits.

They held the gate open for him, then stood there, staring back at Logan. Then they were gone.

He huffed out a long breath. Let his shoulders droop a bit.

Malcolm McLennan had *heard a lot about him*. Great.

Logan joined Narveer and Harper under the tree. 'Someone in the Major Investigation Team can't keep their big gob shut.'

Harper clicked a white tab of gum from a blister pack and popped it in her mouth, voice cold and hard. 'Have you and Malcolm McLennan been friends long, Sergeant? Because you looked *very* chummy.'

'Never met the man till two minutes ago.'

'Could've fooled me. You're not in CID any more, Sergeant, and yet here you are, rubbing shoulders with half the organized crime families in Scotland. Odd that, isn't it?'

Logan folded his arms and leaned back against the tree. 'McLennan says his people had nothing to do with Shepherd's death. Says someone's fitting him up.'

Narveer shrugged. 'He would say that, wouldn't he? Not exactly going to admit to it.'

True.

'I didn't know him, but he knew me. He knew how Shepherd's body had been staged. Someone on the MIT's talking.'

Harper chewed. 'Oh I can believe that. And who's my prime suspect?' Her finger jabbed Logan in the chest. 'You. Who the hell do you think you are? Coming down here and barging in, interfering with *my* investigation.'

'I didn't interfere with anything. It's—'

'What were you trying to do, muddy the waters? Warn someone off? Why are you even here?'

Logan's back stiffened. 'Are you finished?'

'First you're obstructive, then you're useless, then you can't even make a cup of coffee without turning it into a disaster, and now you're talking to *my* suspects behind my back!'

'Oh don't be so—'

'I have given you *every* chance to redeem yourself, Sergeant, but you *still* keep screwing up. If you ever go anywhere near Malcolm McLennan again, or anyone else, without my express written permission, you're finished. Are we clear?'

'He bumped into me! How am I—'

'I said,' she was getting louder with every word, 'are – we – clear?'

Narveer turned away, taking a surprising amount of interest in a lichen-crusted headstone.

Logan stared at her. Let the silence grow. Then pulled on the coldest smile he could. 'Very, sir.'

'And don't think I won't be discussing this with Professional Standards.'

'You do that, *sir*.'

A wave of shadow crashed across the fields, sweeping the sunlight before it. It crested the hill and swallowed the graveyard, plunging it into a gloom that washed all warmth from the air.

Logan stuck his hands in his pockets and pulled his shoulders up to his ears.

Clouds made a heavy grey lid, blanking out the sun.

Twenty minutes, hanging about outside the church, and there was still no sign of John Urquhart. How was Logan supposed to get home?

A handful of mourners lingered at the graveside. OAPs with curved spines and hooked noses. Glittering eyes and hands like claws.

Tiny pale flakes drifted down from the sky, melting as soon as they landed. But when Logan breathed out his breath left vapour trails.

Where the hell was Urquhart?

He worked his way over to the gate, peering round the high churchyard wall at the dozen or so cars still parked along the verge. Urquhart's Audi was there.

More snow.

Sod this. Might as well call for a taxi. He pulled out his phone.

'Laz?' A voice behind him. 'Aye, it is. Thought it was you.'

Logan turned. 'Doreen?' A smile broke out on his face. 'Good grief, Doreen Taylor. It's been … what?'

'Year and a half: Baldy Bain's retirement bash.' She hadn't changed a bit – still looked like someone's plump aunty, dressed in a trouser suit and frumpy brown pudding-bowl haircut. Doreen pointed at the hunched figure next to her. 'You met DC Shand? No relation.'

He held up a long tapered hand. 'Hi.' When he opened his mouth, the reek of long-dead garlic staggered out.

'Iain, this is Sergeant McRae – used to be my acting DI back in CID.' She beamed. 'Logan, Lazarus, McRae. What brings you here?'

Not another one.

'Wanted to see who turned up. You know: rumours.'

She shuddered. 'Tell me about it. Half the druggies in town are convinced World War Three's going to kick off in Tillydrone.'

He pointed at the church. 'You?'

'Much the same. We're in Serious and Organised now. The boss wanted a heads up on who's sniffing about Wee Hamish Mowat's old territory. See if we can nip some of that in the bum before it starts.'

'Right. Right.'

A couple of the wizened old gravesiders shuffled out through the gate and away.

'So...' Logan shrugged. 'You see much of Biohazard?'

'Argh.' She rolled her eyes. 'He's with the Divisional Rape Investigation Unit. Had to share a car with him on a shout last week and I swear to *God* a human being shouldn't be able to produce smells like that, it's not normal.'

Happy days.

'Don't suppose you guys are heading back into town?'

'Before we freeze to death.' She peered up at the sky and flecks of snow settled on her fringe. 'See when I retire? I'm emigrating somewhere warm.'

'Any chance of a lift?'

Logan sat in the back of the pool car, Doreen in the passenger seat, with DC Shand behind the wheel. Driving them along the twisting South Deeside Road. The snow was getting heavier, thickening, highlighting the bare branches of trees on either side.

She turned to look at him. 'You hear the latest? They're talking about merging Aberdeen City and Moray-and-the-Shire back together again.'

Logan groaned. 'What was the point of splitting them up in the first place, then?'

'Exactly.'

His phone dinged in his pocket and he pulled it out. Text message:

```
Sory dude, gt tyed up with R — can
U hang on a bt?
```

John Urquhart.

Doreen produced a hanky and blew her nose. 'Can you imagine how much money we wasted changing everything from Grampian Police? All the signage, all the posters and bits and bobs?'

Be nice to ignore it, but then again he needed Urquhart. No point being in a one-person conspiracy to commit murder.

Logan thumbed out a reply.

```
It's snowing. I'm getting a lift into
Aberdeen.
```

Send.

'Madness, isn't it?' She tucked her hanky away. 'So, all that time and effort, and now we're going to have to change it all back again.'

Shand shook his head. 'Bet they won't let us call it Grampian Police though.'

'Don't see why not. Tayside still get to be called Tayside.'

'True.'

Ding.

```
    Sory its all hands 2 the pumps :( gt
    meatngs 2 orgnize 4 all the factiens!!!

    Cn you get Yrslf back to Banffg or
    d U neeed a hurl?
```

Call that spelling? Maybe Urquhart had chucked a load of
Scrabble tiles in the air and typed out whatever random
order they fell in?
Ding.

```
    Gv me a txt whn U wont to go back.
    Gt smthig 4 U!!!
```

What the hell was that supposed to mean: 'Gt smthig 4 U'?
  'Still it could be worse, I suppose. Remember Big Gary
McCormack the desk sergeant, Laz?'
  'Mmm?'
  Ah right: got something for you.
  'He left when they screwed with the pension and
pay-and-conditions; went and got himself a cushy number
doing Health and Safety for one of the oil companies.'

```
    What is it?
```

Send.
  'Got made redundant two weeks ago. Now he's back trying
to interview for a constable's position. How humiliating is
that?'
  Ding.

```
    Smthig from mr M. VG preznt!!!
```

A present from Wee Hamish Mowat? God knew what that
was. Probably another chess set.
  Logan lowered his mobile and stared out of the window.

The trees died away as the car slowed for the limits into Aberdeen. The granite houses had lost their sparkle beneath the clouds, darkening as the snow hit the stone and melted, leaching away the last of the sun's heat.

Might not be *such* a great idea to have all these messages from one of Wee Hamish's men on his phone. He deleted all Urquhart's texts. Not that it would make any difference – the forensic tech guys would be able to get them back without too much trouble. And even if they couldn't, a quick squint at the phone company's metadata would show who he talked to and for how long.

Should really ditch the sim card and get a burner. Keep it untraceable.

But then... He scrolled down through the saved messages to the ones listed under, 'SAMANTHA'.

> Logan, where the hell are you? Film's about to start. I've got popcorn, but no boyfriend.
>
> Don't make me chat up this guy with hairy ears.

Next.

> Just so you know, I've had a few drinks after work and been to Ann Summers. So brace yourself!

Next.

> I hate Edinburgh. Want to be home! Screw hotels and screw hotel break-fasts and screw forensic conferences. Not doing this again. HOME HOME HOME HOME HOME!

Next.

The thing blared out its ringtone and Logan flinched. It tumbled from his fingers into the footwell. 'Gah...' He snatched it up and pressed the button. 'What?'

'*Sergeant McRae.*' Oh joy, the dulcet tones of Detective Superintendent Harper the Harpy. '*You and I need to talk.*'

'It's my day off. If you want to shout, snipe, or belittle me you can wait till I'm on duty again. Till then, feel free to sod off.'

The pool car slowed as it approached the roundabout.

Silence from the phone.

Probably shouldn't have said that last bit. But you know what? Screw her. Today was bad enough without having to kowtow to some jumped-up, holier-than-everyone, Central-Belt tosser on an ego trip.

An articulated lorry roared across in front of the car, the driver with one hand firmly engaged in trying to remove his own brain via his nose.

Still nothing from Harper. Maybe she'd felt free and sodded off?

'You still there?'

'*Do you normally talk to superior officers like that, Sergeant?*'

'OK, I'm hanging up now.'

'*Sergeant McRae, how dare—*'

'Tell you what, if you're so offended and upset, you go right ahead and put in that complaint with Professional Standards. Have me thrown off the MIT. You won't have to put up with my "incompetence" and I won't have to put up with *you*.' Blood thumped in his ears, the back of his arms itching in time with it. 'Do us both a favour.' He jabbed the call end button with his thumb. Bared his teeth at it. Then thumped his phone down on the seat beside him.

It burst into song again. Same number.

Decline.

And again.

He switched his phone off.

The car crawled up South Anderson Drive. A wee bit of snow and everyone drove like an old wifie, peering out over their steering wheels, doing five miles an hour. Could get out and walk quicker than this.

Doreen swore, then pulled out her buzzing mobile. 'DS Taylor. ... What? ... Yes, no, Boss. ... Yes, we're heading over to the wake. ... Sergeant McRae?' She looked back over her shoulder at him. 'Yes, we're giving him a lift. How did you— ... No, he's right here. You want to talk to him? ... Oh. OK.' Wrinkles lined up between her eyebrows. 'Are you sure, Boss? Don't mean to be funny, but we're supposed to— ... Right. I understand. Soon as we can. ... Yes, bye.'

She put her phone away. 'Change of plan, Iain. We're dropping Sergeant McRae off in Bucksburn.'

Her sidekick groaned. 'But we're going to the *wake*. Little sandwiches, those wee chicken Kiev things, slices of quiche.'

'Bucksburn station, Constable, and step on it.'

Logan sat forward and tapped Doreen on the shoulder. 'I don't want to go to Bucksburn, I want to go to the bus station. I'm going home.'

'Sorry, Laz, orders from on high.'

Sod that.

The traffic groaned to a halt at the junction with Great Western Road, a line of cars and articulated lorries halted at the traffic lights in front of them.

'Fine, I'll get out and walk.' He unclipped his seatbelt and grabbed the door handle.

Nothing happened.

The child locks were on. Of course they were – this was a CID pool car. Couldn't have suspects letting themselves out whenever they felt like it.

'Doreen, I'm not even on duty, I've had a crappy day, and I *want* to go home.'

Colour flushed her cheeks. 'We don't have any choice, OK? Orders are orders.' She tried for a smile. It didn't look very convincing. 'It'll only take a moment. I'm sure it's nothing really, just a quick chat with Professional Standards...'

Friday the thirteenth strikes again.

23

The floral stench of carpet cleaner filled the anonymous waiting room. Probably there to cover the smell of fear, sweated out by previous victims. Posters on the wall extolled the virtues of Police Scotland, each with a posed photo of an officer at some scenic spot. Truth. Reliability. Honesty. Impartiality.

Traffic droned by outside.

Logan paced back to the window.

Snow drifted down in large puffy flakes, thick enough to hide everything beyond a few hundred feet. Cars and buses and lorries, nose-to-tailed each other on either side of the dual carriageway below. Streams of headlights and blood-red tail-lights, moving in a slow-motion shuffle away from here.

Jammy sods.

But then they hadn't been ratted out to Professional Standards by Superintendent Bloody Harper. No, that was a special treat for Logan alone.

He scowled at the crawling traffic.

OK, so maybe it had been a mistake to tell her to sod off and hang up on her. And maybe he could've diffused the situation instead of making it worse. But...

Yeah, probably best to leave that thought there.

Idiot.

He pulled out his phone and turned it back on again. No more texts from Urquhart, thank God. But there was a voicemail from Calamity. Logan set it playing.

'Sarge? Hi. It's Janet. ... Listen, we heard about Samantha, and we wanted ... well, we're really, really sorry. If there's anything we can do, you give us a call, OK? All of us.' There was a long pause. *'If you want to talk to someone, or, you know, go out and get weaselled, let us know. We're thinking of you.'*

'End of Messages. To Replay The Message, Press One. To—'

Logan hung up.

Put his phone away.

Stared out at the traffic.

'So sorry to keep you waiting.' A gaunt woman stood in the doorway, wearing standard police-issue black with an inspector's pips on the epaulettes. Her fringe was nearly down to her eyebrows, but it didn't manage to hide the thick wrinkly creases that made valleys across her forehead. 'We're ready for you now.'

Logan followed her out into the corridor, past office after office – all with their doors shut – and into another room.

They'd made more of an effort in here. Pot plants stood in the corners, historical photographs of Aberdeen hung on the walls, and a couple of windows looked out onto the snow. She waved a hand at one of the comfy chairs arranged around a coffee table with a bowl of individually wrapped mints on it. 'Now, would you like a tea or a coffee before we start?'

OK...

She was obviously down to play Good Cop.

'Thanks. Tea with milk. If that's all right?'

'Not a problem. Well, take a seat, Sergeant McRae, Chief Superintendent Napier will be with you soon as he's off the phone.' She slipped out, closing the door behind her.

So really he'd just swapped one waiting room for another.

But at least an inspector was making *him* tea for a change.

Logan sank into the comfy chair.

Nobody expects the Spanish Inquisition.

She was back two minutes later with a mug and a small plate of jammie dodgers. 'There you go. Won't be long now.' And she was gone again.

Maybe there were hidden cameras in the room, filming his every movement? Maybe Napier and his Minions of Darkness were huddled in an observation suite watching him right now? Waiting for him to incriminate himself.

Well tough.

Logan helped himself to a biscuit.

Wonder what it was this time: telling Superintendent Harpy where to stick her MIT, being at Wee Hamish's funeral, selling the flat to John Urquhart for *way* over the valuation...? Or perhaps it was about a drug dealer getting beaten to death with a claw hammer?

Sit still and drink your tea. Don't fidget. Eat your jammie dodgers.

Two biscuits later, Chief Superintendent Napier arrived, with a file under one arm and a mug in the other. 'Sergeant.' He settled into the chair opposite. Put the mug on the table and opened the file. 'Now, as you may have guessed, a number of people in the Organised Crime and Counter Terrorism Unit are interested in your attendance at Hamish Mowat's funeral this afternoon.' Napier steepled his fingers. 'Would you care to comment on that?'

Logan had a sip of tea. 'I was abducted from my home this morning by three men in a Transit van, forced into a black suit, and driven to a garage somewhere on the outskirts of Aberdeen where I witnessed a man being murdered. I was then driven to the funeral because Hamish Mowat thought of me as a friend and a fitting successor to lead his criminal empire after his death. On the way there I plotted with another individual to kill Mr Mowat's right-hand man.'

Napier smiled, then nodded. 'Well, that's quite under-standable. Now, would you like a pay rise or a knighthood? I've been authorized to give you both, if you like?'

Oh, if only.

Instead Logan lowered his mug. 'We've been getting reports of various cartels and gangs wanting to move into the area following Hamish Mowat's death. After discussing this with Chief Inspector Steel, it was decided that I should attend the funeral.'

Napier raised an eyebrow. 'You discussed this with DCI Steel?'

'Ask her if you like.' Logan pulled out his phone and called Steel.

Two rings, then her voice blared in his ear. *'Where the hell did you get to? I turned up at lunchtime with a big bag of sausage rolls, all set for tea and sympathy, and you were nowhere to be—'*

'Guv, can you brief Chief Superintendent Napier about our plan for me to scope out Wee Hamish Mowat's funeral today?' He put his mobile on speakerphone and held it out.

Silence.

Napier leaned forward in his seat. 'Well, Chief Inspector?'

'Hold on, got digestive biscuit crumbs all down my cleavage.'

He curled his top lip and sat back again.

'Aye, right. The funeral. I sent Sergeant McRae down there to scope out the opposition. I got the feeling these thugs from down south would be up for the service, and I wanted someone on-site to see if they could pick up some info. You know, what with Peter Shepherd being all dead in a Malk-the-Knifey way.'

Had to hand it to her: no one could lie quicker and slicker than Roberta Steel.

'Now is there anything else? Only my boobs are all gritty with biscuit here and I need to get my bra off and give it a good shake.'

If Napier was trying to hide his grimace, he wasn't doing a very good job of it. 'I see. Well … we won't keep you from that.'

Logan switched the speakerphone off and put the phone back to his ear. 'Thanks. I'll debrief you when I get back to Banff.'

'You're no' doing anything with my briefs, Sunshine. My pants

*are off limits. And what the hell was that all about? You better no'
be—'*

He hung up and switched his mobile off again.

Napier closed the folder. 'I'm glad we could get that cleared up so quickly.' Then he stood and stalked across the room to the window and stood there with his hands behind his back, as if he were reviewing the troops. 'And did you learn anything of import at the funeral, Sergeant?'

'Malcolm McLennan thinks someone's trying to fit him up.'

'I see. Speaking of "fitting people up", while we've got you here, I'd like to talk about Jack Wallace.'

Steel's paedophile.

Logan drained the last of his tea. 'What about him?'

'His laptop. Oh, it's full of child abuse images, that's not at issue, but Wallace claims his laptop was missing for a couple of days. He's adamant that someone else took it and put those images on there. That he would never have done it himself.'

'Yes, because *real* paedophiles always own up to what they've done, don't they? Only the innocent ones say they didn't do it.'

'Steel had dealings with Wallace before. She investigated him twice on accusations of rape.'

'Children?'

Napier shook his head. 'Both times the prosecution fell through. The victims changed their minds and withdrew their complaints. And we all know how well DCI Steel takes failure in cases of sexual assault.'

Snow was building up along the window ledge, clumps sticking to the glass for a moment, before melting.

'You see, Logan, the laptop worries me. All those images of child abuse are in two distinct blocks. Half were loaded onto the machine one day, and the rest went on the day after. One would expect, if Jack Wallace really were a practising paedophile, the images would have built up gradually over a period of time. But they didn't, they simply *arrived...*'

He turned and leaned back against the windowsill. 'Which is suspicious, don't you agree? Almost as if someone had placed them there on purpose.'

Logan fiddled with his empty mug. 'Were the pictures encrypted? Had he tried to hide them in any way?'

'The folder they were in was password protected: his mother's maiden name, spelled backwards. All sitting in a subdirectory of his iTunes files.'

So pretty well hidden then.

Which did beg the question: how did Steel find them buried away down there?

Napier flashed his teeth. 'Ah, I see you've finished your tea. Why don't we go and sort that out?'

God, a cup of tea from an inspector *and* a chief superintendent, all in the same day? Well that *certainly* made up for all the other crap that had happened since breakfast.

Down the corridor, third on the left. It wasn't much more than a cupboard with a kettle, a microwave, a toaster, and a wee fridge.

Napier filled the kettle from a bottle of mineral water, and stuck it on to boil. 'Would you like to have a look at the laptop? It's being held here as evidence.'

'Lots of pictures of kids being abused? Not really.'

'I meant the files. You don't have to browse the actual images.'

Oh. 'Would it help?'

'It might help you.'

He made two mugs of tea, and glopped milk into Logan's without asking. Then handed it over. 'No sugar: that's right, isn't it?'

'Er... Thank you.'

Napier opened a cupboard and took out a bag-for-life that was covered with bees and flowers. He reached inside and produced a round metal biscuit tin. Gave it a shoogle. 'Ah, good. The Counter Corruption team haven't got their sticky fingers on them yet.' He levered the lid off. 'I'll pass you on to Karl, our IT whiz, he'll show you anything you need.' Then Napier held the open tin out to Logan. It was full of raggedy brown things. 'Chocolate crispies. I make them with Special K, melted Mars bars and crunched-up Maltesers. Not frightfully good for you, but little treats, now and then.'

'Yes. Right.' Logan blinked at him, then helped himself to one. 'Lovely.'

OK, this was getting creepy.

Napier popped the lid back on and tucked the tin under his arm with the folder, then led the way back out into the corridor. 'Tell me, Logan, do you enjoy being in uniform again? Feet on the streets, dealing with the public?'

He followed Napier down towards the far end. 'It's...' A frown. 'Yes.'

'Good man. I miss it myself. Oh, it's lovely being in a position to influence policy and really *achieve* things on a broader scale, but there's a lot to be said for being on the front line.' He stopped, knocked on one of the office doors, then poked his head inside. 'Karl? That's Sergeant McRae here. Show him anything he needs to see, all right?'

A middle-aged man with a grey cardigan thrown on over his black Police Scotland T-shirt peered out at them from behind a pair of thick-rimmed spectacles. His gaze drifted downwards, then a smile split his round face. 'Do these ancient eyes deceive me, Nigel, or have you made another batch of your famous fudge-and-raisin brownies? Hmmmm?'

Napier held the tin out. 'Chocolate crispies.'

'Ooh, I love those.' He creaked the tin open and helped himself. 'Now, Sergeant McRae, let's get you sorted. Thank you, Nigel, I'll take good care of him.'

'Well, this is where we part company, Logan.' Napier shook his hand. 'I'm afraid I have to deal with a constable who seems to have forgotten that rule number one of using an extendable baton is you do *not* hit people in the head with them. But if you need anything, give me a call.' And then the doppelgänger pretending to be the Ginger Ninja turned on his heel and marched off to distribute his chocolatey treats.

'Shall we, Sergeant?' Karl ushered Logan inside and closed the door behind him. Plonked himself on the other side of a workbench covered in bits of electronic equipment. Laptops, desktops, tablets, mobile phones – all tagged and bearing sticky labels. Another, smaller, bench sat against the wall with a laptop on it, a rainbow swirly screensaver dancing away across the display. 'That's you over there. All set up and ready.'

Logan perched on the edge of a bar stool and poked at the keyboard. The screensaver disappeared, replaced by the machine's desktop. The picture was a line-up of Aberdeen football club players, all done up in their red kit. 'Karl?'

'…by name, Karl by nature.'

'Does Chief Superintendent Napier do a lot of baking things?'

'Every Friday. You really should try Nigel's brownies. Oh my, yes.'

Napier baking? Being nice to people? Having a first name? It was official – that last blow to Logan's head had scrambled his brains. That, or he'd woken up in some alternative mirror-universe this morning.

Nigel.

Bizarre.

Logan moved the mouse arrow over the folder icon and clicked it open. Navigated his way through the computer's hard drive to the iTunes section of the program files. 'Any idea where I should be looking?'

'Try "iTunes dot resources".'

He did and got a screen full of other folders for his trouble. 'Then what?'

'"E S underscore M X dot lproj". Then "printing templates". You'll see a printer icon, only it's not really a printer it's a password-protected RAR file.'

It sat at the top of a list of XML files. Logan double-clicked it and when the password prompt came up, turned back to Karl. 'Do you have…'

He was holding up a Post-it note with 'Hutcheson' written on it in big black letters. 'Only backwards. Capital N.'

Logan picked 'Nosehctuh' out on the keyboard and hit return. Immediately the screen filled with rows and rows of pretty explicit filenames. Some were clearly ordered into groups, as if they formed part of a different photo set. They all had different modified dates, but when Logan ordered them by created date, they fell into two distinct chunks just like Napier had said. And the created dates were all after the modified dates as well.

He leaned back on his seat.

OK, so that didn't prove anything, did it? Jack Wallace might have got them from one of the dodgy scumbags in his paedophile ring. Or maybe he copied them off an older machine? Or had them saved onto a DVD or something?

Didn't mean Steel broke into his house or car, nicked his laptop, then stuck a bunch of kiddy porn on it. Returned it to the house and *accidentally* stumbled onto the folder.

Though let's face it: the files would be nearly impossible to find, given how buried they were in the file structure. You'd really need to know what you were looking for and where, not to mention what the password was. Steel could barely work her own phone, never mind hack her way through a jungle of folders.

And what had she said, when he'd asked her about it? Wallace didn't even try to hide the pictures, as if he was proud of his collection.

Yeah. This was beginning to look dodgier by the minute. 'Karl?'

'Your wish is my command, oh inquisitive one.'

Logan pointed at the laptop. 'These files, all squirrelled away down here in the iTunes folders, that takes some doing, right? Wallace had to be a bit of a computer whiz kid to bury them away there.'

'Oh dearie me, no.' Karl laughed, big and wobbly, like something off a fairground attraction. 'Finding the files is difficult. *Hiding* them, on the other hand, is child's play. You navigate your way down to the bottom of any folder tree that takes your fancy, and Robert is the sibling of your immediate progenitor. My Yorkshire terrier could do it with one paw tied behind his back.'

So maybe even a detective chief inspector could manage.

Steel wouldn't fit him up for fun, though, there had to be a reason.

Logan turned around in his seat. 'Napier said you could show me anything I need to see, right? Well, I need to see everything you've got on Jack Wallace.'

24

'Of course, you know what this is, don't you?'

Logan stared at the crumpled lump in the toilet mirror. 'Shut up.' He finished washing his hands, then ran them under the howling roar of the air dryer.

Mirror Logan shook his head. 'You're only doing this so you don't have to go home and sit there. In the dark. Getting drunk. Worrying about Reuben.'

'Yes, but this is important, isn't it?'

'You killed Samantha this morning, remember?'

'So what: you want I should be home brooding instead?'

'Yes!' A nod. 'At home, right now, not dicking about in Bucksburn station, helping Napier get Steel up on charges. Should be getting utterly and completely hammered...'

A shudder rippled its way through him. Hammered wasn't a term to use today. Not after what happened to Tony Evans.

Deep breath.

The whole top floor was strangely quiet. In most police stations the place would be a barely controlled din of phones and voices and printers. People hanging out in the corridor gossiping and passing on info. But this was like visiting a hospital ward, where the cubicles were full of the soon-to-be dearly departed.

Logan made himself another cup of tea, then headed back

to his temporary office. The place was full of photos – a happy woman looking increasingly rounded, finishing off with what must have been a baby shower. He sank behind the desk. Had a sip of too-hot tea, and frowned at the open file.

Jack Wallace: twenty-nine, blond with a wide nose and big chin. In the attached picture, his eyes were partially hidden by a pair of glasses. Oh, and he'd turned up the collar of his polo shirt, presumably because he wanted to look like a dickhead.

Mission accomplished, Jack.

Logan tapped his fingers on the pile of forms and statements.

Jack, Jack, Jack.

Nothing in there suggested he was into sexually abusing children. No, Jack the Lad was a ladies' man, whether they liked it or not. As long as he was bigger and stronger than them. And it wasn't just the two failed prosecutions for rape – there were about a dozen complaints of sexual harassment and assault. Everything from copping a feel in the lift at work, to ripping off a stranger's blouse in a nightclub toilet then breaking her nose.

No denying it: Jack Wallace was a charmer.

But a paedophile?

All those pictures, hidden away on his laptop. Hidden away and password protected.

Hmmm…

Logan pulled out his phone and flicked through his own photos. There was Samantha, at a beach party in Lossiemouth, grinning like a slice of Edam. Another with her peeling the clingfilm off a new tattoo. One with her lying on her back, on the bed, in her leather corset, grinning up at him.

'And before you say it, I know, OK?' He put the phone down on the desk. 'If you were here, you'd agree with the idiot in the mirror. Well, you're both right. And I don't care.'

No reply.

'And don't look at me like that. What was I supposed to

do?' He shifted in his seat. 'I tried, OK? I tried to kill him and the gun didn't work.'

Samantha's picture sat there. Not moving. Not saying anything.

'Yes, all right: it was cowardly, I admit it. You happy now? I tried to talk Urquhart into doing my dirty work for me, because I haven't got the balls to do it myself.'

Logan scrubbed his hands across his face. 'I don't want to kill anyone.'

Mirror Logan was right, he shouldn't be here, he should be home getting hammered.

Hmmm...

A frown.

The desktop computer came on with a bleep when Logan wiggled the mouse. Typical – its owner had been away on maternity leave for two months, and no one had thought to switch her computer off. No wonder Police Scotland was having trouble saving money.

He logged into the system and ran a search for Tony Evans.

It looked as if Urquhart had been telling the truth. Evans was a small-time drug dealer, never caught with more than nine hundred and ninety quid on him – a tenner shy of getting the lot seized as proceeds of crime. His criminal record was predictably repetitive: possession, possession, possession with intent, aggravated assault, possession, theft from a motor vehicle, possession with intent, theft by opening lockfast places, possession...

And right now, he was probably working his way, in very small pieces, through the digestive system of a couple dozen pigs. No body. No witnesses.

Well, yes, OK – there were witnesses, but Smiler, Mr Teeth, and Captain ABBA weren't going to roll over on Reuben, were they? Not a chance. Urquhart wouldn't rat either.

Which left Logan.

He glanced at the phone. Samantha's picture had disappeared, replaced by a blank black screen.

'What am I supposed to do, march up to Napier and tell him I watched Reuben batter Tony Evans's head in? Oh, and by the way, I didn't stop him. I just stood there like a squeezed pluke.'

No reply.

He put on a passable imitation of Napier's clipped oily tones: 'And tell me, Sergeant McRae, why *exactly* did you leave it this long to inform anyone of Reuben's heinous crime?'

'Well, your Ginger Ninja-iness, that's a very good question. Makes me look a bit suspect, doesn't it?'

'Yes, it does.'

'As if I made the whole thing up?'

'Did you, Sergeant?'

'Wonderful…' Logan sat back in his borrowed seat. 'Maybe I could tell him I'm suffering from Post-Traumatic Stress Disorder? What with the horror of killing my girlfriend this morning, then witnessing a murder.'

Yeah, *that* would work.

He poked the phone. 'Where are you? I sound like a nutter talking to myself like this. At least when you—'

A knock on the door, then Karl stuck his head into the room. 'Sorry, thought you had visitors. I come bearing gifts!' He scuffed in on tartan slippers, then dug into his cardigan pocket and produced a USB stick. 'Ta-daaaaaaa…'

Professional Standards definitely had a weirdo-hiring policy.

Karl leaned over the desk and plugged the stick into a slot on the front of the computer. 'You're very welcome.'

'What is it?'

'Ah, an excellent question. For ten points, and a chance to come back next week, who managed to dig out a copy of the last interview DCI Steel did with Jack Wallace?'

Logan forced on a smile. 'Would it be you?'

'Bing! Correct, you move on to the next round. Thanks for playing.' He stuck his hands in his cardigan, stretching it out of shape. 'I can't get hold of the earlier one, and, to be perfectly honest, I shouldn't have been able to get hold of this one either. Still, ask no questions, nudge-nudge, etc.'

A couple of clicks had the video file playing full screen. It was one of the interview rooms at Aberdeen Divisional Headquarters – number three going by the beige Australia-shaped stain on the wall by the window. Three figures were visible, two sitting with their backs to the camera – one blond spiky haircut and one that looked like a badger who'd been run over by a combine harvester. DS Rennie and DCI Steel. Which meant the man on the other side of the table, facing the camera, had to be Jack Wallace.

His clothes must have gone off for testing, because he was wearing a white SOC oversuit with the hood thrown back. Not a big man, in any sense of the word. Thin, with a pencilled-in beard and narrow eyes, hair scraped forward in a failed attempt to cover a receding hairline. Long tapered fingers fiddled with the elasticated cuffs of the Tyvek suit. He opened his mouth, but nothing seemed to come out.

'What happened to the sound?'

Karl poked a button on the keyboard and the computer's tiny speakers crackled into life.

'...*comment.*' Wallace shut his mouth again.

'It was on mute, dear fellow. Mute.' Karl straightened up and rubbed at the small of his back. 'Just drop the USB stick off when you're done with it. Things are like gold dust here.'

Steel opened the folder in front of her. '*And do you live at twenty-seven Cattofield Crescent, Kittybrewster, Aberdeen?*'

'*No comment.*' The voice was flat and expressionless, as if he couldn't really be bothered.

'Good luck, contestant.' A salute, then Karl turned and scuffed out of the room, leaving Logan alone with the computer.

'*Did you go to Auchterturra Lights nightclub on Justice Mill Lane, Aberdeen, last Friday night?*'

'*No comment.*'

'*Did you see anyone there you knew?*'

'*No comment.*'

247

'*Did you approach this woman and offer to buy her a drink?*'
Steel pulled out a photograph and slid it across the table.
Difficult to make out from here, but it looked like a head-
and-shoulders shot of a woman with long blonde hair.
'Claudia Boroditsky.'

'*No comment.*'

Yeah, this interview was going well.

'*Did you repeatedly attempt to dance with her?*'

'*No comment.*'

'*Did she tell you that she wasn't interested, because she had a
boyfriend?*'

'*No comment.*'

'*At eleven forty-five when she left the nightclub, did you follow
Claudia Boroditsky?*'

'*No comment.*'

'*Did you make sexually threatening comments to her on Westfield
Road?*'

'*No comment.*'

'*Did you attack her on Argyll Place and pull her into Victoria
Park?*'

Wallace barely moved the whole time. Just sat there,
picking at the sleeves of his white oversuit. '*No comment.*'

'*Did you punch her in the face, breaking her cheekbone?*'

'*No comment.*'

'*Did you repeatedly kick her in the chest and stomach?*'

'*No comment.*'

'*Did you produce a knife and hold it to her throat?*'

'*No comment.*'

'*Did you tell her that if she screamed you'd "gut and skin her
like a rabbit, then send the bits to her parents"?*'

'*No comment.*'

Steel's hands tightened on the folder, making the edges
curl. '*Did you tear off her skirt and blouse? Did you cut away her
underwear with your knife?*'

'*No comment.*'

'*Did you rape her?*'

'No comment.'

'Did you rape Claudia Boroditsky?'

'No comment.'

'Did – you – rape – her?'

Wallace seemed to think about that, his head on one side as he looked down at the photograph on the interview room table. Then he sat back. His face was as lifeless as his voice. *'No comment.'*

Logan's breath billowed out in a pale cloud. He stuck his free hand into his trouser pocket and hunched his shoulders. Shuffled his feet. Still didn't help. The air was so cold, every breath was like being stabbed with frozen knitting needles. 'Because I wanted to go, OK?'

DCI Steel snorted down the phone at him. *'You wanted to go to Wee Hamish Mowat's funeral? What the hell is wrong with you, Laz, you lost your marble?'*

The snow fell in slow lazy flakes, covering the pavement, piling up on top of the bus shelter. Drifting down between the crawling traffic.

'It's "marbles". Plural.'

'You're no' in possession of plural marbles. If you had one more screw loose everything would fall apart. No wonder the Ginger Ninja was after you.'

'Yeah, well…' He peered around the side of the bus shelter, back towards town. Cars and trucks and lorries and, dear Lord, was that the actual *bus?* The number 35 had finally crawled into view. And only twenty minutes late.

Which was pretty impressive, given the state of the traffic.

'So where are you?'

'Aberdeen. Waiting for the bus.'

'The bus? Why didn't you drive, you thick… Actually, I don't care as long as you're on your way home. Got plans this evening: curry and beer-ish plans. And maybe whisky-ish too.'

The number 35 grumbled through the snow. Its heating better be working or there was going to be trouble.

Standing out here in a cheap funeral suit and shiny shoes. Like an idiot.

'We've got sod all out of Martin Milne today, by the way. Thanks for asking.'

'I'm sorry, but *maybe* I've had other things on my mind today.' He dug out his money 'Be back about six. Ish.'

'Did a press briefing with him this morning, so the jackals have dispersed. Don't see Malk the Knife getting Milne to go smuggling anytime soon, though.'

'Going to have a bath when I get in, so give us an hour, OK?'

'Nah, he's going to wait till this blows over a bit. Make his move when he thinks we're no' looking.'

The bus hissed to a stop, the doors opening to let out a red-faced woman and a grey-faced man.

Logan climbed inside and handed over his cash. 'One to Banff.'

'Bit of a risk though, isn't it?'

He took his ticket and worked his way back along the bus to a pair of empty seats. Sat next to the condensation-streaked window. Bucksburn station loomed in the fog.

'I mean, killing Peter Shepherd and leaving his body lying around like that. Course we're going to investigate.'

'I met him today.'

'What, Peter Shepherd? How'd you manage that, ouija board?'

'Not Peter Shepherd, you idiot, Malcolm McLennan. Says someone's trying to set him up.'

'Aye, and unicorns poop teacakes.'

The bus's engine growled and they nudged out into the traffic, joining the slow-motion exodus out of town.

'Could be though. Or maybe he did it so we'd all focus on Milne and his boats, when McLennan's really off doing something dodgy somewhere else.'

'Thanks, Laz, that's sod-all help. Any other parades you'd like to piddle on while you're at it? No? Cool, in that case I'm going to—'

The bus inched closer to the roundabout.

Someone sitting further forward nodded along to the tsssss-tsss-tsssss-tsss-tssss leaking out of their headphones.

'Hello?'

An old lady embarked on a massive coughing session.

Logan checked his phone. Steel had hung up.

Lovely.

The battery icon was down to its last bar. Probably enough charge to last all the way home. Maybe. He stuck his mobile back in his pocket and stared out of the steamed-up window. Snow. Snow. And more Snow.

Should have asked her about Jack Wallace. Asked her why the prosecution collapsed before it got anywhere near the court. According to the files, Claudia Boroditsky withdrew her statement and claimed she'd been confused at the time of the assault. That she couldn't really remember who attacked and raped her. That she'd had consensual sex with Wallace earlier in the evening.

Why didn't that sound convincing? Why did it sound more likely that Wallace had tracked Claudia down and 'persuaded' her to change her mind?

No wonder Steel hadn't been happy about the result.

But was she unhappy enough about it to do him on a trumped-up charge of possessing indecent photographs of children?

Logan drew a skull and crossbones on the bus window, sending tears of condensation crying down the glass.

And who's to say Jack Wallace didn't deserve it?

25

Logan cleared a porthole in the fogged-up window. A thin sliver of sky was squashed between the heavy grey clouds and the cold white earth; the setting sun made blood-spatters across the fields, lengthening the shadows behind the drystane dykes. Wind rocked the bus, hurling snow in great sweeping curtains.

The woman sitting in front of him shifted her phone from one ear to the other. 'Oh, I know. ... I know. He's all right, in general, but in bed? Honestly, he couldn't find a clitoris with two Sherpas and a sat nav.' All done at the top of her voice, as if there were nobody else on board.

The rest of the bus was a mixture of OAPs and youngsters, fiddling with their mobile phones and tablets. Each one off in their own private little fortress. A spotty man in a cagoule was actually reading a book. But he had a beard so no one wanted to sit next to him.

'Oh, I know. ... Awful. I know size isn't meant to matter, but it was like being sexually molested by a Chihuahua.'

Fog reclaimed the porthole, fading the world back to monochrome as the sun disappeared.

'I swear to God, Jane, I thought having an affair would be more exciting. Dancing, champagne, clubs, romantic dinners, kinky hotel-room sex. He just wants to stay in watching boxed sets of *Last of the Summer Wine*.'

Logan's phone burst into song, and he pulled it out. Disappeared from the world like everyone else on the bus. 'McRae.' But at least he had the common sense to keep his voice down.

'*Mr McRae, I have a call for you from Mr Moir-Farquharson, one moment please.*'

Moir-Farquharson? Oh that was great. An afternoon with the Ginger Ninja, and now a call from Hissing Sid. Today was a gift that just kept on giving. Like syphilis.

And what kind of dick got their receptionist to make phone calls for them, anyway? It wasn't the seventies.

'*Mr McRae?*' The voice was like a razorblade sliding down an exposed throat. '*Sandy Moir-Farquharson, I need to talk to you about Mr Mowat's estate.*'

OK, seriously: enough with the blessings today.

Logan closed his eyes and massaged his forehead. 'Now's really not a good time.'

'*The will is going to be read on Monday morning, ten o'clock as per Mr Mowat's instructions. As you're the executor, I shall be requiring your attendance.*'

'I can't—'

'*Mr McRae, need I remind you that Mr Mowat's bequests include a sum of six hundred and sixty-six thousand, six hundred and sixty-six pounds, sixty-six pence to be paid to yourself? As such, it might be considered churlish of you to not perform your duties.*'

Oh God... The two-thirds of a million pounds.

How do you forget something like that?

By not wanting to think about it, that's how. By running away from it, scared that anyone would find out.

Arrrrrrgh...

'*Mr McRae? Are you still there?*'

Logan turned his face to the window and lowered his voice even further. 'I told you I didn't want his money.'

'*And I told you it doesn't matter what you do or do not want. Mr Mowat has left this portion of his estate to you, as is his right. It will be paid to you. There is provision for its management, but how you*' *choose to dispose of it after that is entirely your own affair.'* A sniff. *'Any normal person would be delighted and grateful to inherit such a large sum.'*

He cast a quick glance around him. No one was lugging in, they were all far too busy with their own phones. 'I'm a police officer!'

'And now you can be a very rich police officer. Monday, Mr McRae, ten o'clock at my office.' He hung up.

Logan swore at the phone for a while, then switched it off and rammed it back in his pocket. Sagged in his seat, looking up at the ceiling of the bus. His bones rattled along with the engine's diesel drone.

Two-thirds of a million. Because twenty grand over the asking price for his flat didn't look bad enough.

And there was no way Reuben wouldn't be there to hear Hamish's will being read. To find out what they'd all got. Then he wouldn't have to worry about landing Urquhart in it by clyping about the flat, he'd use the inheritance to destroy Logan.

The snow squeaked and crunched beneath his damp, shiny shoes. More fell from the dark orange sky in slow lazy arcs, like the drifting feathers of a shot bird. They flared in the streetlights' glow, then faded, building up in ridges along the tops of the gravestones in the little cemetery. Sticking to the walls of the ancient buildings.

Logan paused for a moment outside the Market Arms. Warm light spilled from the windows, bringing with it the muffled sound of music and laughter.

Tempting.

A shiver rattled its way through him, making his teeth click.

Home. Central heating up full pelt. Hot bath. A big dram of Hamish Mowat's whisky.

He hurried down the street, shoulders up around his ears, hands deep in his pockets.

Past the grim Scottish houses, past the grim Victorian police station, then across the grim car park. The sea was a smear

254

of black through the falling snow, grumbling against the invisible beach.

Around the corner, and…

Logan stopped where he was, on the pavement, looking up at the Sergeant's Hoose.

A light burned somewhere inside, oozing out of the bedroom window.

Great. Steel had let herself in again. So much for a bit of privacy.

He took out his keys, but the front door wasn't locked. It swung open when he turned the handle, the snib disengaged.

You'd think a Detective Chief Inspector would have *some* idea about home security.

He clunked the door shut behind him and clicked the button for the snib. It clacked home. 'Hello?'

The central heating pinged and gurgled.

Light spilled down the stairs from the landing.

Logan peeled off his funeral-suit jacket and draped it over the banister. Undid his tie. Dug out his phone. 'You know you left the door off the latch, don't you?'

He kicked off his wet shoes and stood there in his wet socks. 'Hello?'

The jacket dripped on the laminate flooring.

'Hello?'

OK…

He tried the kitchen.

No Steel.

Then the living room.

Still no Steel.

Typical, she'd sodded off and left the house lying wide open so any druggy could wander in and steal all his stuff. But the TV was still there, and the DVD player, and the answering machine with its winking red light.

Maybe the snow had kept all the thieving gits from stalking the streets trying door handles?

Logan stripped off his trousers and squelched over to the

bookcase and plugged his mobile into the dangling charging cord. Then pressed the button on the answerphone.

'MESSAGE ONE:' A woman's voice replaced the electronic one. 'Mr McRae? Hi, it's Sheila here from Deveronside Family Glazing Solutions again. I'm afraid there's been a bit of a mix-up with your windows.'

Of course there had.

He unbuttoned his clammy shirt.

'Your order's been checked by Dennis and they're all out by about fifteen mil. I'm really sorry. We've no idea how it happened, but we're getting them remade now. Please accept our apologies; we'll get them to you as soon as we can.'

Bleeeeeep.

God's sake.

'MESSAGE TWO:' There was a pause. 'Logan?' Louise from Sunny Glen cleared her throat. 'I just wanted to let you know that the funeral directors have collected Samantha. I gave them the photo you wanted. I'm sure they'll do a sensitive job. And again, I'm so sorry for your loss.'

Yeah, everyone was sorry. Everyone was *always* sorry.

'Don't forget, if you need to talk to someone, Debora is very good. She's helped a lot of families and—'

Delete.

'MESSAGE THREE:' Logan peeled off his soggy socks. 'Mr McRae? Mr McRae, it's John. John Urquhart. Look, you need to give me a call, OK? Like ASAFP. Soon as you get this.'

Delete.

No way he was leaving something like that knocking about on his answering machine for Napier to find.

What the hell did Urquhart want that was so urgent?

'MESSAGE FOUR:' Steel's gravelly tones graced the living room. 'I know you're in there, so answer the sodding door. My key's no' working and I'm freezing my nipples off.'

Bleeeeeep.

What? Why would her key not work? Of course her key worked – she kept letting herself in.

'*Message Five:*' Steel again. '*It's no' funny, Laz. I know you're in: I can hear you moving about in there! Answer the door.*'

Bleeeeeep.

Logan turned and stared towards the front door. Steel could hear someone moving about inside…

'*Message Six:*' She was back. '*Laz, I get it – you're upset, you're sulking, but…*' A sigh. '*Look, you don't have to sulk on your own. I'll sulk with you, you know that. Give me a call.*'

Someone was in his house.

Bleeeeeep.

'*You Have No More Messages.*'

Bloody hell – it had to be Reuben. That's why Urquhart wanted him to call back. Reuben was in his house. And there was Logan, shivering in his sodden pants.

Not a very dignified way to die.

He padded out into the corridor. Shifted the wet suit jacket out of the way.

His equipment belt still hung over the post, complete with CS gas canister and extendable baton. He liberated both and checked the last door on the ground floor.

It opened on a room stuffed with dusty box files, the air thick with the stench of dirt and mould. He eased the door closed and crept up the stairs, freezing at every creak and groan beneath his bare feet.

Up onto the landing and its burning light.

The guest-bedroom door lay open. No Reuben.

Bathroom: no Reuben.

Logan licked his lips, then clacked out the extendable baton to its full length and barged into the master bedroom, CS gas up and ready…

No Reuben.

He clicked on the light.

The bed was made, the curtains drawn: exactly as he'd left it this morning.

Maybe he'd forgotten to turn the landing light off before he'd left for Wee Hamish's funeral? It was all a bit rushed,

257

what with the three guys bundling him into the back of a Transit van. But it wasn't dark then, so why would he have the light on in the first place?

And Steel had *heard* someone...

He lowered the baton. A wooden box lay in the middle of the duvet. It was about the same length and width as a shoebox, but a lot thinner. Polished oak, from the look of it, with brass hinges and catch. A small leather handle, like a briefcase.

Logan dug into the wardrobe and pulled out a pair of itchy police trousers. Fished about in the pockets until he found a pair of blue nitrile gloves. Snapped them on.

Please don't be Tony Evans's severed fingers. Or any other part of his anatomy.

Click. The catch snapped open and Logan opened the box.

A semi-automatic pistol sat in a lining of black foam, cut to match the outline of the gun. What looked like a silencer sat above it and a spare clip and about two dozen bullets were lined up alongside with a small cleaning kit. The smell of gun oil dark and pungent.

Someone had taped an envelope to the inside of the box's lid, addressed 'To Mr McRae'.

He sank onto the edge of the bed.

A wee furry head appeared between his pale legs, meeping and purring as she rubbed against him.

'Hiding, were we? So much for having a guard cat.' Logan reached down and ruffled the fur between her ears. Then opened the envelope, reading out loud to her. '"Dear Mr McRae. Sorry, you were out so I kinda let myself in – brackets, think you should seriously consider a better door lock, some dodgy people about, close brackets." You don't say. And he's spelled "seriously" wrong.'

Cthulhu settled down on the rug, bent almost double, legs stuck out in front of her, making shlurping noises as she washed her white furry tummy.

'"Mr M wanted you to have this. Don't worry, it is

completely clean and has never been fired. He wanted you to have this because of You Know Who. All the best, JU."'

Logan chucked the note onto the bed. 'Well, at least that explains who left all the lights on.'

A clean gun: no prior convictions.

Typical.

So Urquhart didn't want to get his hands dirty after all.

Logan puffed out a long, shivery breath, then picked the thing up. Solid. Cold. Heavy. He racked back the slide. Brass flashed and a bullet span from the ejector port. Of course that didn't mean the thing actually worked. What happened in the garage this morning had proved that.

'I don't want to kill him.'

He stared at the ceiling. 'For God's sake, give it a rest! "I don't want to kill him.", "I don't want to kill him." Shut up.' Deep breath. 'We don't have any choice.'

'But—'

'Do you want him to go after Jasmine and Naomi? Is that what you want?'

No reply.

'Didn't think so. And now we've got a gun.'

He turned it back and forth in his hand.

Have to take it out into the middle of nowhere and squeeze off a couple of rounds to make sure. Turning up to murder Reuben with an untested gun was just asking to be fed to the pigs.

The semiautomatic snapped up, pointing at the open wardrobe.

'You can do this.'

One bullet, right between Reuben's ugly little eyes and—

The doorbell rang.

Logan flinched.

Squeezed out a breath.

Thank God the safety was on.

He crossed to the window and peered out at the road below. No sign of a Transit van, but a rumpled figure in a high-viz jacket stared back up at him, mouth working on what was probably a family-sized bag of swearing. Snow stuck to Steel's hair. She raised both hands and the carrier bags that dangled from them.

Right.

He stuffed the gun back in its box, snatched up the ejected bullet and stuck it in there too. Then slid the lot under the bed, with the dust and balls of cat hair.

The doorbell went again, long and loud as Steel mashed the button and held it down.

'All right, all right, I'm coming.' Logan got as far as the bedroom door before stopping.

Yeah, probably better put on a dressing gown. Confronting Reuben in his pants was one thing, Steel was quite another.

26

'Pass the oniony stuff.'

Logan picked up the polystyrene container of bright-scarlet relish and held it out. Heat pounded out of the radiator, filling the kitchen with warmth, enhancing the earthy spicy smell of takeaway curry. 'Still think the candles are a bit weird.'

Tealights flickered away on the working surface, a couple on the windowsill, still more in various wee holders on the table – tucked in between the cartons.

'It's no' meant to be romantic, you halfwit. Candlelight's appropriate for sitting shiva. And don't think I've forgiven you for locking me out in the snow.'

'Told you: I was in the shower.' He helped himself to a glopping spoonful of bright-orange curry laced with shining green chillies. 'In case you didn't notice, Samantha wasn't Jewish, and neither is chicken jalfrezi.'

Steel shovelled in a shard of papadum, crunching through the words. 'I think Detective Superintendent Harper fancies you.'

'Away and boil your head.'

'All she does is mutter about you under her breath. Logan McRae, this, Logan McRae, that. Aye, when she's no' giving *me* a hard time. How come it's my fault we're no' making progress catching Peter Shepherd's— Gah!' A blob of onion fell from the end of her papadum and tumbled into her lap. 'Bugger.'

'She can go boil her head too. Woman's a menace. All she does is moan and whinge.'

'Nah, she *loves* you. She wants to have your *babies*.' Steel plucked the rogue bit of onion from her trousers and ate it. 'Tell you, we were sat in that damn pool car for two hours today, watching Martin Milne's place, and she wouldn't shut up asking questions about you.'

Logan ripped off a chunk of naan bread. Dipped it in the thick orange sauce. 'I hung up on her today. Told her to feel free to sod off.'

'Ah, so you fancy *her* too. You should pull her pigtails – maybe she'll show you her knickers behind the bike shed after PE.'

'You can feel free to sod off too.'

'Oh she's obsessed with you, sunshine. According to Narveer, she's been watching you for a *long* time. Ever since the Mastrick Monster. Got a file and everything.' Steel shovelled in another mouthful of lamb dansak, grinning as she chewed. 'Fiver says Harper gets her hands on your onion bhajis by the end of the week.'

'Seriously: sod off any time you like.'

Steel poured the last of the shiraz into Logan's glass. 'No more wine.'

He took a swig. 'We're having the funeral on Monday. It's in Aberdeen, if you want to come?'

She clunked the bottle on the table, next to the other empties. 'Think I should go get more?'

'Nah, I'll go.' He threw back the final mouthful then hauled himself out of the chair. Carry-out containers, crumpled beer cans, and carrier bags littered the work surfaces. Plates piled up in the sink. He wobbled a bit. Steadied himself with a hand on the table. 'Why?'

'So we can drink it.'

'No: why's Harper the Harpy keeping a file on me?'

'Told you, 'cos she wants to shag your scarred little backside off. Ooh, Logan, do me harder, yeah, like that … mmmm. Pass the Nutella, etc.'

Woman had a one-track mind.

Logan grabbed a hoodie from the washing basket in the corner of the kitchen. Gave it a shake and pulled it on. 'White or red?'

'Yes.' Steel dug into her pocket and came out with a wallet. Produced a small wad of twenties. 'And get some whisky. Nice stuff, nothing you can clean paintbrushes with.'

He folded the notes and slipped them into his pocket. 'Seriously, why's Detective Superintendent Harpy keeping tabs on me?'

'And some crisps.'

Logan lowered the carrier bags to the floor and thunked the door closed behind him. 'I'm back.' He ran a hand through his hair, flicking off the chunks of snow. Shrugged his way out of the high-viz jacket. 'Hello? You still there?'

If she wasn't, tough: he was drinking her wine anyway.

He slipped off his snow-crusted shoes and padded through to the kitchen in his socks.

Steel was at the table, a frown on her face, fingers of one hand drumming on the tabletop, phone in the other.

'What's bitten your bumhole?' Logan unpacked the bags onto the table. 'Bottle of Chardonnay, bottle of Merlot, and…' He plonked a beige cardboard tube next to the bottles, popped off the metal lid, and pulled out the contents. 'One bottle of Balvenie, fourteen-year-old, aged in old rum casks.'

She licked her teeth and stared at him.

'What? What have I done now?'

'Kinda wondering that myself.' She pointed. 'You already had a bottle of whisky.'

The Glenfiddich he'd got from Hamish Mowat sat on the table beside her.

'And now we've got more.' The Merlot's top came off with a crackle as he unscrewed it. 'Sure you don't want to stick to wine for now? You know, pace ourselves.' It glugged into the glasses, thick and dark and red.

'I looked it up on the internet.'

He went back into the carrier bags. 'Got bacon frazzles, Skips, and some sort of cheesy tortilla things. Or there's Monster Munch.'

'Glenfiddich 1937 Rare Collection. Where did you get this?'

Must be serious: she hadn't even smiled at the mention of Monster Munch.

Logan sat in the chair opposite. Took a sip of wine. 'What's wrong?'

'You got any idea how much this bottle's worth?' She picked it up, holding it like a newborn baby half-full of syrupy amber liquid. 'Last time one of these was on auction it went for forty-nine *thousand* pounds.'

Logan stared back. Swallowed. '*How* much?'

'Where'd you get it from, Sergeant?'

'Forty-nine grand? For a bottle of whisky?'

Her mouth made a thin, cold line. 'Is this why Detective Superintendent Harper is so keen on knowing all about you? How does a duty sergeant, way up here on the Aberdeenshire coast, afford something like that?' She leaned forward and thumped her fist on the table, making the bottles rattle. 'Damn it, Logan, I *trusted* you!'

'Are you kidding me? Have you seen the piece of crap I drive? It's a Fiat Punto with more rust than metal on it. My kitchen cupboards are full of supermarket own-brand lentil soup!' He snatched the bottle from her. 'If I had forty-nine grand knocking about, do you really think I'd spend it on *one* bottle of whisky?'

She folded her arms. 'I'm waiting.'

'It was a gift, OK?' He looked away. 'From Hamish Mowat.'

Silence.

Steel bit her lips for a moment. 'So, a dead gangster gives

you a forty-nine thousand pound bottle of whisky, and you wonder why a detective superintendent from the Serious Organised Crime Task Force has a file on you?'

'It's not *like* that.'

'THEN HOW IS IT?'

He covered his face with his hands. 'I didn't *do* anything. I didn't know the whisky cost that much. We had a drink out of it, then I was given the bottle to take home.'

'You're a bloody idiot.'

'I – didn't – know.' Logan slumped. Forty-nine grand. *And* the money for the flat.

Ha. As if that was the worst of it. If Steel thought this was bad, she'd hit the roof when she found out about Hamish's last will and testament.

Six hundred and sixty-six thousand, six hundred and sixty-six pounds, and sixty-six pence kind of put the rest of it into perspective.

'Gah...'

Maybe she was right: maybe that was why Harper had a file on him. They *knew*.

Oh God.

Might as well go into work on Monday and resign before they get disciplinary proceedings underway. Take Wee Hamish's money and sod off somewhere warm, where they don't extradite police officers who've taken two-thirds of a million quid from gangsters.

Steel sighed again. 'Well, don't just sit there – get the glasses.'

Logan scraped his chair back from the table. 'I got on with him, OK? He fed me info on rival gangs and I put them away.'

She frowned at her fingers, ticking them against one another. 'Forty-nine thousand quid; twenty-eight drams in a bottle; that's forty-nine less twenty-eight ... twenty-one ... hundred and ninety-six...'

'I wasn't working for him. I wasn't doing favours for him. I was arresting drug dealers who needed arresting anyway.' Logan dug two tumblers out of the cupboard – the crystal ones, seeing how expensive the Glenfiddich was. 'And I arrested *his* people too, when I got the chance. That was the deal: no preferential treatment.'

The glasses went on the table.

Steel squeaked the cork from the bottle. 'One thousand, seven hundred and fifty quid a dram.' She poured. 'Call it three and a half grand for a double.'

He sat at the table. 'I mean it.'

She shook her head. 'I know you do, Laz. But if Harper gets wind of this, you're screwed.' Steel raised her glass in toast. 'Here's to getting rid of the evidence.'

'Any ... left?' With the curtains closed and the collection of tealights on the mantelpiece, the living room was warm and cosy. Like a hug. Or a stomach full of takeaway curry, beer, wine, and *very* expensive whisky.

Steel blinked, then picked up the bottle and upended it over her glass. A thin stream of amber splashed into the bottom, dripped twice, then stopped. She sooked on the end, working her tongue into the neck to get out every last drop. Then sat back on the couch and squinted at him. 'You better ... better no' be ... perving on me, Laz. ... Like ... like something out ... out of a porn flim.'

'Porn film. *Film*. You said "flim".'

'No didn't.'

'Yes did.' He covered his mouth as a smoky belch rattled free. 'What do we do ... with the bottle?'

'Forty-nine ... *thousand* pounds.' She gave it a shoogle. 'Never drunk whisky that ... spensive before.'

Logan lurched to his feet. 'I'll get the ... Balvenie.'

The floor was a bit wobbly beneath his feet, but he planted them wide apart and rode it out, lurching through the kitchen. Cthulhu hunched over her mat in the corner, crunching on cat biscuits.

'Hello, sweetie. Hello. Who's Daddy's ... special kittenfish? Hmm? Who's Daddy's love?'

She kept eating.

'Be like that then.' Through in the lounge the phone rang. Ringity ring, ring, ring. Logan picked the new bottle off the table, taking care in case it was as wobbly as the floor.

He made it as far as the lounge door, before the ringing stopped and the sound of his own recorded voice burst out of the machine. *'Hi, this is Logan. I'm not answering the phone right now, but leave a message and I'll try to get back to you soon as I can.'*

Steel was licking the inside of the Glenfiddich bottle again.

'Sergeant McRae?' Oh great, that Central-Belt accent could mean only one thing. *'It's Detective Superintendent Harper. ... It's Niamh.'*

'Oho!' Steel stopped suckling and winked at him. 'Niamh. Told you: she *loves* you. Smoochie smooch-smooch.'

'Shut up.' He lurched across to the answering machine, still clutching the Balvenie. 'What do you want, Harpy woman?'

Silence from the machine.

'Logan, I think we've got off on the wrong foot. Clearly you're a capable officer.'

Maybe Steel was right?

The wrinkly wreck pulled herself upright. 'Going for a pee. If she ... if she propositions you, let me know.'

'I think we need to talk. Tomorrow, when you get into work, let me know. We have things to discuss.'

A grin from Steel. 'Like rubbing each ... each other *all* over with *marmalade* and licking ... licking it off.' The doorbell rang and she blinked at the wall. 'I'll get it.'

'I may not have been entirely fair with you. So. Yes. Well.'

She lurched from the room, singing away to herself. 'Lazarus and Niamh, up a tree, H – U – M – P – I – N – G.'

'Anyway. We'll talk tomorrow.'

Bleeeeeep.

OK, that was ... odd. She should've been shouting the odds, berating him for telling her to sod off. So this afternoon she complained about him to Professional Standards, and now she was calling him up to try and mend bridges and build fences? Or was that the other way around?

Out in the hall, Steel was still going strong. *'First comes sex, then comes sneezes, then there's itching 'cos you've caught diseases.'*

Maybe opening the Balvenie wasn't the best of ideas?

Probably.

The front door clunked, and her voice took on its usual smoky growl. 'Aye? Are you—'

A clatter.

A thump.

A muffled grunt.

Logan dumped the bottle on the couch and sprinted out into the hall.

Steel lay on her side, curled up in the foetal position, arms covering her head as a big bastard in a grey boilersuit and blue ski mask stamped on her ribs. Groaning every time a boot landed.

'GET OFF HER!' Logan grabbed at the equipment belt – still hanging over the end of the newel post – fumbled at the catch holding the extendable baton in place, and dragged the length of metal out.

Ski Mask stopped laying into Steel and lunged at him instead.

A flick of the wrist and the baton clacked out to its full length but not fast enough. Ski Mask barrelled into Logan, sending them both smashing back onto the stairs, the treads stabbing into Logan's spine.

Hands grabbed at his head, shoving his face into the treads.

Another pair of hands. Ski Mask had a friend.

Logan swung the baton, but the friend grabbed his wrist, twisting the arm up behind his back. Red hot nails hammered into the shoulder joint, prising the bone and muscles apart. 'AAAARRRGH!'

The pair of them dragged him over onto his front. Forcing his other arm round to join the right. Piling on the pressure until lines of burning wire tore their way from Logan's wrists to his shoulders. The baton tumbled from his numb fingers and clattered against the laminate floor.

They hauled him upright, the pair of them pulling him around so he was facing the front door and Steel – struggling to her knees by the coat rack.

Her voice was thin and shaky. 'Laz? Laz?' Blood covered the lower half of her face, more pulsing out of her battered nose. Dripping from her split lip. 'Unnngh...' She wobbled there, eyes fuzzy and unfocused.

Logan whipped his head forwards, then back again – hard and fast, looking to connect with one of the bastards' face. But they weren't stupid enough to stand that close.

The pressure on his arms increased and those burning wires forced a growl out between gritted teeth. Made his legs sag. 'Get off!'

The big guy laughed. 'Aye, right.' The voice was familiar: Smiler. The chatty one from the back of the Transit van.

His wee friend stepped in front of Logan. That would be Captain ABBA, with the stupid sideburns and ponytail, both hidden behind a black ski mask. 'Either you hold still and shut up, or I'm gonna slice you open, understand?' An eight-inch blade gleamed in the hall light, then came down to rest against Logan's throat.

He froze.

'Good boy.'

The front door opened and number three came in. Thin and slightly hunched as if all that time playing on a Nintendo DS had curved his spine. Mr Teeth. He closed the door behind him. Nodded at Logan. 'Aye: in case you're wondering, like, this is by way of a warning.'

He grabbed a handful of Steel's hair then battered her head off the wall hard enough to dent the plasterboard. Did it again.

Mr Teeth let go and she slumped to the floor.

Logan struggled forward and a sharp line clawed at his throat.

'Oh no you don't.' Captain ABBA twisted the blade, making the line sting. 'You stand there and you *watch*.'

His mate knelt astride Steel, one hand wrapped in her hair, the other coiled into a fist that snapped forward and battered her head back. Again. And again. *Thud. Thunk. Thud.*

Then Mr Teeth let go of Steel's hair and sat back. 'There we go.'

Her head lolled to the side, blood dripping onto the floor.

Smiler leaned in close. 'You do what you're told, McRae. Cos if you don't: what happened here tonight? That's going to look like a Christmas party at your nan's house. OK?'

Mr Teeth nodded at his mates. 'We done?'

'Almost.' Captain ABBA lowered the knife, then hammered a fist into Logan's stomach, taking his legs out from under him as fire and ice rippled through the scarred muscle.

Smiler let go and Logan slid down the balustrade, hauling in great jagged gasps of air. The world screamed, like a million wasps had gone off at the same time.

Thump. The hallway twisted through ninety degrees, leaving him lying on his side on the laminate floor with tiny black dots circling around the ceiling. Getting bigger. And louder. And then...

Darkness.

... sounds. Grunting...

Dots swirling around the swinging lightbulb overhead...

... muttered voices too faint to make out...

An engine starting...

UP. GET UP AND HELP HER!

Logan forced himself over onto his front.

Gritted his teeth and pushed himself up onto his knees.

Flecks of snow twisted in through the open door.

Steel lay where she'd been left, slumped as if someone had cut all her strings.

Logan hauled himself upright, using the balusters. Staggered over to the door, one arm wrapped around his burning stomach.

White blanketed the parked cars, thick flakes shining in the streetlights' glow. No sign of Reuben's thugs. No sign of the Transit van.

Logan stepped out onto the pavement, but a groan behind him made him stop.

Steel.

Inside, he slammed the door shut and knelt beside her. 'You're OK. Are you OK? Hello?'

'Urgh...'

He brushed a strand of damp grey hair away from her face. Her nose was squint, blood thick on her top lip and down the side of her cheek nearest the ground. One eye was swelling already, the skin around it angry and red.

'Gnnnngh...'

Logan grabbed his phone and called the police.

27

'It's OK, Sergeant, you can see her now.' The nurse pointed at the double doors in the corner.

'Thanks.' He creaked his way out of the plastic chair, standing up in stages like opening a Swiss Army knife.

'You sure we can't get you something? Only you look—'

'I'm fine.' Logan reached up and ran his fingers along the line of gauze taped across his throat, where Captain ABBA's knife had been. 'Barely a scratch.'

'Right, well I'm sure you know best. I'm only a healthcare professional after all, what would *I* know?' Then she stuck her nose in the air, turned around, and marched off.

Logan hissed out a breath, then limped across and pushed through into a corridor that stank of disinfectant and despair. Steel's room was halfway down – her name written on a little whiteboard outside it, like the prison cells in Fraserburgh. He opened the door and stepped inside.

The private room was dark, except for the reading light over the bed. It drained the colour from Steel's skin, leaving it grey and creased. At least, where it wasn't blue and purple. She was lying back, with about half a dozen pillows jammed in under her head. They'd smeared something over her swollen eye – making the bruised skin glimmer

– and stuck a thick strip of white tape across the bridge of her nose, holding down a wodge of gauze.

He eased himself onto the edge of the bed. Tried not to wince. 'You look … well.'

Steel's one good eye narrowed. 'My node hurds.'

'They say it'll take a couple of weeks, but you won't even know your nose was broken.'

'Ad my ribs.'

'They're going to keep you in overnight for the concussion, but other than that, you're fine.'

'Feel lige sombone's burdig pee-stayned maddresses in my hebd.'

Logan patted her leg beneath the blanket. 'Susan's on her way up. Should be here soon.'

The one good eye widened. 'Nooo. Don'd wand her to see me lige this.'

'Tough. She'd kill me if I kept it secret.' He gave the leg a squeeze. 'Did you get a good look at them?'

'Tell her I'mb *fide*!'

'She's coming whether you like it or not. Now, can you ID who attacked you?'

A one-sided frown. 'Big basdard, with a sgee mask ond.'

'Yeah, that's what I saw. Three of them.' He stared up at the ceiling tiles. 'Been a hell of a day, hasn't it?'

'I hade Bandff.'

Another squeeze. 'Get some sleep. And thanks. For staying with me and drinking too much.' He pulled on the best smile he could muster. 'I appreciate it.'

Steel sank back into the pillows. 'You're sudge a big girl's blouse…'

Logan slipped back out into the corridor and closed the door behind him. Closed his eyes and swore.

'How is she?'

When he opened his eyes again, Rennie was right there

in front of him, along with DS McKenzie. The pair of them looked as if they'd just heard the family dog had died.

'She's fine. A bit battered and bruised, but nothing permanent.'

McKenzie moved towards the door, but Logan put an arm out.

'Best not. Let her rest.'

'Right.' McKenzie nodded, setting that curly brown bun of hers wobbling. 'OK.'

Rennie pulled out his notebook. 'Any idea who did it?'

Oh yes. But even if he told them, what good would it do? Even if they *could* find out Smiler, Mr Teeth, and Captain ABBA's real names, what would happen? Would Reuben's three stooges go down quietly, or would they drag Logan kicking and screaming with them?

He shrugged. 'They wore ski masks and boilersuits. One big, muscly; one thin; one short-arse.'

McKenzie had a quick look up and down the corridor, then lowered her voice. 'You know what this means, don't you? Malk the Knife's boys are spooked by the investigation.'

Rennie bared his teeth. 'Ooh, that's not good.'

'They know we're getting close and they're trying to warn us off.' She leaned closer to Logan. 'Did they say anything?'

'Thought you were supposed to be babysitting Martin Milne.'

A sneer. 'Think this is a *bit* more important, don't you, McRae? Now answer the question: did – they – say – anything?'

'The one who attacked Steel, said it was a warning.'

'I *knew* it. Maybe…' She trailed off as an orderly squeaked by pushing an empty porter's chair. Waited for him to fade from view. 'We should let Detective Superintendent Harper know. If they came for Steel, they might be after her too.'

'Good point.' Rennie pulled out his phone and dialled. Listened in silence for a moment. Then, 'Super? … Yeah, it's DS Rennie.' He wandered away. 'Look, I know it's late, but…'

DS McKenzie narrowed her eyes. 'And how come you got off without a scratch on you, McRae?'

'What about this?' He pointed at the line of gauze. 'Tried to slit my throat.'

'Yeah, right.' She pulled out her own phone. 'I'll get a guard on the Guv's room.' She walked off in the other direction, leaving Logan on his own outside Steel's door.

He stood there as they got things organized. 'I'm fine, by the way. Thanks for asking.'

Pair of idiots.

As if Malcolm McLennan would get his people to attack a senior police officer investigating a crime *he* was involved in. Talk about a perfect way to draw attention to yourself. You didn't build a huge criminal empire by being stupid.

But Reuben? Oh he definitely *was* that stupid.

Logan headed down the corridor, through the double doors back into the waiting area, and turned his mobile phone on again. Fully charged. According to the home screen there were half a dozen text messages and three voicemails waiting. Well they could wait. He brought up his call history – John Urquhart's number was top of the list. He called it.

Through the waiting room windows, the snow seemed thicker. Taking its time to drift down from the dark marbled sky.

He sank into one of the chairs, in the lee of a drooping cheese plant.

The phone rang. Then, finally, someone picked up. '*Yup?*'

'Urquhart, that you?'

'*Mr McRae! Where have you been? I left messages and every—*'

'You tell Reuben—'

'*—got to watch out, OK? Reuben heard about you being executor for Mr Mowat's will and went berserk. I mean total card-carrying, machete-wielding, berserk. He's going to get people to come after you, says you need to learn your lesson. You've got to—*'

'Too late. They've been.'

'*Ah.*'

'Three of them: the guys with the Transit van.' Logan leaned forward, scrunching himself around the phone. Making his stomach ache. Stoking the fires. 'You pin your ears back, and you take notes: they attacked a friend of mine and they put her in hospital. If I get my hands on them, I'm going to make Jeffrey Dahmer look like Santa Bloody Claus. Are we clear?'

Silence from the other end of the phone.

'You still there? I want names.'

'Yeah... Erm... The guys we're talking about are only obeying orders, Mr McRae. They get told to rough someone up, they don't ask why. They do what they're told.'

'I got the gun.'

A sigh. *'Look, I know where you're coming from, but they're only, like,* minions, *OK? They're replaceable. Reuben's got lots more where they came from.'*

Don't punish the dog that bites, punish the owner.

'I don't care.'

— Saturday Rest Day —

blood on the snow

28

'*...your nonstop Saturday love songs for the next half hour. So, let's kick off Valentine's Day with a bit of Lucy's Drowning, and their big hit from last year: "The Circle of You"...*'

Logan gritted his teeth and fumbled a hand out from beneath the duvet. Thumped his hand down on the snooze button. Then lay there, shivering. A puddle of sweat sat in the centre of his chest, running in lukewarm dribbles down his ribs.

God.

Someone had swapped his heart for an angry rat – it scrabbled at his insides, digging its claws into his lungs. There was another one inside his head, gnawing away on his brain with yellowed teeth.

Didn't matter how expensive the whisky was, the hangover was just as bad as supermarket own-brand Sporran McGutRot.

He rubbed a hand across his clammy forehead and blinked at the ceiling. Allan Wright, Gavin Jones, Eddy Knowles. AKA: Smiler, Mr Teeth, and Captain ABBA.

Come on then, what was he going to do to them?

What *could* he do to them?

Oh it was all bravado and macho posturing last night on the phone, but now? In the cold morning light, with a raging hangover?

'Urgh...'

A third rat clawed its way into his bladder.

Time to get up for a pee, some paracetamol, and about a pint of coffee.

Revenge would have to wait.

A puffball of white chrysanthemums scented the room, almost covering up the sickly hospital odour. They sat in a big plastic vase, at the side of Steel's bed.

She was propped up, with a cup of tea and a scowl. At least it looked like a scowl. Difficult to tell, what with all the bruising and swelling. The strip of white gauze covering her nose was almost fluorescent against the dark-purple skin that surrounded both eyes. One of them about the size and shape of a broken orange. 'What are *you* looking at?' Her pyjama top was a pale sky-blue, with happy penguins frolicking all over it.

A couple of cards stood on the bedside unit – one was from a shop, all pink with 'For My Loving Wife' on the front. The other was obviously handmade. It was covered in wobbly red hearts, bits of glued-on pasta, and enough glitter to choke a thousand fairies.

'Happy Valentine's Day.' Logan unzipped his jacket and the hoodie underneath, then dumped the paper bag from the baker's on the covers. 'Got you some pies and stuff.'

As if that was going to make up for last night.

'Head feels like someone's scooped everything out and replaced it with a fat kid on a pogo stick.'

'On the plus side, you sound a lot better.' He helped himself to a rowie. 'Where's Susan?'

'Give me that.' She snatched the rowie from his hand and ripped a bite out of it. Winced. Chewed. 'They catch those scumbags yet?'

'Early days. Feeling any better?'

'I'm lying in a hospital bed, wearing penguin PJs, suffering a hangover you could sand floorboards with. How do you *think* I'm feeling?'

The door opened and Susan shuffled in, carrying two plastic cups in a cardboard holder. She'd gone all countrified in tweed trousers and a checked shirt, like a slightly chunky Doris Day meets *The Prime of Miss Jean Brodie*. 'Logan!' She crossed and put the holder next to the chrysanthemums, then wrapped him in a hug. It was warm and smelled of home.

She frowned up at him. Then stroked the gauze taped across his throat. 'Does it hurt?' The wrinkles around her eyes deepened.

'Stings a bit, but other than that.' Shrug.

'*Stings* a bit?' Steel made a strange bunged-up snorting noise, then snarled another bite out of her breakfast, talking with her mouth full. 'I could've died. Don't hear me moaning on about it, do you?'

'Yes. All morning.' Susan's hand was warm against Logan's cheek. 'You look tired.'

'He looks like a wannabe drug dealer. A hoodie, for God's sake. How old are you?'

'Don't be rude.' Susan bent down and kissed Steel on the forehead. 'And I've talked to the doctors – you can go home after you've seen the consultant. Isn't that nice?'

'Sooner the better. I'm allergic to penguins.'

'Well I think you look cute.' She stroked Steel's rampant-weasel hair. 'Do you need anything else?'

'My fake fag's out of liquid. And I want a Bloody Mary. And some chips.'

'Chips? What happened to the diet?'

'Sod the diet.'

'No chips. *Or* vodka.' Susan stood. 'You want anything, Logan?'

'Thanks, but I can't stay. Going down to Aberdeen. Thought I'd clear some stuff out of Samantha's...' He cleared his throat. 'Out of the caravan.'

Susan's hand was warm on his arm. 'Stay and have a coffee. I know Roberta's glad you're here, even if she's too rude and grumpy to say it.'

'Hoy! I'm no' rude and grumpy, I'm at death's door.'

'Keep telling yourself that.' Another kiss, then Susan grabbed her coat and headed out the door. 'Back soon.'

As soon as the door swung shut, the frown faded from Steel's face leaving it lined and sagging. 'Pfff...'

'Sore?'

'Ribs look like a paisley-patterned map of Russia.'

He dipped back into the paper bag and pulled out a pie. Handed it over. 'I'm sorry.'

She waved a hand at him. 'Wasn't your fault.'

Yes it was.

The coffee tasted like boiled dirt, but he drank it anyway, washing down the last of his rowie as Steel got gravy all over her chin. Sitting there, the picture of innocence, with two black eyes.

There was no way she'd fitted up Jack Wallace.

Deep breath. 'Look, this thing with Napier...'

'He's a dick.'

'I know, but—'

'He hates me, OK? Man's got terrible taste in women.' She shrugged and got more gravy on her face. 'I wouldn't toe the line in a disciplinary investigation, so he thinks I'm dodgy. Thinks I play fast and loose with the rules. I'm no',' she made quote bunnies with her fingers, '"invested in the process". Whatever that means.'

Logan put the paper bag down. 'What investigation?'

'Nothing important.'

He stared at her.

She polished off the last mouthful of pie, then wiped her mouth with the corner of the bed sheet, leaving a thick brown smear. As if she'd had an embarrassing accident.

The sound of a floor polisher whubbed in the distance.

'OK, OK.' A sigh. 'It was four years ago. A junkie claimed the arresting officer dangled him off the fifth storey of the Chapel Street car park.'

Oh.

Logan sat back. 'It was Magnus Finch, wasn't it?'

'Doesn't matter. What matters is Napier's had a wasp up his backside about me ever since, because he doesn't understand the word "loyalty".'

'Magnus Bloody Finch.' He gritted his teeth. 'He was selling heroin to schoolkids.'

'Told you: doesn't matter.'

'Only they had to go to his squat to buy it. And they had to shoot up there too. He told them it was a safe environment.'

'You got any more pies?'

'A fifteen-year-old schoolgirl got raped. First by him, then by three of his coke-head friends.'

'Laz, it's—'

'I didn't dangle the bastard on purpose. I arrested him, there was a scuffle, and he nearly went over the edge. I just...' Logan cleared his throat. 'I made him give me the names of his accomplices before I pulled him back.'

Steel pulled the paper bag towards her, and went pie diving. 'Ooh, is that a bridie? No' had one of them for ages.'

'You were covering for me.'

'It's what family do.' She took a bite, giving herself a pastry-flake smile. 'Mmmm.'

She'd started a four-year grudge with Napier for him. To *protect* him. And here he was investigating her.

Way to go, Logan.

Steel picked a bit of mince from between her teeth. 'So come on, then: what about "this thing with Napier"?'

He forced a smile. 'Did you know his first name's Nigel?'

The Fiat Punto's wheels bumped up onto the snow at the side of the road. Logan left the motor running for a bit as the snow drifted down onto the rutted surface.

Trees surrounded the car, stretching off into the gloom on either side, lining the forestry road, their branches drooping with thick layers of white. Further in, there was nothing but grey.

He killed the engine and climbed out of the car. Walked around to the passenger side and fished about under the seat for the polished wooden box. Snapped on a pair of blue nitrile gloves, pulled out the semi-automatic pistol and checked it. Magazine was full. Safety catch was on.

Logan screwed the silencer into place, and slipped the gun into a carrier bag. Then he went back into the footwell for the cheap green cagoule he'd picked up in Banff. Pulled it on, and headed off into the woods.

The oak and beech at the roadside gave way to ordered rows of pine, all standing to attention like soldiers on parade. Fifteen to twenty feet in, there was no sign of snow. It hadn't managed to penetrate the canopy overhead, leaving his boots to scuff through drifts of discarded needles. Everything smelled of mushrooms and earth, and the bitter-tar tang of pine.

He picked his way over fallen branches, around the towering shields of roots at the base of fallen trees, past drainage ditches and clumps of jagged gorse.

Should be far enough from anywhere now.

That was the great thing about Forestry Commission land: everyone stuck to the official paths, and there were none for miles around here.

He stopped in the lee of a great fallen spruce – its flat pan of roots still full of dirt and stones – and pulled up the cagoule's hood. Tightened the drawstrings. Then opened the carrier bag, reached in and took hold of the handgrip. Clicked off the safety catch with his thumb. Wrapped the bag's handles around his wrist.

Before, when it was him versus Reuben, one-on-one, shooting the fat bastard would've been murder. But now? After what happened to Steel? After the threats to Jasmine and Naomi?

There wasn't a choice any more.

'OK.' Logan raised the gun and aimed at the trunk of a wooden soldier, left hand cupping the right, pulling with one arm, pushing with the other. Then squeezed the trigger.

Phut.

It kicked, jerking up through thirty degrees, the plastic bag billowing out with the escaping gas from the explosion. A shower of bark burst from the tree, and the bag sagged around his hand – dragged down by the weight of the ejected cartridge.

Another squeeze.

Phut.

The kick didn't seem so bad this time. Another shower of bark. Another empty cartridge rolled about in the bottom of the saggy carrier bag.

One last time for luck.

Phut.

The cartridges clinked against each other as he picked his way through the trees to the victim. Three bullets, all within a circle of about four inches. Good enough.

Reuben was easily twice as wide as the trunk.

Logan placed the carrier bag on the needle-strewn forest floor, there was a ragged hole where the bullet had torn its way through the thin plastic, but other than that, it was untouched. Blackened a bit by the gunshot residue, perhaps, but it was better in there and on the sleeves of the cagoule than all over him. He peeled off the cagoule, turned it inside out and wrapped it around the bag.

The plasticky package went in another carrier, along with the discarded blue nitrile gloves.

All set.

Even with all the windows open, the place smelled of neglect. How long had it been – six months since he was last here? Eight? Something like that.

Snow blanketed the thin strip of woods behind the caravan park, broken by the thick grey mass of the River Don where it wound its way between here and the sewage works, before twisting away under the bridge, off past Tesco's and out of sight.

The sound of traffic growled in through the windows

– everyone crawling around the Mugiemoss Roundabout, getting ready to do battle with the Haudagain. Poor sods.

Logan placed another armful of horror novels in the cardboard box. Stephen Kings mostly, with a smattering of H. P. Lovecraft and some James Herbert thrown in for good measure. The living room was full of the things: lined up on shelves, piled up in corners. Another trip turned up some Dean Koontz and Clive Barkers.

He folded the box lid in on itself and printed 'BOOKS' across it in thick marker-pen letters. Carried the thing through into the hall and stacked it with the other two.

Stuck the next empty box in the middle of the living room carpet.

Right, videos.

His phone rang between *I Spit on Your Grave* and *Texas Chainsaw Massacre*.

'McRae?' He tucked it under his chin and grabbed *Cannibal Holocaust* and *Night of the Living Dead*.

'Sergeant McRae, it's Detective Superintendent Harper.'

Wonderful.

'Sir.' *Friday the Thirteenth Part III* and *The Thing*.

'You didn't turn up for your shift today.'

'That's because I'm not meant to *be* on shift today.' *An American Werewolf in London* and *Student Bodies*. They went in the box.

No reply.

Wolfen, The Howling, Videodrome, Children of the Corn, A Nightmare on Elm Street. Never let it be said that Samantha didn't find a theme and stick with it.

'Logan, I heard what happened last night.'

Oh, so he was 'Logan' now, was he?

'I know. Rennie called you.' *Razorback, Day of the Dead, Fright Night.* The cases clattered on top of the ones already in the box. Not that anyone would want them down the charity shop. Who watched videos any more? Who even had a video player?

'Anyway, I wanted you to know that we've got a guard on DCI Steel's room. She's going to be fine. And when they release her, there'll be a car outside her house too.'

Yes, Harper the Harpy was a pain in the backside – and an idiot for thinking this was anything to do with Malcolm McLennan – but at least she was looking after Steel. Had to give her credit for that. 'Might be an idea to get that car outside her house soon as possible. They might go after her family. Maybe get someone to keep an eye on Jasmine at school?'

In case Reuben decided to send another 'message'.

'Right. Good idea.'

This time the pause went on for a while.

Eaten Alive!, The Watcher in the Woods, The New York Ripper, Poltergeist.

'Logan, I meant what I said. You and I: we got off on the wrong foot.'

He dumped the videos in the box and settled onto the mildewed couch. 'You've got a file on me.'

'Yes.'

'Why?'

The shelves were full of ornaments too. Dragons, and skeletons, and ankhs, and incense burners, and trolls. The tackier the better, as far as Samantha was concerned. As long as it was a bit gothic, she loved it. Logan reached out and picked a snowglobe off the windowsill. It was a replica of the graveyard in *The Frighteners* – mounted on a genuine chunk of New Zealand rock – where the snow was made from tiny skull-and-crossbones. He gave it a shake, making the crypt doors open and pale hands reach out. She'd been so chuffed when he'd bought it for her. Gave it pride of place on the mantelpiece, until she'd found that replica Jason Voorhees hockey mask on eBay.

He dumped the original black-and-white version of *The Haunting* in with the other videos.

OK, if Harper didn't say anything in the next ten seconds he was hanging up. Nine. Eight. Seven. Six—

'*I've been following your career for years. The Mastrick Monster, the Flesher, Jenny and Alison McGregor, Richard Knox… It's been very* colourful.'

'You still haven't answered the question.'

'*All these dramatic high-profile cases; anyone would think you'd be a superintendent by now, chief inspector at the very least. Instead, you're wearing sergeant's stripes in some God-forsaken Aberdeenshire backwater.*'

His chin came up. 'Maybe I *like* being a sergeant. Maybe I like Banff. Maybe I don't want to be a glorified administrator, slash, project-manager, slash, HR stooge? Running investigations at arm's length and never actually *doing* anything.'

She laughed at him, then sighed. '*When are you back at work?*'

Logan put the snowglobe down. 'Tomorrow.'

'*Good.*' She hung up.

God save us.

He huffed out a breath. Then went back to the videos.

'No, no idea. Hold on.' Logan rested the box on top of the Punto, and opened the boot – keeping the phone pinned between his ear and shoulder. He slid the box of clothes in on top of one marked 'ORNAMENTS'.

With the passenger seat as far forward as it would go, and the back seats folded down there was probably room for another two boxes.

Call it one and a half loads to the charity shop, one to the tip… 'Maybe three o'clock? Four? Depends on the traffic.'

From where he stood there was a great view of the tail-back grinding up to the Mugiemoss Roundabout. The snow might have stopped, but everyone was still driving like they'd forgotten their Zimmer frame.

Steel's voice got all muffled. '*He's saying about four-ish. … What? … OK.*' Then she was back at full volume again. '*Susan says it's roast chicken and dumplings.*'

'Look, I can't promise anything, I've still got all this—'

'*No excuses. You're seeing your kids whether you like it or no'.*'

He clunked the boot shut. 'If I turn up and the pair of you sneak off to the cinema, I will *not* be happy.'

'*Oh come on, we only did that one time.*'

'One time? What about when you disappeared to Edinburgh for the night? Or when you went to see *Rigoletto*? Or *Cats*? You invited me round for a barbecue then tiptoed away to see Bill Bailey at the Music Hall, remember that?' He stamped back into the caravan.

'*Well, maybe no' one time, but—*'

'I am not your unpaid emergency babysitter.' He grabbed another box of clothes.

'*Come on Laz, don't be a big whinge. Going to be a lovely evening – good food, family. Do you the world of good. Might even have a knees-up round the old piano, so Jasmine—*'

'OK, I'm hanging up now.'

'*You're such a—*'

He hung up, braced the box against the doorframe, and stuck the phone in his pocket.

Honestly, the woman was a nightmare.

The box of clothes snagged on the lip of the boot, but he put his shoulder to it and forced it past the black rubber strip. One more box to go.

Mind you, it might be nice to see the kids again. Make sure they were OK. And Susan did cook a damn tasty roast chicken.

Yeah, why not.

Even having to put up with Jasmine practising for her grade three piano might not be so bad. At least it'd be more than wonky scales and tortured nursery rhymes this time.

He closed the car boot and headed back inside.

That CLAN charity shop in Dyce was probably the best bet – cut along the back way, past where the paper mill used to be, across the road, under the dual carriage way and through the housing estate. At least that way…

Logan froze.

A noise came from the open doorway to the living room. Like something had fallen over.

But it was all in boxes. There was nothing left *to* fall over.

He stepped through into the room.

29

A blur in the corner of his eye, then someone slammed into Logan's side. They crashed into the caravan wall and bounced. Then banged against the wall again.

A thick hand grabbed at Logan's face, grinding it into the wallpaper as a fist battered into his ribs. Once. Twice. Three times.

Then the room flipped – ceiling, carpet, then ceiling again. Logan smashed onto the floor.

Lay there, flat on his back, struggling to haul in a breath. Fire ripped up and down his side where the punches landed. Argh...

A weight landed on his chest, cutting short the jagged breathing, and when he opened his eyes there was a man sitting on him – knees pinning Logan's arms to his sides. A wee man, with big blonde sideburns and a wide greasy smile. Captain ABBA, AKA: Eddy Knowles.

'Not so big now, are you?' Eddy's fist jabbed forward, cracking into Logan's cheek, bashing his head off the carpet. Another.

Logan thrashed, legs kicking out. 'GET OFF ME!'

The next punch brought searing yellow blobs and a high-pitched whine riding on a wave of frozen barbed wire.

'GET OFF, YOU WEE—' Logan's head snapped hard to

the left, lips burning. Hot copper and salt seeped across his tongue.

Eddy Knowles sat back, reached behind him, and pulled out an eight-inch hunting knife. 'Remember this?' He held it in front of Logan's eyes, twisting it so the blade caught the light. 'Jonesy and Al say, "Hi", by the way.'

A knife. Why did it have to be a knife?

Knots twisted in Logan's stomach as the scar-lines cried out in protest.

'Gnnnt ffffmmm...' Mouth wasn't working. Everything tasted of blood.

The knife traced its way down Logan's cheek, cold and scratching – not deep enough to break the skin.

'Shame it had to turn out like this. But, well, you know what Reuben's like when he gets an idea in his head.'

'Gnnnnnffffmmmmm...'

Captain ABBA swam in and out of focus.

DON'T JUST LIE THERE, DO SOMETHING!

What?

What the hell was he supposed to do?

'Was only a warning last night. A wee something to show you who's boss. But Reuben's changed his mind again.' He leaned forward. 'Nothing personal, but I got to make an example of you.' Eddy placed the knife against the skin under Logan's eye. 'You understand.'

'Fffffk yyyu.'

'Yeah, not so much.' The knife rose into the air, point down.

Logan grabbed two handfuls of Captain ABBA's buttocks and heaved, digging in with his heels, thrusting his hips upwards in a desperate parody of a sexual act. Trying to not get screwed.

Eddy's eyes went wide as he lurched forwards, caught off balance, sprawling on top of him.

Logan shoved him off, grabbed the back of his neck and battered his head into the carpet.

The knife went clattering away across the floor, under the couch.

An elbow cracked back into Logan's ribs.

They rolled on the floor, punching, gouging, snarling. *Bang* into the wall beneath the window. A rain of ornaments crashed down around them.

A fist cracked into Logan's jaw. He rammed his forehead into Eddy's nose.

Grunting, swearing.

His leg caught the edge of the couch, sending it scraping back across the floor, exposing the knife.

Eddy Knowles lunged for it, blood spattering down from his broken face.

And Logan grabbed the first thing he could find – a solid lump of plastic and rock – and swung it at Eddy's head.

Thunk.

He stuttered forward. Then snatched the knife up. Twisted around.

Thunk.

His head battered sideways.

Thunk.

The blade flashed out, leaving a searing line across Logan's stomach.

'AAAAAAGH…' Logan swung the snowglobe again, teeth bared.

Thunk.

Thunk.

Thunk.

And Eddy wasn't moving any more.

Logan slumped back against the wall, fingers fluttering at the front of his T-shirt. Red seeped through the slashed fabric of his hoodie.

Not again. *Please*, not again.

He unzipped it to the point where the knife had cut clean through and peeled the sides apart. A dark-scarlet line stretched across his stomach, joining up several of the puck-ered ghosts of another knife.

Please…

Logan prodded the wound, wincing. It had broken the skin, but that was about it. A lot of blood, but not too much damage.

He closed his eyes and let his head fall back.

Thank God.

Deep breaths. Not dead. Not dead yet.

He opened his eyes again.

Eddy Knowles lay twisted on his side, mouth hanging open, eyes staring off into the corner. The knife rested in his open hand, its tip buried in the carpet. He didn't blink. Didn't breathe.

Oh no.

Logan looked down at the blunt weapon, lying beside him, and picked it up again. It was the snowglobe of *The Frighteners*. The chunk of genuine New Zealand rock was smeared with dark red. Stained clumps of hair stuck to the rough surface.

No.

He dropped it and it rolled away, snow falling, the crypts giving up their ghosts.

No, no, no, no, NO!

'Don't be dead, don't be dead…' Logan scrambled across the dusty carpet and pressed two fingers against Eddy's throat, just below the ear. The skin was slick with scarlet. No pulse.

'BASTARD!' He shoved him over onto his back, clenched both hands together in a single fist and pressed down on the breastbone. One, one thousand, two, one thousand, three, one thousand.

Nothing.

Logan tilted the guy's head back and pinched the twisted mass of bloody gristle masquerading as a nose, sealing the nostrils. Took a deep breath, covered Eddy's mouth with his own and blew. Went back to the chest compressions. Another breath. Compressions. Breath. Compressions…

Then sat back on his haunches.

The body lay there, motionless, spread out on the floor.

Logan grabbed the lip of the toilet bowl, hunching his back as his stomach tried to turn itself inside out. Retching and heaving until there was nothing coming out but bitter reeking strings of yellow bile.

His hands left sticky scarlet smears on the porcelain.

He was screwed. Completely and utterly screwed. Never mind standing there, doing nothing to stop Tony Evans getting murdered, he'd killed someone.

Killed them.

Jesus.

The caravan floor creaked beneath Logan's feet as he paced back and forth, between the bedroom and the living room. The *not* living room. The death room.

Oh dear Jesus.

The water was cold, sputtering from the tap in the bathroom, sending pink spiralling down the sink. So cold it burned.

Logan scrubbed with the soap, working it into a bloody froth.

Something heavy was sitting on his chest – didn't matter how hard he breathed, he couldn't get any oxygen into his lungs.

Why wouldn't it wash away?

He dragged a hand towel from the box in the hall and folded it lengthways a couple of times then pressed it against the slash across his stomach. Hunched over the kitchen worktop, pushing it into his skin.

A thick strip of fabric, ripped off an old sheet, made a bandage to hold it in place.

Logan folded forward until his cheek rested on the cool worktop.

He could do this.

He could.

He had to.

Eddy Knowles lay spread out in front of the couch, one arm up reaching above his head as if forever frozen in the middle of hailing a taxi.

Sodding bastarding hell.

Well, it wasn't as if he'd have got up and walked off, was it?

Logan grimaced. Smelled like a butcher's shop in here.

The body's forehead was lumpen and dented on one side, nearly caved in. Around his head, the carpet was dark and wet – glinting in the cold afternoon light that filtered in through the grubby windows.

Logan's eyes widened. What if someone looked in? What if someone *saw* him?

He picked his way across the living room, inching his way around the stain.

God, there was a lot of blood.

The curtains rattled as he dragged them shut.

Cold water spilled down his chin as he drained the glass. Then filled it again, standing in the galley kitchen. The glass clicked and skittered against the stainless-steel draining board, threatening to jerk free of his hand.

Call the police.

They'd understand, wouldn't they? It was self-defence, he didn't have any choice. The guy had a dirty big knife and orders to make an example of him.

Yeah, because no one would ask why, would they? They wouldn't want to know what a gangster was doing with orders to carve Logan into little chunks. Wouldn't impound the car. Wouldn't do a thorough search.

What's this under your passenger seat, Sergeant McRae? Why it's an illegal handgun, and it appears to have been fired recently. Who have you been shooting, Sergeant McRae?

That would end well.

Logan raised the trembling glass to his lips and drank.

Didn't matter how it ended, it was what had to happen. He'd killed someone.

He let out a long jittery breath.

Or maybe there was another way? Go out to the car, get the gun, come back and put a bullet through his own head. Bang. Every problem solved with one squeeze of the trigger. No more worry. No more guilt. No more grief. No more—

The doorbell rang out loud and sharp in the cold air.

Too late.

Logan lowered the glass.

Should have phoned the police when he had the chance.

He wiped a hand across his chin, getting rid of the water. Deep breath. Hauled his shoulders back. Then answered the door.

But it wasn't a concerned neighbour who'd witnessed everything, or a uniformed officer with a warrant for his arrest. It was John Urquhart.

His face was flushed and shiny, beads of sweat trickling down his cheeks. 'Oh thank ... thank God...' Urquhart folded over, grabbed his knees and panted. 'Thought I'd... Argh... Had to abandon the ... the car at ... Tesco and leg it...' A coughing spasm rippled through him and he abandoned his knees to clutch at the doorframe. 'Traffic...'

Logan looked over his shoulder at the car park. A familiar, dented Transit van sat next to his manky wee Punto.

'Mr McRae, you need ... you need to get ... to get out, OK?' Urquhart peered up at him. 'Reuben's sent someone ... someone to kill... Oh.' A frown. He pointed at Logan's face. 'Is that blood?'

He pushed past, into the caravan. A pause, then the sound of swearing belted out from inside.

Logan found him in the living room, hands on his hips, staring at the body on the floor.

Urquhart got to the end of his rant and sagged. Shook his

head. Glanced back at Logan. 'I know this probably isn't what you want to hear, but I'm impressed, dude. Eddy?' He nudged the body's leg with a shoe. 'He's killed six guys I know of. Cut the nose right off one of them, and posted it to his wife. Mind you, she was running a drug ring in Cults, so, you know.' As if that made it all right.

'It was an accident.'

'You accidentally battered his head into the carpet? Nah, credit where it's due, Mr McRae. I thought you'd be...' A shrug. 'Nice to see you're still alive.'

Logan leaned back against the wall. His knees wouldn't work properly. The guilt was too heavy for them.

'Mind you, that's some lump you've got there.' Urquhart pointed.

'Where?' He reached up and brushed his fingers across the hair above his ear. A bump the size of a Creme Egg throbbed as he touched it. His fingertips came away red and sticky. 'Oh.'

The ringing noise got louder. Was someone else at the door?

Why didn't Urquhart answer it?

'Mr McRae? Are you OK?'

Only it wasn't the doorbell, was it? It was inside Logan's head.

'Mr McRae?' Urquhart didn't seem to cross the intervening space. One second he was standing over Eddy and the next he was standing over Logan. Looking down.

How did he end up on the floor?

Logan blinked. Shook his head. It only made the ringing worse.

Urquhart squatted down. 'How many fingers am I holding up?'

Three ... no four fingers swam in front of his face. 'Four?'

'Yeah, that's probably a concussion.'

Oh good.

'Come on, let's get you onto the sofa.' Urquhart hauled

298

him up by the armpits and walked him over to the mildewed couch. Lowered him down. Then produced a hipflask from an inside pocket and held it out. 'Here.'

Logan fumbled with the cap and took a swig. Sweet fire spread down his throat and across his stomach.

Urquhart took it back, wiped his palm across the neck and took a jolt of his own. 'It's all going to hell, Mr McRae. All going to hell. Reuben's...' He settled on the arm of the couch. 'Remember those meetings I had to set up? Didn't go well.'

'What a surprise.'

'Reuben got into a fight with Ma Campbell's representative. Hacked off both his hands and sent him home with them in a Jiffy bag. The whole thing's racing to rat-shit in a handbasket. Going to be war.' He sniffed, curled his top lip. 'Man, it stinks in here.'

...

'...you OK?' Urquhart was right in front of him again, peering into his eyes.

'Get off me.' Logan pushed him away, but there wasn't any force to it.

'What you doing here anyway? Having a clear out?'

'It's all going to the charity shop. Or the tip.' Logan's stomach took a lurch to the left. 'The person who owned it died.'

'That's too bad.' He looked around. 'Nothing here you want to keep? You know, sentimental value and that?'

Saliva flooded his mouth. He swallowed. Shuddered. 'Think I'm going to be sick again.'

'Yeah, come on, let's get you on your feet.'

Dry heaves crashed through him like a punch in the stomach, leaving him coughing and gagging over the open toilet bowl. He spat out another glob of foul yellow bile.

Urquhart sat on the edge of the bath, one leg swinging back and forward. 'Course, we can't really leave Eddy lying there. And we can't call it in. You imagine how much trouble that'd bring?'

Another heave. Logan's fingers dug into the blood-smeared porcelain.

'Nah, we'll have to get rid of him. Still, not to worry, wouldn't be the first, won't be the last.' He gave a short, snorted laugh. 'That's the great thing about pigs: always hungry. It'll be fine.'

Logan rested his forehead against the cool toilet rim. 'No. No pigs. We can't... Oh, God.' More bile. The retch echoed back at him, amplified by the bowl.

'It's OK. Don't sweat it. You don't want Eddy going pigward, that's cool with me. You're the boss.'

He spat. Wiped his mouth with the back of his hand. Then flushed the toilet.

The rushing water pulled in cool air, chilling the sweat on the back of his neck.

'You all right to stand, Mr McRae? Need help?'

'I'm fine...' No he wasn't. Logan pulled himself up the side of the bath, holding on to it until the world settled down a bit. Then wobbled over to the sink and splashed water on his face. Rinsed out his foul-tasting mouth.

Urquhart took hold of his arm. 'No wonder you're feeling a bit ropey. See most people? If they went up against Eddy they'd be the ones lying flat on their backs in a pool of blood.' He led Logan out into the hall, then through into the bedroom.

The wardrobes hung open and empty, but there were still sheets and a duvet on the bed. The duvet cover had been black with red skulls once, but mildew had spread green tendrils out across the fabric. No point packing them for the charity shop, the whole lot was going to landfill.

'Here you go.' Urquhart grabbed a corner and threw the duvet back, setting loose an explosion of gritty peppery stench. Then helped Logan sit on the bed. 'Lie down. I'll get a cold cloth for that bump.'

'Don't need to lie down.' But he couldn't stay upright. Maybe just for a minute. Until the room stopped spinning. Should probably go to Accident and Emergency.

Instead Logan lowered his head to the mould-bleached pillow.

Not for long. Get up in a minute. Sixty seconds to catch his breath. Wasn't too much to ask for...

Urquhart appeared, holding a tea towel. Knelt beside the bed and pressed it against the hair above Logan's ear. Cold and damp. Soothing the fire. 'Shhh. It'll all be OK. You trust me, don't you?'

No.

And the world went away.

30

'Gnnnph...' Logan sat bolt upright, blinking in the gloom. Caravan. He was in the caravan. In the bed, the duvet rucked around his waist. It was dark.

He fumbled his phone from his pocket. Quarter to four.

Urquhart must have drawn the curtains.

Logan swung his legs over the side and wobbled to his feet. Stood there with one hand on the wall, holding him up.

That gritty mildew smell had gone, replaced by the acerbic chemical stink of bleach.

He picked his way through the caravan to the living room, where the smell was strongest.

Great.

Eddy Knowles's body was gone. Splotches of orangey grey marked the floor where he'd died, surrounded by the carpet's original dark-red colour. More bleached patches over by the windowsill. A big stain of it on the couch.

Logan reached up and touched the lump above his ear. Flinched. Then poked at it again. Swelling was going down a bit. It had stopped bleeding too.

Not that it mattered.

Might as well have died in his sleep as wake up to this.

So what if Reuben dobbed him in for taking money from

Wee Hamish Mowat's estate? John Urquhart had him on a murder. He had the body and, seeing as how the *Frighteners* snowglobe was nowhere to be seen, the murder weapon too.

Logan dragged out his phone, squinting at the screen as it refused to stay in focus. He picked Urquhart's number from his call history and listened to it ring. And ring. And then it clicked over to voicemail.

'Hi, this is John's phone. He's not here right now, but leave a message, OK?'

He opened his mouth ... then shut it again. What was he going to do: leave recorded evidence asking what happened to the body of the man he'd killed? No chance. He hung up.

Should've called the police when he had the chance. Cut a deal.

At least that way he'd have been out in three or four years. But now?

Maybe the plan to go home and blow his own brains out wasn't so bad? Wasn't as if he had anything else going for him right now. Head home, crack open that bottle of Balvenie, and *phut*.

He leaned back against the wall. But then who would look after Cthulhu?

Steel and Susan? Nah, their Mr Rumpole was far too old and too grumpy to accept another cat into the household.

He rubbed a hand across his face. Then flinched as his phone blared out the 'Imperial March' from *Star Wars*.

And everyone thought Friday the thirteenth was bad.

Logan took the call. 'I can't.'

On the other end, Steel was barely audible over the sound of loud music and shouting in the background – as if she was standing in the middle of a nightclub. *'What? Hold on.'* She'd obviously turned away from the phone. *'WILL YOU SHUT THAT RACKET UP? I'M TRYING TO TALK TO YOUR DAD!'* The music died away. *'Thank you.'*

He turned his back on the room and limped out into the hall.

'*Sorry about that. Wee hooligan's going through her heavy metal phase.*'

'I said, "I can't".' He opened the front door and stepped into the snow.

'*Can't what? What can you no'*—'

'Dinner. The whole thing. I can't.' Logan locked the caravan.

The battered Transit van was gone, leaving the box-filled Punto alone in the car park, covered with about three inches of snow. More drifted down from the dirty grey sky.

'*You got any idea how much trouble Susan's gone to, you ungrateful wee sod?*'

'I can't.' He groaned his way into the driver's seat. Slammed the door shut.

'*Don't you "can't" me, you get your backside—*'

'I'm not feeling well, OK? Been sick twice. And my head hurts. *And* my stomach.' Which was an understatement. It was as if someone had sewn fire ants under the skin, leaving them to bite and sting all the way across his abdomen.

He turned the key, treadling the accelerator until the engine caught. Clicked on the windscreen wipers. They ground their way through the snow.

Steel cleared her throat. '*Hey, I had a hangover today too: don't be such a whinge.*'

'It's *not* a hangover.'

He stuck the car in reverse, the wheels slithered then caught.

'*Aye, pull the other one, it's got sheep attached.*'

'Look…' Logan bit his lip. Winced. Then caught a good look at himself in the rear-view mirror. His mouth was swollen and cracked, a good spread of bruises growing over his cheekbone and temple.

There had to be some way to get her to leave him alone. Something that'd wind her up till she stormed off in a huff.

Of course there was: 'The kiddie porn on Jack Wallace's computer, it was buried away. So how come you managed to find it?'

'*Aye, nice try, Hannibal Lecter, but you're no' changing the subject that easy. You want to cancel on your kids, you can do it yourself.*'

'Oh come on, you can barely work the microwave, how are you suddenly a computer hacker?'

He got the Punto facing the right way and crawled out of the caravan park and onto Mugiemoss Road, past the huge ugly grey sheds of the industrial estate.

His stomach churned and gurgled, keeping time with the thumping waves of warm gravel that filled his skull. Probably got a concussion. Probably shouldn't be driving. But what was he supposed to do, hang about in the caravan till Reuben sent someone else after him?

And then Steel was back. '*You really want to know? Fine.*' Some rustling, then the sound of a door closing.

The road was a dirty black, fringed with brown slush – wavy lines of grit clearly visible.

'*I went to tell him to stay the hell away from Claudia Boroditsky. Grimy little sod had form for leaning on witnesses and victims. Liked to throw his weight about like a big man. And there she is, all of a sudden, saying she was confused, it wasn't him. Really?*'

Tiny flecks of snow drifted down, clinging to the walls of the new flats and bookshelf houses.

'*He's giving it, "Told you I never even saw her – nothing to do with me," when the phone goes. And soon as he nips off to answer it, I have myself a wee wander. Didn't have to do any hacking – the laptop was in the study, and the pictures were right there, bold as brass. He'd got it set on slideshow.*'

An eighteen wheeler grumbled past on the opposite side of the road, sending up a wake of muddy sludge.

'*And we're talking some sick stuff here. Really horrible. Arrogant git hadn't even shut the laptop when I rang the bell. Left it sitting right* there.' She sniffed. '*Probably got him all excited, talking to the police downstairs while that* filth *was playing away on his laptop.'*

'So you didn't have to type in a password or anything like that?'

'Course what I really wanted to do was chuck him down the stairs a few times. And how would I know what his password was? What am I, Derren Brown?'

Logan pulled over to the side of the road and sat there with the engine running. From here the fields were a patchwork of white and grey, bordered with thin black lines and the occasional clump of bare trees. The landscape faded as the snow swallowed the middle distance.

He huffed out a breath and ran a hand across his stomach.

The knife's line stung beneath his fingers, like rubbing rock salt into the wound.

Steel started a four-year feud with Napier to cover for him.

And now here he was, press-ganged into investigating her for Chief Superintendent Chocolate Crispies. Somehow it was a lot easier when Napier was just a shadowy Nosferatu figure, lurking and ready to pounce.

Jack Wallace was an arrogant tosser, that much was obvious from the interview footage. Sitting there impassive as everything he'd done was laid out in front of him. 'No comment'ing all the way.

Maybe he wasn't really a paedophile? Maybe it was all about sexual power for him and he didn't care who he exerted that power over? As long as they were weaker than him.

And now Steel was in the firing line because Wallace fancied getting out a bit early. Oh, poor me, I've been set up by the nasty policewoman.

Logan pulled out his phone again and brought up the photo of Samantha at Rennie's wedding. Rested the phone in the gap between the steering wheel and the instruments.

'I know what you're thinking, and you're right.'

No reply.

'You think I'm looking for excuses not to go home. Because if I go home, I've got to face the fact that I'm screwed.'

She was beautiful. Hair as red as fresh blood, skin as pale as the snow. The corset made the top of her breasts swell – one skeleton on either side above the leather, holding aloft a banner with 'QUOTH THE RAVEN, "NEVERMORE"' on it. Bare shoulders showing off the tribal tattoos, brambles, skulls and hearts and jagged swirls.

'Come on, look at me: I can't even kill someone in self-defence without feeling awful. It's like there's a lump of granite inside my chest. How am I going to kill Reuben in cold blood?'

He reached forward and zoomed in on her face.

'She stood up for me. Least I can do is return the favour.'

The Punto's engine pinged and clicked as it cooled.

'I miss you.'

No reply.

He sighed, put the phone back in his pocket and started the car again. Then did a U-turn.

Sod going home.

Peterhead's Asda wasn't very busy at half-five on a Saturday evening. Just as well really. It meant there weren't too many people around to stand and stare as Logan limped and shuffled his way around the clothes department.

He caught sight of himself in a full-length mirror attached to a pillar.

Talk about stop-and-search chic. His cagoule – unwrapped from the handgun in the car park – covered a multitude of sins and bloodstains, but did nothing to hide the hunched, bruised lump of a man reflected back at him.

If they had any sense, store security would be keeping an eye on him. He might as well be carrying a placard with 'I SHOPLIFT BACON AND CHEESE!!!' on it.

He leaned on his trolley and added a pair of jeans to the

black T-shirt, blue hoodie, black socks, and grey trainers already in there. Then limped around to the pharmacy aisle and lumped in two packs of the highest-strength painkillers he could find, a pack of waterproof plasters, and an elasticated bandage.

That should do it.

A big middle-aged bloke in a black V-necked jumper and a tie followed him all the way to the checkouts. Just in case.

The prison officer held the door open, grimacing as Logan limped into the interview room.

'Sure you don't want to see the doctor?'

Logan hissed out a breath as he lowered himself into one of the seats. 'I'm fine, really.'

The room was bland and anonymous. Grey floor, grey walls, grey table, grey seats. A mirrored black hemisphere sat in one corner, like a supermarket security camera, and a panic strip ran around the wall.

'Yes, but...' She pointed at his face.

'Broke up a fight outside a pub at lunchtime.' He tried for a smile. 'You should see the other guy.'

Currently working his way through the inside of a pig. If Logan was lucky.

'Well, OK. If you're *sure*.'

'Positive.'

A nod. 'I'll go get Mr Wallace.'

As soon as she was gone, Logan popped another couple of Nurofen from their blister pack and dry-swallowed them. To hell with the recommended daily dosage. He slipped the packet back in the pocket of his new hoodie. Wasn't easy, changing in the Punto's passenger seat, in a lay-by, but at least he looked a bit less drug-dealy now.

Shame his whole body still ached. And every time he moved, the elasticated plasters pulled at the hair on his stomach.

But other than that, everything was just sodding *peachy*.

It couldn't have been more than five minutes before the guard was back with Jack Wallace.

Prison hadn't put any weight on him, he was still small and thin, the red sweatshirt and grey jogging bottoms almost hanging off him. He'd kept his scraped-forward fringe, but the pencil beard had thickened to a marker pen. Probably not so easy to get precision grooming equipment when you were banged up in HMP Grampian.

The officer pointed. 'Jack, this is Sergeant McRae, he's here to talk to you about your allegations. For the record, again, this interview isn't being recorded, and you've declined to have your solicitor present. Correct?'

Wallace nodded. He looked thin, but when he moved his head it made the skin wobble beneath his chin. As if he'd been much larger once and lost a lot of it in a hurry.

'All right then. Sergeant McRae, I'll be right outside if you need me.'

'Thanks.' Logan waited till the door clunked shut, then shifted back in his seat. Why was it impossible to find a position that didn't hurt? He settled for something that only made the left side of his body ache and stayed there, not saying anything, letting the silence grow.

OK, so it was an old and cheap trick, but it worked. Sooner or later the person on the other side of the interview room table would—

'I didn't do it.' Wallace leaned forward, hands clutched in front of him. 'I don't know why she says I did, but I didn't. I mean, kids?' He bared his teeth and shuddered. 'That's just sick.'

Logan stayed where he was. Mouth closed.

'I don't understand it. I never *ever* looked at a kid like that. Never.' He sniffed, then wiped his eyes on the sleeve of his sweatshirt. 'I don't belong in here. You wouldn't believe the people I'm in with – paedos, rapists, people who shag *sheep* for Christ's sake! Scum.' His bottom lip wobbled, then got pulled in. 'I shouldn't be here.'

Someone walked by in the corridor outside, whistling something tuneless.

'It was that Chief Inspector Steel.' He pronounced her name as if it were made of battery acid. 'She set me up. She stole my laptop and she put that disgusting filth on it so she could arrest me.' He coiled forward, elbow on the tabletop, head in his hands. 'She's had it in for me for *years*. This is her idea of a joke. But it's my *life*!'

'Why?'

Wallace looked up. 'What?'

'Why would she do that? Why you?'

'I don't *know*.' He scrubbed at his eyes again. 'If I knew, I'd tell you, but I don't. I've never done anything. I haven't.'

Logan tilted his head on one side, stretching the muscles in his neck, pulling the strip of gauze tight across his throat. 'What about Claudia Boroditsky?'

Wallace reacted as if he'd been slapped. Sat bold upright, blinking back the tears. 'I never touched her. Never. You ask her – it was all lies. She dropped the charges and they threw it out of court.' He poked the table with a thin finger. 'I should've sued her. Had her done for making false claims. Trying to pervert the course of justice. *I'm* the victim here.'

Yeah, right.

'It's not fair.' He reached across the table, but Logan kept his hands out of reach. 'I didn't rape anyone, and I didn't download child porn. I swear on my mother's grave, that wrinkly old *bitch* set me up.'

And there it was, a flash of the real Jack Wallace: aggressive, woman-hating, outraged and martyred, sexist scumbag. Lying and weaselling. Trying to escape justice yet again.

Well not this time.

Logan stood. 'We're done.'

31

Logan spread out a copy of the *Aberdeen Examiner* on the kitchen table, then unwrapped the semiautomatic from its plastic bags. Took another hit of Balvenie, holding it in his mouth till the warm sweetness turned into numbed gums and tongue.

The cagoule was long gone, stuffed into a bin somewhere between Peterhead and Banff.

His blue nitrile gloves squeaked on the metal as he disassembled the gun, turning it into a jigsaw of metal components. Each one with its place and purpose.

He'd only fired three test shots, but the barrel was furred with soot, outside and in.

A prooping noise came from the doorway, then a small furry body wound its way between his ankles. Tail up.

He reached down to ruffle her ears then stopped.

Had anyone ever been done because the Scene of Crime lot found gunshot residue on a suspect's cat? Probably not. But it wasn't worth the risk either.

'Sorry, Kittenfish, Daddy's busy just now.'

The semiautomatic came apart easily enough. Logan laid out its moving parts across a story about two school kids who'd found a homeless man floating facedown in the boating pond at Duthie Park. The photo of the pair of them

– grinning away after their 'traumatic ordeal' – darkened with blotches of oil from the recoil spring.

Cleaning the gun only took a couple of minutes, so all that time spent on firearms training hadn't been wasted. The gun clicked and snapped together again. Logan hauled back the slide and checked the action. All ready.

Assuming he had the guts to pull the trigger.

Shooting someone *had* to be easier than battering them to death with a snowglobe.

His hands trembled as he placed the semiautomatic back in its polished wooden box.

Soon find out.

He snapped off his gloves and bundled them up with the used carrier bags. Stuck the lot in another bag. Have to head out later, take a route away from the CCTV cameras mounted on the front of the police station across the road, drench them with bleach and dump them somewhere. Maybe in a dog-waste bin, or a random wheelie bin. Somewhere no one would think to look.

Then he bent down, winced, swore, and finally picked Cthulhu up. Held her warm purring body against his chest. Tried to breathe.

'Daddy killed someone today.'

Why was it never like this in the books or movies? The hero gets attacked, the hero kills the attacker, throws out a smart one-liner, and moves on. They never looked like someone had carved a hole in their chest and filled it with frozen gravel.

He kissed the top of Cthulhu's head. 'Let's get you something to eat.'

The Nurofen clicked out of their blister pack. Logan washed both of them down with some more whisky. Then dipped back into the cardboard box on the floor.

He placed Samantha's dark-red skirt – with the black embroidered roses – on the bed, tucking it under the leather corset. Added the black-and-red striped holdups, and the knee-length kinky boots with the gold braiding that made them look like some sort of Napoleonic uniform. The black leather gloves. The only thing left was the Ziploc plastic bag containing all her rings and piercings. He placed it where Samantha's head would have been.

'There you go: the outfit you had on at Rennie's wedding. You'll look lovely in your coffin.'

He sat next to her. Took the glove as if it were her hand.

Stared at the wall. The outlines began to blur.

He laughed – short and strangled.

Ground the heel of his hand into an eye.

Laughed again.

'I'm having a really, really, *really* crap week.'

Deep breath.

It trembled on the way out. Then he swore as the doorbell rang out long and heartless.

'Yeah.'

No prizes for guessing who that would be.

The glove went back on the bed.

He knelt on the floor and pulled out the polished wooden box, took out the semiautomatic and racked a round into the chamber. Clicked the safety off.

Who cared if he got his fingerprints all over it.

The doorbell went again as he thumped down the stairs, gun up and ready.

If Reuben thought this was going to be easy, he was in for a nasty shock.

Wrench the door open, shoot him in the face.

Easy.

He could do this.

Logan's left hand closed around the handle. He leaned forward and peered through the spyhole.

Oh.

It wasn't Reuben, or even one of his thugs, it was Detective Superintendent Holier-Than-Thou Harper.

Perfect end to a perfect day.

The doorbell mourned.

Maybe he could pretend he wasn't in? But then all the lights were on, and presumably you didn't get promoted to detective superintendent by being a moron.

He tucked the gun into the pocket of his new hoodie and opened the door.

She stood on the pavement, her cheeks flushed, the tip of her nose a shiny pink – ears too. A thick padded jacket made her look about twice normal size, the collar turned up against the falling snow. Her breath streamed out in pale grey wisps. 'Hello.' She lowered her eyes. 'Are you going to ask me in, Sergeant?'

He stuck his hand in the pocket, obscuring the semi-automatic's outline. 'Do I have a choice?'

Harper flashed him a lopsided smile. 'Detective superintendents are like vampires. We can't come in unless you invite us.'

Oh God, she *was* coming on to him. Steel was right.

Not that she wasn't attractive, in a perpetually angry, shouty, judgemental, girl-next-door, blonde, big-brown-eyed kind of way. Never really noticed how big her ears were before, but now that they were all pink and glowing they kind of—

'Seriously, Sergeant, I'm freezing out here.'

'Oh, right.' He backed away and ushered her into the house. Shut the door behind her.

Harper had a good look around. 'You live here on your own.'

Not that there was anything wrong with larger ears.

'You want a cup of tea, or something?'

'Yes.'

'Fine.' He pointed at the kitchen. 'Kettle's in there, help yourself. I'll be down in a minute.'

She pursed her lips, then raised an eyebrow, before turning and wandering through into the kitchen.

As soon as she was gone, Logan charged upstairs and

jammed the gun back in its box. Stood there for a moment, in the middle of the bedroom, staring down at Samantha's clothes – laid out for their last hurrah. The last thing she would ever wear, forever and ever, amen.

At least he wouldn't have to worry about Harper jumping him. Nothing killed the mood like a display of your dead girlfriend's clothes in the middle of the bed.

The sound of cupboard doors opening and closing came up from downstairs. Either she couldn't find the mugs, or she was having a nosy. Let her. She wasn't going to find anything: the empty Glenfiddich bottle was safely hidden in the recycling bins behind the public toilets in Oldmeldrum, all she'd turn up were cheap dishes and cheaper tins of soup.

He headed down to the kitchen.

Harper had placed two mugs beside the grumbling kettle. She turned and frowned at him as he entered. 'Rennie and McKenzie told me you'd been attacked last night, but they didn't say someone had beaten the crap out of you. I thought you got away with a tiny cut?'

His hand drifted up to his face. The new collection of bruises and split lip. 'Yeah. Had to break up a fight outside a pub this afternoon. You know what it's like: never off duty.'

'Hmm…' She stepped closer, reached up and pulled his hand away. Staring straight into his eyes. Pursed her lips.

She was going to go in for a kiss.

Well, maybe it wouldn't be so bad an idea to feel *alive* for a change.

He leaned forward.

Then she slapped him. It came from nowhere, fast and hard, leaving a stinging brand burned into his right cheek. 'OW! What the hell was that for?'

'You couldn't even be bothered going to his funeral!' She hit him again. 'How could you be so bloody selfish?'

'What?' Logan backed away, out of slapping range. 'You… Yesterday you were all pissed off *because* I'd gone to his funeral. You *saw* me there!'

'Not Hamish Mowat, you insensitive dick, your own father!'

Logan curled his lip. 'You're off your head. Get out of my house.'

'Did you just not *care*?'

'Really: I want you to leave now. Before I throw you out.'

'HE WAS YOUR FATHER!' Harper closed the gap, hand flashing up. 'He doted on you and you couldn't even be bothered...' She swung for Logan's face. But this time he was ready for it. Grabbed the arm before anything could connect and shoved her backwards.

She stumbled and fell, thumping down against the kitchen units. Sitting flat on her bum glowering up at him. 'Think you're so special, don't you?'

'My father died when I was five, OK? *Five* years old. That's why I didn't go to his funeral. You happy now?'

She blinked up at him. 'When you were five?'

'Not that it's any of your damn business, Detective Superintendent.'

'But...' Little creases formed at the sides of her mouth. 'But he only died two months ago.'

And Logan was meant to be the one recovering from a concussion.

'I think I'd remember my dad being alive for the last thirty-four years. Now get out.'

She shook her head. 'He died two months ago, a fortnight before Christmas. I know, because he was my father too.'

Cthulhu sat on the coffee table, head tilted to one side, staring at the pair of them. They'd each taken opposite ends of the couch, a gap between them big enough to drive a motorbike through.

Harper cleared her throat. Fidgeted with the hem of her jacket. 'You didn't know?'

'Look, I understand that you're upset, but my father died when I was five. I've no idea who your dad was, but unless he came back from the dead they're not the same man.'

316

She pulled out her phone and poked at the screen. Then held it out.

A photo of a grey-haired man with a beard and performance eyebrows grinned back at him, holding up a birthday cake. 'This him?' Logan swiped right and another photo appeared, this one of the same guy sitting in a deck chair in a T-shirt and shorts.

'How can you not recognize your own father?'

Logan dumped the phone on the couch between them. 'Could be anybody.'

'Charles Montrose McRae, born sixteenth October 1954. Check.'

'I don't *need* to check.'

'My middle name's Findon, because that's where I was conceived. It's a McRae family tradition.'

Logan frowned at the man in the deckchair, as the screen went black. 'Mine's Balmoral. They were on a week's caravanning holiday...'

'So check.'

'We visited his *grave*. Every twentieth of May, my mother would bundle me and my brother into the car and we'd go lay flowers on it. He got shot trying to arrest someone for aggravated burglary.'

A short bitter laugh. 'Oh, he got shot all right. That's where he met my mum, recovering in hospital. She was a nurse. Three weeks later they packed up and moved down to Dumfries.'

Logan stared.

'Then she got pregnant with me. Your mother wouldn't give him a divorce, so they couldn't get married. I got to be "Harper the Bastard" all through school.' She bared her teeth. 'I hated you so much.'

'What the hell did *I* do?'

'He never stopped banging on about what a great wee boy you were. Logan this, Logan that. Then you joined the force and that was it: "Look at all these cases your brother solved", "Look at this serial killer your brother caught", "Look at this bit in the papers about your brother rescuing those people off *Britain's Next Big Star*, isn't he great?"' She stopped fidgeting with the couch and held her hand up, thumb and forefinger about three inches apart. 'Kept all the clippings in a scrapbook this thick.'

'This isn't funny.'

'Oh he thought you were *perfect*. Well, if you're so all-fired wonderful, how come you're a lowly sergeant in some Aberdeenshire sheep-shagging backwater? I'm a *Superintendent*. Where's my scrapbook?'

OK, sod this. Logan pulled out his phone and called Sergeant Ashton.

It rang for a bit, then she picked up. *'Fit like, min?'*

'Beaky? It's Logan. I need you to look up an officer for me: Charles Montrose McRae. Date of birth: sixteenth October fifty-four.'

'What, right down to business? No foreplay? No half-arsed stab at spickin' the Doric?'

He put the call on speakerphone so Harper could hear herself being proved wrong. 'Please, Beaky, it's important.'

Sergeant Ashton sighed. *'No one's any fun.'* There was some clicking of keys. *'You'll be chuffed to hear we've got a full house for tomorrow night. I'm anticipating a most successful dunt with a big haul of drugs, and medals for everyone... Here we go: PC Charles McRae. Joined Grampian Police in 1977 ... clean record ... shot in the line of duty four years later. Was he a relative?'*

'My father.' And Detective Superintendent Harper was full of crap.

'Aw, min. I'm sorry.'

'It's OK, Beaky. Thanks for—'

'Hold the horses a minute... That's weird: got another PC Charles Montrose McRae coming up, same D.O.B. Joined Dumfries and Galloway Constabulary, 1982. Retired in 2007, but came back as a PCSO for four and a bit years. Some people are gluttons for punishment, aren't they?'

Sitting on the other end of the couch, Harper stuck her nose in the air.

Logan stared at his phone. 'They're the same person?'

'Bit of a coincidence if they're not. 'Specially with a name like that. Now, anything else your lordship requires, or can I get back to my eightses?'

'Thanks, Beaky.' He ended the call. Cleared his throat. 'But...?'

'See?' Harper picked up her mug, swilling the dregs of tea round. 'Now, we'll still have to work together on the Shepherd investigation, so I expect you to be professional. There will be no favours or special treatment, just because we're related. I'm still your commanding officer and I expect you to follow orders like everyone else. Are we clear?'

'She told us he was dead!' His bloody mother. 'All these years. The lying, manipulative, *cow*!'

'...after the tone.'

Bleeeeeep.

'You lied!' Logan paced back and forth, in front of the mantelpiece, phone rammed against his ear. 'You said he was dead, and he was living in Dumfries the whole time! I grew up without a father, because you were too bloody *selfish* and petty and ... and bloody...' The phone case creaked in his hand. 'We're done. Understand? You're not my mother. You're nothing to me. *Never* call me again.' He slammed the phone back into the cradle so hard it bounced and fell on the floor.

Logan snatched it up and slammed it down again. Stood there, glowering at it.

Sitting on the couch, Harper raised an eyebrow. 'Feel better?'

'No.' He paced back to the other end of the mantelpiece. 'How could he abandon us with that horrible woman? How? What the hell did we do to deserve that?'

A shrug. 'He loved my mother more than yours.'

Not surprising. A rabid Alsatian would be more loveable than Rebecca McRae.

'Thirty-four years. He could've got in touch!'

'I've never really had a big brother before, do they normally moan this much?'

'*Moan?* How would you like it? "Oh, your dad's not dead, he just couldn't be arsed being there your whole life?" Useless, lazy—'

'Don't you *dare* talk about my dad like that!' She stood, fists clenched. 'For your information, he sent letters and cards, presents every birthday and Christmas for *years*.'

'We never got them.'

'Then blame your mother.'

She glowered at him and he glowered back.

The doorbell rang.

Maybe this time it'd be Reuben, come to do them all a favour. And with any luck he'd kill Harper first and let Logan watch.

Another ring.

She folded her arms and stuck her chin out. 'You going to get that, *Sergeant*?'

'Blow it out your arse, *sir*.' Logan turned and marched out into the hall. Peered through the spyhole.

Not Reuben. Calamity's face was all distorted by the wide-angle lens. Tufty and Isla stood in the street behind her.

Oh joy.

Logan opened the door. 'I know it's snowing, but it's the wrong time of year for carol singing.'

Calamity's grin slipped as she stared at him. 'What happened to your face?'

'Cut myself shaving.'

'OK... Anyway,' she held up a bulging bag-for-life, 'we come bearing beer and food.'

'Right. Yes.' He didn't move. 'Look, now's really not a good—'

'Trust me, Sarge.' She lowered the bag. 'I know you

probably think you want to be alone after what happened with Samantha, but this is what teammates are for. It's Valentine's Day, you're all alone, and we're going to support you whether you like it or not.'

Tufty held up another bag. 'I brought sausages!'

Because nothing said, 'I'm sorry you had to kill your girlfriend' like processed meat products.

He stepped back. 'You'd better come in then.'

They bustled past him into the hall, then peeled off various scarves and jackets. Stamped their feet and blew on their hands.

Isla handed him a big lumpy bag full of what felt like tins of beer. 'Least you won't have to put them in the fridge. Bleeding perishing out there.' The other two looked like normal people, out on a cold February night, but not Isla. No, she'd got all dolled up in a short tweed dress with a weird vintage collar and thick black tights. Like something off a Marks & Spencer advert. 'Got some Southern Comfort and Bacon Frazzles too. I mean, who doesn't love...' She stood up straight, eyes widening. Then nodded over Logan's shoulder. 'Ma'am.'

Pink rushed up Calamity's cheeks, turning them the same colour as her nose. 'Ah. Sorry, Sarge. We didn't know you were...' She grabbed her bag-for-life and pointed at the front door. 'We should probably...'

'Constables Nicholson, Anderson, and Quirrel, this is Detective Superintendent Harper. And before you go any further down that line of thought: no. She's my sister.'

Tufty squinted at the pair of them, then a smile blossomed on his thin face. 'Ah, right: I see it now. You've both got the same ears!'

— Sunday Dayshift —

when all is in ashes

32

'...useless unprofessional bunch of *turdbadgers*.' Steel hurled the newspaper down on the conference table.

No one moved. Ten plainclothes officers, four uniforms, all squeezed into the Major Incident Room and all doing their best not to make eye contact with her.

Steel stomped off to the window, blocking the view of Banff bay and the gently falling snow. 'Well?' If anything, she looked worse than she had yesterday. The penguin PJs were gone, replaced by a charcoal-grey suit and red silk shirt, but the bruises had darkened and spread. A pair of truly impressive black eyes sat either side of her bandaged nose, their edges fading to green and yellow. The bruise on her cheek was the colour of over-ripe plums.

She glared at them out of her one good eye, the other still swollen up like a pudding. 'Didn't think so. Well believe me: I'm no' forgetting and I'm no' forgiving this. I find out which one of you gave the *Sunday Examiner* an exclusive, I'll make sure you walk squint for a month. Understand?'

Someone cleared their throat.

Logan leaned back against the wall, keeping as still as possible. Every movement sent needles and knives jabbing through his back, ribs, and stomach.

More glowering from Steel. 'Now, who fancies a bollocking?' She raised a finger and pointed at the assembled officers one at a time: 'Eenie, meenie, miny, mo, catch a slacker by the toe.' The finger stopped with DS Robertson and his sideburns. 'You, Pop Larkin, where's my list of Milne and Shepherd's sexual conquests?'

Pink bloomed across the skin above that ridiculous facial hair. 'It's not as easy as you'd think. I'm trying to get names for all the faces, but—'

'THEN TRY HARDER!' Steel mashed her hand against the table, making everyone flinch. 'This is a murder investigation, not a game of sodding Cluedo. When I tell you to do something, you bloody well do it!'

The blush deepened. 'Yes, Guv.'

'Next! Which one of you idiots is meant to be hunting down the animals who attacked me and Buggerlugs McRae over there?'

There was a pause, then DS Weatherford raised her hand.

Suddenly, Steel was all sweetness and light. 'Ah, Donna. Good. Tell me, Donna, have you caught them yet?'

'Well…' She glanced around the room, but no one would look at her. 'Not as *such*, you see—'

'WHY THE BLOODY HELL NOT?'

Weatherford shrank back in her seat. 'There's no finger-prints! And we can't get DNA back till—'

'AAAARGH!' Steel bashed the table again. 'This is what I'm talking about. Every single one of you: it's not your fingers you need to get out, it's your whole buggering fist!'

Then Harper stood. 'Thank you, Chief Inspector.' She pointed at the actions written on the whiteboard. 'You all know what you've got to do, so go out there and do it. And try to keep your big mouths *shut* this time.'

Chairs scraped back and the MIT team scurried out, heads low, no doubt suitably motivated from being shouted at for the last ten minutes.

Logan waited till the door shut to sink into one of the

vacated chairs. Winced. The knives were out again. He hissed out a breath.

Steel stuck two fingers up at him. 'Don't start. You're getting no sympathy from me. Want to know what pain is? Try this on for size.' She hauled her shirt up, exposing her side. The paisley-pattern map of Russia she'd complained about yesterday was there in all its blue, green, and purple glory. It stood out bright and clear against the milk-bottle skin, disappearing under the line of a scarlet bra.

'God's sake, put it away.' He grimaced and turned his head away. 'Trying to make me lose my Weetabix?'

'Cheeky wee sod.'

Harper took her place at the head of the table. 'All right. I think that's quite enough banter. Let's focus on the problem at hand.' She sat back, steepling her fingers. 'How much damage does this cause us, Roberta?'

Steel sniffed, then picked up the *Sunday Examiner* again. Opened it out so the front page was on display. A big photo of Martin Milne stared out at them beneath the headline, 'MURDER SUSPECT "WORKING WITH POLICE" SAYS OFFICER'. She dumped it back on the table. 'No' exactly great news, is it?'

'Well, I suppose it would be naïve of us to think Malk the Knife wouldn't expect something like this. The question is: does it change anything? Logan?' The smile that accompanied his name was brittle, but at least it was there. Keeping it professional.

He pulled the paper closer.

'An anonymous source on the Major Investigation Team confirms that Martin Milne (30) is working with Police Scotland to identify the people responsible for last week's murder of his lover, Peterhead businessman Peter Shepherd (35). Mr Shepherd's body was discovered in woodland south of Banff...'

Well, if Milne was planning on keeping his relationship with Shepherd a secret, it was too late now.

327

Logan sucked on his teeth, staring at the picture. 'If I were Malcolm McLennan, and I knew the police were watching, there's no way I'd get Milne to smuggle things into the country for me now. Far too risky.'

'So our whole operation is ruined, because someone on the MIT can't keep their big mouth shut.'

'Assuming Malcolm McLennan had anything to do with it in the first place. He denied it at the funeral...' Frowning hurt, but Logan did it anyway. 'What if it's all a big distraction? Killing Peter Shepherd like that, leaving him lying about for people to find, it's a bit high profile, isn't it? We were *always* going to connect his body to McLennan. And then connect Shepherd to Milne. Maybe that's the idea?'

'True.' Harper stared at one of the room's windows.

Outside, the lights of Macduff were just visible through the pre-dawn gloom. Snow clung to the hill over there, pale blue and deep.

Steel prodded at the skin around her swollen eye. 'What about one of the other scummers? Black Angus MacDonald, or Ma Campbell?'

Logan tapped at the table with a fingertip. 'Could be. Campbell's got drugs in Macduff already, maybe this is her way of making sure we're all focusing our attention on McLennan instead of her? Make enough noise and the signal gets hidden.'

'Hmmm...' Harper kept her eyes on the window. 'What about the money Milne and Shepherd borrowed?'

'The only reason Milne thinks it came from Malcolm McLennan is because Shepherd told him it did. They could have been dealing with anybody and Milne wouldn't have known, would he? Plus it means the local mob believe *McLennan*'s the one moving in on their turf, not Jessica Campbell. Any retaliation's going to be aimed at Edinburgh, not Glasgow.'

A knock on the door, and Narveer poked his head in.

Today's turban was a greeny-blue tartan with yellow lines through it. 'Super? That's the Assistant Chief Constable on the phone for you.'

'Thank you, Narveer.' She stood. 'We can't afford to take our eye off Milne, but I agree it's possible this is all sleight of hand. Logan, I want you to look into the Ma Campbell angle. Get descriptions of anyone Milne met with and see if they match. See if we can turn down the noise a bit and let the signal come through.'

Logan nodded. 'Sir.'

'Good work. Now, if you'll excuse me, I have to go explain to our lords and masters why we haven't made any progress on this bloody case since Thursday.'

When Harper was gone, Steel sagged in her seat. 'So, are you two shagging yet?'

He stuck two fingers up at her. 'Did you have to rip a strip off Robertson and Weatherford in front of everyone? Poor sods are doing their best.'

'Come on, I saw her checking you out all through the briefing. Yesterday she thought you were a two-foot wide skidmark on the hand-towel of life, now she's throwing you meaningful glances like they're on buy-one-get-one-free.' Steel grinned. 'You shagged her, didn't you?'

'She's my *sister*. OK?'

'You shagged your sister? You're disgusting. Told Susan we shouldn't have got you that boxed set of *Game of Thrones*.'

He stood. 'You know what? I'm glad your ribs hurt. Serves you right.'

Snow-covered fields drifted by the car windows. Robbed of colour, everything looked dead beneath the grey sky.

'Ooh, I like this one.' Rennie took a hand off the steering wheel and turned the radio up. The sound of some insipid auto-tuned X-Factor-wannabe cover of a Marilyn Manson song glopped out of the speakers.

Logan reached forward from the back seat and flicked his

ear, at almost exactly the same time as Steel clouted him on the shoulder from the passenger seat.

'Ow!'

A glower from Steel. 'If you're thinking of singing along, I'm going to make sure it's falsetto, understand?'

'Philistines.' But he turned the radio down again.

A bright-orange Citroën Saxo lay on its back, half in the ditch at the side of the road and half in the field beyond, scattering a path through the drystane dyke in between. Its oversized spoiler lay six feet away, buckled and torn. A 'POLICE AWARE' sticker graced its upside-down rear window.

Rennie hooked a thumb at it. 'Had one of those when I was a boy racer. Mental car.'

'Why doesn't that surprise me?' Logan watched it slide past: big flared wheel arches, twin exhausts, and alloy rims.

It was the same, every winter. Most people drove like little old ladies at the first sign of snow, but the wee loons still screeched about as if nothing had changed.

Steel turned in her seat, grimacing. 'How come you never said you had a sister?'

'Didn't know till last night.' Logan unhooked his Airwave handset from its clip. Say what you like about having to cart about a heavy stabproof vest all day, but the Velcro straps and armoured panels supported his back and stopped it from moving too much. Which kept the sudden stabs of pain down to a minimum.

'Oh aye? And did you find out before or after you shagged her?'

'Grow up.' He punched the Duty Inspector's shoulder number into the handset and pressed the talk button. 'Bravo India, safe to talk?'

'A McRae always pays his debts.'

'Seriously, you can stop talking now. Your—'

A man's voice boomed from the Airwave's speaker. *'Go ahead, Logan.'*

'Guv, I need in on tonight's dunt again.'

Inspector Mhor sighed. *'Believe it or not, Sergeant, I didn't float into Fraserburgh on a half-buttered rowie.'*

'Guv?'

'Do you really think the dayshift Duty Inspector doesn't talk to the backshift one? Inspector McGregor and I go through the roster every day when I hand over to her, and that includes what's going on with her shift. I know you've been seconded to the MIT.'

'Yes, but—'

'No buts. Sergeant Ashton is running the raid on Ricky Welsh's house. What, did you think that I'd say yes when McGregor said no? I'm disappointed in you, Sergeant.'

The rising sun found a chink in the heavy lid of grey, sending blades of gold carving across the white fields.

'I'm not trying to play anyone off against anyone else, Guv. Detective Superintendent Harper wants me to look into Jessica Campbell's possible involvement in Peter Shepherd's death. The drugs at Ricky and Laura's are the only known link we have up here. So...?'

'And Harper's all right with this?'

'It was her idea.' OK, so that was stretching the truth a bit, but hey-ho.

Up ahead, Whitehills loomed in the distance. Its streetlights gave the place an unhealthy yellow glow.

Still nothing from Bravo India.

They were through the thirty limits before Inspector Mhor's voice came through the speaker again. *'Right. Logan, I'm prepared to put you in charge of the dunt again. But I want a big result from this one – it's costing us a fortune, so make it count.'*

'Will do. Thanks, Guv.'

He twisted his Airwave back into place. Finally *something* was going his way.

Rennie took a right before they got into Whitehills proper, heading down the hill towards Martin Milne's house.

Steel turned and squinted back at Logan again. 'You set that whole thing up, didn't you?'

'Don't know what you're talking about.'

'All that guff about only having Peter Shepherd's word for it – you just wanted your dunt back.'

'You heard Detective Superintendent Harper, she thought it was worth investigating.'

'You manipulative wee sod.' A smile twitched the corner of Steel's mouth. 'I've taught you well, young Grasshopper.'

A line of wire fencing appeared on the right, surrounding the suspended building work. It looked as if they weren't the only ones who'd read that morning's *Sunday Examiner*: the media blockade was back. Three outside broadcast vans and a dozen cars were parked on the part-finished road, trails of exhaust coiling out into the morning air. Some of the rustier cars had their passenger windows rolled down a crack, cigarette smoke joining the exhaust fumes.

Their occupants turned to stare at the pool car as it bumped through the potholes.

Rennie parked in front of Milne's house. 'Boss?'

'See if I catch the rancid wee turd who leaked that story?' Steel curled her lip and scowled through the windscreen. 'Where are they? Supposed to be babysitters minding the roost.'

No sign of a patrol car. No sign of DS McKenzie, *or* her minions.

Steel pulled out her phone and fiddled with the screen. Held the thing to her ear. 'Becky? ... Yeah, I'm great, thanks, bit sore, but can't complain. How are you? ... That's good. Becky, got a wee question for you: WHERE THE GOAT-BUGGERING HELL ARE YOU?'

Rennie flinched, both hands over his ears.

'No, you're not, and I know that because I'm sitting outside the house *right now*. ... Angry? Why would I be angry? Oh, wait a minute, now I remember – I TOLD YOU TO KEEP AN EYE ON MARTIN MILNE! ... Yes, I think you better, Sergeant, and when you get here we'll see how far my left boot will fit up your backside!'

Logan climbed out into the cold, then reached back in for his high-viz jacket.

'No excuses!' She glowered at him with her good eye. 'Door!' Then back to the phone. 'No' you, Becky, McRae's letting all the heat out. Where was I? Ah, right: WHAT THE HELL DO YOU—'

He thumped the door shut and marched up the driveway to the house.

Rennie scampered along behind, catching up as Logan leaned on the doorbell. He pulled out a little squeezed smile. 'How you doing? You know, with Samantha, and Superintendent Harper, and your dad, and everything?'

'Didn't know you cared.' Logan stepped back and peered through the frosted glass at the side of the door. No sign of life.

'No, I mean it. Can't imagine how hard that kinda thing must be.' The smile turned into a frown, then he patted Logan on the shoulder. 'I'm … you know?'

'Yeah. Thanks.'

'So what's it like suddenly having a wee sister?'

Logan leant on the bell again. 'Slightly less annoying than you.'

A grin. 'So, what's the plan?'

'You heard Steel: Malcolm McLennan's not going to make contact with this lot hanging about.' He pointed at the phalanx of cars. Some of the occupants were already out, cameras poised. 'Go check every single road tax, tyre, brake light, and anything else you can think of.'

The bottom lip protruded a half-inch. 'Why me? You're the one in uniform, surely you should be... Erm.'

Logan stared at him.

He cleared his throat. 'Right. OK.' Then turned and marched back down the drive again, intercepting the vanguard as they made it as far as the pavement outside the house. 'All right, ladies and gentlemen, I'm going to need to see your driver's licences.'

The door opened and a rumpled Katie Milne blinked out at Logan. 'Do you have any idea what time it is?' Her gaze slid over his shoulder and she sagged. 'Oh God, not them *again*. Why can't they leave us in peace?'

'Mrs Milne, I know it's early, but we need to have a word with your husband. There's a story in today's paper that you're probably going to want to discuss too.' Which was an understatement. Hey, your husband was having an affair with his business partner and as many women as they could talk into having a threesome with them.

Happy Sunday.

33

Martin Milne's eyes got wider and wider as he read the front page of the *Sunday Examiner*. His bottom lip wobbled when he turned the page and saw the rest of it. 'Oh God...'

They'd left the curtains shut in the living room, so the press couldn't leer in through the windows. A pair of standard lamps cast a cheery glow on the ceiling completely out of keeping with the horrified expression on Milne's face.

'How did... Who? It's...' He lowered the newspaper, then jerked up in his seat – turning to face the closed door. 'Has Katie seen this?'

'No' yet, no.' Steel winced her way down onto the couch, hissing like a deflating balloon. 'But it's only a matter of time.'

'But I *trusted* you!' He grabbed his head with both hands, forcing the hair back from his face. 'How could... Oh God...'

Logan took the newspaper back and folded it, hiding the offending front page. 'We'll find out who spoke to the journalist and we'll make sure they're properly punished. If you want to make a formal complaint we have guidelines to help you through the process. Here.' He reached into a pocket of his stabproof vest and pulled out a leaflet. Handed it over.

'What's my wife going to say? What's Katie going to think when she finds out?'

Steel pursed her lips. 'My guess? She'll no' be too happy about you shagging a bloke. Doubt she'll be too keen on the other women either.'

He crumpled the leaflet. 'This is all your fault!'

'Aye, with all due respect, Martyboy, I'm no' the one who forced you into bed with Peter Shepherd and half the slappers between here and Ellon. That was all you.'

'Oh God.'

Logan took out his notebook. 'Can you describe the people who gave you and Peter the loan?'

Milne glared up at him. 'Are you *insane*? I'm not helping you any more. I trusted the police and you told a newspaper who I was sleeping with! Private, personal details.'

A sigh. Then Logan lowered himself onto the edge of the couch, the stabproof vest making sure he sat bolt upright. 'I'm sorry, Martin, but you can't back out of this now.'

'I want you out of my house.'

'Let's say you don't cooperate with our investigation. Do you think Malcolm McLennan will forget about the two hundred and twenty-five *thousand* pounds you owe him? No, he'll make you smuggle things into the area for him whether you like it or not. And we'll be watching you.'

'I don't—'

'Sooner or later we're going to catch you bringing in a boatload of drugs – or counterfeit goods, or weapons, or illegal immigrants – and we're going to arrest you and put you away for sixteen to twenty years. And Malcolm McLennan isn't going to be very pleased about losing a shipment, is he? He'll be even less pleased when you try to cut a deal to get out of prison before you're fifty.'

Milne bit his bottom lip and stared down at his hands.

'Or maybe you'll refuse to smuggle anything for him, because you know we're watching you. He won't like that either; all that money you owe. What do you think the chances are of you being found in the not too distant, battered to death, naked, with a bag over your head?'

Milne's voice was barely audible. 'Why can't you just leave me alone?'

Steel shook her head. 'Never going to happen, Martyboy. That ship sailed soon as you fessed up in the cells. You help us, or you're screwed.' She gave him a big grin. 'Now, any chance of a cuppa? I'm parched.'

The little boy sat at the kitchen table, wearing thick socks and fleecy pyjamas with dinosaurs on them. A graze sat on his left cheek, about the size of a walnut, the skin scabby and brown as it healed. His face was creased with sleep and his blond hair stood out at all angles, so the resemblance was uncanny when Steel sat down next to him and pushed a piece of jam-smeared toast and a big glass of milk in front of him.

'There you go, Ethan. You eat that up like a good wee boy.'

He turned his head to the door.

Muffled shouting filtered through from the living room. Not clear enough to make out actual words, but the tone obvious. Katie Milne wasn't pleased about her husband's extramarital activities.

Logan tucked his phone between his shoulder and his ear as he rinsed out his mug and placed it on the draining board. 'We've got descriptions of three I-C-One males, two in their late twenties, one early forties. Couple of distinguishing features we can run past the National Crime Agency, see if we can't get a match.'

'*Good.*' Rustling came from the speaker, as if Harper was rummaging through a pile of paper. '*What about names?*'

'No luck. Milne says they always referred to each other by number: One, Two, and Three. "One" was the older guy.'

'*Hmmmm... So definitely organized. How did Milne take the article in the paper?*'

The sound of something smashing against the wall made Ethan flinch, toast halfway to his mouth.

'He and his wife are discussing it now.'

'*Logan?*'

'Yes, sir?'

'*I appreciate you keeping our relationship professional at work – I know a lot of people would have a problem with taking orders from their little sister – but when we're off duty you can call me Niamh. OK?*'

'OK.'

'*Good. Right. Well, get cracking with the IDs and we'll see if your theory pans out.*' The line went dead.

His little sister. Yeah, that still sounded weird.

He put his phone away. 'Time to head.'

Steel held up a finger. 'Just a minute.' Then she scooted around in her chair, until she was facing the wee boy. 'Ethan? Can you tell your Aunty Roberta what happened to your face?' She pointed at her own cheek, mirroring the scabby patch.

The little boy shrugged, then stared at his toast. 'Fell down.' His voice was tiny, barely more than a whisper.

'Where did you fall down?'

'Outside.' He picked at his toast. 'Some boys pushed me.'

'Wee shites.' Steel sighed, then popped a couple of pills from a blister pack, washing them down with a scoof of Ethan's milk. She levered herself to her feet. 'Right, wee man, we're off. Make sure you look after your mum. Can you do that for your Aunty Roberta?'

The six-year-old lowered his eyebrows, pursed his lips and nodded.

'Good boy.'

Out in the corridor, the sound of fighting was much clearer.

'*HOW COULD YOU? YOU FILTHY, DIRTY, PERVERTED—*'

'*Now you just sound homophobic.*'

'*HOMOPHOBIC? I'LL GIVE YOU HOMOPHOBIC, YOU CHEATING BASTARD!*'

'*OW! Don't—*'

Something smashed.

Logan nodded at the living room door. 'Think we should break it up?'

'Nah.' Steel hoiked up her suit trousers. 'Do them good to let off a bit of steam before she chucks him out of the house. Besides, I'm starving – time for second breakfast.'

'*I HATE YOU!*'

They slipped out and shut the front door behind them.

'Ooh, bleeding hell.' Steel wrapped her arms around herself and shivered. Then narrowed her eyes.

A patrol car had pulled up at the back of the press pack. Two faces blinked out through the windscreen, one with curly brown hair, the other grey. DS McKenzie and DC Owen.

Steel produced her phone. Listened to it ring with a big smile plastered across her face.

In the patrol car, McKenzie flinched, then took out her own mobile.

'Becky. Sweetheart. Can you guess what I'm thinking? ... That's right. ... No, I don't think so. I think I'll aim for right up to the knee. ... That's right.'

McKenzie's face drooped.

'Aye, you better believe it. But as all these lovely members of the press are watching, I'm going to give your lazy wee bumhole a temporary reprieve. Milne's getting chucked out of the family home and you're sticking to him like sick on a ballgown. ... Because I don't want Milne disappearing, suitcase in hand, *that's* why. Probably going to crash at a friend's house, but in case he fancies hopping a flight to Rio, you're watching him.'

In the car, McKenzie folded forward and rested her head on the dashboard.

'And while you're at it, get onto DS Robertson – tell him to get his comedy-sideburn-wearing arse down here and babysit the wife and kid. Now did you get all that, or do I have to tattoo it on your lower intestine with my size nines? ... Good girl.' Steel hung up. 'Right, where's the Boy Blunder?'

Logan pointed.

The media encampment didn't look too happy. A lot of them stood about with faces like a spanked backside, glowering as Rennie squatted down beside an ancient Volvo estate and poked at its tyres.

Steel made a loudhailer from her hands. 'HOY! CAPTAIN KWIK-FIT, WE'RE LEAVING!'

'What hacks me off is how she lied all those years.' Logan leaned forward, poking his head between the front seats. 'How could anyone be so self-centred, so *awful* a human being, that they thought it was OK to make two wee boys think their dad was dead?'

Snow drifted down, melting as it hit the pool car's windscreen.

Steel tucked her hands into her armpits. 'What's keeping Rennie? Can he no' see I'm wasting away here?'

An old man hobbled out of the Tesco, humping two hessian bags in one hand, working a walking stick with the other.

'Thirty-four years and not so much as a word.'

'Bet he comes back with the wrong grub.'

'There was a headstone and everything! Right there in the graveyard with his name, date of birth and death carved on it. How sick would you have to be to get a headstone made?'

'Should've sent you instead. Rennie'll be back with a pair of tights, a grapefruit, and a pack of ice lollies.'

'Then drag your two kids to lay flowers in front of it every year? She faked his *grave*!'

Steel puffed out her cheeks. 'Yes, your mother's a heartless, vindictive, nasty, complete-and-total swivel-eyed loony, we get it. Now where's my pies?'

'Thanks. Your support means a lot to me. I've just found out the father I thought was dead since I was five *wasn't*. Oh and he had another family that apparently was nice enough not to abandon. And while we're at it, he died two months ago.'

'You lost a dad you thought was dead anyway, and gained a sister. By my reckoning, you're ahead on the deal.'

340

'Ahead? What's wrong with you?'

She shrugged. 'Might be the pills. Or, it might be you being a whiny little bitch. How many years have you been on the job? All you had to do was look your dad up on the system. You didn't bother.'

'I thought he was dead. Why would I look him up?'

'Oh, I don't know. Because he was your *dad*?'

Logan sat back, folded his arms and stared out of the window. 'You're a lot of help.'

A sigh. 'Laz, it's no' my fault you've got a pineapple wedged up your bum. This thing with Samantha, it was only two days ago. That takes some getting over. You need some time off. Go away for a bit.'

'And who's supposed to catch Peter Shepherd's killer?'

Steel stared at the ceiling. 'Such a martyr.'

'I am *not* a martyr.'

'Yeah, because the whole MIT, the entire might of B and A Divisions – they can't solve a murder. Only the *great* Sergeant Logan McRae can do that.'

Outside, the snow fell.

A couple walked past, arm in arm. Couldn't have been more than thirteen or fourteen years old. Young and in love. They'd learn soon enough.

Steel took out her fake cigarette and popped it in her mouth. 'Take some time off.'

'I went to see Jack Wallace yesterday.'

She blew a puff of steam at the windscreen, turning it opaque. 'Oh aye?'

'Sends his love.'

'Good. Hope he's getting *lots* of love himself. Aye, from some big hairy bloke giving him fourteen-inches of non-consensual prison-issue-sausage after lights out.' Another puff. 'Couldn't happen to a more deserving arsehole.'

Rennie bustled out of the Tesco, clutching an armful of something.

'About time.' One more puff, then Steel put her e-cigarette

away. She kept her voice light and neutral. 'Any reason you felt the need to go see our friendly neighbourhood kiddy-fiddler, Laz?'

Rennie hurried across the street, high-stepping through the snow.

'Believe it or not, I was looking out for you.'

Her voice didn't change. 'Were you now?'

The driver's door opened and Rennie climbed in behind the wheel. 'Holy Mother of the Sainted Aardvark, it's cold out there.' He handed his armful to Steel, then stuck the keys in the ignition. The engine roared into life, heaters howling lukewarm air into the space, spreading the crackling scent of hot pastry. 'Brrrrrr…'

''Ello, 'ello, 'ello, what's all this then?' She pulled a package from the bag. 'Hot Cornish pasties? Well, DS Rennie, looks like you just became my favourite sergeanty type. Sorry, Laz. No hard feelings.'

Yeah, right.

'OK, thanks anyway.' Logan hung up the desk phone and frowned at the computer screen. Then hit print.

The Sergeants' Office seemed to have become the dumping ground for a collection of blue plastic crates that smelled vaguely of fish.

Logan picked up his empty mug and headed out into the main office.

No one there. The blinds were open: snow drifted down from a coal-coloured sky, the waters of the bay had receded, leaving a dark curve of wet sand behind.

A grinding whirring noise burst from the big photocopier/printer and two dozen sheets of A4 clicked and whined into the tray. He left them there and went to make a cup of tea.

The TV was on with the sound turned down to a murmur. A balding Italian chef smeared fillets of white fish with a snot-coloured paste then wrapped them in ham.

Logan chucked a teabag in his mug and stuck the kettle on.

Someone had obviously decided that the station's resident gnome wasn't classy enough and given him a bright-blue bowtie. They'd replaced his paper dagger with a magic wand and—

'Can I not get *two* minutes peace?' Logan pulled out his ringing phone. 'McRae?'

'Is this Sergeant Logan McRae?'

Why did nobody ever listen? 'Can I help you?'

'It's Detective Inspector Bell.'

A smile cracked its way across Logan's face. 'Ding-Dong, it's been years. How's CID treating you?'

'You own a static caravan, don't you: 23 Persley Park Caravan Park, Aberdeen?'

Oh God. The smile died. They'd found Eddy Knowles's body.

Barbed wire wrapped itself around Logan's chest, tightening and tightening until there was barely any breath left.

He was screwed.

'Logan? Are you there?'

He cleared his throat. Stood up straight. 'That's my caravan.'

Here it came.

Hand yourself in to the nearest police station where you'll be detained on charges of murder and attempting to pervert the course of justice by illegally disposing of a body.

'I've got some bad news, the fire brigade did what they could, but by the time they got there… I'm sorry.'

'Fire brigade?' The barbed wire snapped and air rushed into his lungs.

'The fire investigation team are looking through what's left, but it's pretty much burned to the ground. At least no one was hurt, right?'

'Was it… Did someone…?'

'Officially, I can't say – ongoing investigation – but off the record? Apparently there's traces of an accelerant. Looks like it was torched on purpose.'

'Christ.'

So that was that. His whole life with Samantha had been consumed by flames. First his flat, now her caravan. There was nothing left but her body.

'You know I've got to ask this: can you confirm your whereabouts last night, Sergeant McRae?'

Logan blinked at the TV, a wee bloke with curly hair was turning a little bird in a frying pan. 'Home. I was at home. In Banff.'

'And can anyone corroborate that?'

'Three police constables and a detective superintendent. We had beer and sausages.'

'Yeah, as alibis go that's a pretty good one. I'll let you know if anything comes up this end, but in the meantime I'll text you the crime number and you can get on to your insurers.'

Logan puffed out a breath. 'Yes. Thanks, Ding-Dong.'

He hung up.

They hadn't found Eddy's body. Urquhart hadn't screwed him over.

Thank Christ.

'Any chance of a coffee?' Inspector Mhor sidled into the room, hands in the pockets of his black police-issue trousers. The canteen lights sparkled off the big polished dome of his head. With the two small ears, small mouth, button nose, and hairy eyebrows, he looked a bit like a surprised egg.

Logan swallowed. Nodded. 'Guv.'

'You OK?'

'Sorry. One of those days.' He pulled another mug from the cupboard.

Mhor leaned against the wall. 'How's preparation for the dunt coming?'

'Good, thanks: we're going in at half-eleven tonight. As long as everyone turns up on time.'

'Have you told Beaky she doesn't have to come in early?'

'Next on my list, Guv.' She wasn't going to be pleased, but tough. At least she'd get a lie-in. 'Soon as I've spoken to Detective Superintendent Harper.'

The kettle juddered and rattled, then fell silent.

'Logan, I want you leading from the rear on this one, understand? You look like someone tied you to a washing machine then threw you down an escalator. Battered police officers don't fill the public with confidence.'

'Guv.' Coffee, sugar, hot water. He handed the mug over.

'Cheers. And for God's sake do something about the Response Level warning, will you? Someone's changed it to "Dalek Attack Imminent". Nightshift are a law unto themselves.' Mhor took a sip, grimaced, shuddered, then turned and sidled off. 'Urgh. Like licking the underside of a broken-down bus...'

34

Logan swapped the warning of Dalek attack for a more traditional 'NORMAL', then headed upstairs with his pile of printouts.

DS Weatherford bustled past on the landing, clutching a file box, grey fringe stuck to her shiny forehead. 'I'm doing it, I'm doing it.'

He watched her go. 'I didn't say anything!'

'Aaaargh...'

A happy workforce was a *productive* workforce.

Harper was on the top floor with her sidekick, the pair of them sitting side-by-side at the conference room table poking away at laptop computers.

'Sir?'

She looked up. 'Sergeant McRae.' Her voice had all the warmth of a mortuary cadaver. 'What have you got for us?'

Fine. If that was the way she wanted to play it – he could do cold and professional too.

Logan held up the printouts. 'No direct matches, *sir*, but they've sent me every near miss in the whole UK. I'll get Milne to go through the photos, see if he recognizes anyone.'

Narveer held out his hand. 'Let's have a squint then.'

He passed them over and the Inspector flicked through them.

'I understand you're organizing a drugs raid for tonight, Sergeant.'

Logan nodded. 'Ricky and Laura Welsh. Word on the street is they're acting as agents for Jessica "Ma" Campbell. She's trying to move in on Hamish Mowat's old territory. If we can get our hands on one of Campbell's representatives it might help with the Shepherd case.' Well, assuming it wasn't the guy Reuben sent back to Glasgow with his hands in a Jiffy bag.

Narveer poked a finger at a picture of a young man on the printout. 'Big Willie Brodie. I did him for assault and possession with intent – what, eight years ago? God, doesn't time fly?'

'And you didn't tell me about this in advance, because…?'

'Didn't I?' Logan hooked a thumb over his shoulder. 'The operation's been planned since Wednesday. We were going in long before we knew there was any connection with Peter Shepherd's murder and—'

'*Possible* connection.'

'Has to be worth a go, doesn't it?'

Narveer laughed and poked another picture. 'Crowbar Gibson! Thought he was dead.'

Harper pursed her lips and frowned at Logan. 'I think it's probably best if Detective Inspector Singh and I accompany you on this raid.'

Sod.

'Of course, sir.'

'Now is there anything else?'

'No, sir.'

'Sergeant?' Narveer pulled his chin in, then held up the last sheet of the pile. 'Before you head off, are we *really* worried about Daleks attacking Banff?'

Inspector Mhor was right, the nightshift had a lot to answer for.

'*You scheming, underhand, lowlife, son of a rancid—*'

'Oh come off it, Beaky, it was never your dunt in the first

347

place.' Logan slipped in behind the wheel of his rusty Punto. It was like sitting down in a fridge. 'Tell you what, you want it? You can have it.' He turned the key and whacked the heater up to full.

'*Really?*' Suspicion dripped from her voice. '*Why? What's wrong with it?*'

'Nothing. It's *all* yours.'

'*Laz, I'm warning you.*'

A sliver of clear glass appeared at the bottom of the windshield, creeping upwards with glacial slowness.

'There's nothing wrong. Oh, and good news: Detective Superintendent Harper will be tagging along, and so will her sidekick DI Singh. Kick-off's at half-eleven. Make sure you wear warm socks.'

'*Seriously? I've got to do a dunt with a superintendent and a DI breathing down my neck?*'

'Don't forget the Chief Inspector from Elgin doing his "down with the common man" thing.'

'*Gah… It'll be a cluster-hump of credit-stealing egomaniacs, all pulling rank on each other. You know what? I've changed my mind. You can keep it.*' She hung up.

'Thanks a heap.'

The blowers were still churning away at the fog and ice. Going to take a while.

Of course what he *should* be doing was sorting out the insurance on the caravan. He let his head fall back against the rest and glowered up at the Punto's ceiling. Yes, because *that* wasn't going to look suspicious, was it?

Oh, Mr McRae, I see you became the legal owner of the static caravan when you switched off your girlfriend's life support. And two days later you're making an insurance claim because it's burned to the ground. Hmm…

No doubt about it, this was turning out to be a *spectacular* year.

Hadn't even got the damn thing on the market before someone torched the place.

The question was: who set the fire? Which one of Reuben's minions?

Well he didn't need a team of fire investigators to find out. Logan poked John Urquhart's number into his phone and waited for him to pick up.

'Yello?'

'Who burned down my caravan?'

'Mr McRae? Dude. How you feeling today?'

'Which one of Reuben's little helpers did it? I want a name.'

'That was a serious bash on the head you got.'

'Give me a sodding name!'

Silence from the other end of the phone.

The clear glass inched higher.

'It wasn't Reuben who did it, it was me.'

'It was *you*? What the bloody hell did you—'

'Thought you'd be pleased! The caravan was spattered with blood: yours and Eddy's. DNA everywhere, signs of a struggle... Now there's no forensic evidence tying you to anything. You said all that stuff was going to the charity shop or the tip anyway, so I torched the lot.'

'Ah.'

'Doesn't matter how hard they look, no one can put you and Eddy together in the same place. He's gone, the snowglobe's gone, the crime scene's gone. You're in the clear.'

If only it was that easy.

Wind rattled the hotel room window, hurling clumps of sleet against the glass.

Martin Milne sat on the end of the single bed with his head in his hands.

A small, drab hotel room in a small, drab hotel, with views out over the churning sea. Just the place if you wanted to gear yourself up for a suicide attempt. Which, going by the state of Milne, was a distinct possibility.

His voice wasn't much more than a whisper. 'She threw me out.'

Now there was a shock.

Logan pulled the printouts from his jacket pocket. 'I need you to look at some faces for me, Martin. See if any of them are the men you spoke to about the loan.'

'Said I was poisonous.' Milne took the photos. Frowned.

'We need to find these people, Martin. It's important.'

'I'll never get to see Ethan again. He's my world...'

Yeah right. If Milne was that concerned about his son he wouldn't have been running away to Dubai with Peter Shepherd. Abandoning the poor wee sod to grow up without a father. Made you sick.

Logan folded his arms. 'Martin? Where were you? After they killed Peter Shepherd, where did you go?'

He moved on to the next photograph. 'Where did I go?'

'You went missing for four days. Everyone was worried about you. *Katie* was worried about you.'

'She's never going take me back, is she?'

Of course she wasn't.

'Give her time.'

A nod. 'After...' He bit his lip. Sniffed. 'I hid in the woods the first night. Too scared to sleep in case they came back. Next day it poured rain, I walked and walked and walked.' Milne frowned. 'An old man gave me a lift to Turriff in his van. Got myself a B-and-B and stayed in my room with the curtains shut.' His chin came up. 'And then I realized how selfish I was being. I had to go home and protect my family. Protect my son.' The chin dropped again. 'How am I supposed to protect him if she won't let me in the house?'

Logan put a hand on his shoulder. Tried for a consoling smile. 'Katie's angry. Probably feels betrayed, lied to, used. It'll take her a while to get past that.'

A nod.

'You want to keep Ethan safe, don't you?'

Another nod.

'So look at the pictures and see if you recognize the men you and Peter spoke to.'

Milne took the printouts and frowned at the faces. Took his time.

Muffled voices came through the wall from the room next door, followed by the jingly sound of a cartoon on the TV.

Out in the corridor, someone marched past.

Milne pointed at one of the pictures. 'This kind of looks like the guy they called Three.'

'Anyone else?'

He shook his head. 'Wasn't really paying attention when I met them.' A small laugh burst free, strangled and ragged. 'Pete and me had been talking all morning about running off to Dubai together. They're not keen on … you know, men being together, but Pete said we could make it work. If we were discreet. And the money was *great*.'

Logan stared at him. 'And what about Ethan? While you're off earning heaps of cash in Dubai, what happens to your son?'

Milne picked at the bedspread, keeping his eyes on his fingers. 'We were going to take him with us.'

Aye, right.

'There were only *two* visas, Martin.'

'I got a ninety-day one for him online. See if he liked living with us in Dubai before making it permanent…' A shrug. 'Don't suppose it matters now.'

Logan took the printouts back and drew a number three on the photo Milne had chosen. The man in the picture had swept-back brown hair and a proper soup-strainer moustache. As if he were channelling an Eighties porn-star.

Milne wiped at his eyes. 'Don't suppose *anything* matters now.'

Becky was waiting for Logan as he stepped back into the corridor. 'McRae.'

He closed the door to Milne's hotel room. 'DS McKenzie.'

She jerked her chin towards the exit. '*She* out there, is she?'

'What, Steel? No.' He tucked the folder of mugshots under his arm. 'Look, whatever the pair of you are fighting about, it's got nothing to do with me. I just go where I'm told.'

'Scrotum-faced old cow.' Becky folded her arms. 'All she does is shout and whinge and make sarcastic comments.'

'Yup.'

'You know she screwed up the overtime log for January? The *whole* month. Again. How am I supposed to put two kids through university and pay the bloody mortgage if she keeps screwing up the overtime?'

Logan held a hand up. 'Preaching to the choir. You want some advice?'

'No.'

'Fine.' He turned and walked to the exit. Got as far as the door before Becky thundered down the corridor after him.

She grabbed him by the arm. 'OK, what?'

'Steel can't be arsed doing the paperwork, so she makes a mess of it till someone steps in and does it for her. You want your overtime paid? You're going to have to take one for the team, or talk someone else into it.'

Becky's face crumpled. 'But it's *her* job!'

'I did it for nine years. Tell me about it.' He pushed through into the hotel reception, a bland beige space with dying pot plants and an ugly carpet.

'I hate being a police officer!'

Join the club.

Sleet spattered the windscreen. A couple of people hurried by the car, heads down, shoulders up, teeth bared. They didn't look at the funeral home.

Logan propped the printout up against the steering wheel. 'According to the National Crime Agency, it's one Adrian Brown, AKA: Brian Jones, AKA: Tim Donovan.'

'*Hold on.*' Harper made rustling noises down the phone. '*Right, got him. Adrian Brown; thirty-two; five nine; form for assault, assault, theft, more assault, and to keep things interesting – assault.*'

A light came on inside Beaton and Macbeth.

'Sounds lovely, doesn't he?'

'He's meant to be with the Manchester Goon Squad, what's he doing all the way up here?'

'Might not be. Milne said it "kind of looked like" Number Three, so not a hundred percent on the ID.'

'Hmmm... And how is our sacrificial goat?'

'Milne? Wallowing in a great big tub of self-pity.'

'Serves him right.'

She had a point. Milne was all set to abandon his wife and run off with someone else to a land faraway. And there was no way Katie would have let him take Ethan. No, that was probably going to be a midnight flit to the airport and off to Dubai before she woke up.

Still, at least Ethan would've *had* a father, growing up.

Yeah. Well.

Logan cleared his throat. 'Anything else, sir?'

'Did you make it clear what would happen to him if he didn't cooperate? If Malk the Knife, or Ma Campbell, gets in touch and he doesn't tell us, I'll make damn sure he goes down for a long time.'

'He's already cracking under the pressure. Push him too far and he'll break.'

'Don't try to teach your little sister how to suck eggs, Sergeant. This isn't my first organized crime op. I need results, not excuses.'

'Sir.'

And she was gone.

Were sisters always this much of a pain in the backside?

He folded the printouts and stuffed them in his pocket, along with his mobile phone, then dug into the glove compartment for the Jiffy bag. Took a deep breath, scrambled out of the car, and made a run for the funeral home.

Andy was waiting for him with the front door open. 'Mr McRae.' His black suit was immaculate, the shirt so white you could have used it in a washing powder advert. He stuck his hand out and Logan shook it.

'Thanks for opening up, Andy. I appreciate it.'

A small shake of the head. 'Nonsense. It's no trouble at all.' As if he usually wore a suit on a Sunday, on the off chance. 'If you'd like to follow me?' He led the way through the reception area to a gloomy room with a single spotlight.

It glowed down on an open casket – polished black wood with a red silk lining.

Something lodged in Logan's throat, as if he'd tried to swallow a stone.

Samantha was laid out, on her back, hands folded over her stomach. They'd dressed her in all her finery, the leather corset, the skirt, the gloves.

He stepped closer.

Her head looked strange. Unfamiliar. As if... He reached out and stroked her forehead, where the dent should have been. 'You fixed it.'

'We wanted to do you proud, Mr McRae.'

'She's beautiful.' Just like she was in the photo from Rennie's wedding. Make-up perfect: warpaint and piercings. They'd even managed to make her skin look like living flesh again. Samantha's tattoos stood out bright and clear, as if they were brand new.

'Would you like a moment?'

'Please.'

'I'll be right outside if you need anything.' Andy turned and glided from the room, as if he was mounted on silent castors.

Logan pulled on a smile. 'Alone at last.'

No reply.

He held up the Jiffy bag. 'Present for you.' He dug out the hardback copy of Stephen King's *The Stand* and tucked it into the coffin beside her. 'Got it online. It's signed.'

He stood there. Shuffled his feet. Put a hand on her bare shoulder, then flinched that hand away. Samantha's skin was cold to the touch.

Well of course it was. She might look like she was asleep, but that didn't mean Andy hadn't taken her body from the mortuary fridge while Logan was on the phone in the car park outside.

Not sleeping, just dead.

'Sarge?'

Logan looked up from his computer. Blinked a couple of times. 'Rennie.'

Rennie crept into the Sergeants' Office, carrying two mugs of tea and a manila folder. 'Tea.' He put the mugs down on the desk, then checked over his shoulder before handing Logan the folder. As if they were spies meeting up in a car park to swap state secrets.

OK.

'You don't have to call me "Sarge", we're the same rank.'

'Force of habit.' Rennie settled into the seat opposite. Grinned. 'Go on then, open it.'

Logan did. Inside were a wodge of printouts and a gold-and-red packet about the size of an old-fashioned video cassette. He raised an eyebrow. 'That what I think it is?'

'Oh yes.'

'Close the door.'

While Rennie was hiding them from the prying eyes of the outside world, Logan ripped his way into the Tunnock's tasty caramel wafers. Tossed one onto the other side of the desk and helped himself to another. 'To what do we owe the honour?'

'She Who Must Be Feared And Obeyed. Says when we're done with tea and treats we're to sod off and grab some snooze-time.' Rennie unwrapped his chocolate wafer and took a big bite, getting little flecks of brown all down his chin. 'Make sure we're all rested and ready for tonight.'

The wafer turned to blotting paper in Logan's mouth. 'Tonight?'

'The drugs raid?'

'Oh God.' Logan curled forward and thunked his forehead on the desk.

'What?'

Perfect, because having Harper and her sidekick tag along wasn't bad enough.

Thunk.

'What's, "Oh God"?'

He left his head against the cool wooden surface. 'You and Steel want in on my drugs raid.'

'Yeah, well, you know. If it proves important to the investigation into Peter Shepherd's death, Steel wants—'

'To muscle in on any credit going.'

'I wouldn't exactly put it that—'

'She's out of luck. You can inform Her Royal Scruffiness that I've already got Detective Superintendent Harper, Detective Inspector Singh, and a Chief Inspector from Elgin on board. There's going to be more top brass on this dunt than *actual* police officers.' He straightened up. 'I should've let Beaky have it.' Logan frowned. 'Wonder if it's too late?'

Rennie tore another chunk off his wafer. 'It'll be like old times. You, me, and the Holy Wrinkled Terror – on the path of truth and justice. Kicking in doors and taking names.'

Thunk.

'What? Why are you banging your head off the desk?'

Thunk. Thunk. Thunk.

35

'*...after the news. But first it's nine o'clock and things are hotting up on* Britain's Next Big Star *as Jacinta and Benjamin face sudden death—*'

Logan killed the telly and swigged back the last dregs of his tea. 'Right, you little monster – Daddy has to go dunt in someone's door.' He scooped Cthulhu off the sofa and turned her upside down. Gave her a kiss on her soft white tummy. 'Whose daddy loves her? Is it you? Yes it is, *your* daddy loves— Not again.'

Cthulhu wriggled free as his phone blared out its anonymous ringtone. She jumped to the floor, all four feet making a loud *thump* as she touched down. About as graceful as a dropped microwave.

He pulled out his phone. 'McRae.'

A sharp, loud voice stabbed into his ear. '*How dare you call and leave abusive messages on my phone, Logan Balmoral McRae! I am your* mother *and you will not—*'

He hung up. Then brought up his call history and blocked her number. Glowered at the screen for a bit.

Sod her.

Logan hauled his stabproof vest on over his police-issue fleece, got into his equipment belt, and topped the lot with his high-viz jacket. What every sharply dressed man about town was wearing this season. On with the hat, then out into the driving sleet.

His phone went again as he hurried across the car park. Tough.

Logan pushed his way through the tradesman's entrance and into the warmth of the station. Stamped his feet free of gritty grey snow.

Laughter boomed out into the corridor from the canteen. *'Come on then, what did you do?'*

'Only thing I could – threw up on it.'

More laughter.

He kept going, through into the main office. No one around. And with any luck it would stay that way till everything was sorted.

Logan slipped off his jacket and stepped into the Sergeants' Office. Stopped. Tried *really* hard not to swear.

Harper was sitting in his seat, an open file on the desk in front of her. 'Sergeant.'

'Sir.'

She pointed. 'You're supposed to leave your equipment in the locker room. Officers are *not* authorized to take police property home with them. Especially not extendable batons and CS gas!'

Logan hung his jacket up, leaving it to drip on the carpet tiles. 'And it's lovely to see you too, Niamh.'

'Don't you dare *Niamh* me, Sergeant, you're—'

'One: my shift doesn't start for another fifty minutes, so I'm not on duty. You asked me to call you Niamh when I'm not on duty. Two: the Sergeant's Hoose belongs to Police Scotland, so my equipment belt has remained on police property since I left here at five. And three: I *do* have permission. Check with Inspector McGregor.' He scritched off his stabproof vest. 'Now, is there anything else I can help you with?'

'Hmmm...' Harper pursed her lips and swivelled left and

358

right in his seat for a moment. 'Is everything organized for the operation this evening?'

'Why do you think I came in early?'

The Operational Support Unit van rocked on its springs as another gust of wind punched it in the ribs. Every seat in the van was taken – Tufty, Calamity, Isla at the back; the three officers from Elgin and their Chief Inspector in the middle, the four-man OSU team in the front, which barely left standing room for Harper, Narveer, Steel, Rennie, Logan, and the Police Dog Officer. Which was a shame, because she absolutely *reeked* of wet dog and it was impossible to get away from the smell.

Everyone in the van was dressed in full armoured ninja black – with kneepads, gauntlets, and elbow guards. Well, everyone except Harper and Steel, who looked as if they'd just crashed a very strange fancy-dress party.

Five minutes and it was already getting muggy in here, thick with the smell of stale clothes, damp dog, and warm bodies. The windows fogging up.

Logan pulled out his plastic folder of paperwork and held it up. 'One last time.'

A groan from one of the Elgin contingent.

'I don't care if you've heard it before, you're hearing it again. Ricky and Laura Welsh have form for violence, so watch yourself. They're unlikely to have firearms, but their Saint Bernard makes Cujo look like Basil Brush – anyone who doesn't have their Bite Back with them will *not* be allowed in that house until the dog's been made safe. Am I clear?'

A smattering of, 'Yes, Sarge.'

'Good. Sergeant Mitchell, you're up.'

The huge figure sitting in the passenger seat pulled his helmet on. It grazed the van's ceiling – he was that big. '*Mesdames et Messieurs*, grab your bonce protectors and gird your loins. In the immortal words of the Bard: *il est temps*

359

de mettre sur le maquillage, il est temps d'allumer les lumières!'

The other three members of his team gave a synchronized bark of 'Hooah!' and fastened their helmets.

Logan cracked open the van's side door. 'You heard the man.' He backed out onto the sleety road as everyone did what they were told.

Well, everyone except Steel and Harper. And Narveer, but then there was no way he'd get a crash helmet on over his turban.

The smell of soggy canine got worse for a moment as the Police Dog Officer picked her way past, heading for the other van and its contingent of Alsatians and Labradors.

Steel and Harper joined Logan out on the road.

'You're no' serious about that Saint Bernard, are you?' Steel's words billowed out on a cloud of fog, turned a pale yellow by the streetlights.

'Thing's massive. Looks like someone crossed a velociraptor with a highland cow.' He fastened on his own helmet – pulling the chinstrap tight – unlocked the Big Car, and slipped behind the wheel.

Steel stuck her hand up. 'Shotgun!' Then scrambled into the passenger side, leaving Harper with the back seat.

Soon as she climbed in, Logan clicked the button on his Airwave. 'Shire Uniform...' Ah, no he wasn't. Stubby was duty sergeant for as long as he was seconded to the MIT. 'Sorry, force of habit. Sergeant McRae to Sergeant Mitchell. Operation Kermit is on.'

'Roger that, we're rolling.'

The OSU van pulled away from the kerb and turned left at the end of the street. After a couple of beats, the dog van followed it.

Logan pulled on his thick leather gloves.

Harper leaned forward and poked him on the shoulder. 'What are we waiting for, Sergeant?'

'You to put your seatbelt on. Sir.'

Steel produced her e-cigarette and puffed on it. 'Brother

Sergeant and Sister Sir. Oh, the family fun you whacky kids have these days.'

'I see.' A click from the back seat. 'Right, well, go ahead.'

Mitchell's voice came over the speakers. *'Easy now... Baz: Big Red Door Key. Davy, you and me are first in. Carole, you've got the hoolie bar.'*

Logan eased the Big Car out and took the same left as the vans.

Most of Macduff was in darkness, just the ribbons of streetlights holding everything together. A right. Then another left onto Manner Street.

Not a living soul to be seen. The only blot on the stillness was the two big white vans in yellow-and-blue police livery.

'Ready when you are, Sergeant McRae.'

He pressed the button again. 'And we're clear. Go, go, go!' The Big Car roared forward as Logan rammed his foot hard down.

Granite cottages flashed by on either side, the North Sea a wall of solid black dead ahead. He slammed on the brakes and the Big Car slithered on the sleety tarmac, stopping with two wheels up on the kerb. He jumped out.

A swarm of ninjas burst from the OSU van – the huge figures of Sergeant Mitchell's team taking the lead. One of them clutched a mini battering ram, another held an elongated crowbar with a dirty big spike sticking out of it. Everyone else piled up in a big lump behind them.

The Dog Officer's van skidded to a halt, less than a foot from the other van's bumper. She leapt out onto the kerb then hauled open the sliding side door as Logan joined the back of the queue.

One of Mitchell's team swung the Big Red Door Key and *BANG*, the cottage door went crashing in.

The other one – Carole? – swung the hoolie bar, shattering the living room window with the spike, raking the pick around the frame to dislodge the loose glass. Ripping the Venetian blinds away from their mountings.

The Dog Officer charged past Logan, one hand wrapped around the lead of her massive Alsatian.

And they were in.

A dark house. Narrow corridor with doors leading off to either side and one at the end.

'POLICE, NOBODY MOVE!'

Barks went off like gunshots in the confined space.

Then answering barks from deeper inside the house. Deep and huge.

Logan shouldered the door on the left and burst into a double bedroom. Unmade bed, wardrobe door lying open, socks and pants scattered on the floor. No sign of Ricky or Laura Welsh.

Back into the hall. Almost.

It was crowded with bodies in riot gear and the sound of elbow pads thumping off the walls. Then swearing as something kicked off at the front of the line.

'GET THAT BLOODY DOG!'

'AAAAAARGH!'

'SHE'S GOT A KNIFE!'

Screw this.

Logan forced his way past Tufty, and out the front door. Grabbed Isla by the stabproof vest. 'You, with me!' He pounded down the pavement and skittered around the side of the terrace, nearly losing his footing on the sleet-crusted paving slabs.

There – an eight-foot wall with a wheelie bin in front of it.

He scrambled up and over, tumbled down the other side and crashed into a deformed snowman, knocking its head off. Got to his feet as Isla clattered down into the dark beside him, flat on her back.

'Aaagh...' Flailing arms and limbs.

Logan ran for the adjoining wall between this garden and the one next door.

'It's OK, I'm fine, I'm fine...'

Over the wall.

He landed and a security light blared on, illuminating a swing set and a shed.

One more to go.

He fought his way over a wooden fence and into Ricky Welsh's back garden about two seconds before the kitchen door battered off its hinges. Someone in riot gear crashed out backwards, wrestling with a Saint Bernard the size of a hairy Godzilla. They rolled into the rectangle of yellow light cast through the kitchen window.

It was Claire, the huge woman from the Operational Support Unit, her mouth wide open in a snarling scream as the dog tried to take her head off.

Teeth flashed, saliva spattering her faceguard, huge paws pressing her into the lawn. Claire's hands jabbed out, wrapping around the Saint Bernard's throat, elbows locked, holding it back. 'AAAAAAARGH! GET IT OFF, GET IT OFF, GET IT OFF!'

Ricky Welsh burst from the ruined doorframe, hurdled both dog and officer, and sprinted for the back wall – a six-foot-tall stretch of granite and crumbling harling topped with six inches of snow and ice.

Logan fumbled in his stabproof's pocket for the tin of Bite Back. Pulled it out and sprayed half the can at the St Bernard's muzzle. It blinked and made whimpery mewling noises. Backed away, shaking its head. Confused and disorientated.

Now, everything stank of cloves.

Isla thumped into the garden, landing on her feet this time.

Then the Dog Officer and her Alsatian exploded out of the kitchen, the big dog barking on the end of its lead.

Logan pointed at the back wall. No sign of Ricky Welsh. 'That way!'

The Dog Officer battered past, going the long way around to keep her Alsatian away from the dissipating cloud of Bite Back. Over the wall. And away.

He sprinted after them, breath burning in his lungs. Sweat made tiny rivers down his back, between the shoulder blades, as he clambered up the wall. He paused at the top, one leg hooked over the other side.

Isla scrambled up beside him. 'Where is he?'

Ricky Welsh had cleared the garden it backed on to, making for a break between two of the houses. One more fence and he'd be out.

Then the Dog Officer released the hounds. Well, hound.

Her Alsatian raced free of its leash and cleared the wall Ricky had just clambered over in a single leap. Crossed the lawn in a couple of bounds. Then lunged for Ricky's flailing legs.

Its teeth snapped shut on an ankle.

Ricky screamed.

Isla cheered.

He tumbled backwards into the snow and curled into a ball, with his arms crossed over his face, flinching at every bark of the big dog.

The officer caught up with her Alsatian, shoved Ricky Welsh over onto his front and cuffed him. Then looked up, grinned, and gave them two thumbs.

Result.

It was about time something went right for a change.

36

Logan walked through the shattered doorway into Ricky Welsh's kitchen. Not exactly the tidiest in the world. Certainly not now anyway.

He stepped over the battered remains of a chair. 'You OK?'

'Urgh...' Claire, from the OSU, was hunched over the sink, splashing water on her face. 'Covered in Saint Bernard dribble. How can one dog produce so much slobber?'

'Told you it was huge.'

She raised her dripping face. 'Thanks for spraying Cujo, Sarge.'

'Nah.' He left her to it and picked his way through the shattered remains of a small kitchen table and out into the hall. Muffled voices came from somewhere above his head. Lots of grunts and hissing. The occasional thump. Someone swearing.

The stairway was as narrow as the corridor. It doglegged around, emerging in what had to be an attic conversion. In the gap between two rooms, three officers in their riot gear were pinning a woman to the ground. Barely holding her in place. They piled on her back and legs, forcing her into the shabby carpet.

Laura Welsh was big, thickset. Ginger curls covered her face as she hissed and wriggled. Three small red hearts were tattooed between the knuckles of her right hand, stretched tight across her clenched fist.

The Chief Inspector from Elgin had his knee on her shoulder, jamming Laura's other wrist against the floor with both hands. 'I'm not telling you again – calm down!'

Nicholson lay across Laura's legs. She grinned up at Logan. 'I love knocking on doors.'

More wriggling.

The guy at the head of the piley-on scowled. 'You're not helping, Constable.'

'Sorry, Guv.'

Logan whipped out his limb restraints and helped Nicholson secure Laura's legs – one set binding her knees together, the other her ankles. Then he stood back as the others finally managed to get her hands cuffed behind her back. 'Everyone OK? Anyone hurt?'

A flash of freckled skin, green eyes bulging, teeth bared, lipstick smeared. 'I'LL KILL THE LOT OF YOU!'

The Chief Inspector flipped up the visor on his crash helmet, exposing a chubby face with a squint nose. 'Are you honestly trying to make things worse for yourself, Mrs Welsh? Because threatening to kill four police officers isn't going to look good when they haul you up in court.'

'GAH!' Then she pulled her head back and slammed it into the dirty carpet. Lay there, face against the floor, hissing breath in and out through her teeth.

'There we go.'

Through the open door, behind Chief Inspector Chunky, lay a small bedroom. It was a shambles of clothes and cardboard boxes. Narveer sat on the edge of the bed with his head thrown back, one hand holding onto his turban, the other pinching the bridge of his nose. Blood made a bandit mask across the lower half of his face.

Logan poked his head into the room. 'You OK?'

'No.' The word all bunged up and growly.

He wasn't the only one in there – two of the Elgin officers

were snapping the cuffs on a pair of men who were doing a lot more cooperating than Laura Welsh.

The bigger of the pair wore skinny jeans and a couple of hoodies, a blue one on over a red one. His hair was shorn at the sides and quiffed sideways in the middle. It went with the neck beard and horn-rimmed glasses.

Mr Hipster's friend had a granddad shirt, braces, and a brown waistcoat – as if he was auditioning for a Mumford and Sons cover band. He even had the 1940s haircut.

Logan nodded at them. 'Names?'

Mr Hipster licked his lips. 'I know how this looks, but we were just...'

Mr Mumford blinked at his friend. 'Yeah ... there was ... an advert in the paper for a mountain bike? We, erm, came round to see if it was any good.'

'You know, to buy it and that?'

'Mountain bike.' Mr Mumford jerked his eyes towards the landing and lowered his voice. 'No idea what's going on here, but *really* don't need a mountain bike that badly.'

'Yeah, so if we could, you know, head off? That'd be cool.'

'Completely cool.'

Smiles.

No chance.

'Well?' Harper hadn't moved from the back of the Big Car, sitting there with her seatbelt on and her arms folded.

Logan closed the driver's door and peeled off his gloves. 'Drug dog's going through the place now. Our friend the Chief Inspector has decided to supervise the search.'

Steel puffed a faceful of steam across the car at him, e-cigarette glowing from the corner of her mouth. 'Which means the thieving git wants to take all the credit.'

'And Narveer?'

Logan shrugged. 'Don't think his nose is broken, but better safe than sorry.'

'Agreed.' Harper unfastened her seatbelt. 'What about our two house guests?'

'Nick McDowell and Steven Fowler. Sticking to their mountain-bike stories.' He drummed his fingers against the steering wheel, frowning out through the windscreen. The sleet had stopped at last, giving way to a bitter wind that rattled the streetlights. A couple of houses had people at the windows, staring out, having a good old nosy at the police vehicles. 'Don't know why, but Steven Fowler rings a bell.'

'So do a PNC check.'

Logan glanced in the rear-view mirror. 'I did *actually* think of that, sir. He's got a couple of parking tickets: that's it. Never been arrested. Far as I can tell, he's never even been cautioned.'

But still...

Steven Fowler.

Steve Fowler.

Stevie... Oh crap.

Stevie Fowler – the guy Reuben wanted him to collect a package from. Collect a package and hide it until further notice.

Oh that was just *great*.

Logan's 'loyalty test' was under arrest, and now—

'Sergeant?'

He blinked.

Harper was leaning forward between the seats, staring at him.

'Sorry.'

Steel was at it too. 'You OK, Laz? Only you look like someone's stuffed an angry hedgehog up your bum.'

'Just a ... twinge that's all. From breaking up that fight yesterday.'

'Tell me about it. Could barely get my bra on this morning.' She untucked her shirt. 'You should see my ribs, Detective Superintendent, they're—'

'Actually,' Harper pulled in her chin, 'I think I'd better go check on Narveer. Excuse me.' She fumbled with the door handle and clambered out of the car. Hurried along the pavement towards Ricky and Laura Welsh's place.

Steel grinned. 'Think your sister fancies me.'

'Yes. Because you're *so* desirable.'

'And don't you forget it.' She puffed on her fake cigarette. 'While you were off playing policeman, I regaled her with the sexual conquests of my youth. Edited highlights, anyway.' A sigh. 'Did I ever tell you about Mrs Morgenstern? She was thirty-four, I was fifteen. She was my piano teacher and I was horny as a—'

'Can we not do this?'

Steel sniffed. 'Thought you boys liked a bit of hot girl-on-girl action?'

A gap opened up through the clouds, letting a cold slab of moonlight crash against the street, bathing it in frigid grey light.

Stevie Fowler.

What the hell was Logan supposed to do now? Never mind the fact that whatever Fowler should have handed over for safekeeping would probably end up in the evidence store; would Reuben expect Logan to let him go without so much as a slap on the wrists? Because there was *no* chance of that happening. Not with Harper and Narveer and Steel and the Chief Inspector from Elgin falling over each other to find someone to prosecute so they could take the credit.

Reuben already wanted him dead, this *really* wasn't going to help.

Oh he was so screwed.

'Anyway, so one day Mrs Morgenstern turns up for my lesson wearing this pencil skirt and silk blouse and – oh my hairy armpits, Laz, you should have seen her *breasts*.'

Urquhart. Call Urquhart and explain what happened.

'Every time she bent over the piano it was like diving into Loch Cleavage. God, you could've drowned in there.'

369

This wasn't Logan's fault. *Fowler* had screwed up, not him.

'So I tell her I'm having difficulty with my fingering and she says—'

Logan's phone blared out its anonymous ringtone. He dragged the thing out. 'Sorry, got to get this.'

Whoever it was, it had to be better than *Confessions of a Teenaged Lesbian Piano Student.*

'McRae.'

'Logan? It's Eamon.' A pause. *'Your brother?'*

He turned his back on Steel and climbed out of the car. 'Let me guess, Mother's been bending your ear.'

'I don't know why you've got to antagonize her the whole time, Logan. She phoned me in tears, saying you'd shouted and sworn at her. How could you be so insensitive and—'

'Did she tell you *why* I was swearing, Eamon? Did she let that tiny nugget of truth escape, or was it all lies like usual?' He slammed the car door. 'Well?' His breath rolled out in a cloud of fog, before being torn away by the wind. Cold air nipped at his ears.

'Logan, she's your mother. *You can't—'*

'Dad didn't die when he was shot. He got better and sodded off to Dumfries with a nurse. Settled down and had another family. You've got a wee sister, Eamon: you're not the youngest any more.'

Dark furious barks exploded inside the Dog Officer's van. Difficult to tell if it was Cujo or the Alsatian. A second later it didn't matter, because the other dog joined in – doubling the noise.

'All those years she dragged us along to put flowers on his grave and he wasn't even dead!'

Still nothing from the other end of the phone.

'She lied to us, Eamon. We could've had a father growing up, but she *lied*.'

The barking was getting louder, each dog egging the other on.

Logan slammed his palm against the van's cold metal

bulkhead. 'SHUT UP, THE PAIR OF YOU!' It didn't work. If anything, they got louder.

Curtains twitched in the house opposite.

Maybe it wasn't the best of ideas to be ranting and raving in the middle of the street, where anyone could see him, film him, and upload it to YouTube. He turned his back on the van and marched back to the Big Car. 'You still there?'

'I don't know what you're trying to prove, Logan, but it's not funny. Grow up, phone Mother back, and apologize.'

'Don't be such a mummy's boy.'

'All right, I'm hanging up now.' And the line went dead.

What a shock: Eamon took her side. Well sod him too. Logan wiped the condensation from his phone's screen and blocked Eamon's number too.

He stood and glowered down Manner Street. The sea shone, down the end, between the buildings, like a polished headstone.

Thirty-four years.

Thirty-four sodding years.

Steel was still puffing away as he climbed back into the Big Car. 'Aye, aye, Captain Cheery's back.'

Logan slammed the door closed. 'Don't start.'

'You ever wonder why you're such a miserable git?'

He turned and stared at her. 'Please, *do* tell me. Is it because I got the crap kicked out of me yesterday? How about: someone tried to slit my throat the night before that? Or maybe it's because someone burned Samantha's caravan down today?' Getting louder with every word. 'Oh, tell you what – and I'm going out on a limb here – how about it's because I had to kill my girlfriend on Friday? YOU WANT TO PICK ONE?' Spittle glowed in the dashboard lights.

Steel took a good long draw on her e-cigarette. Dribbled the steam out of her nose, long and slow. 'Are we finished, or is there a wee bit more tantrum in there?'

'I'm having a bad week, that OK with you?' He folded his arms and thumped back in his seat. And that wasn't even

371

mentioning the guy he'd seen killed and the guy he'd killed himself. A long breath rattled its way free. Surprising he could even function at all. 'This isn't easy.'

She sighed, then gave his shoulder a squeeze. 'You're a silly sod, Laz, you know that, don't you?'

And then some.

Tufty put a hand on Ricky Welsh's head and pushed it down as he guided him into the back of the Big Car. Making sure he didn't mess up those flowing shoulder-length locks of his by battering them against the doorframe.

Once in, Ricky sat all squinted over to one side, unable to sit properly because of his hands being cuffed behind his back.

Soon as Tufty had fastened Ricky's seatbelt for him, Logan started the car's engine and fiddled with the rear-view mirror until their new friend's face filled the reflection. 'You're not going to give us any trouble, are you, Ricky?'

'Bloody dog tried to rip my leg off.'

'Your dog tried to rip my officer's *face* off, so we're probably even.'

'I'm in agony here, OK?'

Steel wriggled down in the passenger seat as Tufty climbed in on the other side of Ricky. 'How long till Fraserburgh?'

Logan turned on the windscreen wipers, grinding away a gritty swathe of ice. 'Half an hour?'

Outside, two of Mitchell's team were struggling Laura Welsh into the OSU van. They'd put a spit hood on her – it made her look as if she was wearing a baggy nylon condom on her head. The other two, Stevie Fowler and Nick McDowell were being loaded into a second patrol car.

'Course you know what's going to happen, don't you, Ricky?' Steel pointed as Harper climbed into the car with Fowler and McDowell. 'That pair of hipster halfwits will spend the next thirty minutes spilling their guts to Detective Superintendent Harper. All the way from here to Fraserburgh, trying to cut a deal by landing you and your *charming* wife in the crap.'

The OSU van pulled away from the kerb, headlights scrawling their way across the granite houses as it did a three-point turn.

'What do you think, Sergeant McRae? How long's our Rickyboy going to get sent down for?'

Logan did a three-pointer of his own, following the van. 'Good question. Had to be, what, sixty grand's worth of heroin in there? Kilo of amphetamine. Plus nine thousand-quid bricks of resin...' He sucked a breath in through his teeth. 'Fiver says eight years.'

'Eight years? Aye, if the Sheriff's in a *really* good mood. Five quid on twelve to fourteen.'

'Deal.'

She reached across the car and shook his hand.

Ricky curled his lip. 'Yeah, good try. I'm completely bricking it back here. Woe is me, etcetera.' He shifted from side to side in his seat. 'Amateurs.'

Ah well, it'd been a longshot anyway.

Logan took them out through the town limits, following the OSU van on the road to Fraserburgh.

One last go. 'Ricky?' Logan caught his eye in the rear-view mirror. 'Hamish Mowat only died on Wednesday and you're already climbing into bed with Jessica Campbell? Not very loyal, is it?'

No reply.

'How do you think Reuben's going to feel about that? Think he's going to be happy?'

Ricky Welsh squirmed for a moment, then shrugged. 'No comment.'

'What do you think he's going to do to you when he finds out?'

'No comment.'

Maybe Harper would have more luck with Fowler and McDowell? Who knew, maybe Fowler would keep his trap shut about delivering a package for Logan? And maybe pixies and fairies would scamper out of DCI Steel's backside and buy them all fish suppers for their tea.

Ricky Welsh was probably right, 'no comment' was the only way to go.

37

Steel yawned, showing off grey fillings and a yellow tongue, then slumped in her chair. 'Time is it?'

Logan checked. 'Nearly half one.'

Fraserburgh station was coffin quiet, not so much as the creak of a floorboard to break the spell. Wind battered the windows in the Sergeants' Office, hail crackling against the glass. Outside, the streetlights bobbed and weaved, their pale-yellow glow blurred by the weather.

'Half-one...' Steel slumped even further, trouser legs riding up to expose pale hairy shins. 'Bored. Knackered.'

'So go home.'

'*And* my ribs hurt.'

He shut down his computer. 'So – go – home.'

'Feels like someone's given me a going over with a lawn-mower.' At least that would explain the hairstyle.

'There's no point hanging around here. One: we have to wait for everyone's lawyers to turn up. Two: then we've got to wait for them to coach their clients in the ancient art of denying everything. Three: Harper says she's sitting in on all the interviews, so it'll take *hours* before it's done.' He stood and stretched, wincing as it pulled at the bruises along his back. 'Might as well Foxtrot Oscar, go home, and get some sleep.'

Another yawn. 'Harper? You no' on first-name terms yet? After all those years you spent swimming about together in your dad's testicles, think you would've developed some sort of bond. Calling each other "Sir" and "Sergeant". No' natural.'

'Why is every woman in my life a pain in the backside?'

Steel grinned. 'Your own fault for being part of the oppressive patriarchal hierarchy.' She scratched at her belly. Frowned. 'I want chips.'

'Good for you.' He fastened his equipment belt, then Velcroed on his stabproof vest. 'Now are you coming or not?'

'Chips.' Steel banged on the arms of her chair. 'Chips, chips, chips, chips, chips!'

So this was what having a toddler was like.

'Suit yourself. But don't say I didn't—'

A knock on the door, then Narveer poked his turban into the office. His eyes were swollen around the bridge of his nose, a circle of black flecks crusting each nostril. 'Sergeant McRae? Detective Superintendent Harper would like to see you downstairs regarding the two gentlemen we arrested at the Welshes'. Interview Room Two please.'

Ah.

She'd found out about him and Stevie Fowler.

Well, it had to happen sooner or later.

'Right.' Deep breath. A nod. Then he followed Narveer out into the corridor, back straight, chin up.

All the way down the stairs, the Detective Inspector peered at him. Not saying anything.

At the bottom he stopped, put a hand on Logan's arm. 'Sergeant McRae, I understand this is probably very difficult for you.'

Now there was an understatement.

'But I need you to see it from the Super's point of view.'

Her brother was involved in organized crime. Yeah, that would probably be a bit embarrassing for her. But it wasn't as if she didn't have plausible deniability, was it?

'Sergeant McRae, Logan, just because she's known about

you for years, it doesn't mean she's used to the *reality* of the situation.'

She wasn't the one who'd end up doing eight years in HMP Glenochil with all the other dodgy police officers and vulnerable prisoners.

'Give her time, OK? She's a *much* nicer person when you get to know her.'

What?

Logan licked his lips. 'You sure about that?'

'She's been an only child her whole life, well, except for the spectre of you and your brother. And now here you are,' he poked Logan in the shoulder, 'in the flesh.' A shrug. 'Given how much she hated you last week, she's come a long way.'

Yeah…

'Anyway, better not keep her waiting.' Narveer led the way through the station, along its creaky galleon floors, to a bland door with a big '2' painted on it and a laminated sign: 'NO PERSONS TO BE LEFT UNATTENDED IN THIS ROOM AT ANY TIME'.

Narveer knocked, then opened the door.

Harper was sitting there, on her own. Violating the signage. She tried on a smile. 'Sergeant McRae, I want you to sit in on the interviews with Fowler and McDowell. I need a result on this one. You did a good job bursting Martin Milne, let's see if you can do it again.'

Oh great.

Sit in a little room, trying to get the guy who was meant to deliver an illegal package to him to incriminate himself without mentioning Reuben, or Logan, or the illegal package.

Because that was going to go *so* well.

And it'd be videoed, so they'd have him on record fiddling the truth.

Wonderful.

Eight years for being concerned in the supply of controlled drugs – Contrary to Section 4(3)(b) of the Misuse of Drugs

Act 1971, M'lord – and another eight for trying to pervert the course of justice.

Hurrah.

'Are you all right, Sergeant? Only I thought you'd be pleased at this show of faith.'

'Yes.' He pulled on a smile of his own. It hung there like a scar. 'Thank you.'

Screwed, screwed, screwed, screwed, screwed.

'For the record, I am now showing Mr Fowler exhibit Sixteen A.' Harper held up an evidence bag full of small white pills. 'Do you recognize these, Steven?'

The interview room smelled of aftershave and tobacco, both of which oozed out of Fowler as if he'd been drenched in them. He'd been stripped of his hoodies, sandshoes, and skin-tight jeans and given a white SOC suit instead – rustling every time he moved. 'Are they pills of some kind?' Playing it wide-eyed and innocent.

At least it made a change from the usual 'no comment'.

'Seriously, Steven?' She glanced at Logan. 'Can you believe this guy?'

Fowler shrugged and spread his hands. 'What am I supposed to say? They look like some sort of pill to me.'

'What kind of pill?'

'I'm doing my best to cooperate. I could have lawyered up and I didn't, did I? I really want to help, but me and Nick were only there to look at a mountain bike. If I'd known they were drug dealers we'd never have gone. Honestly.'

Harper stared at him. Then wrote something down in her notebook, tore the page off, folded it, and handed it to Logan: 'Feel Free To Actually <u>Contribute</u> At Some Point.'

Well, there was probably no point putting it off any longer.

Logan cleared his throat. 'Have you been in the market for a mountain bike for long, Steven?'

'Yeah. Totally.'

'I see. Good. And what do you do, when you're not shopping for second-hand bicycles? Got a job?'

Pink bloomed in Fowler's cheeks. 'Not at the moment.'

'I see.'

He shifted in his seat, then ran a hand across his sideways quiff as if checking it was still there. 'I'm not on benefits or anything, OK? Got made redundant last week, that's all.'

'I see.'

'Me and Nick worked as roustabouts for two years ... then the oil price, you know?'

Silence.

'Wasn't our fault. Everyone says they're tightening their belts, yeah? Well, *their* belts are cutting off *our* circulation. How am I supposed to support my kids with no job?'

'I see.'

Fowler leaned forwards, shoulders scrunched up around his ears. 'It's not easy out there. Yeah, I got my redundancy, but it's not going to last, is it? Got to make your own way in the world, can't rely on handouts, can you?'

Logan tapped his pen against his notebook. Tap. Tap. Tap. Like a metronome.

Fowler stared at it. 'Man's got to work. That's what we wanted the bike for. Going to start a messenger service in Aberdeen. Point-to-point for oil companies and that, you know?'

Tap. Tap. Tap.

'I mean, everyone's got packages they need delivered, right? Letters and bids and tenders and things. Stuff you can't email.'

Tap. Tap. Tap.

'And that's why we were there. Need to buy a couple of bikes to get it off the ground.'

Tap. Tap. Tap.

He wrapped his arms around himself. 'See. Nothing weird about it. Just two blokes trying to pay their way.'

379

Tap. Pause. Tap. Pause. Tap…

Harper sighed. 'Interview suspended at one forty.' She pressed the button, then stood. 'I suggest we take a comfort break and reconvene in five minutes. Sergeant McRae will look after you.'

As soon as the door shut behind her, Logan leaned forward, mirroring Fowler. 'Steven? I know who you are.'

Fowler blinked at him.

'You're already delivering packages, aren't you? That bit of your story was true.'

He bit his top lip and stared at the tabletop. 'Don't know what you mean.'

'Oh come off it, Steven, I know, OK? Reuben – the package, hiding it?' He picked up the notebook and slammed it down again. 'I *know*.'

Fowler flinched. His shoulders trembled. 'I don't… It… We…'

'You were supposed to drop off a package.'

'Oh Christ…' He scrubbed a hand across his face, as if he was trying to rub some life back into it. 'Who told you?'

'Well?'

'Yes. There was a package.' Fowler scooted forward in his seat, talking low and fast. 'Look, it hasn't been easy, OK? The redundancy. It's… I *need* to make money. I've got two kids and an ex who thinks I'm made of the bloody stuff. So I do a bit of delivery driving, it's no big deal, is it? A bit of picking up and dropping off?' He bared his teeth. 'Only I need a lot more than picking-up and dropping-off money. So I thought, why not? I mean, it's not like this Reuben guy's going to shop me to the police if I nick his drugs, is it? How's he even going to know?'

Really?

'I think he *might* notice.'

'No, think about it: I pull a fast one at the handover, I keep the stuff but give *them* fake pills. Nick films it on his phone, so it all looks cool. See? We gave the guy the stuff, so it must be *them* what stole it, not us. We're in the clear.' Fowler bit his bottom lip. 'All's fair in love and dealing, right?'

'All's fair? Have you any idea what Reuben does to people who steal...' Logan narrowed his eyes. Wait a minute: give the guy the stuff? The *guy*. Not *Logan*. Steven Fowler had no idea who he was. 'What about this guy you were meant to deliver the package to?'

'What about him? Probably some drug-dealing scumbag. Not like anyone's going to miss him.' Fowler raised his nose. 'If you think about it, I'm doing society a favour.'

He didn't have a clue.

'Who is he: the guy who's getting the package? Name?'

A shrug made the SOC suit crackle. 'First parking spot, west of Portsoy, half-two Tuesday morning is all I got. No names.'

The details were exactly the same as Urquhart had given him. Only Urquhart had trusted Logan with Stevie Fowler's name.

He really didn't know.

A smile crept across Logan's face.

Fowler pulled his chin in and sat back. 'What? What's so funny?'

Maybe he could get away with this after all?

Harper sighed her way back into her seat. Clicked the button on the recording unit. 'Interview recommences at one thirty-seven.'

Logan gave her a grin. 'Mr Fowler would like to make a statement, wouldn't you, Steven?'

He twisted his head to one side, shoulders up. The sideways quiff was developing a distinct droop. 'Yeah.'

'Just tell Detective Superintendent Harper what you told me.'

Fowler puffed his cheeks out, then nodded. 'OK, here's the thing...'

*   *   *

381

Harper stared down the corridor as Fowler was led back to the cells. Then she turned to Logan. 'How did you do that?'

He closed the interview room door. 'Got lucky, I suppose.'

'No. I was only gone for six minutes and when I got back, there he was singing like a parakeet. You did the same thing with Martin Milne.'

'You want to take a quick pop at McDowell too? Let him know Fowler's trying to dob him in as the brains of the operation.'

Tiny creases appeared between her eyebrows. 'Why are you still a sergeant?'

'Say, fifteen minutes to grab something from the vending machines? Then I'll get McDowell into number three.'

'You should be a DI by now, at the very least. You're three times the cop that wrinkly disaster is.'

Logan shrugged, then headed towards the stairs. 'Tried being a DI once, didn't like it. Either you're a dick and make someone else do all your paperwork and rosters, or you've got sod-all time to do any investigating.'

She shook her head, following him up to the canteen. 'You really do take after Dad, don't you?'

'No idea.'

38

Dark fields whipped past the Big Car's windows, banks of grey snow lining the road.

Sitting in the passenger seat, Steel didn't bother to stifle the yawn that made her head look like a flip-top bin. 'Knackered.'

'Well you should have gone home when I said, shouldn't you?' Logan pressed the button on his Airwave. 'Sergeant McRae to Constable Nicholson, safe to talk?'

There was a pause, then, *'Aye, aye, Sarge.'*

'How's it going, Calamity?'

'Like a grave. Not a creature is stirring, not even a druggy. Must be the weather.'

'Good. Tufty behaving himself on his last night in nappies?'

'He's brought in fancy pieces. And I mean, really *fancy.'*

Steel thumped Logan on the arm. 'Make sure they save some for us. I'm starving. Had nothing to eat but two packs of Wotsits and a Toffee Crisp since midnight.'

'Wanted to check in and make sure everything was all right.'

'Thanks, Dad.'

'We'll be back in time for threeses.' He let go of the button.

The tarmac glittered with frost that flared in the headlights then disappeared back into the night.

Steel dug her hands into her armpits. 'Have you got a deep-fat fryer back at the house?'

'No.'

'Chip pan?'

'No.'

'What kind of Scotsman are you?'

More fields.

They drifted through the limits at Crudie, dropping to fifty. Not that there was much of it: the place was little more than a scattering of houses spread out along the road. If it weren't for the dirty big signs at either end with 'CRUDIE ~ PLEASE DRIVE CAREFULLY' on them you'd barely know it was there.

Logan glanced across the car. 'I saw the interview, by the way. You and Jack Wallace.'

'Oh aye?'

'Seemed like a lovely man. You know, apart from all the sexual assaults and treating women like they're punchbags.'

'Wallace is a prince all right.' She shook her head. Then turned and stared at Logan. 'You're Napier's bitch now, aren't you?'

'Well what did you want me to do, refuse to help him? That wouldn't look suspicious, would it? At least this way I'm on the inside, I can ... finesse things.'

She slid further down in her seat, then plonked both feet up on the dashboard. 'Blah, blah, blah.'

'Look, Napier says he'd be just as happy exonerating you. And it's not like you actually *did* anything, is it?'

No reply.

Logan glanced at her again. 'Did you?'

'Course I didn't.' She pursed her lips and hummed for bit. 'Once upon a time, in the fabled granite city of Aberdeen, there lived a man named Jack Wallace. Now Jack Wallace wasn't a very nice man, in fact he was a complete and utter bastard. He liked to attack women, beat, and rape them. It made him feel big and clever.' Steel turned her face to the window. 'One sunny evening in May, Wallace drugged and raped a seventeen-year-old girl called Rosalyn Cooper. And if that wasn't bad enough, he filmed it on his phone and used it to blackmail her into a "relationship".' Steel made quote marks with her fingers. 'So he could keep on raping and battering her without having to bother shelling out for drugs.'

Logan tightened his grip on the steering wheel. 'He *filmed* it?'

'Now Rosalyn thought her mother and father would blame her for the attack, and they would throw her out of the house and never speak to her again. And Wallace told her everyone would call her a slut and a whore and she'd never get a job or any friends ever again. And she was so scared and traumatized, she actually believed him.'

Steel dug out her e-cigarette and took a long slow drag, setting the tip glowing bright blue. 'Then one day, a brave knight rode in on a big white horse with a sharny arse, and she said, "Come on, Rosalyn, you're no' to blame here. It's that scumbag Wallace who's at fault. We'll do him for rape and make sure he gets locked away for years and years and years." But Rosalyn was too scared to press charges, because if she did it would all come out and her parents would know and they'd never love her again. And the brave knight told her they could get round that. They could make it work. But she was too scared.'

'What happened?'

Steel blew a line of steam at the windscreen. 'It wasn't even the first time he'd done it. The first poor cow he filmed ended up in a secure ward doped up to the ears because spiders kept crawling out of her fingertips. Completely – and utterly – broken.' A small laugh broke free, but there was no humour in it. 'So Rosalyn did the only thing that made sense to her: she climbed into a very hot bath with a bottle of vodka and a craft knife. Her little brother found her next morning. Apparently he sees a therapist twice a week now.'

More fields.

They passed the turn-off to Gardenstown.

Logan shook his head. 'So get a search warrant, find the phone, and show the footage to the Procurator Fiscal! Get the scumbag charged.'

'You really think I've no' tried that? Can't get a warrant on the word of a dead girl.' Another line of steam hit the windscreen. 'And even if I could, what'd that prove? She's drugged in the video: she's no' fighting back, and it's no' as if she can testify in court, is it? We'd never get a conviction.'

More fields – wide, flat and rolling beneath the icy moon-light.

'Tell you, Laz, I've *never* had a better day than when I turned up at Wallace's house to give him a hard time and found a ton of kiddy porn just sitting there on his laptop.' This time the laugh had a lot more joy in it. 'I mean, a *slideshow* for God's sake! Wee shite was probably gearing up for a good wank when I turned up and spoiled the romantic mood. And now he's got six years of spanking his raping wee monkey cock in a prison cell. Assuming he can get it up without staring at images of abused kids, or beating the crap out of some poor woman. Serves him right.'

Hard to argue with that.

Steel grinned across the car at him. 'You know what? I'm in such a good mood I'm even prepared to put up with oven chips, if you've got any?'

Logan peered out of the bedroom window at the street below. Steel wound her way along the road, having had to settle for cheese on toast and a large Balvenie instead. When she'd disappeared from view, he shut the curtains and pulled out his mobile.

Dialled John Urquhart.

The phone rang and rang and rang. Then finally, '*Mmmph? Hello? What?*'

'You can tell Reuben the delivery's off.'

'What? Who's...' A cough rattled out of the earpiece. 'Mr McRae? What time is it?'

Logan's eyes flicked to the clock-radio – 03:32. 'The delivery's off. Stevie Fowler got himself arrested in a drugs raid four hours ago.'

Urquhart yawned, then swore. 'He got himself arrested?'

'He was never going to deliver the package, it was all a scam so he could steal the drugs and sell them to a local dealer.'

'Oh, Reuben's going to love that. Is there—'

'And before you ask: no. He's confessed in front of a detective superintendent from the Serious Organised Crime Task Force. There's no way in hell he's walking free.'

Urquhart made a noise like a deflating mattress. 'That's … unfortunate. And did Mr Fowler happen to mention where he'd got the package from in the first place?'

'And where he was meant to deliver it. Good job he didn't have my name, or I'd be in the cell next door by now.'

'And the package is...?'

'The kilo and a half of amphetamines? He'd already sold it. It's evidence.'

A sigh. 'Mr McRae, you know how Reuben's going to react, don't you? He doesn't like people who steal from the organization.'

'Really? Because I don't like people who threaten my kids and SEND THUGS ROUND TO KILL ME!' Logan slammed his palm into the wallpaper.

'I understand where you're coming from, Mr McRae, but you really have to put that behind you and move on.'

'Move on?'

'Seriously, dude, chill. I had a word with the Reubenator and smoothed things out. Told him he can't kill you 'cause you're the executor for Mr Mowat's will. He bumps you off and everything'll take forever to sort out.'

'And what happens after the will's executed, he sends someone else?'

'That's how the system works: the big dog eats the small dog. You don't like getting bit? Be the bigger dog.'

Logan settled onto the edge of the bed. 'I'm supposed to just forget about it?'

'*No, you're supposed to bite back.*' A pause. '*So, we'll see you tomorrow?*'

Tomorrow?

Oh, right, the reading of the will. 'Don't think I've got any choice.'

Not now.

Logan hung up and switched off his phone.

He stood there, frowning down at the bed. Then knelt beside it and fished out the polished wooden box. Should really give the gun a proper wipe down, make sure there were no fingerprints on it.

Tomorrow was going to be a big day.

— Monday Dayshift —

I, being of sound mind and body…

39

'And we *finally* have some good news.' Standing with her back to the whiteboard, Harper pointed the remote. The screen on the wall opposite filled with a satellite image of the coast. Gardenstown was marked with a big arrow, as if no one in the room would know what the place was.

The two arms of the harbour made a broken triangle, poking out into the sea like a cartoon nose and jaw – with mooring jetties for teeth.

Harper pressed a button and a red laser dot appeared, then swept towards the harbour entrance. 'We got a phone call from Martin Milne at half six this morning. Malk the Knife's people have been in touch.'

A rumble of conversation went around the room.

Standing against the wall, by the door, Logan shifted from one foot to the other. Something hard and spikey was frolicking across his back, digging its claws into his spine. He took another swig of water from his mug. Didn't seem to matter how much he drank today – his mouth was still like a desert, head throbbing like an overripe boil full of burning pus.

'Narveer?'

Her sidekick stood and read from a sheet of paper, voice slightly rounded and mushy. Forced down a bruised and swollen nose. 'At four o'clock this afternoon, the *Jotun Sverd* will leave Peterhead harbour and rendezvous with a private yacht sixty miles east of Bora in the Moray Firth. The crew will take on board a number of sealed crates and conceal them in containers already on board.'

The screen changed to a photo of a small supply boat – about a third as big as the usual neon-coloured monstrosities – with superstructure at the front and a railed loading bay at the back. Like a floating pickup truck. It probably would have taken two full-sized containers, but they'd managed to fit about eight of the smaller ones on it, each emblazoned with 'GEIRRØD CONTAINER MANAGEMENT AND LOGISTICS' and their angry Viking logo.

Logan took another swig.

It wasn't as if he could blame a hangover. One whisky and that was it.

No, the churning sensation in his stomach and head was probably down to what he'd hidden beneath the passenger seat of his rusty old Fiat Punto. Sealed away in a freezer bag, sealed inside *another* freezer bag, with a brown-paper evidence bag over the top of that.

One semiautomatic pistol of Eastern European extraction, with a full magazine of bullets and a silencer.

All ready to bark in Reuben's face.

'The *Jotun Sverd* will then make its way north of Gardenstown and wait there until six o'clock tomorrow evening, when it'll come into the harbour and be met by a Transit van. Malcolm McLennan's men will then unload the merchandise and take it away.'

He ran a hand across his face, it came away damp.

'Thank you, Narveer.' Harper pointed the remote and the aerial view was back, but zoomed in so the harbour filled the screen. 'We will be positioned here,' the red dot swept to the left-hand side, 'here,' right, 'and here. A secondary unit will cover the access roads in and out of Gardenstown.'

Everything had seemed so clear last night. He wasn't doing

it for himself any more, he was doing it to stop Reuben sending someone after Jasmine and Naomi. He was doing it to save Steel from another beating. He was doing it to stop a turf war between the Aberdeen mob and everyone else. He was doing it because no one else would and it needed to be done.

It really did.

It was all decided.

So why could he barely breathe?

'You'll get your team assignments tomorrow.' Harper put the remote down. 'Now, any questions?'

Steel sidled up next to him, kept her voice low. 'You all right?'

Someone's hand went up – Becky. 'Did we get a result last night?'

'Yes and no, DS McKenzie. Two individuals arrested at the Welshes' house have confessed to selling class A drugs and are giving up their supply chain, thanks to Sergeant McRae.'

Everyone turned to look at him. Lots of nods and smiles.

His stomach lurched, saliva flooding his dry mouth.

Don't be sick. Don't be sick.

He swallowed it down.

'As for Ricky and Laura Welsh, it's "no comment" all the way. So far there's nothing concrete to connect them with Ma Campbell or the murder of Peter Shepherd. That doesn't mean we're going to stop digging though.'

'Seriously, Laz,' Steel put a hand on his arm, 'you look like you're about to blow chunks.'

'I'm fine.' Liar.

Harper held up her hand. 'Right, you all know what you're doing, so go out there and do it.'

The assembled hordes shuffled from the room.

Harper and Narveer settled at the conference table, scrawling notes across piles of actions. Steel wandered over to the window, mobile phone clamped to her ear.

Logan blew out a shaky breath. 'Well, if you don't need me, I'm going to—'

'No you don't.' A sniff, then Harper straightened up. 'Sergeant, while I appreciate your assistance last night, I want you to get something perfectly straight: I expect members of my team to turn up for work sober and functioning. *Not* hungover and useless.'

'I'm not hungover.'

'How am I supposed to catch Peter Shepherd's killers if my officers are the walking dead after last night's binge drinking?'

'I'm – *not* – hungover!'

'And while we're at it, what did I say about you coming to work in plainclothes? I was perfectly clear: you're—'

'Hoy!' Steel held the phone against her chest. 'Much though I hate to break up this family bondage session, your big brother's telling the truth. Mr Grey-and-Sweaty here looks like a puddle of sick because he's off to bury his girl-friend today. Hence the ugly suit.'

'Ah.' Harper closed her mouth.

'Now, if you don't mind, I'm trying to have phone sex with my wife here. I'll tell you all about it later, if you like, Super? Blow-by-blow?'

'No. Thank you.' The muscles worked in Harper's cheeks, clenching and unclenching, as she gathered up her actions and stuffed them into an awkward pile. 'That won't be necessary. Narveer, we'd better go … out.'

The DI kept his face expressionless. 'Yes, Super.' He followed her from the room, pausing only to throw a wink back at Steel from the doorway, before sealing the pair of them in.

Logan sagged against the wall. 'Thanks.'

'What time's the funeral?'

He pointed at her phone. 'Aren't you keeping Susan waiting?'

'Nah, it's only Rennie – he's away to the baker's for break-fast butties. You want booby-trap or sausage?'

'Sausage.' Maybe it'd help settle his stomach? 'Funeral's at twelve.'

'Brown or red?'

'Red.'

A nod, then she was back on the phone. 'Aye, and another sausage butty with tomato sauce. ... Of course he wants both sides buttered, have you never seen MasterChef? ... Good. ... Get on with it then.' She stuck her phone back in her pocket. 'Susan's coming, and she's bringing Jasmine and Naomi. Apparently Jasmine insisted. Says you need her there to hold your hand.'

'That's ... very kind.'

'Tell you, Laz, she's turning into a right little control freak.' Steel settled on the edge of the conference table. 'You OK?'

'No.'

'Know what you're going to say?'

'The eulogy? Yeah.' He rubbed at his face, then sighed. 'Got to head into town early. Make sure everything's sorted with the church and the lawyers and the cemetery. And I've *still* got to sort out the insurance for the caravan.'

'You know Susan and me are here for you, right? If you need someone to lean on, you've got people on your side, Laz. All of us. Even Rennie. I know he's a useless wee spud most of the time, but he means well.'

Logan nodded. 'Thanks.'

'Now: have your butty, then sod off and go do what you've got to. I'll clear everything with your wee sister.' A grin burst its way across Steel's face. 'And if she gives me any trouble, I'll tell her about the time I went caravanning in the Lake District with a dental hygienist, and the *Bumper Book of Lesbian Fun*. Ah, the glory days of youth...'

'Sarge?'

Logan looked up from his sausage butty, and there was Tufty, hanging his head around the Sergeants' Office door. 'Officer Quirrel, I presume?'

He limped into the room. 'And on the last and final night, verily didst the brave Probationer do battle with a ravening wolf and recover the fair maiden, Tracy Brown.'

'You found Tracy Brown?'

Tufty leaned on the desk and raised his gimpy leg off the carpet an inch. 'She was holed up with a married man in Strichen. His wife was off to Disneyland Paris with the kids for a week, so Tracy and him were having a nonstop humpa-thon till they got back.'

'Typical. Too busy shagging to notice the whole northeast of Scotland is plastered in missing posters with her face on them. Why do we bother?' He bit another mouthful of sausage and bun, tomato sauce making a dribbly bloodstain across the back of his hand. Chewing around the words, 'What about the wolf?'

'Bloke had a poodle. But it was massive. At *least* two foot tall with teeth like carving knives.'

Logan pointed a finger at the limpy leg. 'Get that seen to.'

'Course, soon as Big Donald Brown finds out someone's been riding his wee girl like she's the *Indiana Jones et le Temple du Péril* roller-coaster, he's going to go *balistique*.'

'Might be an idea to put a grade-one flag on the house. Just in case.'

'Will do.' Tufty puffed out a breath. 'You hear we got a fatal RTC last night? Wee boy in his pimped-out Peugeot lost it in the snow on the Fraserburgh road. *Bang*, right into a telegraph pole. Little sod walked away, but his girlfriend?' Tufty grimaced. Shook his head.

'Every winter. They prosecuting?'

'Bloody hope so.' He hooked a thumb over his shoulder. 'Anyway, you coming to Whitehills with us? Drookit Haddie, fish, chips, beer. They might even break out the karaoke machine.'

'I'd love to, but I can't. It's Samantha's funeral.'

Tufty's eyes went wide. 'Oh crap. I'm sorry, Sarge. It... Yeah. OK. I'm sorry.'

Him and everyone else.

'Don't worry about it. You go have fun. It's not every day you get to become a proper police officer. We're proud of you, Tufty.'

'Sarge.' He limp-shuffled his feet for a moment, then leaned forward and patted Logan on the shoulder. 'If you need anything. You know.' A shrug. A nod. Then Tufty cleared his throat. 'Right, better go get my gaping wound seen to before they have to amputate my whole leg.'

'You do that.' Logan polished off the last bite of butty, wiped his hands on the napkin it came wrapped in, then sooked his fingers clean. Stood.

No point putting it off any longer.

By the end of the day there would be something much darker red than tomato sauce on his hands.

The song on the radio faded away, replaced by someone who sounded as if they'd not taken their medication that morning. *'Hurrah! Wasn't that terrific? We've got the news and weather coming up at the top – of – the – hour with* Sexy *Suzie. Don't miss it. But first, here's a blast from the past: anyone remember H from Steps? Well—'*

Logan killed the engine and the rusty Fiat Punto pinged and rattled.

He checked his watch: nine fifty. Ten minutes.

Blew out a long rattling breath.

Come on. This wasn't difficult. People did this all over the world every day. Gun. Forehead. Trigger. Bullet.

'Yes, but I can't do it in a solicitor's office, can I?'

He glanced at himself in the rear-view mirror. 'Well of course you can't, Logan. That would be stupid.'

'Not to mention all the witnesses.'

'Exactly.'

He chewed on the ragged edge of a fingernail, working it smooth. 'Have to get him somewhere private. Somewhere you can get rid of the body.'

'Where though? Where's he going to go with a police officer? A police officer he tried to have killed two days ago. He's going to *know* something's up.'

'And what about the body? How do we get rid of it?'

Logan blinked at his reflection.

'Are we really doing this?'

'You know we've got no choice. Be the bigger dog.'

'What about the pig farm? Kill two birds and one fat violent bastard with one stone. People die out there all the time. What's one more meal for the pigs?'

'True. Very true.'

'But how do we get him out there? He has—' A knock on the car window sent him flinching back in his seat. 'Jesus!'

He turned, and there was John Urquhart, smiling in at him.

Logan undid his seatbelt and climbed out into the bitter morning air. 'Mr Urquhart.'

'Mr McRae. Glad you could make it.' He stuck out his hand for shaking and nodded at the manky Fiat Punto. 'Hope I didn't interrupt your phone call.'

'Phone call?'

'Don't know about you, but I always feel a right nutter talking on a Bluetooth headset. Everyone thinks you're talking to yourself.'

'Yes. Not a problem.' Logan locked the car, as if anyone would be desperate enough to steal a rusty pile of disappointment when it was surrounded by all these Audis, Jaguars, and BMWs.

The car park was tucked off Diamond Street – which didn't exactly live up to its name. Instead of sparkling, the road was lined with the backs of buildings: half facing out onto Union Terrace, the other half Golden Square. Leaving a dark narrow canyon of grey and old brick.

Urquhart patted the roof of Logan's car. 'Suppose you'll be upgrading after today.'

It took a moment for that to sink in: Wee Hamish's bequest. Two-thirds of a million pounds. 'Probably not.'

'Right. Got you. Don't want to arouse suspicions. Clever.'

Logan put a hand in his pocket, steadying the gun. 'Better get this over with. Got a funeral to go to.'

'Yeah, totally.' A nod. Then he led the way to a black-painted door in the corner of the car park, with an intercom mounted beside it. Pressed the call button. 'Mr Urquhart and Mr McRae for Mr Moir-Farquharson. We have an appointment?'

There was a pause, then the unit buzzed and the door popped open an inch.

Urquhart leaned on it, exposing a short corridor with a flight of stairs at the end. He held the door for Logan, dropping his voice to a whisper as soon as they were inside. 'I told Reuben about Stevie Fowler. He is *not* happy.'

'What a shock.' Logan kept his hand on the gun. It was still in its bags, but the outline of the thing was clear enough. No idea if it would be fireable though – not without jabbing his finger through the freezer bags to pull the trigger.

'He's getting worse. And yeah, I know that sounds hard to believe, but it's like breakdancing in a sodding minefield right now.'

Logan stopped at the foot of the stairs and stared at Urquhart. 'So we kill him.'

A frown. Urquhart licked his lips. 'Mr McRae, it's—'

'We get him out to one of the pig farms and we put a bullet in him. Let the pigs take care of the rest.'

Silence.

Urquhart stared down at the shiny black tips of his shoes. 'Mr McRae, I'm not supposed to take sides, OK? I'm meant to be impartial, like, you know, the Civil Service? You and Reuben, you're the Tories and Labour, whichever side wins is the next government. My job's to make sure the country still runs. Implement policy, and that.'

'Impartial?' Logan poked Urquhart in the chest. '*You* were the one who told me to kill him!'

'Yeah, well.' A shrug. 'You know, that's impartial advice, isn't it? Just saying what Mr Mowat thought.'

'So, what, you're happy for me to shoot Reuben, as long as you don't have to get your hands dirty? That it?'

'I can't take—'

'You said it yourself: he's getting worse. What's it going to be like when he starts a war?'

'But—'

'This is what Hamish wanted. What other option do *we* have?'

Urquhart dragged in a deep breath. Stared at his shoes again. 'We don't.'

'Tonight. Tell him we have to talk about Steven Fowler nicking his drugs and selling them to Jessica Campbell, and we have to do it at the pig farm so no one knows we're meeting. Can you sort it?'

A nod. 'Think so.'

'And no witnesses. You, me, and him there: no one else.'

Urquhart nodded. Bit his bottom lip. 'Does this mean you're taking charge? Because—'

'Hello?' The door at the top of the stairs opened and a middle-aged woman with lacquered hair and 1950s Dame Edna glasses. Her pink cardigan was buttoned all the way up. 'Is there something wrong?'

Urquhart waved at her. 'Sorry, had to tie my shoelace. Be right up.'

'Well, the reading is about to start and Mr Moir-Farquharson is a very busy man.'

'Of course.' He hurried up the stairs and Logan followed him, through into a reception area lined with historic views of Aberdeen in gilded frames, mounted on dark mahogany panelling.

She waved a hand toward the door on the far side of the room. 'Mr Moir-Farquharson is waiting for you.'

'Of course.' Urquhart gave a short bow. 'Thank you, Mrs Jeffries. Always a pleasure.'

Logan opened the door.

It was a conference room, with a long oak table down

the middle and views out through a pair of mullioned windows to the heart of Golden Square. Which was basically one big pay-and-display car park with a few trees around the central bank of parking and a statue in the middle. All drab and squashed under the pale-grey sky.

Reuben stood by a side table, helping himself to a cup of tea and a raisin whirl. The expensive suit managed to even out some of the bulges, but he still looked massive. Dangerous. His hands dwarfed the thin china cup. His scarred face turned, eyes drifting up Logan, then down again. A grunt. 'About time.'

A tall, dapper man sat at the head of the long table in a dark suit that looked even more expensive than Reuben's. The hair at his temples was solid white, beneath a lid of greying black. Distinguished. Patriarchal. The only thing slightly out of kilter was the squint nose. He checked his watch, then pulled on a thin smile. 'And we can begin.'

The only other person in the room was a shrunken woman with pink-tinged hair and hands taloned with arthritis. Skin hung in loose wattles from her chin to the neck of her tweed jacket, her face like a scrunched-up chamois leather, her eyes polished onyx buried in the folds.

Sandy Moir-Farquharson dipped into a leather briefcase and came out with a leather folder. Opened it like a tomb. And began to read. '"I, Hamish Alexander Selkirk Mowat, being of sound mind and body, do hereby declare this to be my Last Will and Testament…'

40

'Sign here, and here...' Moir-Farquharson pointed, and Logan scrawled his signature in the appropriate places. 'And here.'

Outside the conference room window, the skies had darkened to the colour of a burned body. Thick white flakes drifted down amongst the cars parked outside, falling on Porsches and manky Fiat Puntos alike.

'And here. And lastly, here.'

Logan did.

The solicitor took the documents back and blew on the signatures, as if they'd been done with a quill rather than a Police Scotland biro. 'Now, if you'll excuse me, I shall instruct my colleagues to set the wheels in motion.' He stood. 'Thank you for your patience, everyone.'

The little old lady nodded, setting her wattles swaying. 'He was a good man and all.'

Reuben hadn't moved for the last half hour. No sign of life, except for the muscles in his jaw clenching and unclenching.

She sighed. 'And *very* generous. Three hundred thousand pounds, just for cleaning his house.' She brought out a handkerchief and dabbed at a wrinkly eye. 'A braw man.' She waved one of her claws at Urquhart. 'Can you help me up?'

'Of course, Mrs P. You lean on me.' Urquhart got her to her feet and guided her across the wooden floor with its fancy rug and out into the reception.

As soon as they were gone, Reuben bared his teeth. 'Two-thirds of a *million*.'

Logan stared at the ceiling – moulded and pristine, with a modest chandelier. 'Nothing to do with me: it's what Hamish wanted.'

'Pin your lugs back, McRae: you screw about with this will, you stand in the way or delay *anything*, I'm going to carve—'

'For God's sake, Reuben, give it a rest.'

'Who the hell do you think you're—'

'Yes, you're all big and scary. Well done.' Logan's hand wrapped around the evidence bag in his pocket, feeling the outline of the gun. Its weight. 'You think this is easy for me? I'm a police officer. This is all profits from crime and I'm supposed to divvy it up between a bunch of thugs and gangsters. How's that going to look?' He shook his head. 'Should hand the whole thing over to the National Crime Agency and let them deal with it.'

A growl rumbled across the table.

'Don't worry: I won't. I promised Hamish.' Logan gave up on the ceiling and looked at the glowering lump of hate and gristle sitting opposite instead. 'We need to talk about Stevie Fowler.'

A big fat finger poked across the table. 'I want that bastard out on bail. I want him where I can get at him.'

'Not possible. Too many top brass were there when he was arrested. They know about his confession. Hell, they're falling over each other to claim credit for it. He stays where he is.'

'When I say I want him out, I want – him – out!'

'And I say, he's not going anywhere.' Logan tightened his grip on the gun. 'If you want him, you'll have to go after him where he is.'

403

'Wow.' Urquhart sauntered back into the room, closing the door behind him. 'Mrs P, eh? What a woman.' He helped himself to a chocolate mini-roll, popping the thing in his mouth whole, chewing with his mouth open. '"Cleaning house", eh? Never heard it called that before.'

Reuben's finger swung down and ground itself into the desk, as if he was stubbing out a cigar. 'Where are my damn drugs?'

'Same thing. They're evidence and everyone knows about them.'

He lunged like a Saint Bernard, back hunched, huge paws on the table. Barking, spittle flying: 'I WANT MY BLOODY DRUGS BACK!'

Urquhart's eyes bugged. 'Shhhh! Jesus, Reuben, you want everyone in Aberdeen to hear? Come on, calm the beans, man, yeah?'

Reuben glowered at him.

'You know it makes sense, right? Calm. We can't talk about this here. Too many ears.' He licked his lips and snuck a glance at Logan. 'How about we meet up later, just the three of us? Sort out what we're going to do about that two-faced git, Fowler, and his thieving mate. Stealing from us and flogging it to one of Ma Campbell's dealers? Who does he think we are, Clangers?'

The big man stayed where he was.

'Reuben – calm – dude. We can sort it. Mr McRae's on the team, aren't you, Mr McRae?'

Logan let go of the gun. 'Of course I am.' He nodded at the copy of Wee Hamish Mowat's will he'd got in his executor's pack. 'I know you don't like what's in there, but it ties me to the organization. I'm up to my ears whether I like it or not.'

A grunt, then Reuben stood up straight, towering over the pair of them. 'Where?'

'Call it midnight, when no one's about.' Urquhart gave a small shrug, as if it wasn't important. As if this was the most natural thing in the world. 'How about ... West Gairnhill Farm? That's good, isn't it? Secluded.'

'Fine. Midnight.' Reuben jabbed his finger at Logan again. 'Be there.' Then he turned and lumbered from the room like a well-dressed grizzly bear. And every bit as deadly.

As the door swung shut, Logan slumped in his seat and covered his face with his hands. 'Gah.'

Urquhart blew out a long breath. 'If it were done, when 'tis done, then 'twere well it were done quickly.' So he couldn't spell in a text message, but quoting Shakespeare was OK? 'Anyway, better get off.' Urquhart let out another elongated sigh. 'Places to go, people to kill.'

'No, I wanted to make sure everything was OK, that's all.' Logan leaned against the windowsill, looking down at the street below as Reuben's rounded figure hunched its way towards a dark-blue Bentley.

On the other end of the phone, Andy had his professional voice on, the pronunciation crisp and calm. Soothing. *'Everything's under control, Mr McRae. We brought Samantha down an hour ago, so don't worry – she'll arrive on time. And I've checked with the church, they have all the Order of Services ready to hand out and the organist has been practising his rendition of "Welcome to the Black Parade". Apparently it sounds like quite something on a completely refurbished three-manual Willis organ.'*

'Thanks, Andy.'

'Anything I can do to help, please give me a call.'

The conference room door opened and Sandy Moir-Farquharson, AKA: Hissing Sid, slipped in. 'Mr McRae, thank you for staying behind.'

'Sorry, Andy, got to go.' He hung up and put his phone away as Moir-Farquharson sat at the head of the table again.

'Now, there are a few things we need you to do as executor of Mr Mowat's will, then there's the matter of the bequest he left you.'

The two-thirds of a million.

Logan sat. 'What if I don't want it?'

'Then you're free to give it away to charity. Mr Mowat has made provision for the money to be held in escrow, awaiting your retirement from the police. That way you would not be ... embarrassed by the sudden arrival of such a large sum in your bank account.'

'In escrow?'

'Essentially, there will be nothing connecting you to the aforementioned bequest until you cease to be a serving police officer. Should you decide to retire to the Dordogne, for example. Or perhaps the Isle of Man? Then the bequest will be made at your disposal.'

Logan drummed his fingers on the tabletop. 'Nothing connecting me to it at *all*?'

Moir-Farquharson pointed. 'Please stop doing that.' Then straightened his tie. 'Your affairs will be treated with the utmost discretion. And you know how discreet we can be here.'

That much was true. Getting anything out of Hissing Sid was like trying to remove a granite boulder from a cliff face using a broken toothpick. Even *with* a warrant.

'I only require from you guidance as to how you wish the money employed while it's in escrow. Mr Mowat made allowance for investing a portion in a managed fund, for example. It could provide you with a very acceptable pension, should you wish.'

Which was more than working for the police did these days.

Logan picked a point over Moir-Farquharson's shoulder and stared at it. It was another of the old photos of Aberdeen, mounted in a gilded frame. Holburn Street from the look of it. 'Do you remember telling me that Hamish had... That he'd said you'd defend me, in court, if anything happened?'

'I am aware of Mr Mowat's wishes, yes. Why, is something likely to, as you put it, "happen"?'

'Possibly.'

'Ah.' Moir-Farquharson hooked his thumbs into the lapels of his jacket, as if he were wearing his silks and about to stride forth across the courtroom. 'Would I be right in surmising that the something in question relates to Mr Mowat's former associate, Reuben?'

'Might do.'

'Indeed.' He nodded. 'Mr McRae, I normally restrict my counsel to advice of a strictly legal nature, but if I may make so bold: when engaged in any business, it is always preferable to be the one *conducting* a hostile takeover than to be on the *receiving* end. I would imagine, in the circumstances, your options are very much limited to staging one of your own, or putting your affairs in order.'

Brilliant.

The sausage butty was a stone in his stomach, dragging it down.

'Thank you.'

Moir-Farquharson reached into his pocket and produced a small white rectangle with the company logo on it. 'My card.' A smile spread itself across his face. It was like watching a python preparing to devour a small child. 'I would, of course, be only too happy to assist you in drawing up a new will, should you choose the latter option.'

Of course he would.

Rubislaw Parish Church wasn't exactly packed. The pale wood pews hosted a scattering of men and women, no more than about forty of them. Some were in uniform – probably given an hour off work to attend – but most were in an assortment of black clothes. Some in suits, some in jeans. And Logan barely recognized any of them.

Steel turned and waved back at him from the front row, pointing to the empty seat beside her. Susan sat on her other side holding onto a wriggling Naomi. Jasmine was last in line, staring up at the vaulted ceiling with her mouth hanging open, as if she'd never seen anything like it in her life.

Andy appeared at Logan's shoulder. 'Mr McRae? We're ready for the pallbearers, now.'

'Thanks.'

The walls were painted a cheerful yellow, with big flower arrangements of red roses and white lilies, lots of black ribbons. They were a bit gothic for the cheery interior, but what the hell.

He turned and followed Andy back out of the front door, where a couple of stragglers were hurrying up the pavement and through the gates. The church's façade was stained nearly black with dirt, and soot, and exhaust fumes. A clock-tower steeple rose on one side – running about fifteen minutes late – looming over the heavy stonework and narrow windows. It was sealed off from Queen's Cross roundabout by a shoulder-high hedge on one side and a low gate on the other, as if that would keep out the Godless masses. Next door, the three-storey granite buildings had been given a clean, which only made the church look grimier.

Even the snow looked less pure. It drifted down, clinging to the bushes and walls, dulling the paintwork of the gleaming black hearse parked outside the church – back door open.

'Crap, crap, crap, crap, crap, crap…' Three slightly wobbly figures ran up the pavement, cheeks pink, breath trailing behind them in cloudy wisps. Isla, Tufty, and Calamity. All dressed in their Sunday best.

Isla slithered to a halt on the icy path in her four-inch heels. 'Sorry, Sarge. Took longer to get here than we thought. Traffic's a nightmare.'

Calamity gave Logan's shoulder a squeeze. 'You OK, Sarge?'

Couldn't help but smile. He pointed at Tufty. 'I thought you were all off celebrating Pinocchio here becoming a real boy.'

'Nah.' Isla waved a hand at him. 'We're a team, Sarge. We got your back.'

Up close, the smell of beer, wine, and sloe gin surrounded the three of them. There was a distinct whiff of wet dog too.

Logan frowned. 'You didn't drive, did you?'

'Got a lift off Syd Fraser. He's parking the van.'

Well, at least that explained the smell of dog.

The first notes of Samantha's favourite song rang out from inside the church, made huge and dark by the organ.

Andy appeared at his elbow. 'Mr McRae? It's time.'

A hand on Logan's shoulder made him flinch. He took a step back and blinked.

Right.

'Laz, you OK?' Steel peered up at him, the wrinkles deep between her eyebrows.

He cleared his throat. 'Yeah. Fine.'

Snow swept across the graveyard, wind rattling the empty trees – driving the icy flakes into his skin like tiny icy daggers.

The plot had a good view down the hill, across the road, past the roundabout, the caravan park where Samantha used to live, over the river to the sewage works, and off to the fields beyond. Half one in the afternoon and the big Danestone Tesco had all its lights on, blaring like a beacon through the gloom. The roads were clogged, a solid stream of headlights going one way and tail-lights going the other.

Steel tucked her hands into her armpits and sniffed. 'Nice ceremony. Shame about the turnout.'

A handful of people hurried down the curving paths, towards the line of parked cars at the cemetery gate.

'She was in a coma for five years. People move on.'

'Suppose so.' Steel stamped her feet and turned her back on the wind. 'Thought your wee sister could've bothered her backside to turn up though.'

'She's got a murder inquiry to run.' He brushed the cold damp earth from his hands. 'Besides, I only met her on Thursday. Barely know the woman.'

'Still should've turned up.' Steel hunched her shoulder and rocked from side to side. 'Gah, can't feel my bum.'

'Go. Get warm. It's OK.' He pointed down the hill at the cars. 'I just want a minute.'

She patted him on the back. 'Don't be daft. Never wanted

to feel my bum anyway. Christina Hendricks's arse on the other hand, I'd grope the hell out of that. You'd need both hands, mind.'

'Honestly, it's OK. Go.'

'Sure?'

'Sod off.'

A shrug. Then she slouched off, leaving him alone at the graveside.

A dozen handfuls of part-frozen earth had done nothing to hide the lid of Samantha's coffin.

'This is turning into a habit. Two funerals in four days.' He stuck his hands in his pockets. 'Hope you like it here. Thought it would be better than some anonymous council job. At least you know the area.' He copied Steel, turning his back on the wind. The snow made pattering sounds against his suit jacket, like hundreds of tiny feet running all over him. 'You can see your old house from here... Well, you could if someone hadn't burned it down.'

The wind moaned through the trees and between the headstones.

'Anyway, yeah...' Logan frowned. Bit his bottom lip. 'Don't suppose they'll let me visit much, you know: after they catch me, prosecute, and send me down for sixteen years. Assuming Reuben doesn't pull a fast one and kill us both.'

A thick eddy of snow whipped past, dancing among the dead flowers and ceramic teddy bears. Down by the round-about, someone leaned on their car horn, as if that was going to get the traffic moving at more than a snail's crawl.

'You know, you *could* say something.'

The high-pitched pinging rattle of an approaching train sang through the frozen air, getting louder and louder until it was swamped by the diesel roar of the train itself. It clattered by on the line up the hill, between the cemetery's top edge and the dual carriageway beyond. A ribbon of flickering lights and bored faces, staring out of the carriage windows at the falling snow.

410

'Mr McRae?'

Logan didn't turn around. Didn't have to. 'Mr Urquhart.'

'Sorry I couldn't make the service.' Urquhart stepped up beside him, a bouquet of black roses in his hand. 'Thought she might like these.'

'Thank you.'

'Yeah.'

The flickering strobe of passing carriages faded, leaving them alone in the snow.

Urquhart squatted down, then dropped the black roses onto the black coffin lid nestled in its black grave. He stood and wiped his hands together. 'We're all set for tonight. The guys who run the pig farm will stay well away till I say otherwise, and they've got half a dozen porkers who haven't been fed for a couple of days. So Reuben turns up, we go for a little walk.' Urquhart made a gun from his thumb and fingers. '*Pop*. Munchity crunchity.'

'What, no Shakespeare this time?'

'Nah, a time and a place, right, Mr McRae?'

Mr McRae.

Logan puffed out a cloudy breath – it was torn away by the funeral air. 'I think, John, as we're conspiring to commit murder, you can call me Logan, don't you?'

41

Might as well not have bothered having a wake. It wasn't as if the funeral was oversubscribed, and only half of the attendees made the trip across town to the burial. And only a dozen of *those* made it to the Munro House Hotel in Bucksburn, even though it wasn't even five minutes from the cemetery.

The function room carpet was a muted red tartan, faded by the passage of feet and years. Its wood-panelled walls were thick with landscapes of Glencoe and paintings of grouse and deer. Two stags heads, mounted on opposite walls, glared out with gimlet eyes as if they were about to charge each other.

The remaining twelve people milled around the buffet table, looking swamped in a room that probably held five hundred on a good day.

But then this wasn't a good day.

Steel popped a wee pastry thing into her mouth, talking as she chewed. 'Good spread.' She helped herself to another vol-au-vent from the tray, nestled amongst all the tiny pies and sausage rolls and mini Kievs and filo prawns and the bowls of crisps and pickled onions and untouched salad. 'You're staying with us tonight. And before you say anything, Laz, that's no' a polite invitation it's an order.'

Logan stared down the table at the dwindling mourners. 'There's enough food here for about sixty people.'

She held up her glass – filled nearly to the brim with whisky. 'And don't think we don't appreciate it. And the free bar.' She clinked it against his mineral water. 'Slàinte mhath!'

The young man threw his head back and laughed. 'Oh God, and the *smell*!' He took another scoof of what looked like Coke, but reeked of rum. 'Tell you, you think a septic tank would be bad enough, but try throwing in a decomposing corpse!'

The woman with him grimaced at Logan. 'Sorry about this, he's had—'

'No, wait a minute, wait a minute.' Mr Rum-And-Coke stifled a belch. 'So there we are, in like chest waders, and we're like up to our knees sloshing about, trying to find all the bits of this dead girl, and Samantha slips, right?' Another laugh. 'She slips and it's like in slow-motion and you can see it in her face, she's going down, but she's damned if she's going down alone—'

'Come on, Billy, we should get going, it's—'

'—reaches out to steady herself and grabs Fusty Frankie, and he's like, "Holy crap!"'

'Billy, come on, you—'

'And *he* grabs me, and I'm like, "Aaaargh!" and I grab Gordie's leg, cos he's not down in the tank, he's up on the ground above us—'

'Billy!'

'—and there's screaming and swearing and down we all go...'

'Sarge?' Someone tapped Logan on the shoulder, and when he turned, there was Calamity. 'Sorry we can't stay, but we're back on shift at ten and if I don't get Tufty and Isla back to Banff soon they'll be sod-all use tonight.' She grimaced. 'Isla's been on the Baileys, and you know what she's like with a drink in her. Probably going to get The Smiths' greatest hits all the way home.'

Logan nodded. 'Thanks for coming.'

413

'What are friends for?' She leaned forward and kissed him on the cheek. 'Let us know if you need anything, OK?'

And then there were five.

Logan struggled his way through yet another testicle-sized Kiev and washed it down with a mouthful of mineral water.

'Laz! Laz, Laz, Laz...' Steel marched over to him, back fence-post straight, one arm swinging completely out of time with her legs – which seemed to have developed an opinion of their own about how knees actually worked. 'How come you're not drinks? Got to drinks. It's a *wake*.' She held up a tumbler half full of amber liquid. 'Is only Grouse, but I *like* it. Good for you.'

'No. Thanks. Don't really feel like it.'

'You sure?' She blinked at him, then threw back a mouthful. 'Is there any crisps? Oooh, never mind, I spy sausage rolls!' And she was off.

Susan wrapped an arm around Logan's waist and gave him a lopsided hug. 'I'm really sorry, but the little monster needs her bed.' Naomi nestled in the crook of her other arm, looking for all the world like a cross between ET and some sort of pink grub. Blinking and making big wet toothless yawns.

Logan kissed the top of Susan's head. Her hair smelled of oranges. 'Don't be. Thanks for coming.'

She let go and backed up a pace. 'And you're sure you're OK taking the big monster home?'

They both turned.

Steel was over by the bar again, one leg wandering back and forth, while the other kept her upright. She was pouring from a litre bottle of Bells, and, to be fair, getting most of it in the glass.

'She needs a day off, doesn't she?'

Susan sighed. 'You're preaching to the clergy, Logan.' Then she turned and waved at Jasmine. 'Come on, Horror, put the Nintendo away, we're going home.'

'Don't suppose you want to take some of this food home with you?'

She picked up a wee individual cheese-and-ham tart, grimaced, then put it down again. 'I hate to let it go to waste, but we're all on diets.'

Steel wobbled over and wrapped her arm around Logan's shoulders, whisky slopped out of the glass in her other hand. 'I love you. No, I do. You're a ... a good *person*. For a man.'

The last mourner at the wake raised an eyebrow at Logan. 'And with that, it's time for me to go.' He shook Logan's hand. 'I'm really sorry about Sam. She was one of the best Scene Of Crime officers I ever worked with.'

'Thanks.'

'Nooo!' Steel sloshed more whisky at him. 'Stay! We'll have ... have a drinks.'

A pained smile, and he grabbed his coat and left.

Logan took the glass off her. 'Come on, bedtime.'

'But is *whisky*.' Reaching for it.

'No more whisky. Home.'

'Nooo...' She lurched out into the middle of the room and did a wobbly three-sixty with her arms out, squinting at the empty room. 'Where everyone gone?'

'Can we *please* just go home?'

'Hungry.' Her eyes widened. 'Ooh, sausage rolls!'

God's sake.

Logan let her scoop up a couple of pockets' full of assorted funeral food, then steered her down to the car.

'Yeah.' Logan shifted his grip on the phone, fingers already going numb as snow whipped in through the bare trees' branches. 'Look, I've told them to leave the food out, and the function room's paid for till five. So anyone who wants it, is welcome.'

On the other end of the phone, Napier's weirdo IT guru made lip-smacking noises. *'That's very generous of you, my dear*

Sergeant McRae. The Magnificent Karl, and all associated officers of Bucksburn station, salute you! We'll make sure it gets a good home. Oh my, yes.'

Which meant the locusts would descend and the hotel would be lucky if the function room still had its carpet by the time they finished.

'Thanks, Karl.' He hung up and slipped his phone back in his pocket, keeping his hand there. Shivered.

Ding-Dong hadn't been kidding: there was almost nothing left of Samantha's static caravan. The axles and some drooping bits of metal sat amidst piles of blackened stuff. Bits of wall, bits of floor. Something that used to be a washing machine, its plastic door melted to a vitrified amber. All dead. All slowly disappearing under a duvet of snow.

He nudged at a mound. A charred Dean Koontz novel emerged, followed by what was left of a thick paperback with a zombie on the cover.

Nothing but ashes and death.

But then, what else did a life leave behind?

He kicked the books into the wreckage.

The question now was: what to do till midnight?

No point going all the way back up to Banff, to come all the way back again. Might as well take Susan up on her offer. Hang out, drink some tea, maybe watch a film. Then slip out, kill Reuben, and feed him to the pigs. Do it right and no one would know he'd even left the house. No one except for John Urquhart.

Still have to figure out what to do with him.

Logan turned back to the car.

Steel sagged in the passenger seat, head lolling against the window, mouth wide open. Snoring hard enough to make the Punto's roof vibrate.

Oh joy.

Logan pulled up outside Steel's house, behind the patrol car. Climbed out into the snow.

The street was quiet, expensive, secluded – a cul-de-sac lined with old granite buildings and trees on both sides. Their canopy of naked branches blocked about half of the flakes that spiralled down from the darkening sky, but let plenty through to pile up on the roofs and bonnets of fancy four-by-fours and family saloons.

Snow crunched beneath his feet as Logan picked his way along the road to the patrol car and rapped on the driver's window.

It buzzed down, exposing a square face with thick eyebrows. 'Help you?'

Logan showed her his warrant card. 'Sergeant McRae. Anything happening?'

'Nah. Kids came home from school about twenty minutes ago, Tesco van dropped off shopping at number twelve, other than that: quiet as the grave.' A sniff. 'Freezing our backsides off here.'

'It's OK, you can Foxtrot Oscar. I'll stay over and keep an eye on the place. Just make sure someone's back here for nine-ish tomorrow.'

She curled her lip and raised one of those family-sized eyebrows. 'Yeah...' Then reached for her Airwave. 'Think I'll check with my guvnor first, if it's all the same to you.'

'Be my guest.' Logan hooked a thumb back towards his manky rusting Punto. 'But before you go, you can give me a hand getting DCI Steel inside.'

'Ummmph...' Logan dumped Steel on her bed, then stood back panting. 'She's heavier than she looks.'

'Why do you think we're all on diets?' Susan hauled one of Steel's legs up and undid the boot on the end.

The bedroom looked like something out of a catalogue: the bedding toned with the carpet and the curtains, the wallpaper went with the two chairs, and the wooden bed frame, wardrobe, vanity unit, and ottoman all had exactly the same twiddly bits.

He stepped over to the window as Susan got to work on the socks. 'Hour and a half it took to get here. Traffic's appalling.' The front garden was almost swallowed by snow, the shrubs and bushes fading into soft outlines. Thick plumes of white purred from the patrol car's exhaust, then it pulled away from the kerb. Off to fight crime. Logan smiled and turned his back on the scene. 'And the *snoring*. Dear God, it was like being battered over the head with a chainsaw.'

'Welcome to my world. Give me a hand with her jacket?'

They ate in the kitchen.

'Nothing fancy, I'm afraid.' Susan put a big bowl of pasta down in front of him, studded with mushrooms and flecks of bacon. Then she sat and watched him eat, her own plate untouched. 'Are you feeling all right, Logan? Only you seem a bit … you know.'

'This is lovely, thanks.' He shovelled in another mouthful and tried for a smile. 'I'm OK. You know: been a tough week.'

'Well, if you need someone to talk to.' She reached across the breakfast bar and took his hand.

'Thanks.' But two people in an illegal conspiracy was probably enough.

'Come on, Monkeybum, time for bed.'

Jasmine stuck her bottom lip out and pulled on a kicked-puppy expression. 'But I'm watching *Adventure Cat* with *Dad*.'

On the TV, a round fuzzy cat in a weird hat leapt off a space jukebox and ninja-kicked an oversized rat dressed as the King of Transylbumvania.

If Police Scotland really wanted to make inroads into the drugs trade, arresting everyone involved in children's television would probably be a good start.

'You heard your mum.' Logan switched off the telly, then plonked a palm down on top of Jasmine's head and ruffled

418

her hair. 'Teeth, then bed. And if you're good I'll read you some of your favourite book.'

'But, Da-ad...' Head on one side, making her eyes as big as they possibly could be – eyelashes fluttering.

Yeah, she was going to cause fights in pubs when she was older.

'No *Skeleton Bob and the Very Naughty Pirates* for you then.'

'Oh ... poo.' Then she hopped down from the table and went to do her teeth.

Logan checked his watch: eight o'clock.

Four hours to go.

Logan settled on the edge of the Peppa Pig duvet – covering Daddy Pig's genitalia-shaped head – and picked the book up from the windowsill. 'Are you sitting comfortably?'

It was strange, but after working with Detective Superintendent Harper, the family resemblance was actually pretty clear. OK, so the hair colour was different – Jasmine's dark brown versus Harper's off-blonde – but they both had the same strong jaw, the same lopsided smile. The same big ears.

Jasmine frowned at him. 'Why do you always say that, before you read a story?'

'Because I'm old.' His hand drifted up, feeling the outline of his own ear. It wasn't really that big, was it? Oh, sodding hell: it was. God, they were a family of elephant people.

He opened the book to a lurid illustration of a wee skeletal boy in a knitted pink suit and feathery pirate hat, on a boat, sword-fighting against what looked like octopus tentacles. 'Ahem.' He put on a cod West Country accent.

'"The following tale, Dear Reader, I fear,
Is probably not for your sensitive ears,
The old and the wobbly, the scared and the sick,
Had better read something else pretty darn quick,
For this is a tale that's both scary and true,
Of how Skeleton Bob joined a most *scurvy* crew..."'

*   *   *

Rasping snores thundered through the wall, making the paintings on this side vibrate. Logan lay flat on his back, on the bed, fully dressed except for his shoes, with the evidence bag resting on his chest. Heavy. Pushing down on his heart.

A faint yellow glow oozed in through the curtains, picking out the edges of more catalogue furniture.

He pulled out his phone and checked the time: quarter past eleven. Give it another five minutes.

Surely Susan would be asleep by now? Then again, how anyone could sleep next to that racket was anyone's guess. They said love was blind, but apparently it was deaf as well.

Four minutes.

Shadows made patterns on the ceiling, barely visible in the gloom. There an open grave, here a severed hand. Was that a claw hammer encrusted with blood and hair?

Where the hell was Samantha when you needed her? Someone to hold his hand and tell him he was doing the right thing.

He was, wasn't he?

OK, not the *right* right thing, but it was this or … what?

Couldn't even go to the Procurator Fiscal and get Reuben done for battering Tony Evans to death. No body, no witnesses. And even if he *could* get Reuben sent down for eighteen years, Logan would be off to a cell of his own. Where Reuben could have him shanked in the laundry room. Raped and strangled in the showers. Stabbed in the exercise yard.

Two minutes.

So grow a pair of man-sized testicles and do what needs to be done.

Easy as that.

God…

How could people like Reuben just kill people and not worry about it? Why didn't it keep *them* awake, staring at the horror-film shadows on the ceiling?

One minute.

OK that was long enough.

Logan slipped off the bed and picked up his shoes. Eased out into the corridor. Closed the door, slow and gentle.

The snoring didn't miss a beat.

He crept downstairs and out into the night.

42

'You know what this is, don't you?'

The Fiat Punto rattled its way along a narrow country road, windscreen wipers moaning their way back and forth across the glass, smearing the snow as it melted.

Logan glanced at himself in the rear-view mirror. 'Stupid?'

'What if it's a trap? What if Urquhart's set you up?'

'Could be.'

A tiny row of houses crawled past on the left. Two or three lights were on, but other than that they were dark. Nearly midnight, and with luck nobody would be wandering about, taking down number plates.

Mounds of grimy white lined the tarmac. The road hadn't been gritted, but it had been ploughed which made it *slightly* easier to drive on. Logan's Punto rattled through the troughs, doing no more than twenty, heater up full, blowers at maximum.

'Not too late to turn around and go home.'

He didn't dignify that with an answer.

'Is this doing-both-sides-of-a-conversation thing more or less healthy than talking to a hallucination of a woman who's in a coma? Because I'm guessing less.'

Mirror Logan shrugged. 'What about Urquhart? I mean, assuming he isn't actually on Reuben's side – he's going to hold this over you for the rest of your life. He'd have you on murder.'

'He already has – Eddy Knowles, remember?'

'That wasn't our fault.'

'We killed him.'

A thick black line emerged through the snow ahead. That would be Gairnhill Wood.

'OK, you have to stop talking to yourself in the plural. Bad enough as it is.'

'All right: *you* killed him, doesn't matter if you meant to or not. No one's going to buy self-defence if you conspired to get shot of the body.'

'Which I didn't.'

'Yeah, but who's going to believe that?'

'True.'

The woods swallowed the Punto. Its headlights made a tiny smear of life in the darkness.

Not far to go now.

'So how does Urquhart turn *me* in without implicating himself? He's the one who got rid of the body.'

'Allegedly.'

'Hmmm… There is that.'

'Here we go.'

A sign hung on chains by the side of the road: the silhouette of a pig with '← WEST GAIRNHILL FARM' printed above it in faded letters.

Logan touched the brakes and the Punto slithered a bit, then slowed. He took the turning at a crawl.

'Are you sure you're sure?'

'No. Now shut up.'

Trees lined both sides of the farm road like long-dead sentries. The Punto rocked and thumped through potholes hidden by the snow, following the tracks of at least two other cars.

'They're already here.' He bashed the steering wheel with the palm of his hand. 'Damn it. Should've got here an hour ago. Scoped the place out. Been waiting for them.'

'Don't be an idiot: it's Reuben's farm, his people live here. If you'd turned up early they'd have clyped on you. Or taken you in and given you a cup of tea. Either way, you were never getting the element of surprise. Now shut your porridge-hole and let me concentrate.'

The road bumped and lurched through the woods to a clearing where the land fell away downhill, overlooking rolling fields and jagged clumps of forest – all smothered beneath a layer of dirty white.

An old-fashioned farmhouse with gable ends and a slate roof loomed beside a cluster of agricultural buildings. Somewhere for keeping a tractor; another piled high with hay; and three long low buildings, ugly and naked, pinned to the ground by rows of blazing halogen lights. The pigsties.

Urquhart's Audi sat next to a big red Land Rover that looked showroom clean under a thin dusting of snow.

Everyone was here.

Logan parked on the other side of the Audi.

Right.

He pulled on his stabproof vest. Might not help against a bullet, but at least it was something. A brand-new cagoule went over the top, hiding it, then he snapped on a pair of blue nitrile gloves and opened the evidence bag. Slipped the second freezer bag off – leaving the gun one layer of protection. Then took a biro and poked it through the plastic, wriggling the pen about until the hole was big enough to get his finger around the trigger. The slide hauled back with a clack. Safety off. Logan eased the semiautomatic into the cagoule's pocket.

With the silencer attached a quick draw was out of the question, but it was a pig farm, not the OK Corral.

'Right.'

Deep breath. It wasn't easy with the stabproof vest hugging his ribs.

'Come on. You can do this.'

Out.

The air crawled with the brown sickly-bitter stench of pig shit, bolstered by the sharp tang of fermenting urine. Steam rose from the three long buildings, caught in the glare of the lights. Grunts and squeals rang out from inside.

It was a bit like walking into an episode of *The X-Files*.

Logan tightened his grip on the gun and followed the footprints in the snow to the sty furthest from the house.

Not too late to turn around.

Not too late to run.

And then it was.

The big metal door clattered back and John Urquhart smiled out at him. 'Mr McRae, cool, glad you could make it.' He'd dressed for the occasion: suit, shirt, tie, heavy black overcoat. Not exactly the best outfit for killing someone and disposing of the body. 'Come in, come in.'

Logan was going to die here, wasn't he? Die and be eaten.

Come on. Not dead yet.

Logan nodded, put his other hand in his pocket – hiding the blue glove – then followed Urquhart inside.

Out there, the cold had obviously dampened the smell, because in *here* the stench of pig was so thick it coated the inside of his mouth with a greasy sour film. It was warm too, condensation trickling down the corrugated iron. Rows and rows of naked pink backs filled the sties on either side, three or four to a bay. Metal gates bolted into breezeblock walls.

Reuben stood at the far end, arms crossed over his massive chest. He'd ditched the expensive suit for scabby green overalls, the shiny leather shoes for a pair of manky rig boots. A black holdall sat at his feet. He jerked his head up, setting those scarred chins wobbling. 'You're late.'

Wrong – bang on time. 'Nice to see you too, Reuben.' Kind of surprising – how calm his voice sounded. As if this was any other meeting, in a pig sty, with a killer and his right-hand-man.

Logan turned and leaned back against the nearest sty, where he could see Reuben and Urquhart at the same time. Kept his hands in his pockets.

'Rightiehoo.' Urquhart beamed. 'So, Stevie Fowler, yeah? What to do?'

'Kill him. You steal from me, you die. That's how it works.'

'Yeah, OK, one vote for death. Mr McRae?'

'We—'

'NO!' Reuben kicked a sty gate with his steel toecaps, setting the metal ringing and the pigs squealing. 'This isn't a bloody democracy. I say Fowler dies, you make it happen. End of.'

Urquhart's smile slipped a bit. 'Right. OK. Got you. Fowler gets an accident in prison, and—'

'Not an accident.'

'Come on, Reuben, let's be sensible about—'

'NO BLOODY ACCIDENTS!' His face flushed, teeth bared, flecks of spittle flashed in the harsh light. 'He suffers and everyone gets to see what's left, and they talk in frightened whispers about the moron who thought he could screw with me!'

Urquhart licked his lips. 'OK, OK, you want him messy dead? We'll get him messy dead. But the cops are going to know it was us, Reuben. They're going to come after us.'

'So what?' He pointed a thick finger at Logan. 'We got someone to make it all go away.'

Logan turned a bit to the left, so the semiautomatic in his pocket was more or less in line with Reuben's stomach. 'No, you don't.'

He bared his teeth. 'Don't think you heard me properly, McRae.'

'I'm not one of your minions, Reuben. I'm not going to make things go away. I *can't* make things go away.'

'You bloody well—'

'It doesn't work like that any more!' Logan jabbed a finger back at him. 'This isn't *The Godfather*, police officers can't just

426

make investigations vanish. People notice, the media notice, the Procurator Fiscal notices.'

Reuben frowned at Logan's hand. 'What's with the gloves?'

Why draw this out? Get it over and done with.

Kill him.

'Scared of getting your hands dirty, McRae?'

Take the gun out and *shoot* him.

Do it.

'What the hell did Mr Mowat ever see in you? Heir to the throne my arse. You haven't got the balls to...' Reuben raised an eyebrow and stared at the gun. Then snorted. 'Aye, right.'

The semiautomatic was getting heavier with every heartbeat, and every time he tried to swallow, his throat closed up. The silencer's black cylinder wavered, then drifted up to point at Reuben's chest. 'I'm sorry.'

'Genuinely? You think this *scares* me?'

Urquhart backed away a couple of steps. 'Guys?'

Reuben laughed. Then squatted down and opened the holdall at his feet. 'See, the trouble with people like you, McRae, is you're all gob and no panties. Think a gun makes you a big man? Nah.'

'I'm not screwing about. Put your hands behind your head.'

'What makes you a big man, is being a *man*.' Reuben pulled a sawn-off shotgun from the bag and stood. 'Gun's only a tool.'

Urquhart backed off some more. 'Come on, let's not do anything we're going to regret, right?'

'Reuben, hands behind your head. *Now.*'

'A tool's only as good as the craftsman who wields it.' He cracked the shotgun open and slid two cartridges into the breech. 'Mr Mowat told me that. Wise man, till it came to you.' *Clack*, the shotgun was closed again. 'See, you're weak, so—'

Logan shot him.

The silencer's *phut* didn't even echo.

Reuben rocked back on his heels, but he didn't go down. He stared at the spot of red seeping into the leg of his overalls, turning the green material a dark purple. 'You...' He glared at Logan. Then the shotgun came up.

Buggering hell.

Logan dived over the wall of the nearest sty, battering down amongst the huge pink bodies as a loud *BOOOOOM* reverberated back from the corrugated metal walls, followed by a clatter of shot.

Chunks of breezeblock sparked into the air, falling as gritty dust.

The pigs squealed, dirty hooves scrabbling at the straw bedding as they tried to get away. But the sty was barely big enough to turn around in. They barged against Logan, knocking him down, snouts and teeth flashing all around him.

'GET OUT HERE YOU WEE SHITE!'

BOOOOOM.

Gah...

How could he miss? The guy was huge and all he'd managed to hit was a *leg*?

Clack, then the hollow rattle of empty shotgun cartridges hitting the concrete floor.

Now.

Logan snapped up to his knees, bringing the gun up two-handed. *Phut. Phut.*

Only Reuben wasn't where he was meant to be.

Clack.

For a big guy, he moved incredibly fast. He'd got himself inside one of the other sties, sawn-off shotgun up and ready.

Logan ducked again.

BOOOOOM.

Something stung his cheek, like a wasp.

Up.

Phut.

Reuben grunted as red spread across his left shoulder. *BOOOOOM.*

The blast clattered against the breezeblocks as Logan dived amongst the pigs again.

'YOU'RE DEAD, MCRAE, YOU HEAR ME? YOU'RE DEAD AND EVERYONE YOU KNOW IS DEAD!'

Clack. More shotgun cartridges hitting the floor.

Logan stuck his arm above the parapet and pulled the trigger. Not aiming, just hoping. *Phut, phut.*

'DEAD!'

He scrambled to his feet, and there was Reuben.

The big man had Urquhart, holding him up by the armpits, arms wrapped around his chest. Urquhart's head lolled to the side, blood darkening the front of his suit jacket.

Logan brought the gun up. 'Put him down.'

Reuben still had the shotgun in his hand, only he couldn't point it without letting go of Urquhart. 'This is all *your* fault.'

Couldn't get a clear shot with Urquhart acting as a human shield.

'Put – him – down.'

The big man backed towards the far door, dragging Urquhart with him. 'This isn't over, McRae.'

'I'm warning you, Reuben: put – him – down!'

'This isn't over by a *long* way.'

He stepped out through the door, letting in a whirl of snow, slamming it shut behind him.

Logan vaulted from the sty and ran, gun up and ready. Reuben wasn't getting—

BOOOOOM.

The shotgun blast ripped through the corrugated iron door, grabbed Logan by the chest and hurled him to the concrete floor.

'Unnngh…'

The smell of fireworks fought against the piggy stench.

His whole front screamed in searing agony, like he'd been trampled by a burning elephant.

'Ow...'

It took three goes to get to his knees.

The front of his cagoule was shredded, the stabproof vest beneath it torn and tattered. Bits of stuffing poked out, exposing the buckled armoured plate.

Every breath was laced with jagged shards of hot copper.

'Arrrgh.'

He pulled himself up one of the sties and stood there, one hand holding his chest, the other holding the gun.

By the time he lurched out through the punctured door, Reuben's Land Rover was nowhere to be seen.

43

Logan peeled off his shirt and dropped it to the bathroom floor. Locked the door. Shuddered in the darkness. Then pulled the cord.

The light on the medicine cabinet flickered on, casting a bluish-white glow, pushing back the gloom. It washed the colour from his skin, turning it pale and ghostly. A walking corpse. Shot in the chest.

He stepped closer to the mirror, where the light was brightest.

It had been what, an hour since Reuben tried to blow a hole in him? And the bruising hadn't come up yet. But when it did, it would be *huge*. His whole chest was red and swollen, with purple contusions in the middle where the majority of the shot had hit. When he prodded them, it was like rubbing vinegar into a fresh cut. Thank God the blast had to travel through that metal door first, or the stabproof vest wouldn't have stood a chance. The guys who ran Reuben's pig farm would've been cleaning up his innards for days.

Bee-sting lumps speckled his cheek – six or seven of them, all about the size of a Smarty, each one with a dark dot at the centre, as if he was a teenager again, covered with blackheads. It hurt, but Logan squeezed one of them between his thumbnails until a tiny pellet plopped into the sink, leaving a plume of pink as it sank through the water.

One was barely an inch below his left eye.

Lucky he wasn't blinded. Lucky the door had been there. Lucky he wasn't pig food.

Yeah. He was a lucky, *lucky* guy.

He gritted his teeth and squeezed out the other flecks of shot. Then opened the bathroom cabinet as tiny rosebuds of blood bloomed on his cheeks and chin. A dusty old ceramic bottle of Old Spice was half-buried behind all the moisturizers and exfoliants and cleaners and hand cream. He eased it out and splashed a couple of shakes into his palm – like Henry Cooper used to do on the adverts – rubbed his hands together, then patted at the bleeding holes.

Dear ... sodding ... *Christ*, that stung.

Logan closed his eyes hissing breath in and out. In and out. Until it settled to a steady throb. Arrrrgh... That hurt more than being shot.

A brittle laugh burst free, but he stamped on it. Forced it down.

Shuddered.

Almost killed someone tonight. Not by accident. Not in self-defence. On purpose. Premeditated.

And who knew, maybe he *had* actually killed someone: maybe he'd killed John Urquhart? Maybe Urquhart had caught one of those random unaimed bullets? Or maybe he'd not backed away far enough when Reuben brought the shotgun out?

The bathroom mirror was cold against his forehead.

Idiot.

Why did he have to miss that first shot? This would all be over by now.

Well done, Logan.

Sterling job.

The distorted, bruised, and battered Logan stared back at him from the mirror. 'Maybe you missed because Reuben was right: you don't have the balls to kill anyone.'

'I don't *want* them.' He lathered up with antibacterial

432

handwash, then slathered it onto his face, working it into all the stinging pellet holes. Making them scream. Then shouted them down with a second dose of Old Spice.

Arrrrrgh...

The freezer downstairs produced a packet of petits pois, the drinks cupboard a half-empty litre of Famous Grouse. Logan pressed the former against his burning face and the latter into service as an anaesthetic.

Four ibuprofen and the same again of aspirin hadn't made a dent in it, but the second dram of whisky worked its magic. Or it might have been the frozen peas numbing his skin. Either way it didn't ache *quite* as much.

Of course, Reuben would come after him with a vengeance now. The gun-without-a-firing-pin incident was bad enough, but this? Tonight? He'd be like a rabid dog.

Maybe they'd have a few days while Reuben recuperated from his two bullet holes? Enough time for Logan to call his new lawyer and put his affairs in order.

That or flee the country.

A groan came from the kitchen doorway, followed by something out of a George Romero film. It was Steel, wearing a fluffy grey dressing gown, with penguin pyjama bottoms sticking out beneath, arms sticking out in front, and her hair sticking out in every other direction. Only she didn't try to eat Logan's brains; she shuffled over to the sink and turned the cold tap on full. Then dunked her head under it.

He topped his glass up, and screwed the cap back on the bottle.

She was still trying to drown herself in the sink.

Logan took a sip, rolling the whisky around his mouth, numbing it from the inside.

And finally Steel emerged from beneath the cascade of cold water looking almost completely unlike a shampoo advert. Instead of flinging her hair back in a glorious golden arc, she slumped against the sink, water running down her face and dripping onto her grey fuzzy dressing gown and the floor. Like a cat who'd just been fished out of the toilet bowl. 'Pfff...'

He toasted her with his glass.

She wiped her face on a sleeve and squinted. 'What?'

'Didn't say a thing.'

'Got a head like a... Like a...' Her shoulders sagged even further. 'No, can't be arsed.'

Logan stood and pulled another glass from the cupboard. Filled it from the dispenser built into the fridge. Held it out. 'Here.'

She took it with both hands and gulped it down. 'More.'

He refilled it and she guzzled that one too. And the next.

Then Steel settled into a chair on the other side of the kitchen table. Her eyes seemed to have difficulty both focusing on the same spot, and something was wrong with her mouth – all the words were soft and mushy, as if she was pushing them through a sieve. 'I think I might've died in my sleep.'

'Whose fault is that?'

'Why did you let me drink so much whisky? It's like there's a ceilidh in my skull and only fat people in hobnail boots got invited.' Another mouthful of water. 'They're doing an Orcadian Strip the Willow.' Her top lip curled as she sniffed. 'And why does it smell like an auld mannie's pants in here?'

Logan lowered the bag of petits pois. 'Cut myself shaving.'

She shook her head, then grabbed onto the table. Blinking. 'Gah. Stop the world...' A deep breath, then she relinquished her grip. 'I – am definitely – not – going – to be – sick.'

'You're still drunk, aren't you?'

'No. Maybe. Kind of.' Steel burped, then grimaced and shuddered. Had another mouthful of water. 'I'm sorry about Samantha. She was a total Hottie McSexyPants. And I'm no' just saying that! See if I wasn't married and she hadn't been in a coma?'

434

'Go back to bed.'

'Can't. When I lie down the walls chase each other round the room.' She drained the last drops from her glass. 'More.'

Logan filled it. 'Think I might give it up. Move somewhere warm and far away.'

'Don't be daft.'

'I mean, what's the point? We spend ninety percent of our time dealing with five percent of the people. Barely scratch the surface.' He knocked back a mouthful of Grouse, sucked air in through his teeth. 'I'm not a very good police officer.'

'If you move, how you going to watch Jasmine and wee Naomi grow up?'

'Not very good at all.'

'Don't whinge, Laz. I hate it when you whinge.' She sniffed. 'Makes you sound like Rennie.'

'Yeah.'

'And we *do* make a difference.' She put down her water and picked up his whisky, raised it to her lips. The colour drained from her cheeks and she put it down again. 'Nope.'

'Don't think Detective Superintendent Harper really wants a big brother.'

'Look at all the scumbags we put away every year. You got those people-traffickers last year. And that guy who was beating up auld wifies for their pension money.'

'Don't think my brother Eamon wants one either.'

'Wah, wah, wah.' She finished her water, stuck it back on the table with another burp. 'We got anything to eat?'

He pointed at the fridge. 'Sausage rolls, mini Kievs, and some of those tiny quiches. They're a bit pocket-fluffy, but Susan cleaned the worst of it off.'

'Done.' She slumped over to the bread bin and extracted a Glasgow roll. Then raided the fridge. 'And you want to make a difference? Make one. Don't sit there moaning about it.' The roll got split open and buttered on both sides. 'Don't see me with my thumb in my gob moaning on about scumbags I can't put away, do you?' Four sausage rolls went on the bun, followed by a couple of the Kievs. 'No, because Roberta Steel doesn't take "no comment" for an answer.' Everything got slathered in tomato sauce, then she took a big bite, talking as she chewed, 'You get a problem, you find a solution, Laz. That's what the big girls do.'

He stared down into his whisky. 'I'm in trouble.'

'See when Jack Wallace intimidated his way out of a rape charge, did I go whingeing away with my tail between my knees? Bet your sharny arse I didn't. I *did* something about it.' She thumped down into the seat opposite again and jabbed the table with a finger, leaving a smear of tomato sauce behind. 'And yeah, maybe I should've slipped someone a hundred to break every bone in his body instead. Got them to chuck him in the harbour to sink. But that'd be wrong, right?'

'I think Reuben's going to...' Logan frowned. 'Wait, you *should* have done that?'

'The important thing is, he's no' on the loose attacking women any more. Wee shite's where he belongs.'

'What *did* you do?'

She waved a hand at him, and took another bite. 'Come off it, like you've never bent the rules to get the right result. Course you have.'

'I...' More than she'd ever know.

'Exactly.' She drained her water. 'You should've *seen* Wallace when we told him there wasn't enough evidence to prosecute. Strutting about like there was a rooster up his backside. "Look at me, I won. And I'm going to do it again, because you're all too thick to stop me." Aye, well who's thick now?' She popped the final chunk of funeral-leftovers butty in her mouth and stood. Stuck the kettle on. 'You want tea?'

'You fitted him up.'

'Course, could've done him for pretty much anything, but kiddy porn's a classic, isn't it? You get done for being a paedo,

436

that's with you for the rest of your life; that stain doesn't wash off. Nah, he's got to live with it till the day he dies. Now he knows how the women he attacked feel.' She rattled a couple of mugs onto the worktop. 'And with any luck some nice obliging nonce will shank the wee bastard in prison and take him out of the food chain for good.'

Logan stared at the back of her head as she fiddled about with teabags and spoons. 'Where did you get the images?'

'Oh, you'd no' *believe* the things you can confiscate if you know the wrong people.'

Oh God.

Logan buried his face in the bag of frozen peas. 'You fitted him up.'

'Got loads of those photos left too, you know: if you ever need someone off to the jail?'

'That's not "bending the rules"! That's snapping the damn things in half, then setting them on fire, then peeing on the smouldering ashes.' Gah. He threw the petits pois down on the countertop. 'How many times have you done it? How many people have you sent to prison on faked evidence?'

Steel dug out the steaming teabags and hurled them into the sink. 'We hold a position of *trust*, Laz. It's no' about following the rules or ticking the boxes on this or that procedure, it's about justice. Proper justice for the poor sods out there getting brutalized and attacked and raped and killed.'

He threw his arms out, as if blocking the way. 'We've got rules for a reason! You can't—'

'Justice! And yeah: so I fitted Wallace up, so what? He bloody well deserved it.'

'Napier was right.'

'Napier's a dick.' She slopped milk into the mugs, then thumped one down in front of Logan hard enough to send a beige wave slopping over the side. 'And he's got sod all on me.'

'The created dates on the images show they were all copied onto his machine in two batches.'

'Doesn't prove anything. If Napier had evidence he wouldn't need you crawling about like a cut-price Columbo.'

'God's sake.' He sat back.

She sat forward. 'OK, so it was wrong. You happy now? I – was – wrong. But what the hell was I supposed to do? Jack Wallace raped Claudia Boroditsky, he raped Rosalyn Cooper. She *killed* herself because of him. It's what he does.' Steel poked the table again. 'You want people like that running about when Jasmine's growing up? Stalking her in nightclubs? Following her home?'

'It's not—'

'But it's OK. Don't you see?' A smile bloomed across Steel's face. 'You're on the *investigation*. You can make sure Napier gets sod all, and if anything *does* come up, you lose it. And you make sure it stays lost.'

'Christ.' He closed his eyes and rested his forehead on the bag of defrosting peas.

'You *owe* me that, Logan. You owe me.'

The ceiling seemed like miles away in the gloom. Logan lay on his back, staring up at it. Every breath ached, but it was difficult to tell if the pain was from the battering his chest and ribs had got, or if it was something deeper. Something under the skin. Something malignant.

She'd fitted Wallace up.

So what? *He'd* killed Eddy Knowles. Tried to kill Reuben too. And failed.

Who came off worse in that comparison: the police officer who breaks the rules to get a rapist off the street, or the one who tries to murder a mob boss to save his own skin?

It wasn't as if he'd had any choice though, was it? It—

'Oh shut up.' His voice barely bruised the silence.

'Yes, but I *didn't* have any—'

'What's the point of going over and over this? You think you did what you had to. So does she.' Logan checked his watch. 'It's two in the morning. Go to sleep.'

'Jack Wallace wasn't going to kill her, though, was he?'

The bed creaked beneath Logan as he hissed and grunted his way over onto his side. 'Got to be at work tomorrow.'

'Napier's not going to stop, you know that, don't you?'

For God's sake.

Logan sighed.

'Of course he isn't.' The house was graveyard quiet.

'So what are we going to do?'

'Thought I told you about that: no plurals.'

'OK, so what am *I* going to do? Cover for her, or tell the truth?'

'She'd cover for you.'

'Maybe she shouldn't.' The pillow was soft against his bruised face. 'You can't fit people up. If you do, you're no better than Reuben, or Malcolm McLennan, or Jessica Campbell. The rules are there for a *reason*.'

'So tell the truth.'

'I *can't*.'

'What did you tell Reuben? We can't make evidence disappear, the police force doesn't work that way any more. The law applies to everyone. Him, me, even Steel.'

'Look, let's … sleep on it. See how we feel in the morning.'

'I feel sick.'

Snow clattered against the bedroom window.

'So do I.'

— Tuesday Dayshift —

welcome to the end of days

44

Detective Superintendent Harper raised an eyebrow. 'What happened to her?'

Steel slumped at the end of the conference room table, head buried in her hands. Not moving.

Logan shrugged. 'Coming down with a bit of a cold.'

The sound of voices came from the locker room below their feet, singing from the shower room across the hall, someone coughing a lung up on the landing outside. The sounds of Banff station lurching its way through another day of MIT infestation.

'Hmm...' Harper stared at him. 'And you? Break up another fight outside a pub?'

He pointed at the sticking plasters, freckling his face. 'Need to buy a new razorblade, this one's blunt.'

Becky eased her way into the room, holding a tray covered in mugs. She bared her teeth. 'Right.' The smile she pulled on wouldn't have fooled a house brick as she thumped the tray down on the table. 'Anything else I can get you, or should I go and maybe do some actual police work?'

'Thank you, DS McKenzie.' Harper helped herself to a coffee. 'While we've got you, how about an update on Martin Milne?'

'Climbing up the walls. Worried about his wife and kids.

Moaning about how someone should be organizing Peter Shepherd's funeral.' She scowled at the tray of mugs as Logan picked up a coffee and a Lemsip for Steel, then grabbed a tea for himself. 'If we weren't watching him round the clock, Milne would be off.'

'Suppose we'd better pay him a visit.' Harper sipped at her coffee, grimaced slightly. 'This is great, thanks. If you pass DI Singh on the way down, let him know I'm looking for him.'

'Yes, Super.' Becky turned and flounced off, curly brown hair bobbing along behind her like an angry pompom.

Logan nudged Steel's shoulder. 'Drink your drinks.'

'Urgh.'

Harper sniffed. 'Tell me, Detective Chief Inspector, does your sudden illness have anything to do with the funeral and *wake* yesterday?'

Steel surfaced barely long enough to show off her two black eyes and the bags underneath them. 'It was howfing it down with snow the whole time. Talk about freezing? Still can't feel my toes.' She even threw in a cough or three for good measure.

'Quite.' Harper turned to face the whiteboard, where someone had drawn out the harbour at Gardenstown along with the surrounding streets and the only two roads out of town. An assortment of fridge magnets were stuck to the board. 'Remind me again, who's the Eiffel Tower?'

Logan checked the list. 'DI Singh's team. You're the penguin in a sombrero, Rennie is the canal boat, DS Weatherford is Thomas the Tank Engine—'

'I have *never* known a police station that had to resort to stolen fridge magnets.'

'I'm the Christmas tree, and DCI Steel is the old boot.'

'Hmmm...' Harper edged closer. 'She doesn't really have a cold, does she?'

'Been mainlining Strepsils and Lockets all the way up here.' Which was a lie.

Harper stared at the board. 'This has to work. The top

brass are already complaining about the budget on this investigation, if this is another disaster...' She bared her teeth. 'I need a result, Logan. I need it tonight.'

'It's only been a week since we turned up Peter Shepherd's body. Give it time.'

'A week's a long time in politics and Police Scotland.' She folded her arms, narrowed her eyes at the hand-drawn map and the fridge magnets. 'Are we missing anything?'

'What about DS McKenzie and DS Robertson? Logan dipped into the Tupperware box. 'We've got a lump of cheese or a sheep playing the bagpipes.'

'Better make it the bagpipes for McKenzie, she moans enough.'

Logan stuck that magnet on the smaller scrawled map in the corner – Milne's hotel. The block of cheese went on the other little map – the part-built development where the Milne family home sulked. 'Shame we can't co-locate them. Be a lot easier to manage one locus than two.'

'True. It would free up bodies for the swoop as well.' Harper picked up a marker pen and twirled it between her fingers and across her knuckles, like a tiny baton. Back and forth, back and forth. 'Give McKenzie a shout and tell her we want Milne back in the family home whether the wife likes it or not. I doubt anything's going to happen, not right away. Malk the Knife will want a few days to work on his revenge. Robertson can run the babysitting team.'

Logan settled on the edge of the conference table, next to her. 'Assuming it's actually Malcolm McLennan behind it.'

She turned and frowned at him. 'Why do you always do that?'

'I'm only saying we should keep an open mind.'

'No, not that. You never call him Malk the Knife, it's always Malcolm McLennan.'

'An old friend once told me you shouldn't use silly nicknames for your enemies: it's disrespectful. And when you treat your opponent with disdain, you underestimate them. And when you *underestimate* them, you give them an advantage.'

She looked him up and down. 'Might not be as daft as you look, Logan Balmoral McRae.'

'Thanks, sir.'

Back to the map. 'Anyway, it's not as if we've got anything on the *Jessica* Campbell angle. Ricky and Laura Welsh still aren't talking.' She stood. 'Get a car. When I've spoken to Narveer, we'll go make sure Milne isn't trying to wimp out on us.'

Harper grabbed a folder from the table and marched off.

As soon as the door shut behind her, Logan sagged. Dug out a packet of paracetamol and washed three of them down with a swig of tea. They did nothing to blunt the ache radiating across his chest.

Steel hadn't moved.

'Drink your Lemsip.'

'Urgh...'

'Don't know why you bothered coming into work today.'

Steel raised her head from the conference table. 'I'm dying.'

'What did I tell you this morning? Stay home, call in sick. But *no*, you had to play the brave little soldier.'

'Be nice to me, I'm *dying*.'

'And what happened? You snored, gurgled, and farted all the way up here. It was like sharing a car with a malfunctioning septic tank.'

She wrapped her hands around the mug of Lemsip and slurped at it. Then frowned at him with bleary bloodshot eyes. 'Did we *do* anything last night?'

Logan turned his back on her and fiddled with the fridge magnets on the whiteboard instead. 'Do anything?'

'Yeah, I had this weird feeling we got in a fight or something. And when I woke up my dressing gown was all soggy.'

'No. Don't remember that.'

'I can't have peed myself, 'cause it was only wet on the front.'

Logan repositioned the old boot, putting it further away from the Christmas tree. How could she not remember admitting she'd fitted up Jack Wallace? 'Right. Well, I'd better go get that car sorted.' He hobbled out of the room, nearly colliding with DS Robertson in the corridor.

Robertson backed off a couple of paces, a manila folder held against his chest as if that was going to save him from the impending bollocking when Steel got her hands on him. He nodded at the Major Incident Room door. 'Is the Creature from the Lesbian Lagoon in?'

Logan grimaced. 'I wouldn't if I were you. She's likely to go off like Semtex this morning.'

'Not *again*.' He shifted his grip on the folder and fiddled with one of those ridiculous sideburns of his. 'I've got IDs and interviews for some of Milne and Shepherd's sex partners.'

'Only some?'

'Not my fault it's taking forever, is it? You try getting members of the public to identify someone based on a photo of them humping two blokes. Not as if you can go on *Northsound* and say, "We're looking for a double-jointed busty brunette, with a caesarean scar and a hairy mole on her bum, who enjoys kinky threeway fun," is it? *And* I've got Milne's family to look after.'

Logan glanced up and down the corridor, then leaned in and lowered his voice to a whisper. 'This goes no further than you and me, OK? But...' Another check. 'Have you thought about actually going and *asking* Martin Milne?'

'But Steel—'

'Doesn't need to see your working, she just wants results.'

Which was how she'd got into trouble with Jack Wallace in the first place.

He had a quick check in the corridor outside the locker room. No one about. Then ducked inside. The room was packed with tall, thin lockers in varying shades of battleship grey, green, blue, and beige. They lined the walls, with an island

447

stretching out between the two windows. A hanging rail was set up behind the door, festooned with stabproof vests and high-viz waistcoats, all bearing their owner's numbered epaulettes.

Logan flicked through them till he got to the vest that used to belong to Deano. Well, he was retired now, he didn't need it. One last check to make sure no one was watching, then Logan unbuttoned the epaulettes and replaced them with his own.

No one would ever know. Well, unless they did a stock check, and even then there was no evidence that he'd been the one who nicked it.

His own stabproof would quietly disappear, taking with it its tattered front-piece and dented armour plate. Like the cagoule, gloves, plastic bags, and bullet casings had. Leaving nothing to tie him to last night's fiasco.

Nothing except two eye witnesses, one of whom might well be dead by now. The other of whom would be plotting a very nasty, very bloody, revenge.

Logan pulled the new stabproof vest on, fiddling with the big Velcro tabs until it fit. All those years and it had adapted to Deano's body shape. It'd take a while to train it to his own. And for some reason, the pockets were full of Starburst wrappers.

He ditched them in the bin, then nipped downstairs to the Sergeants' Office.

Beaky wasn't in, so Logan slipped into the seat and logged onto the computer. Scanned through the notifications for the last twelve hours. No sign of anyone being admitted to hospital for gunshot wounds in Aberdeenshire, or Aberdeen City.

Well, there wouldn't be, would there. Reuben had his own private wee NHS to take care of himself and his people. Go to a hospital with a nine-millimetre hole in you and the doctors were obliged by law to inform the police. Much better to go private.

448

So was John Urquhart alive or dead?

Logan stared at the screen for a bit, then logged out. Grabbed the Big Car's keys from the box, and *almost* made it outside.

'Sergeant McRae?'

He turned, and there was DS Weatherford, still looking sweaty and harassed. The bags under her eyes had darkened, matching the stains beneath her arms. She shuffled her feet. 'DS Robertson tells me the guvnor's a bit … delicate this morning?'

Understatement of the year. 'One way of putting it.'

Weatherford glanced over her shoulder. 'It's not my fault. I've tried everything. They won't prioritize the DNA results unless we fast-track them, and there's no budget for it. How am I supposed to catch the people who assaulted the pair of you? *How?*'

Logan patted her on the shoulder. 'Take a deep breath. Then go upstairs and tell Steel she needs to put up the extra cash, or stop being a pain in your backside. She'll appreciate the honesty.'

'Really?' Weatherford's eyebrows went up an inch. Then she licked her lips and nodded. 'OK. Honesty. Pain in the backside. I can do this.'

'And if she shouts at you, try to think nice thoughts till she stops.'

With any luck, given the state of Steel's hangover, any yelling would hurt her more than it hurt Weatherford. If nothing else it would keep the ensuing bollocking to a minimum.

'Oh God…' The DS turned and fidgeted her way back along the corridor.

Logan shook his head and stepped outside.

The air was crisp and harsh, biting at his ears as he unlocked the car and climbed in behind the wheel. Took out his mobile phone and called John Urquhart's number.

Listened to it ring.

'*Yellow?*'

'John? It's Logan.'

'*Mr McRae? You OK? Reuben said—*'

'Thought you might be dead.'

'*Nah, just a scratch. Didn't get far enough away from the Reubenator's shotgun. My own stupid fault. Couple of stitches and I'm right as rain.*' A sigh. '*More than I can say for the Armani, though. Whole suit, completely ruined. Overcoat too.*'

'What about Reuben?'

'*Ah… Yes. Reuben.*' Urquhart made a hissing noise. '*He's a wee bit hacked off. You know, what with you shooting him and everything.*'

'I tried, I really did.'

'*Never seen him so angry. I mean, we're talking Chernobyl in green overalls here.*'

Of course he was.

Well, it wasn't really that surprising, was it? If you shoot someone twice they were hardly likely to be your bestest friend forever.

'*Might be a good idea for you to get out of Scotland for a bit, Mr McRae. Somewhere far away, where Reuben can't get his hands on you. Cos if he does, it's going to be long and slow and horrible. Trust me, I've seen it.*'

The side door to the station opened and Harper marched out with Narveer trailing in her wake. Today's turban was a cheery yellow-and-black check, like Rupert Bear's trousers.

'*And you better keep that gun on you till you go, you know what I'm saying? He's pulling in favours.*'

Not much chance of that. Harper and Narveer were hardly going to let him nip home for five minutes. What? Oh, nothing much: got to feed the cat and pick up a firearm in case a gangster needs shooting. Again.

Yeah, probably not.

Narveer opened the back door. 'Morning, Logan.'

Logan gave him a wave, keeping his voice neutral. Nothing to see here, just a standard-issue innocent phone call.

'Anyway, I've got to go. But if you hear anything, let me know, OK?'

'*Stay safe, Mr McRae. Safe and far, far away.*'

Logan hung up and slipped the phone into his pilfered stabproof vest as Harper climbed into the passenger seat. 'All set?'

She nodded at him. 'Let's go pay Mr Milne a visit.'

DS McKenzie sat on the end of the bed, munching her way through a wee packet of complimentary shortbread, getting crumbs down her shirt. She'd released her hair from its angry pompom, letting it curl and coil around her scowling face.

Logan nodded at the adjoining wall to the next hotel room. 'How did Milne take it?'

'You'd think we were asking him to swim the Atlantic. *Apparently* Mrs Milne is not the forgiving type.'

'On the bright side, it means you'll get to be in on the swoop.'

'He's such a bloody whinge. No one *made* him get a loan from gangsters, did they? Deserves all he gets.'

Logan peered out through the window at the car park below. An old man was out shovelling grit onto the snow, giving it dark brown streaks. 'They going to put him in witness protection?'

'You know what? I genuinely couldn't give a toss.' McKenzie crumpled up the wrapper and lobbed it at the bin. It didn't even get halfway there. 'Steel won't let me do the overtime paperwork unless I do the shift rosters as well. Says it'll be good practice for when I get promoted.' Her top lip curled. 'Lazy, useless, wrinkly, disaster area.'

'Could always transfer out to another division.'

'And let her win?' Becky tore her way into another wee packet of shortbread. 'You ever wonder why we bother, McRae?'

Every. Single. Day.

He left her to her sulk and headed next door.

A suitcase sat in the middle of the bed, an array of socks and pants and shirts arranged around it, all neatly folded and ready to pack. Milne stood with his back to the TV, arms crossed, jaw set, bottom lip poking out as Harper settled into the room's only chair.

'Come on, Martin, we've been over this.'

Narveer had taken up position by the en suite, leaning back against the wall. 'Your family's safer if you're all in the one place.'

Dirty photos jumbled across the hotel desk – the stills from Shepherd and Milne's sex sessions. Some had names written in the corner of the image in jaggy biro letters, others nothing but a row of question marks. It looked as if DS Robertson hadn't wasted any time getting his finger out. At long last. Maybe it would save him an arse-kicking when Steel's hangover passed, but Logan doubted it.

All those different women: blondes, brunettes, redheads, thin, not-so-thin, positively chunky, light skin, dark skin, olive skin, young-ish, middle-aged, old. Milne and Shepherd didn't seem to have a type. Well, other than anyone who was prepared to say yes to a threesome.

A few of them looked familiar, but then B Division wasn't exactly Greater Manchester. Rural area like this, you rubbed shoulders with everyone sooner or later. Pretty certain he'd stopped the school-teachery type, with the black bun and PVC stockings, for having bald tyres on her Fiat Panda. And the large woman with the knee-highs: was it her shed that had been broken into, or was she the wheelie-bin dispute with the next-door neighbours?

Milne shook his head. 'I should never have got involved.' His voice was about an octave higher than it had been, trembling at the end as if he was having difficulty keeping it under control. 'I should've kept my big mouth shut. What if something happens?'

'They're going to be all right, Martin.' Narveer gave him a wink. 'Trust me: we've done this before, loads of times.

There's a car in front of the house right now, no one's getting anywhere near Katie and Ethan.'

'But—'

'You're doing the right thing, Martin.' Harper pointed at the array of clothes. 'This is for the best.'

A couple of others Logan couldn't put a name to: a young blonde woman looking over her shoulder and grinning at the camera while Shepherd spanked her; a large woman with a Y-shaped scar on her top lip and a thing for black lace; and a grey-haired lady with an *Iron Maiden* tattoo all over her back... Wait, was that Aggie? Shepherd's neighbour? It was. So apparently she did a bit more than just nip in and feed Onion the cat from time to time.

Milne ground a palm into one eye socket. 'Katie *hates* me.'

Shock horror.

'She needs time to adjust, that's all. Now, come on, get packed and we'll take you over there. OK?'

He stared at his feet. 'I should never have said anything.'

A sigh, then Harper sat forward. 'Sometimes it's not easy doing the right thing, Martin. Sometimes there's risks and there's costs, but that doesn't change anything – it's still the right thing to do. And we have to do it, because if we don't, then everything falls apart and everyone suffers.' She smiled. 'Do you see?'

Milne nodded, eyes still fixed on his shoes.

'Good. Now, you get packed.'

45

Logan rested his forearms on the steering wheel as Narveer escorted Martin Milne up the drive to his house. No sign of the media today. The small development was buried under a couple feet of snow, everything anonymized by the rounded white blanket. The only thing not covered in snow was the other patrol car, parked up at the junction. Its occupants sat upright, making a big show of being vigilant, as if they hadn't been reading newspapers and eating crisps when Logan had pulled up in the Big Car.

Reuben was pulling in favours. That meant whatever was coming his way, it was coming soon. Someone brighter might attack the people he loved first, destroy everything around him, but not Reuben. He wouldn't have the patience. No, he'd want his revenge up close and personal. And he'd want to be there to see it happen.

Mind you, that didn't mean he wouldn't eventually get around to punishing the people Logan cared about... The patrol car parked outside the house would keep Susan, Naomi, and Jasmine safe for a while, but Police Scotland wouldn't keep it there forever. And as for Steel...?

He cleared his throat. 'Did you mean what you said?'

Harper looked up from her mobile phone, thumbs tapping away at the screen. 'About what?'

'Doing the right thing.'

'Course I did.' Back to the phone. 'Look at Auschwitz, or Rwanda, or Somalia, all that human suffering because people didn't do the right thing. They pretended it was nothing to do with them, they looked after number one. That's how civilization dies.'

Milne and Narveer had reached the front door. They stood there, waiting on the top step.

'No matter what it costs?'

'No matter what it costs.'

The door opened and Katie Milne blocked their way, arms folded, face lined and heavy. She looked as if she'd aged ten years since Sunday.

Milne put his suitcase down and held out his arms, as if he was expecting a hug.

She slapped him.

'What if it costs you everything?'

'Then you do it anyway.' Harper put her phone away. 'But Milne's not *losing* anything, he threw it all away when he cheated on his wife and decided to run away with his boyfriend.'

Katie landed another couple of blows before Narveer stepped in and broke it up. He grabbed both her wrists and spoke to her – the words inaudible from inside the Big Car. Whatever he was saying, it seemed to be working. Her shoulders dropped, then her head. Then she turned and walked into the house, leaving the door open behind her.

Narveer patted Milne on the back, watched him pick up his suitcase and shuffle inside, then followed him.

Then you do it anyway.

Logan checked the dashboard clock. 'That's it gone twelve. Do you want to—'

The phone in Harper's hand launched into some hip-hop song and she swore. Held it to her ear. 'Boss. How are you— Yes. ... Yes, I know. ... We're all—' She glanced across the car at Logan, then turned in her seat to face the window, showing him her back. 'I understand that, sir, but everything's in hand. Soon as they unload the boat at Gardenstown, we'll arrest Malcolm McLennan's people and— ... Yes, sir. ... That's the plan. We'll—' She put her other hand over her eyes, fingers digging into her temple. 'I know that, sir. Yes. ... OK. We'll keep you updated. ... Bye.' Harper lowered her phone to her lap. 'Oh joy.'

Logan turned the key in the ignition. 'Pressure?'

'It never changes. Doesn't matter how high up the tree you climb, there's always another monkey further up trying to crap on you.' She puffed out a breath. 'Maybe we should head over to Peterhead and have another crack at Laura and Ricky Welsh? See if we can find something concrete linking them to Jessica Campbell.'

He made a seesaw motion with one hand. 'Doubt they'll say anything. They used to deal for Hamish Mowat's operation, if it gets out they're playing on Campbell's team someone's going to have a pop at them in prison. Doesn't matter how tough you are if they stick a homemade knife in your back.'

'Maybe you can work the same magic you used on Martin Milne and Steven Fowler?'

It was worth a go. 'I can try.'

Anything to put off the phone call he had to make.

No matter what it costs.

Ricky Welsh had a scratch at the tattoo encircling his neck. Its ink had faded to a gritty blue on his yoghurt-pot skin. He tipped his head to one side, letting his hair swing. 'No comment.'

Logan pulled the next photo from the folder. 'I am now showing Mr Welsh a photograph of exhibit D, nine blocks of cannabis resin, each with an estimated street value of one thousand pounds.' He slid the picture across the table. 'Do you recognize these, Ricky?'

'No comment.'

Sitting next to him, Welsh's lawyer couldn't have looked

more bored if he'd tried. The bald patch on top of his head was spreading along with his waistline. His suit a bit shiny at the elbows. He'd gone to university for this? Where was the strutting about in front of the jury, making rousing speeches and jabbing his finger at things? Scoring points and rescuing the innocent from travesties of justice. Instead, he was trapped in a cramped over-warm room, on a snowy Tuesday afternoon, in Fraserburgh, with a client who'd probably spent more time in court than he had.

'We found these in your living room, Ricky.'

'No comment.'

'If you didn't put them there, who did?'

'No comment.'

Harper sighed. Checked her watch. As if that was going to make any difference.

Logan put another photo on the table. A surveillance shot of someone's mum, chunky and unthreatening, wearing a grey jacket over a floral dress. Her afro was streaked through with grey spirals, skin the colour of polished mahogany. 'Do you recognize this woman, Ricky?'

His eyes flicked to the picture and away again. 'No comment.'

'No? We have information that the cannabis resin in your house belongs to her.'

The solicitor yawned. Sighed.

'No comment.'

Yeah, this was going to take a while.

Logan ran a hand through his stubbly hair. Blew out a breath. It thickened in front of his face, turning into a cloud of white that slowly faded into the falling snow.

The prison car park had been ploughed and gritted, mounds of dirty white piled up in the far corner like a mini mountain range. A lot of effort for the half-dozen cars sitting there, their paintwork slowly disappearing under the fresh fall.

He shifted his phone from one hand to the other and blew onto his frozen-sausage fingers.

Come on: one last bit of good before Reuben came for him and took it all away. Make the call.

Can't.

No matter what it cost, remember?

Yes, but—

Either it's the right thing to do, or it isn't. Pick one.

A big fat seagull waddled across the tarmac, glaring up at him as if he'd done something to offend it.

The phone in his hand rang, making him flinch so hard he almost dropped it. 'Hello?'

Harper's voice came from the speaker. *'Logan? That's them bringing Laura Welsh up now. Maybe we'll have more luck with her than Ricky?'*

'It couldn't go any worse, could it? I'll be there in a minute.'

'OK.'

The line went dead.

Logan scrubbed a hand across his face, setting the bruises and tiny punctures stinging. Then turned and marched inside.

'No comment.' Laura Welsh barely fit in the interview room chair.

Her solicitor was nearly sideways in his seat, trying not to get squished by those broad shoulders. A small man in a pinstriped suit that needed a bit of a clean. His fingers skittered along the edge of his notepad, the pen almost vibrating as he wrote 'No Comment' in it. Probably wondering who he'd offended at the Scottish Legal Aid Board to make them lumber him with Laura Welsh.

Logan tried the photo of Jessica Campbell again. 'Do you recognize this woman, Laura?'

'Aye. Is it Oprah Winfrey?' She grinned, showing off a couple of gold incisors. The patch where she'd thumped her forehead into the landing carpet had scabbed over, making dark parallel lines in the pale freckled skin.

'Do you think Hamish Mowat would have liked you and

458

Ricky switching sides? Getting your drugs from Jessica Campbell? That's—'

'I object.' Mr Nervous sat up straight. 'My client has...'

Laura Welsh stared at him, the grin turning into a growl.

He cleared his throat. Lowered his eyes to his trembling pen. 'Yes.'

She smiled again. 'Wee Hamish is dead. Did you no' hear?'

Harper leaned forwards. 'We found nine thousand pounds' worth of cannabis resin in your house, Mrs Welsh. Do you know how many years that'll get you?'

Laura didn't even look at her, she raised a big hand and pointed instead. The hearts tattooed between her knuckles, flexed. 'I don't know you. Keep it that way.'

Silence.

Logan straightened the photograph. 'So you've changed sides.'

'See, soon as Wee Hamish Mowat died, that was it. Chaos.'

'What about Reuben?'

'Oh, he's a great man with a knife, or a hammer, but running things? You imagine what it's going to be like now Wee Hamish is gone? Going to fall apart.'

Mr Nervous fidgeted with his pen. 'Mrs Welsh, I really think—'

'See if I have to tell you again...'

He shrank about a foot. 'Sorry.'

Laura nodded. 'Sergeant McRae and me are just having a chat about general stuff. Putting the world to rights. Right, Sergeant McRae?'

'Right.'

'Way I hear it, everyone's picking sides. Smart money's on Glasgow.' A shrug. 'Or Edinburgh.'

'What about the Hussain Brothers? Liverpool Junkyard Massive? Black Angus MacDonald?'

She curled one side of her face up. 'Nah. On a hiding to nowhere with that lot. Black Angus couldn't organize a piss-up at an AA meeting. Rest are all wannabe hardmen.'

'Reuben's not going to bow out gracefully.'

'Scar-faced fat bastard wants to start a war. How's he going to do that when all his troops have sodded off to Ma Campbell or Malk the Knife? Be nothing but him and a couple morons pissing into the wind.' She flashed Logan those gold incisors again. 'Desperate last gasps of a dying regime, Sergeant McRae. And there won't be a civil war when it topples: Edinburgh and Glasgow will divvy up Aberdeenshire and that'll be it.'

Until Jessica Campbell and Malcolm McLennan decided they wanted a bigger slice of the cake.

'And Reuben?'

'Sooner or later, he's going to end up dead. Question is how many people he takes with him.'

Harper leaned in. 'You seem to know a lot about the goings on up here, Mrs Welsh.'

A shrug. 'I hear things.'

'And did you hear who attacked Sergeant McRae and Detective Chief Inspector Steel on Friday night? Was it Jessica Campbell's people, or Malcolm McLennan's?'

Laura's grin was back. 'No comment.'

Harper tucked the folder under her arm, staring down the corridor as Laura Welsh was led away back to her cell. Then Harper turned and slammed her boot into the interview room door. 'Damn it!'

'Can't say we didn't try.'

'No comment, no comment, no *bloody* comment.' She took a deep breath and hissed it out. 'Right.' Shook her head and made for the exit, straightening her shoulders as she marched towards the double doors. 'It doesn't matter. We'll find out who's behind it all soon as they turn up to collect the cargo at six. We'll still get a result.'

True.

She pushed through into the stairwell, and stopped, frowning at the window. Snow drifted across the prison car park, whipped into mini cyclones by the wind. Rattling the lights on their pillars and making them sway. 'Better get the car warmed up, Sergeant. We'll head back to Banff and make sure everything's set for the swoop soon as I've updated the powers that be.'

'Sir.'

She followed him down one flight, then pulled out her phone and disappeared into the admin block, leaving him alone in the stairwell.

Logan waited till she was *definitely* out of earshot. 'Thanks a bloody heap.'

So he could freeze his ears off, marching outside in the snow to get the Big Car all warm and toasty for her.

Bloody Superintendents were all the same.

He thumped down the stairs, and signed out at the reception desk. Then shoved his way out into the snow.

It was like being machine-gunned with tiny white blocks of Lego, stripping the air from his lungs. The wind battered him, making him lurch like a Monday-morning drunk across the gritted tarmac to the Big Car.

Gah. Just because Peterhead was a hundred and twenty miles north of Moscow it didn't have to show off about it. Polar bears had it warmer than this...

He fumbled his keys out with numb fingers and scrambled inside. Started the Big Car up and cranked the blowers to full, huffing warm breath into his cupped hands.

Barely half four, and it was more like the middle of the night out there. Snow hammered the car, rocking it on its springs.

He slipped his hand into his pocket and felt the outline of his mobile phone.

Do it.

No.

For God's sake, *grow* a pair!

Harper was right: the only thing that stopped everything falling apart was people doing the right thing, instead of the easy thing.

461

Yes, but...

The blowers roared.

Steel had fitted Jack Wallace up. She'd manufactured evidence. Lied in court. Perverted the course of justice. She'd crossed the line. Yes, Wallace *deserved* to be in prison, but he deserved to be there for what he'd done, not for what he hadn't. That was how it worked.

So do the right thing. 'I don't want to.'

No matter what it costs, remember?

A deep breath, then Logan pulled out his phone; called up his contacts list and dialled Napier.

It rang and rang.

Still not too late to hang up.

And rang and rang.

This was stupid. Hang up.

And rang and—

'*Chief Superintendent Napier.*'

All the moisture evaporated from Logan's mouth.

'*Hello?*'

He clicked off the blowers. Licked his lips. 'Chief Superintendent, it's Logan McRae. I need to talk to you about Jack Wallace.'

46

Harper checked her watch. 'They're late.'

The harbour lights cast pale writhing shadows, distorted by the falling snow. Not a breath of wind. Thick white flakes drifted down onto the Big Car's bonnet, melting away with the heat of the engine, even though it'd been turned off for nearly quarter of an hour.

Logan twisted the key far enough to get the windscreen wipers going. The view wasn't that much better with the snow cleared. From here, tucked in between two bland grey buildings, the harbour walls made a lopsided triangle that sulked beneath the cold night sky. About two dozen small boats sat along the jetties jutting out into the water, not a single light between them.

He pressed the button on his Airwave. 'All units, check in.'

'DI Singh: no movement.'

'DS Weatherford: no movement.'

'DS Rennie: nada for us.'

'DS McKenzie: no movement.'

Silence.

Logan pressed the button again. 'DCI Steel, check in please.'

Her voice cracked out of the handset. *'I'm bored, I'm tired, I'm cold, and Spaver here keeps farting. Other than that? Sod all.'*

Harper shook her head. 'And they made *that* a Detective Chief Inspector?'

He looked away. Fixed his Airwave back on its clip. 'Sorry I couldn't get anything out of Laura Welsh.'

'At least you tried.' She pursed her lips, frowning as if she could taste something sour. 'It'll be over soon. All we need is a result this evening and everything will be fine again.'

Narveer's voice came over the speakers. *'Hold on, we've got something. Lights on the water.'*

'About time!' She scooted forward and peered out through the windscreen. 'Can't see anything.'

'Yup, we've got visual – small container ship. It's the Jotun Sverd.'

'Hallelujah.' Harper picked up her Airwave from the dashboard. 'All right, everyone, listen up. We stay put till Malcolm McLennan's goons offload the cargo. I want them red-handed, so no one moves before it's all in their vehicle.'

Logan tapped his fingers along the steering wheel. 'You wouldn't think the harbour was big enough for a supply boat, would you? Will it even make it through the entrance?'

'We'll find out soon enough.'

The ship's lights appeared through the snow, getting closer.

'Logan?' Harper kept her face forward and voice light and neutral. 'When this is all done, do you want to come visit down in Dumfries? I think Mum would like to meet you.'

'Erm ... yeah, that would be nice.' Assuming Reuben let him live that long. 'I'll need to find someone to look after Cthulhu, though.'

The boat got bigger and bigger, its orange hull standing out against the black water. It was nowhere near as big as the full-sized supply boats – the whole thing would have fitted into a tennis court, with room to spare. Spotlights bathed the small deck in a harsh white glow, picking out four offshore containers with the Geirrød Viking logo on them.

Its engines growled into reverse, slowing the thing to a crawl as it approached the harbour entrance. But instead of trying to squeeze in, the ship swung around, so its stern was facing Gardenstown, then backed up alongside the jutting arm of the sea wall.

One last growl, and the engines fell silent. A couple of men jumped up onto the wall and tied the ship in place.

It wouldn't have been much use on a stormy night, but with the sea like a slab of dark marble, it would be good enough for offloading, even if it did block the harbour entrance.

Harper rubbed her hands together. 'Not long now.'

'Where the hell are they?' Harper checked her watch again. 'It's been twenty minutes.'

'Maybe they're struggling through traffic somewhere? You know what it's like when it snows – everyone drives like tortoises.'

She puffed out her cheeks. 'Tell everyone to check in again. McLennan's men have to be *somewhere*.'

Logan drummed his fingers on the steering wheel and scowled out at the falling snow. Reuben was out there right now, plotting. Planning his revenge.

Question was: when?

Tomorrow? The day after? A week from now?

Tonight?

The flakes glowed for a moment as they passed through the sphere of yellow cast by the bulkhead light fixed to the building next to the Big Car. Then faded to blue-grey again.

Might be an idea to not be at home when he turned up. Maybe he could beg a bed at Calamity's? Or Tufty's parents' house?

Or he could appropriate one of the cells in the station. Wasn't as if anyone used them these days.

Cthulhu would hate it, but it was better than the alternative: the pair of them waking up at four in the morning to find three figures in ski masks looming over the bed with sawn-off shotguns and machetes.

Or they could get a B-and-B sorted for the night. Get another one for the night after that. And another after that. Keep moving so no one knew where they were.

On the run from now till Reuben's thugs caught up with him.

'Logan?'

'Hmm?' He blinked. Turned.

Harper was staring at him. 'If you don't stop drumming your fingers, I'm going to break them. OK?'

He took his hands off the wheel. 'Sorry.'

Harper sagged in the passenger seat. 'This whole thing's a complete disaster, isn't it?'

'Give it time.'

'Gah.' She took her watch off and placed it on the dashboard, in a tiny sliver of streetlight. 'Forty minutes. They should have been here, unloaded, and gone by now.'

True.

Logan shrugged. 'They might be playing it cautious. Scoping out the harbour, making sure there's nothing suspicious going on. Or maybe they're running a bit late?'

Or maybe he'd been right in the first place, and this was all a set-up.

He looked across the car at Harper.

Yeah, probably best to keep that to himself.

'I told you so,' probably wouldn't go down too well.

Steel's voice growled out of the speaker. '*Aye, no offence, Super, but are we planning on spending the night here? Cos if we are I want a sexy WPC instead of Spaver McFartypants.*'

Harper picked up her Airwave. 'This channel is for operational use *only*.' She pinched the bridge of her nose and screwed her eyes shut. 'Is DCI Steel always this much work?'

'Pretty much.' Logan set the windscreen wipers going again, clearing two lopsided grey rainbows through the snow. Nothing had changed – the *Jotun Sverd* still sat at the harbour entrance, all lights blazing like an industrial Christmas ornament. 'We should've brought a Thermos of tea.'

Logan sat forward in his seat, arms on the steering wheel. 'Maybe we need to go back to the idea that we're being screwed with.'

Harper reclined her seat and stared up at the ceiling. 'Do you have any idea how much this operation is costing?'

'It was always a bit too obvious, wasn't it? Shepherd's body is left lying about for us to find, it leads us to Martin Milne, which leads us to the money they owed, which leads us here.' He shook his head. 'It's like someone's handed us a join-the-dots picture and left us to get on with it.'

'Only the picture's a great big knob, wearing a police hat.'

'So what do you want to do?'

She scowled. 'Kick Martin Milne in the balls. *Hard.*'

Logan fiddled with his Airwave, taking it off the closed channel and back onto the normal one. 'Sergeant McRae to Control. Have we got any suspicious activity reported in B Division tonight?'

A man's voice crackled back. *'How suspicious is suspicious?'*

It would be something big, if it needed a distraction this size. 'Banks, building societies, anywhere you'd get a big financial score. Luxury car showrooms, that kind of thing? It'll be nowhere near Gardenstown.'

Harper clapped her hands over her face. 'I'm going to look like a proper moron if they clear out a bank while I'm sat here twiddling my thumbs with *twenty* officers and a dog team.'

'Hud on, I'll have a lookie.'

The *Jotun Sverd* just sat there, all bright lights and shiny paintwork.

'Do you think Milne knows? I mean, he had to arrange the boat.' Logan frowned. 'But they had to pick up the stuff from a yacht... Why go to all that trouble?'

'Aye, Sergeant McRae? No sign of anything suspicious reported. You want me to give you a shout if something comes in?'

467

'Thanks.' He switched his handset to the operation's channel again, then settled back in his seat to wait.

'*DS McKenzie: no movement.*'

Logan wiped the windscreen. Still nothing.

Harper had the seat all the way back now. 'They're not coming, are they?'

He checked his watch. 'Twenty to eight.'

'Argh. Nearly two hours late. Why would you set all this up and not turn up for *two* hours?' She reached into her jacket and pulled out her phone, dialling without sitting up. 'Hello, Narveer? ... Yes. ... Not a thing. ... Yeah, I'm coming to that conclusion as well. ... OK. ... We'll give it till eight – if nothing's doing by then, we're going in. At least tonight won't be a complete bust. ... Yeah, OK. Bye.' She put her phone away and glanced across the car at Logan. 'You get the gist?'

'Yup.' He hooked a thumb over his shoulder. 'You want me to get onto the team watching Milne's house? Make sure the wee sod's still there?'

'He better be. Because if no one turns up, he and I are going to have *words*.'

Harper hunched forward, nose nearly touching the dashboard, staring at her watch. 'Eight o'clock.' She bared her teeth. 'They're not coming. Assuming they ever were.'

Logan struggled his way into the high-viz jacket, zipping it up to the neck, then fastened his seatbelt. 'Maybe someone tipped them off?'

'Bet it was Martin Bloody Milne.' She clunked her seat upright and put her own belt on. 'Call it.'

He didn't bother unclipping his Airwave, just pressed the button and spoke into his shoulder. 'All units, confirm: the swoop is on.'

'*DI Singh: ready.*'
'*DS Weatherford: ready.*'
'*DS McKenzie: ready.*'

'*DS Rennie: Geronimo!*'

Then silence.

Not again.

'DCI Steel, confirm.'

Nothing.

'DCI Steel, I repeat: *confirm.*'

A loud, wet raspberry rattled out of the handset. '*I'm awake, are you happy now? Was having a lovely dream, too. Helen Mirren, a thing of cherry-flavoured lubricant, and a Toblerone...*'

Logan put his peaked cap on. 'Swoop is on in five. Four. Three. Two. One. Go!'

He cranked the engine over and clicked on the lights, foot down. The Big Car surged forward, out between the grey buildings and onto the harbour.

The council might have gritted the roads, but they hadn't bothered with the harbour wall. It slithered beneath the Big Car's wheels, the rear end swinging out as they fishtailed towards the *Jotun Sverd*.

Harper grabbed the handle above the door. 'In one piece, Sergeant! I don't want to end up at the bottom of the harbour!'

He eased up a little, flicked it into four-wheel-drive. Blue-and-white lights strobed all around them as the other vehicles moved into the harbour, making the falling snow glow and flicker.

Logan slammed on the brakes, skidding to a halt right next to the boat, then scrambled out into the cold night.

Someone peered at him over the supply boat's bulwark. An older woman, wearing bright-red overalls and a hard hat. Greying hair tied back in a ponytail. 'Hello?'

He hopped over the rail and dropped the three foot onto the deck. 'Hands where I can see them.'

She pulled in her chin. 'Okeydokey...' Then put her hands up, as if this was a robbery.

Harper landed beside him, followed by Narveer and his two constables. Then Rennie and his lumpen thugs.

A man appeared at the railings behind the bridge – round

and squat, in a thick padded jacket. 'What the hell's going on?'

More and more police officers landed on the deck, like pirates in high-viz jackets. Rennie and his thugs swarmed up the stairs to the bridge. 'Nobody move!'

'I demand to know what the hell is happening here!'

Harper marched into the middle of the deck, between the containers, and pointed up at him. 'You the captain?' Heavy flakes of snow settled on her shoulders.

'And *you* are?'

'Detective Superintendent Harper. I have a warrant to search this vessel.'

He shrugged. 'Knock yourself out.' He leaned on the railing. 'Suzie? Show the cops around, will you? I've got a Pot Noodle on the go.'

Suzie raised her eyebrows at Logan. 'Can I put my hands down now?'

Harper kicked the nearest container. 'We'll start with this one.'

'Okeydokey.' She wrestled with the catch, forcing it down and around, then hauled the big metal door open. 'There you go.'

Logan followed Harper to the container's entrance, looking over her shoulder at the hollow, empty space.

That wasn't right.

Harper curled her hands into fists. 'Open the other ones.'

The Dog Officer pulled his face into a lopsided grimace. 'I can go over the place again, but...' A shrug. A Labrador sat at his feet, big pink tongue lolling out one side of its idiot grin. 'Sorry.'

Harper swore, then stared off down the corridor. Inside, the ship smelled of diesel and air freshener. 'OK, thanks.'

Logan leaned against the wall. 'Nothing at all.'

She scrubbed a hand over her face. 'You tried the cabins and the offices?'

'Everywhere. Even the bulkhead storage compartments.'

'God damn it.'

Narveer ambled over, ducking to avoid losing his Rupert Bear turban on the doorframe. 'Super? We've done PNC checks on the crew: the only one with any form is the deckhand, Elaine. Got drunk on a hen night last year and lamped someone in the Aberdeen McDonald's.'

Harper stared at the ceiling for a moment – white-painted metal, lined with rivets. 'Make sure the captain's in his office.'

'Ma'am.' He turned and ducked out through the door again.

She sighed. 'It's not looking good, is it?'

'Well … no. Not really.'

Harper pulled herself upright. 'Come on, let's go speak to the captain.'

Logan followed her through the metal corridors, down the stairs and below deck. A line of cabins wrapped around the hull, with the captain's office in the middle.

She didn't bother knocking; barged right in. 'All right, I'm running out of patience here, so let's cut the social niceties. Where's the shipment?'

The room was barely big enough for a couple of filing cabinets, a desk, a plastic pot plant, and a visitor's chair. The captain folded his arms across his rounded stomach, using it as a shelf. Tiny brown splodges marked his shirt: the ghost of Pot Noodles past. 'What shipment?'

'The one that's meant to be in the containers!' She leaned on the desk, looming over him.

'There's not meant to be *anything* in the containers.'

Logan closed the door behind him. 'You were supposed to pick up a number of sealed crates from a yacht, sixty miles east of Bora, and hide them in the containers.'

'Nah.' He shook his head, setting his chins wobbling. 'Think I'd remember something like that. You've got the wrong boat, mate.'

Harper slammed her hand down on the desk, making a cup of tea tremble. 'Martin Milne told you to pick up those crates and deliver them here!'

'Don't be daft. Martin told us to pick up four empty containers and take them out for a putter about the Moray Firth for a bit. Run a couple of fire drills with the crew and a man overboard. Then make for Gardenstown and wait for him. He's bringing fish suppers for everyone.'

'Fish suppers?'

'Yeah, well, it's meant to be a procedural awareness exercise thing. Something to do with new operational rules the oil companies want to bring in. Waste of time, if you ask me, but what do I know?'

Logan settled into the visitor's chair. 'So no yacht?'

'No yacht. Look, if you don't believe me, examine the ship's log. We've got GPS trackers and everything gets stored on the computer so the clients can audit it. Be my guest: audit it.'

Harper stood on the bridge, hands behind her back, looking down at the prow of the ship. 'Nobody at all?'

The senior team gathered in a ragged semicircle behind her: Eiffel Tower, Canal Boat, Christmas Tree, Old Boot, and Thomas the Tank Engine. The only one missing was Sheep Playing the Bagpipes.

Rennie leaned against one of the swivel chairs bolted to the floor. 'The crew all back the captain's story. Empty containers, pootling about, fire drills, and fishing dummies out of the water. Oh, and they're getting really hacked off about the lack of fish and chips.'

'Can't say I blame them.' Steel stuck her hands in her pockets. 'Could go a fish supper right now. Maybe some mushy peas too. Oh, and a pickled onion.'

Harper ignored her, pointing a finger at Narveer instead. 'What about the logs?'

He checked his notebook. 'GPS says they never went anywhere near where Milne said the yacht would be. Assuming there ever was a yacht. And there's CCTV on all decks too – they didn't rendezvous with anything.'

'BLOODY HELL!' She gripped the console, shoulders hunched. Hissed out a breath. 'Options?'

Narveer sighed. 'Think we're going to have to take this one on the chin. We were working on information we believed to be reliable. It's not our fault.'

'Oh aye, the top brass will buy that.' Steel gave him a cheery grin. 'Known for their understanding nature are our glorious overlords.'

Logan stepped up beside Harper. 'What if Malcolm McLennan was telling the truth at Hamish Mowat's funeral and his people had nothing to do with Shepherd's death? What if it *was* Martin Milne all along?'

She turned and stared at him. 'So, what: you were right in the first place?'

'I didn't say that.'

'Narveer, send everyone home. And tell the captain his boss won't be turning up this evening, because he's going to be in a sodding police cell.' She turned and marched towards the door. 'Sergeant McRae, you're with me.'

47

Logan gave Narveer a shrug, then hurried after Harper, out into the snow, zipping up his high-viz jacket and pulling on his peaked cap.

McKenzie was down on the main deck, wandering back and forth in front of the containers, mobile phone clamped to her ear, breath trailing along behind her in the frigid air.

'Sir?' Logan reached out and grabbed Harper's arm. 'Are you sure you shouldn't be taking DI Singh with you? He *is* your sidekick, after all.'

'Narveer is a big boy, Sergeant, believe me, he'll be fine. Which is more than I can say for Martin Milne.' She climbed down the stairs to the main deck. 'Grab DS McKenzie. Tell her I want Milne's house locked down tighter than a pair of cycling shorts.'

'Sir.'

She clambered up onto the dockside and stamped through the snow to the Big Car.

McKenzie was staring up at him, still on the phone, wearing an expression that suggested she'd just stepped in something.

Logan picked his way down the stairs, the metal treads clanging beneath his feet. 'Becky?' He pointed at the Big Car. 'Harper needs you: we're pulling Martin Milne.'

She put a hand over the bottom of her phone. 'Why me? *Robertson's* on babysitting duty.'

'Because you ran the team looking after him. She wants a full lockdown till we get there.'

Her eyes narrowed. Then she went back to her phone call, turning her back on him and keeping her voice down.

'Sometime tonight would be good, Becky. You know what detective superintendents are like if you keep them waiting.' He crossed the deck and climbed up onto the harbourside. Stood there until she finished her call, and joined him.

Her curly brown hair was flecked with snow. 'This has been a complete cocking farce.'

'Yup, and now we get to go apportion blame.' He climbed into the Big Car and started the engine. Set the blowers on full to clear the fogged-up windscreen.

McKenzie slipped into the back. Pulled out her Airwave. 'DS Robertson, safe to talk?'

'*Fit like, Becky? How'd the swoop go, you get them?*'

'Shut up and listen. I need a sit-rep on the Milne house.'

'*All present and correct: no one in or out. No sign of any suspicious vehicles in the area.*'

'They up and doing?'

'*Lights are on, but the curtains are drawn. Think they're watching telly and trying to kid on he never shagged his business partner.*'

'Good. Keep them on lockdown, we're paying a visit.' McKenzie put her handset away. 'Everything's set.'

Harper nodded. 'Thank you.' Then frowned. 'Is there something else?'

She clicked on her seatbelt. 'Thought I'd tag along for the ride.'

'I think Sergeant McRae and I can handle it.'

'Sure you can.' A cold, unpleasant smile uncoiled across her face. 'But I wasted days looking after Milne, and if the wee sod's screwed us over I want to be there when he gets his collar felt. And if we're *really* lucky, he'll resist arrest for a bit first.'

'Fair enough.' Harper pointed at the windscreen as the fog finally cleared. 'Let's go see what he has to say for himself.'

Logan did a five-point turn, keeping their speed to a crawl and steering well clear of the sudden drop into the dark water. As they faced the right way, a set of blue flashing lights appeared on the road above the harbour, working its way down. 'Sir?'

She reached across the car and put a hand on his arm. 'Hold it here for a minute.'

The car got closer, then disappeared behind a squat row of cottages, before emerging again, driving onto the dock. It stopped beside the Big Car, and the driver's window buzzed down. Logan buzzed his down too.

Oh no.

Napier looked up at him. 'Sergeant McRae.'

Not now. Not *here*.

'Chief Superintendent.'

'Tell me, is Detective Chief Inspector Steel available?' He wasn't smiling. Wasn't rubbing his hands with glee. Instead his shoulders drooped, mouth pulled down at the edges, a slightly pained expression on his face. 'I'm afraid I need a word.'

'She's on the ship.'

'I see.' He bit his bottom lip and frowned for a moment. Then nodded. 'Thank you, Sergeant.'

The window buzzed up and the patrol car pulled forward a dozen feet, until it was alongside the boat.

'All right, Sergeant, we can go now.'

'Actually,' Logan unclipped his seatbelt, 'I'll only be a minute, OK?' He scrambled out of the Big Car, and picked his way through the snow to the patrol car as two of Napier's colleagues boarded the *Jotun Sverd*, leaving their boss on the dockside. 'Sir?'

Napier turned and nodded at him. 'Not the best of days, Logan. Not the best.'

'What's going to happen to her?'

'We found a flash drive covered in her fingerprints. It's got exactly the same set of images she *discovered* on Jack Wallace's laptop. The "last modified" dates match.' The tip of Napier's nose was already going red. 'A report has been submitted to the Procurator Fiscal.'

'They're going to prosecute?' Logan marched off a couple of paces, then back again. 'But she's—'

'This isn't what I wanted, Logan, it really, *really* isn't. Every time I have to arrest a fellow officer...' He sighed, the breath turning into a cloud. 'Well, there you go. That's my problem, isn't it?'

'What's going to happen to her?'

Napier wiped flecks of snow from the shoulders of his black police-issue fleece. 'She'll be charged with perverting the course of justice. Jack Wallace will be released from prison and his conviction quashed. In all likelihood, he'll sue Police Scotland and win. And the next time he rapes someone we'll have to start all over again, but it'll be three hundred percent more difficult because his lawyers will be screaming "harassment".' Napier shook his head. 'This is why we have *rules*, Logan.'

Up on the boat, Steel emerged from the bridge, slouching along with her hands in her pockets, e-cigarette poking out of the side of her mouth. Napier's people were behind her. No handcuffs, no frogmarching.

Napier patted Logan on the shoulder. 'Perhaps you shouldn't be here for this bit.'

No matter what the cost.

The two officers helped Steel up onto the dockside, then stood back.

She took a good long draw on her fake cigarette. 'Well, well, if it's no' the Dark Prince of Professional Standards himself. What can we do you for, this sharny night, Nigel?'

Napier stared at her for a moment, then put his hands behind his back. 'Detective Chief Inspector Roberta Steel, I'm detaining you under Section Fourteen of the Criminal

Procedure – Scotland – Act 1995, because I suspect you of having committed an offence punishable by imprisonment.'

She glanced past him at Logan. 'Oh aye?'

'Please, get in the car.'

'What if I don't want to get in the car? What if I want to kick off, right here?'

He closed his eyes and gritted his teeth. 'Please, just get in the car.'

'I've done sod-all and you know it.'

'That's for a court to decide.'

She jabbed a finger in Logan's direction. 'Tell him, Laz. Tell this lanky strip of gristle he's got the wrong woman.'

One of Napier's people stepped up and took hold of Steel's arm. 'Let's not make this any harder than it has to be, OK?'

'Laz?'

The other one stepped up, and between them they steered her towards the patrol car.

'Laz, *tell* them!'

They opened the back door and eased her inside, one putting a hand on top of her head so she wouldn't bash it.

'LAZ! TELL THESE BASTARDS WHAT—'

Clunk. The car door shut, taking her angry voice with it.

The snow-covered landscape hissed past the Big Car's windows, headlights glittering back at them from wet tarmac. Every time the windscreen wipers travelled across the glass, they squeaked and moaned, as if someone was murdering a lot of mice one at a time.

Harper was staring at him.

Logan kept his eyes on the road.

'Well, Sergeant, are you going to tell us what that was all about?'

'DCI Steel is consulting on one of the Chief Superintendent's cases.'

Trees drifted by in the distance, their branches drooping under the accumulated frozen weight.

'Hmmm...'

Sitting in the back seat, McKenzie kept her mouth shut, thumbs busy poking away at her mobile. Texting or playing Candy Crush.

Harper scowled out at the darkness. 'I can't believe we've been so *stupid*. There never were any gangsters, were there? All that rubbish about getting a loan from Malcolm McLennan – Milne made it up.'

'He falls out with Peter Shepherd, they fight, it gets out of hand, and next thing you know, he's got a body to get rid of.' Logan changed down for the hill. 'So he comes up with the idea of staging it to look like the photo in *The Blood-Red Line* and framing McLennan for it. Tells us McLennan loaned them two hundred thousand so we won't do him for embezzling the cash – suddenly *he's* the victim. A nice neat little package.'

'And I should have listened to you in the first place.' She banged a hand on the dashboard. 'Idiot.'

Harper's Airwave gave its four point-to-point beeps. *'Ma'am, it's Narveer.'*

She pressed the button. 'Go ahead.'

'I've sent the Jotun Sverd*'s crew on their way. No fish suppers for them.'*

'What about everyone else?'

'There's a couple of house fires in Peterhead, and a factory unit's gone up in Fraserburgh. Sounds like wilful fire raising. Everyone on duty's en route. I've disbanded everyone else. No point totally spanking the overtime budget.'

The road wound up, then plunged down like a roller-coaster.

'Thanks, Narveer. We'll need to get started on the paperwork first thing tomorrow. See if we can justify the almighty cock-up and expense.'

'Will do. Do you ... with— ... isn't for— ... next...' Then hissing. Then nothing at all.

Harper slapped the Airwave against her palm. 'Work you stupid lump of plastic.'

McKenzie shifted forward. 'It's the hollow here. No reception.'

Through a gap between the hills, the sea was a slab of clay, framed by snow-flecked woods.

Logan took them around the corner, and slowed. A woman stood at the side of the road, wearing jeans, a Barbour jacket, and a knitted bunnet. She waved her arms over her head, caught in the on-again off-again flash of a Range Rover's hazard lights.

He stopped and buzzed down his window. 'Broken down?'

Her cheeks and nose glowed bright pink. 'There's been an accident – a car's left the road. Please, you have to help them!'

'Hold on.' Logan pulled the Big Car up onto the verge, behind the Range Rover, then jumped down into the snow. Reached into the back for his high-viz jacket and peaked cap. 'Becky, can you get the warning signs out of the boot and stick them up round the corners? Don't want some idiot rallying their way into the back of us.'

McKenzie put her phone away. 'OK.'

'There's a spare high-viz in there too.'

The woman tugged at his sleeve. 'Please hurry.'

Logan took out his torch and crunched his way through the snow to the front of the Range Rover. A pair of tyre marks cut through the dirty white crust, heading over the edge. He played the beam down the ravine and across the trees, then stopped. Red tail-lights reflected the torchlight back at him.

He peered closer. It looked like a hatchback, about thirty feet down the gorge, tipped up on its side, crumpled between the trunks of two trees. Maybe a Clio or a Fiesta – something boy-racery with an oversized exhaust, the number plate half hanging off.

'Right,' he turned back to the woman in the Barbour jacket, 'I need you to get back in your car and head up the hill. Soon as you get to the top, call nine-nine-nine. Tell them…'

She wasn't looking at him, she was staring at the Big Car.

Someone lay in the road, on their front, not moving.

It was Harper. Facedown on the tarmac, as if she fancied a nap.

What, had she fallen out? Slipped on the snow?

Logan took a step towards her, then stopped as something hard pressed into his back.

A thick, dark voice sounded over his shoulder. 'Well, well, well, if it isn't Sergeant Logan McRae.'

He licked his lips. 'Reuben.'

The Range Rover's back doors opened and two men climbed out: one huge and solid, the other thin and knife-like. Smiler and Mr Teeth, AKA: Allan Wright and Gavin Jones. The remaining two-thirds of Reuben's Transit van team since Eddy Knowles got his head caved in. They were both wearing black leather gloves. Both holding semiautomatic pistols.

So this was it.

Reuben jabbed him in the back again. 'You're supposed to be dead.'

Every inch of Logan's skin fizzed, the hair stood up on his arms and head, his mouth was full of wasps. 'Tried it once. Didn't like it.' He eased around.

Reuben had his sawn-off shotgun in one hand. The other held a crutch – stainless steel with a grey plastic cuff – keeping the weight off that leg. 'Did you really think you were going to get away with it? Pulling a gun on me, like I'm some sort of prick?'

Funny, but now that the moment was here, it was almost calming. No need to worry about when Reuben would make his move, when he'd get his revenge, because it was *now*. There was something liberating about that.

Logan nodded back towards the Big Car. 'Detective Superintendent Harper and DS McKenzie have nothing to do with this.'

'What, you think you're going to play the big hero? "Save them, it's me you want?" That kind of crap?'

Someone crunched through the snow behind him, getting closer. Then another familiar voice. 'Can we get this over with?' It was McKenzie.

'Oh for God's sake. You're working for *Reuben*? Seriously?'

'Told you: I've got two kids to put through university and a police pension that won't cover the mortgage when I retire.' She stepped around him, putting herself behind Reuben and the shotgun. 'If you're working up to a lecture about loyalty, don't bother. I know what you did to DCI Steel, McRae – she might be a useless old bag, but you wouldn't know loyalty if it gave you a lap dance.' Becky stuffed her hands in her pockets and sniffed. 'Come on, Reuben, time's wasting. Do him and get it over with.'

'What?' Reuben grinned. 'And miss out on all this fun?'

The shotgun flashed up, the barrel smashing into the bridge of Logan's nose. It sent him staggering backwards, arms windmilling as the snowy verge disappeared beneath his feet. And he was gone...

48

Hot yellow orbs flashed across the dark sky, screaming and jabbing as Logan went crashing through branches and bushes, tumbling over and over, their jagged limbs clawing at his face and hands.

Then a loud *crump* and he was on his front in the snow, head-down on the hill, tangled in the undergrowth.

Ow...

'Oh for God's sake. Are you happy now?' McKenzie's voice cut through the silence.

'You listen up, you curly-haired wee bitch, you are here because I *own* you. Understand?'

Logan rolled over onto his back and tried to blink away the ringing in his ears.

Up.

Get up and run.

Yes, because being bright fluorescent-yellow in the woods wouldn't get him shot at all, would it?

He unzipped his high-viz jacket and struggled out of the thing. Rolled away as the sawn-off barked. A rain of pellets clattered through the branches. One bit at his hand, but not hard enough to break the skin.

That was the trouble with a sawn-off, it was great for close quarters – you could clear a room with one with a single blast – but over longer distances? The shot spread out too far, too fast.

Logan scrambled behind the upturned Fiesta as the shotgun barked again, pinging and clanging against the dented bodywork. Everything tasted of hot pennies. He ran a hand across his mouth – it came away warm and slick and black in the moonlight. Blood dripped from his burning nose, the world stank of meat and peppercorns.

Reuben's voice boomed out. 'COME OUT, COME OUT, WHEREVER YOU ARE, MCRAE!'

No chance.

He dragged out a hanky and wadded it against his bleeding nose.

Could head down the hill. Stick to the trees and make it as far as the sea. Might get a signal on the Airwave down there. Call in the cavalry.

'LET'S MAKE THIS EASY, SHALL WE, MCRAE? YOU COME OUT AND TAKE YOUR MEDICINE LIKE A BIG BOY AND I WON'T KILL YOUR DETECTIVE SUPERINTENDENT FRIEND. HOW DOES THAT SOUND?'

Terrible. He'd probably kill them both anyway.

Logan peered around the Fiesta's boot.

Reuben stood at the road's edge, caught in the Range Rover's headlights, using his shotgun as a pointer – directing Allan Wright and Gavin Jones down the slope. They were harder to make out than their boss, almost vanishing as they picked their way through the snow and bushes. Gavin Jones on the left, Allan Wright on the right.

OK, stocktake.

Logan patted his equipment belt: one set of limb restraints, one set of handcuffs, one extendable baton, and a can of CS gas. Throw in an Airwave handset that wasn't getting a signal and that was it. God knew where the torch had got to, probably buried in the snow somewhere.

A hard crack sounded from the left, followed by a ringing thud that vibrated through the Fiesta's bodywork.

A voice from the right, Wright: 'YOU GET HIM?'

There was a pause, then Jones shouted back. 'DON'T KNOW.'

What good were limb restraints against guns?

Should've listened to Urquhart and taken the semiautomatic with him.

Yes, because that worked *so* well last night, didn't it?

'That's what you get for being a bloody wimp.'

Logan unhooked his CS gas. 'Oh that's helping, is it?'

'If you'd killed Reuben when you had the chance, instead of fannying about, you wouldn't be in this mess.'

'Shut up.'

'You shut up.'

Two men armed with handguns, one armed with a sawn-off shotgun.

Turn around and get the hell out of there.

Laughter echoed down the hill. 'HEY, MCRAE, MCKENZIE TELLS ME THIS ISN'T ANY OLD DETECTIVE SUPER-INTENDENT: SHE'S YOUR *SISTER*! OH THAT'S PRICELESS.'

Another hard *crack* from the left, closer this time. The bullet sizzled through the air over his head.

'WELL?'

'DON'T THINK SO.'

'MAYBE WE SHOULD—' There was a crunch and the popcorn crackle of breaking branches. 'AAAAAAAArgh!' Then a thump.

'AL?' Jones crashed through the undergrowth off to the right. 'AL? YOU OK?'

'Argh...' The sound of someone spitting. 'THODDING HELL.'

'WHAT HAPPENED?'

'I BIDT MY TUNG!'

Reuben's voice bellowed over the top. 'YOU KNOW WHAT I'M GOING TO DO TO YOUR SISTER, MCRAE?'

The crunching sound of feet on frozen snow was getting louder. A minute or more and they'd be on top of him.

Don't just crouch there – *do* something.

Logan took a deep breath and backed away from the Fiesta. The trees were thin and spindly, nothing thick enough to stop a bullet.

'I'M GOING TO CARVE HER LIKE A SUNDAY ROAST AND FEED HER TO THE PIGS, ONE SLICE AT A TIME, WHILE SHE WATCHES.'

He ducked, creeping into a clump of whin. The dead seedheads hissed at him. Another six foot further on, the ground dropped away, plummeting into the darkness. Edge of the world.

'YOU THEE HIM?'

'HOW? DARK AS A BADGER'S ARSE DOWN HERE.'

'YOU LIKE THAT, MCRAE? OR YOU GOING TO COME OUT AND BE A MAN?'

The guy on the left, Jones, had reached the overturned Fiesta. He was a vague dark outline against the bushes and patches of snow, sharp nose swinging from side to side, as if he were scenting the air. He whirled around three hundred and sixty degrees, his gun up at head level, twisted on its side – gangsta stylie.

Idiot.

No sign of idiot number two.

Logan ran a hand across the ground. Sticks. Twigs. Dirt. Rock. It wasn't big – barely the size of his fist, but it'd do.

He threw it off to the right, deeper into the woods. It clattered and rattled through branches, its final thunk swallowed by the snow.

Jones spun around and a flare of light exploded from the end of his gun, illuminating him in all his thin and pointy glory. The *crack* echoed around the ravine.

Logan blinked. Blinked again. But the flash was a hard burst of yellow-white, etched across his eyes.

'JONETHY: YOU GET HIM?'

'MAYBE.' Gavin Jones was even less visible than before, hidden by the shot's afterimage. 'YOU SEE ANYTHING?'

'WHAT'S KEEPING YOU PAIR OF IDIOTS? FIND HIM!'

'You think it's that easy?' Jones's voice was barely a mutter. 'You limp your fat arse down here and kill him yourself.' He picked his way down the hill, crackling through the bushes.

Closer. Closer. And then he was level with Logan's clump of whin ... and then he was past.

Logan flipped the cap off his CS gas, pulling the canister from its holster. The coiled bungee cord holding it to his equipment belt tightened as he stood up and aimed. 'Hello, Ugly.'

Jones span around. 'Jesus—'

Logan mashed his thumb down on the trigger.

'AAAAAAAAAARGH! AAAAAAAAAAARGH!' He folded in half, both hands covering his face, the gun still clenched in one fist. 'MY EYES! AH JESUS...'

Logan helped him take his mind off the CS gas by kneeing him in the groin.

'JONETHY?' Wright's thick lispy voice wasn't far away – slightly further uphill to the right. 'JONETHY! YOU OK?'

'WHAT THE HELL'S GOING ON DOWN THERE?'

Gavin Jones crumpled to the ground not far from the cliff edge, moaning and whimpering.

The gun was easy enough to take off him. Logan dragged him into the whin bush, pulled his hands behind his back and cuffed them.

One down.

'JONETHY!'

A quick frisk through his pockets turned up a spare clip for the semiautomatic.

That evened the odds a bit.

He gave Jones a kick, setting him off again, then crept uphill, using the swearing and crying as cover.

'JONETHY?' A shot rang out. Then another one. And another.

Logan hit the ground, scrambling on all fours back to the car.

Wright crashed through the bushes, firing off two more shots. 'Thodding hell...' He was downhill now, his silhouette crouching over his mate. 'HE'TH GOT JONETHY!'

'DO I HAVE TO DO *EVERYTHING* MYSELF?' Up on the road, Reuben moved to the edge of the verge, the sawn-off glinting in the headlights. 'WHERE IS HE?'

Logan stayed where he was. Not moving. Keeping his breath as quiet as possible.

McKenzie marched over to Reuben, hands jabbing out, emphasizing the words. 'Are you happy now? He gets away and we're all screwed!'

'MCRAE?'

'Oh give it up. I *told* you to kill him and get it over with, but would you—'

Reuben rammed the butt of his sawn-off into her face hard enough to lift her off her feet. She crumpled out of sight, groaning. Then he took a short limp forward, good leg swinging back then snapping forward. There was the crunch of boot meeting flesh. And another one. One more for luck.

He stood back. Bent down and rubbed at his bad leg. '*You* work for *me*, bitch. Understand?'

No reply.

'UNDERSTAND.' Another kick. Then he took his crutch and prodded something hidden by the verge. Probably McKenzie. 'Oh.'

Allan Wright was still crouched over his mewling friend.

Logan took a deep breath.

Do it now, while they were both distracted.

One down, two to go.

He scrambled upright and charged, leading with his shoulder. Crashed through the whin, setting the seedheads rattling.

Wright almost made it to his feet before Logan battered into him, sending him sprawling. He hit the ground and bounced. Rolled over, snarling, then his eyes went wide – two big circles of white in the darkness – as he went over the cliff edge.

His hand flashed out, grabbing, wrapping around Logan's ankle.

'Aaagh...' The world flipped backwards, crashing and rolling, and then they were falling.

Cold air rushed past Logan's face, then something hard crashed into his side, flipping him over. And again. And again. Swearing and screaming his way down into the dark, surrounded by the clattering snap of breaking branches, thuds, and grunts.

One last crash and then a moment of agonizing silence followed by a deafening THUD.

Oh God...

Flat on his back, eyes screwed tight shut.

His arms and legs felt as if they'd been battered by crowbars, the whole of his chest screaming in pre-bruised agony.

Every breath was like being punched in the ribs.

'Ow...'

Be lucky if he hadn't broken his back. Probably going to die here, lying at the bottom of a gully, covered in gunk and dirt and broken bits of tree. Body eaten by foxes and crows. Nothing left but shards of bone and a tattered police uniform, to be swallowed by the cold dark ground.

A high-pitched whine filled his head, getting louder as the woods grew darker. And darker. Then silence.

At least if he was dead it wouldn't *hurt* any more.

That would be something...

Logan exhaled one last broken-glass breath and let the darkness take him.

49

Cold.

Something wet rolled across Logan's cheek. Then another cold kiss. And another.

He opened his eyes.

The world was grey, with little white spots drifting slowly towards him. Like a long dark tunnel filled with flakes of ash.

So, this was what death looked like?

Well, why not?

Last time he'd been unconscious for this bit. Or maybe, because the surgeons had managed to get his heart started again, he'd just never got this far?

Either way, surely it wasn't meant to be this *cold*?

A tingle grew in his arms and legs, like the opening bars of a symphony for pins and needles. But instead of that hard itchy electrified wave, the melody was one of ache and pain. Getting louder with every second.

'Buggering hell...' The words came out on a cloud of white. He squeezed his eyes shut. 'Ow...'

Not dead then. Dead people didn't hurt this much.

Logan rolled over onto his side and everything snapped back into its proper place.

He wasn't floating down a dark tunnel full of ash after all: he was lying at the bottom of the gully, the ground around him covered in snapped twigs and bits of broken branch. Trees reached up into the falling snow, their tops disappearing into the grey.

A dark voice boomed through the night. 'WELL?'

The voice that replied was a lot closer. 'I FOUND AL! HE'S NOT BREATHING!'

'DO I LOOK LIKE I GIVE A TOSS ABOUT AL? WHERE'S MCRAE?'

Oh great. They'd come looking for him.

Get up.

Sod off, it hurt too much.

No: up.

Logan groaned his way onto his front and forced himself to his knees. The landscape swam. A gentle probe of the back of his head brought his hand away dark and sticky, his fingers smelled of raw meat. Probably cracked his skull.

Be dead for real in a minute, from intracranial bleeding.

That or Reuben's thugs.

'FIND THE BASTARD!'

Jones's voice dropped to a mutter. '"Find the bastard." "Find the bastard."' He was getting closer. 'Can barely see, never mind find anybody.'

One last heave and Logan was on his feet, one arm wrapped around a branch to keep himself upright.

'Should've sodded off soon as Mr Mowat died. Should've taken that job with Doogie. Could've been driving lorries all over Europe by now, but *no*.' There was a crash, then some swearing.

Logan ran his free hand over his equipment belt. The baton was still there, but all that was left of the CS gas was the coiled bungee cord. It ended in a frayed tuft where the canister had been ripped off on the way down through the trees. No idea where the gun had got to.

'YOU FOUND HIM YET?'

'Course I haven't, you fat dick.' Then, much louder, 'HE'S PROBABLY SNUFFED IT!'

'I DON'T WANT "PROBABLY", I WANT *DEFINITELY*! FIND HIM!'

'All over Europe, but noooo.' Closer: couldn't be more than twenty feet away. '*You* had to stay with the team, because Eddy said we should.'

Logan shrank back behind a tree that wasn't really big enough. Mind you: the Police Scotland ninja-black outfit might be a liability in the height of summer, but here? At night, in the dark, when it was snowing? Couldn't have camouflaged himself much better if he'd tried.

A thin figure emerged from the gloom, picking his way between the bushes and boulders that littered the bottom of the ravine. Gavin Jones. 'Yeah, and did Eddy hang around? Course he didn't.'

He wasn't wearing the handcuffs any more – they must have got the keys off McKenzie – but he *had* got himself another gun. Or maybe it was Wright's gun?

Logan unclipped his baton and slid it out, slow and quiet.

Couldn't extend it, that would make too much noise, so he wrapped his fist around the handle and held the thing facing down against his knee.

'No, the two-faced bummer legged it when the going was good, didn't he? Talked *us* into staying then did a runner.' Jones stumbled over something in the dark and nearly went headlong. 'GAH! BLOODY SODDING ABOUT, IN THE BLOODY DARK, BASTARDS!'

'YOU FOUND HIM?'

'NO I HAVEN'T SODDING FOUND HIM!' He shoved his way through a bush. 'Sod this. And Sod you. Soon as I get back to the road you can shove your job. Don't need this crap.'

One more bush and he was level.

His eyes were all swollen, the skin puffy and dark, shiny trails of snot glimmering on his top lip. But that was getting a face full of CS gas for you.

Logan flicked the baton up and the extendable section shot out with a *clack* over his shoulder. Then down again, hard, cracking it across Jones's wrist. The gun clattered to the ground as Gavin Jones screamed – mouth open wide, full of those squint little teeth. 'AAAAAAA—'

He snapped the baton up again. The vibration shuddered up his arm as the metal bar cracked into Jones's face. There was a *crunch* like someone crushing a bag of crisps.

Gavin Jones crumpled to the ground, mouth still open. Only now the squint little teeth were nothing more than jagged stumps in ruptured gums.

Still breathing, but definitely unconscious.

'WHAT THE HELL WAS THAT?' Reuben's voice echoed into silence.

The snow fell.

'JONESY, WHERE'S MCRAE?'

It settled on the boulders and the trees.

'JONESY?'

Logan collapsed the baton against a boulder and put it away. Then knelt in the dark, running his hands over the cold earth till he found the gun.

'MCRAE? I KNOW YOU'RE THERE!'

He turned and limped back towards the cliff face.

'I'M GOING TO KILL YOUR SISTER! YOU HEAR ME?'

Leaned his cheek against the cold rock.

Took a deep breath.

Right, let's try that again.

Logan eased himself over the top of the cliff and lay on his back, panting.

His arms were on fire, hands cut and scraped by the rocks and branches, punctured by long dead thistles. Both legs ached. So did his head, and his back.

Let's face it, *everything* hurt.

His breath hung above his face.

Come on. Almost there.

He wobbled to his feet. Spat out a thick glob of white. Then lurched up the hill.

That crashed Fiesta lay a good forty or fifty feet off to the left.

Logan froze.

Reuben was still there. Still standing at the edge of the road, peering down into the darkness, clutching his sawn-off in one hand and his crutch in the other.

Moron. A sensible person would have sodded off by now, taken his hostage and his battered bent cop and worked on an alibi. But not Reuben. He was too busy getting revenge.

No wonder Wee Hamish didn't want him taking over.

Logan climbed the slope, bent double, grabbing handfuls of cold damp grass to pull himself up. By the time he reached the road, he was on his knees, pulse thumping in his throat, keeping time with the drums in his skull.

The trees and snow and tarmac throbbed in and out of focus.

Be nice to lie down here for a bit. Three or four days, maybe.

The road curled around to the right, hiding the Big Car and Reuben's Range Rover behind a massive clump of gorse.

Nearly there.

Come on.

Logan struggled to his feet and stood with his head back, arms hanging loose at his side, steam rising from his sodden black fleece. Then pulled the gun from his pocket and staggered on. 'What's the plan?'

'Shut up, you idiot, he'll hear you.'

Good point.

OK: here's the plan. We walk up to Reuben and we shoot him in the head. No screwing about. No hesitating. No 'accidentally' shooting him in the leg instead.

Headshot.

Bang.

Blood and brains all over the road.

OK?

OK.

What about the body?

We can sort that when we get to it.

Right.

The Big Car appeared from behind the gorse bush's spiny fronds, emergency flashers blinking orange light.

Not far now.

Logan flicked the safety catch off and stepped out into the middle of the road.

He raised the gun and limped past the Big Car. 'Reuben.'

The big man stood with his back to the slope. He'd ditched the crutch – now his hand was wrapped up in a big fist of long blonde hair. The other held the sawn-off shotgun against Harper's forehead. 'Took your time, McRae. Been waiting ages.'

She was kneeling on the tarmac, her eyes narrow and wrinkled at the edges as if she were having difficulty focusing. Twin lines of dark red ran horizontally across her cheek. Arms behind her back. Which explained where Mr Teeth's handcuffs had gone.

Logan aimed. 'Let her go.'

'Or what?'

'I won't miss this time.' He kept limping, closing the gap, keeping the gun pointing at Reuben's big fat scarred face. 'Let her go.'

'Nah.'

McKenzie's body lay on the verge with its head turned to one side. There wasn't much left of her features: the whole front of her face was a raw bloody pulp, screamingly red in the Big Car's headlights. The woman with the knitted bunnet – the one who'd flagged them down claiming there'd been an accident – squatted beside McKenzie, going through her pockets.

Classy.

Reuben ground the shotgun's barrels into Harper's skin. 'See, this wee bitch here? I'm going to paint the woods with her brains. BANG!'

She flinched, and so did Logan.

Reuben laughed, belly and chins wobbling. 'Then I'm going to do the same to you. And *then* I'll track down your kids and do them too. Because you're *weak*.'

Logan pulled the trigger and the Range Rover's rear window shattered. The handgun's BOOOM reverberated back from the trees. 'Let – her – go!'

The woman in the bunnet scrambled back, one hand on her chest. 'Jesus...'

Reuben grinned. 'Thought you weren't going to miss?'

Harper raised her chin. 'Shoot him.'

'Shut up, darling, the grown-ups are talking.' Reuben twisted the fist in her hair until she screwed her eyes closed, breath hissing out through her clenched teeth. It caught the headlights and billowed bright white.

'Come on, Reuben. It's not her you want, it's me. She didn't screw you over and make you look like a moron, did she?' Logan limped closer. 'That was *me*.'

Closer.

'Think you're getting a rise out of me, McRae?'

'Wee Hamish didn't think you had the brains to take over. He was right, wasn't he?'

Closer.

'You want to see brains? How about your sister's?'

Closer.

'It's all falling apart, isn't it? All your dealers are defecting to Malcolm McLennan or Jessica Campbell. You inherited an empire and now you're king of sod-all.'

Closer.

Stevie Wonder couldn't miss at this range.

'Say good bye, McRae, you're—'

Logan shot him in the face.

50

Narveer sucked on his teeth for a bit. Then shook his head. 'A right cocking mess.'

Really? What gave it away?

A pair of ambulances blocked the road with their boxy white bodies, blue-and-white lights flickering on and off – catching the snow as it fell.

Logan ducked under the yellow-and-black cordon of tape: 'CRIME SCENE DO NOT ENTER'. He pointed at the ambulance furthest away. 'I'm going to take her home, if that's OK?'

The DI puffed out his cheeks. 'Professional Standards are on their way. Going to be the mother, father, and maiden aunt of all internal investigations.'

'Yeah, well.' Logan looked back along the road, where someone in a white SOC suit was photographing Detective Sergeant Becky McKenzie's body. 'Been a rough night all round.'

Torches swung along the slope below them, wielded by more figures in oversuits – ghosts in the dark, hunting for evidence.

A patrol car sat inside the cordon, behind the Big Car. The woman in the back seat glowered out at them, knitted bunnet wedged down over her ears. Not bright enough to do a runner before reinforcements turned up. Reuben certainly knew how to pick them.

She bared her teeth at Logan, through the glass.

He waved back. 'Hope your handcuffs are so tight your fingers fall off.'

Narveer shook his head. 'She can't hear you.'

'It's the thought that counts.'

'Yeah... You really need some time off, don't you?' He put a hand on Logan's shoulder and steered him towards the ambulances. 'Go. Get the boss home before she starts trying to take over the investigation.'

Logan ran a hand over his face. 'Suppose we'll both be suspended from active duty, till it's dealt with.'

'Probably.'

By which time he'd probably be in a cell looking at sixteen years.

Logan limped along the road, past the Range Rover with the shattered back window, and on towards the ambulances.

The one nearest had its back doors firmly shut, and he stuck up two fingers as he hobbled past to the other one.

Harper sat on the tailgate, a bottle of water in her hand and a silver blanket around her shoulders as if she'd just run a marathon. She blinked at him, then batted the paramedic away. 'Get off.'

The wee man in the green overalls dumped a stained clump of cotton wool into a kidney dish, then pulled out another, using it to clean the blood off Harper's cheek and forehead. 'You've probably got concussion. Any idea how serious that can be? Because the answer's *very*.'

The other ambulance growled as it pulled away. Accelerating as it passed them, its siren cutting through the snowy night.

Logan groaned to a halt. 'Touch and go, but they'll do their best.'

Harper sniffed. 'Can't believe you shot him in the head.'

'Think I should've let him kill the pair of us instead?'

'It's going to take *weeks* to shampoo him out of my hair.'

'Look into the light.' The paramedic knelt in front of Harper and shone a pencil torch in her eyes. 'Can you hear any—'

'Seriously, if you don't sod off right now, I'm going to arrest you.'

'Fine. If that's what you want.' He put the torch away. 'It's your funeral.'

She climbed down onto the snow. The ambulance tyres had left four lines of black tarmac showing through, but everything else was slowly disappearing under a pall of white.

A roar of rotor blades *whupped* by overhead, a spotlight from the helicopter catching the trees in freeze-frame.

Logan led her over to one of the patrol cars arrayed along the road. 'How's the head?'

'Sore. Yours?'

He touched the wad of gauze taped over the egg growing out of his skull. 'Yes.' He opened the door and helped Harper up into the passenger seat, then limped around to the driver's side. Sagged for a minute, then started the engine. Clicked the headlights up full beam.

She turned in her seat, looking back towards the cordons and the vehicles and the ghosts. 'What did you mean?'

Logan pulled the car away from the verge, one back wheel *vwipppping* on the snowy grass till the tyre took hold. 'You can stay in the spare room tonight. Paramedics said you're not supposed to be alone in case you die.' At least it was safe to go home now, and he and Cthulhu were spared having to live out of a series of anonymous bed-and-breakfasts.

'You told him, I wasn't the one who screwed him over and made him look like an idiot.'

'The paramedic?'

'The big ugly fat guy with the scars.' She tugged at a clotted coil of hair. 'Mr Wash-And-Go.'

'No I didn't.'

A very clean grey van appeared over the crown of the hill, with 'BEATON AND MACBETH' in discreet lettering on the side. Andy and George waved at him as they passed. With one body at the foot of the cliff and another on the roadside, it was going to be a busy night for the duty undertakers.

Harper faced front again. 'You did, I heard you.'

'No, I said I made him look like a moron.'

'And?'

As they crested the hill, Logan's phone started dinging and bleeping – text messages coming in after all that time in the gully.

'And I was trying to piss him off. Get him angry and distracted.'

'Yes, but why pick that?'

'Worked, didn't it?'

'You know there's going to be an inquiry.'

And he was screwed whether Reuben regained consciousness or not. Gavin Jones would probably last about fifteen minutes before spilling his guts, and it would all be over for Sergeant Logan Balmoral McRae. 'Good.'

He flicked the windscreen wipers up a notch, clearing the glass as the snowfall thickened.

The world was a swirling mess of white and grey – visibility down to a dozen feet. Logan dipped the headlights. It helped a bit.

She cleared her throat. 'Thank you. For not letting him blow my head off.'

A shrug. 'What are big brothers for?'

The wipers squealed and groaned.

The grey-white world slid by.

'Logan? When—' Harper's Airwave handset gave four beeps.

'*DS Robertson to Detective Superintendent Harper, safe to talk?*'

She sighed, then pulled it out and pressed the button. 'Go ahead, Robertson.'

'*Yeah, listen, Boss: are you still needing us to lockdown the Milne place? Only my guys were meant to be off-shift half an hour ago. Someone coming to relieve us?*'

Harper turned and widened her eyes at Logan, giving him a flash of teeth. 'You stay where you are, Robertson – I'll OK the overtime. Sergeant McRae and I are on our way.'

'*Boss.*'

Logan sighed. 'We've been involved in a fatal shooting. They won't want us on active duty. We—'

'Has anyone *officially* said you can't take part in an active investigation?'

'Not officially, no.' He kept his eyes on the road. 'Sure you don't want to go home?'

'Oh I'm absolutely positive. I've had a *very* bad day, and Martin Sodding Milne is going to find out what that feels like.'

Logan pulled up outside number six, Greystone View.

The lights of Whitehills were blocked out by the blizzard, thick sheets of heavy snow howling in on a wind that hammered the trees and gardens. A gust rocked the patrol car on its springs. He killed the engine.

Snow moaned and hissed against the roof.

Another patrol car was parked in front of them and the passenger door popped open, disgorging a skeletal lump in a high-viz jacket. DS Robertson hurried over, bent almost double by the wind. He rapped on the car window and Logan clicked the keys in the ignition far enough to buzz it down.

The wind growled.

'Thought you'd forgotten about us.' Flakes of white clung to his ludicrous sideburns, weighing them down.

'Any movement?'

'Sod all. Light's been on all night, but the curtains have barely twitched. No one in or out, as per.'

Harper clunked her door open and climbed into the snow. Stuck her hand out. 'DS Robertson, can I have your cuffs?'

A shrug. 'Don't see why not.' He passed them over as Logan buzzed up the window and creaked his way out of the car. It was as if his joints had all rusted on the twenty-minute drive over here. The muscles in his arms and legs ached, his back complaining as he struggled his way into a high-viz jacket. He puffed out a breath and waited for the worst of it to pass.

'You OK?' Robertson was frowning at him. 'Only you look like crap.'

'Yeah. Hang on for ten minutes, OK? Just in case.' He turned his shoulder to the wind and fought his way up the drive, cold leeching through his damp boots into his damp socks.

Harper stamped along beside him, using him as a windbreak.

Logan leaned on the bell. Turned his back on the blizzard. Snow thumped into his shoulders, threatening to tear the peaked cap from his head. 'Samantha was right, I should have gone to Spain.'

'What's in Spain?'

'Complications.'

The door remained firmly closed.

He tried the doorbell again, keeping his thumb on it.

Harper moved in closer, so she was sheltered from the snow. 'Sod this. Not standing out here like a pair of idiots while Milne sits in there laughing at us.' She nodded at the door. 'Sergeant, I have reason to believe Martin Milne's family is in danger and we should force entry. Agreed?'

Logan tried the handle.

Locked.

He mashed the bell again. 'Don't think I'm really up to kicking it down.'

'Hold on.' Harper put a hand on his arm as a shadow fell across the glass beside the door.

There was a *click*, and then the shadow faded again.

This time, when Logan tried the handle, the door swung open, letting a flurry of snow twirl into the hall.

They hurried inside, shutting the door behind them, just in time to see Katie Milne disappear into the kitchen, what looked like a bottle of champagne in one hand.

Logan followed her, pausing to check the lounge and the downstairs bathroom on the way. No sign of Milne.

Katie had her back to them as they entered the kitchen, putting two mugs down in front of the rattling kettle. 'Is tea all right? I don't have any coffee.' Her voice was soggy – slow and muffled – as if her mouth wasn't working properly. She raised the bottle of champagne and swigged from it. 'Or there's wine, if you'd rather?'

Logan unzipped his jacket. 'Mrs Milne, where's your husband?'

She turned. Her chin was covered in dried blood, bottom lip all swollen and cracked. Which explained the voice. A single white tooth sat on a saucer by the sink. 'He's in the garage.' She pointed at the far wall, then took another swig. Blinked in slow motion. 'Would you like biscuits?'

Harper nodded. 'Sergeant, invite Mr Milne to join us.'

Logan limped back out into the hall, following the vague direction of the pointed finger down to a door at the far end. It opened on a breezeblock garage, with a dark-blue Aston Martin parked in it.

Milne was on the floor.

He lay face-down on the concrete, naked, with both hands tied behind his back. Torso and legs covered in bruises. Wine bottles lay scattered around him, a couple of them broken, the heady winey smell mingling with the butcher-shop tang of blood and offal. A black plastic bag was duct-taped over his head.

51

Katie Milne ran a finger along the countertop. 'They came in the back way, over the garden wall. Didn't see them till they were barging in through the French doors.'

Two cups of tea sat on the table, untouched.

Harper stared. 'And they killed him? Right there, in front of you?'

'They said I had to watch as punishment.' She reached into a pocket and came out with a small white plastic tub. The kind that pills came in. 'I had to tell everyone what happened to people who couldn't be trusted.'

'Notebook, Sergeant.' Harper snapped her fingers at Logan. Back to Katie. 'Can you describe them?'

She shook her head. 'They were wearing ... I don't know, masks or something.' Katie dropped the container into the bin. Took another swig of champagne then went to put the bottle down, but missed the worktop. It hit the floor and shattered, spattering out frothing wine that hissed and fizzed against the tiles.

Logan didn't bother with the notebook. 'And then you cleaned the kitchen?'

'What?' Katie turned towards the fridge and its display of childish drawings.

'Where's Ethan?'

'Didn't you hear me? They killed my husband.'

He pointed at the floor. 'You say they came in from the garden, which is under about two feet of snow, but the tiles are bone dry.' Well, everywhere except for the bit covered in champagne. 'So's the laminate in the hall *and* the garage floor.'

She took a picture of a cow jumping over a rainbow from the fridge door. 'Ethan's always been very sensitive.'

'Mrs Milne? When all this happened, why didn't you alert the patrol car parked right outside?'

'They always tell you children are so resilient, don't they? That they can get over anything, given enough time.'

'Did you kill your husband, Mrs Milne?'

'Don't be ridiculous.' Her voice was getting slower. More slurred.

'Logan?' Harper picked up four bits of paper from the kitchen table. It looked as if they used to be a single sheet, torn into ragged quarters, one side covered in neat blue handwriting. 'Listen to this: "Dear Katie. I can't go on like this. I'm tired of being scared all the time, I'm tired of the threats and the violence. I'm tired of never knowing what's going to set you off. By the time you read this, Ethan and I will be long gone."'

Katie shook her head. 'No.'

'"I should never have lied for you. As soon as we're out of the country I'm going to tell the police that gangsters didn't murder Peter, it was you. I'll tell them I only helped you cover it up because you threatened to kill yourself and my son."' Harper looked up from the torn letter. '"You need help, Katie. You need to tell the police what you've done. Ethan deserves better than this."' She lowered the fragments to the table. '"Martin".'

'How could he be so *selfish*.' Katie held the picture against her chest. 'Taking my baby from me. My baby.'

Logan's eyes flicked to the bin. The empty tub of pills. Oh no...

'Where's your son, Mrs Milne? I need to see him right now.' Logan waved a hand at Harper. 'Go: search the bedrooms.'

'You should have seen Ethan's face when he found out about his father.' She stared down at her hands. 'Broke my heart.'

Harper scrambled out into the hall, pulling out her Airwave. 'DS Robertson, I need you in here!'

A copy of the *Aberdeen Examiner* sat on the worktop, by the kettle. Someone had been having a bash at the crossword. Katie flicked it over, exposing the front page. 'HUNT CONTINUES FOR STUDENT EMILY'S KILLER' above a photograph of a young woman in a leather jacket grinning away outside a pub somewhere.

Katie picked it up and knelt by the broken champagne bottle, spreading the newspaper out beside her and dropping shards of green glass onto it. Wine soaked into the paper, darkening it. 'He told me it was only the one time. That it was a mistake, he loved *me*. We were a family.'

'Mrs Milne, please: where's Ethan? Is he safe?'

'I mean, Peter Shepherd? Martin and Peter, together? He'd been in my house *so* many times. He was Ethan's godfather. How could they *do* that?' She shook her head. 'They were going to take my baby from me.'

'LOGAN!' Harper's voice boomed out from somewhere deep inside the house. 'LOGAN, CALL AN AMBULANCE!'

Katie Milne wadded up the newspaper and dumped it in the bin. Then put the drawing back on the fridge. 'He was always so sensitive.'

52

'Here.' Logan held out a plastic cup full of vending machine coffee, topped with a scummy disc of foam masquerading as milk.

Harper took it. 'Thanks.'

'They were out of KitKats, so I got you a Double Decker.' Logan eased himself into the plastic seat next to hers, groaning and grunting all the way. 'Gnnn...'

'You OK?' She ripped the top off the orange-and-purple wrapper and took a bite of chocolate.

'No.'

'Me neither.'

A man in light blue hospital scrubs squeaked his way down the corridor and stopped in front of them. Checked his clipboard. 'Detective Superintendent Harper? Good. Yes. Well, I'm happy to say that Mrs Milne's going to be fine. We pumped her stomach and it looks like she didn't take anywhere near enough Loprazolam to cause any real damage.'

Logan took a sip of his own horrible coffee. 'What about her son?'

'Ah.' The nurse clutched the clipboard to his chest and pulled on a pained smile. '*Unfortunately*, Mrs Milne gave Ethan a lot more sleeping pills than she took herself. We're doing everything we can.'

Harper stood. 'Is she fit to be discharged?'

'I don't see why not.'

'Good.' She dumped her coffee, untouched, into the bin. 'Logan, get the car. Mrs Milne's got some answering to do.'

Harper walked back up the corridor, the squeal and groan of the station's floorboards accompanying her like an ominous soundtrack. She stopped in front of Logan and sagged against the wall. 'Still with her solicitor. Don't know what she thinks she's going to achieve. Maybe cop a plea for diminished responsibility?' Harper stifled a yawn. 'Anything from the hospital?'

'Not yet.' Logan checked his watch. 'Twenty past two.' He puffed out his cheeks. 'We should really sod off. Been a long, *long* day.'

'I'm going nowhere.' She wrinkled her top lip and sniffed. 'Urgh… Why does everything smell of black pudding?'

He pointed at the dark clots of Reuben in her hair. 'That would be you.'

A shudder. 'Right, that's it: I'm off to find the station showers. Gah…' She marched away, stiff-backed, arms held out from her sides as if she were wading through something horrible.

Katie Milne's solicitor could do worse than go for diminished responsibility. Clearly the woman was off her head. Killing her husband was bad enough – and maybe understandable in the circumstances – but what she'd done to her son? No sane person gave their six-year-old child an overdose of sleeping pills.

So yes, diminished responsibility.

A good lawyer could probably get her six years, an honest lawyer would make sure she never set foot in the real world again. But a *great* lawyer?

A great lawyer would make sure it never got to court in the first place.

Logan turned and headed to one of the empty admin offices. No furniture, no filing cabinets, nothing but uneven carpet tiles and the peppery smell of dust. He closed the door and pulled out his wallet.

Sandy Moir-Farquharson's business card was wedged in between Logan's library card and a receipt for high-strength painkiller. He called the emergency contact number on the back and listened to it ring.

Twenty past one in the morning, and the lawyer sounded wide awake: '*Hello?*' No rest for the wicked.

'Mr Moir-Farquharson, it's Logan McRae.' Deep breath. 'I'd like you to represent a friend of mine. She's in custody right now.' And yes, she was guilty, but... But what? He'd done worse things himself? He felt ashamed? He wanted a shot at redemption?

Probably far too late for that.

Still, it was worth a try.

'*I see. Well, before I make a decision, Mr McRae, I shall need to know who this friend is and what they're alleged to have done.*'

'Her name's Detective Chief Inspector Roberta Steel.'

The microwave dinged and Logan fished out his bowl. 'Ow! Ow! Ow!' It clattered onto the worktop. 'God, that's hot.' The stolen beans glooped and bubbled. He smothered them with stolen hot sauce and stolen cheddar. Then buttered his stolen toast and took the lot over to the line of tables.

A serious-looking woman frowned out of the canteen's TV, mouth moving silently while the ticker below her scrolled: '19 DEAD IN DAMASCUS CAR BOMB ATTACK... GOVERNMENT MINISTER RESIGNS OVER "HOSPITALGATE" SCANDAL... BENJAMIN AND *JACINTA* LEAVE BRITAIN'S NEXT BIG STAR...'

Logan left her on mute and dipped a bit of toast into his spicy cheesy beans. Chewed as he turned the page. Mrs Milne's police record was restricted to two parking tickets, one for speeding, and a caution over a trolley rage incident in the Peterhead Asda six months ago.

The canteen door opened, then clunked shut. Followed by a sigh. Then the sound of the vending machine whirring into life. A rattle, *hiss-click*, then more sighing. Narveer settled on the opposite side of the table, clutching a tin of Irn-Bru and a bar of Dairy Milk. 'Logan.'

'Inspector.' Another bite of bean-dipped toast.

'What a nightmare...' He clicked the top off his fizzy juice and stifled a yawn. 'Anything from the hospital?'

'Nothing they can do but wait and see.'

'Poor wee soul. I remember when our eldest was that age – came down with meningitis. Thought we were going to lose him.' Narveer shuddered, then clunked a bite of chocolate. 'Never been so scared in my life. Can you *imagine* forcing sleeping tablets down your wee boy's throat? Doesn't bear thinking about.'

And the whole thing cast Ethan's being the clumsiest kid in school in a different light. All those bruises, cuts, and scrapes. The broken arm. How much of that was Mummy? How much of it done to punish Daddy?

Next up was the manila folder full of dirty photographs. Logan spread them out on the table, making a fan around his bowl.

Narveer pointed. 'Catching up on the case?'

'Yup.' He scooped out another mound of beans.

'Have I done something to offend you, Sergeant?'

'No. Sorry. It's been a long, long, *long* horrible day.' Logan sat back. 'I'm doing interview prep.'

'Let me guess, Niamh won't let you go home?'

'Be a shame to abandon the whole thing now.' More beans. 'Far as we can tell, Mrs Milne found the note before Martin could disappear. He was all packed and ready to go – two suitcases for him and a backpack for Ethan. Probably thought he could sneak out the back way while we were all hanging about Gardenstown harbour like a bunch of morons.'

'Hmph.' Narveer polished off his chocolate, then wiped his hands down the front of his jacket. Pulled over the photos. 'This DS Robertson's work?'

A nod.

510

'God, his penmanship's appalling. What's this say?' He held out a picture of Milne, Shepherd, and a woman who had her hands wrapped around Milne's throat as she brought the full length of her strap-on to bear.

'"Diane McMillan." That's a D.'

'It is? Oh. "No police record, works as a learning support coordinator. At home with her husband when PS went missing – Alibi confirmed."'

Logan finished his pilfered beans and wiped the bowl clean with the last of his pilfered toast. 'At least he checked.'

'True.' Narveer flicked through the rest. 'You think these will help?'

'Probably not.' He stood and walked his empties back to the kitchen area. Dumped the bowl and plate in the sink. 'You want a tea?'

'Please. Then maybe we should...' He stood. 'Niamh.'

Harper slouched into the canteen, rubbing a towel through her hair. 'Inspector Singh.' She'd ditched the bloodstained suit, replacing it with a black police T-shirt and standard-issue trousers.

'Sergeant McRae's making tea, if you want one?'

'Not the way he makes it.' She dumped the towel on the back of a chair. 'Katie Milne's solicitor says we can interview her now.'

Logan dumped his teabag back in the box and returned to the table. Gathered up the PNC report and the photographs, stacking them up into a ... pile. Wait a minute. He frowned, tilted his head to one side and stared.

Then spread the top three photos out again.

One was Aggie with her *Iron Maiden* tattoo; one was the redhead in the stripy stockings; and one was the young blonde woman, looking back over her shoulder at the camera – three biro question marks were lined up in the bottom corner. Identity unknown.

'Logan?'

No.

Couldn't be.

Could it?

'Sergeant: I said it's time to go interview Katie Milne.'

He span around. 'Paper. I need a newspaper.' There were a pile of them on the coffee table, in front of the TV with its mute newsreader. *Daily Mail*, *Telegraph*, *Press and Journal*, *Scottish Sun*. The front pages were a mix of political scandals, showbiz gossip, and atrocities in the Middle East.

Damn it.

'Sergeant McRae, are you—'

'Ah!' Logan lurched over to the recycling bins, lined up between the kitchen area and the vending machines. He knelt, ripped the cover off the paper bin and rummaged inside – throwing hand towels and printouts and sandwich wrappers and cereal boxes and scrunched-up envelopes over his shoulder.

'Have you gone mad? Narveer, stop him!'

Where the hell was... Ah. Perfect.

Logan stood holding a copy of that morning's *Aberdeen Examiner* aloft as if it were Excalibur itself. 'Got it!'

He slapped it down on the table, face up: 'HUNT CONTINUES FOR STUDENT EMILY'S KILLER' above the photo of Emily Benton. 'You see?'

Narveer held up his hands. 'OK, Sergeant, I think it's maybe time you went home and got some sleep.'

'Look.' He poked the newspaper with a finger, then the photo from Shepherd's collection. 'That's why she looks familiar.' The young woman getting spanked was grinning back over her shoulder, half of her face hidden. But it was her.

'Yeah... No. Don't see it.'

Logan dragged out his Airwave. 'Control, I need to speak to someone about the Emily Benton post mortem. Right now.'

'*Hold on...*'

Narveer grimaced, looking across the explosion of paper debris radiating out from the recycling bins. 'You said it yourself, it's been a long day. You've been through a lot and—'

A broad Doric accent thumped out of the Airwave's speaker. '*Aye, fa's this?*'

'Sergeant McRae, B Division. You got Emily Benton's PM photos?'

'*Aye.*'

'I need any distinguishing features.'

'*We can have a bash. ... Tum-tee, tum-tee, tum-tee... Right, here we go: scar on outside of left ankle, strawberry birthmark inside of right thigh, crown on second molar lower left.*'

Harper picked up the photograph and squinted at it. Then held it out to Logan. 'There.' A strawberry birthmark, just visible on her inner thigh, below Shepherd's spanking hand. If you didn't know what it was, it could easily be mistaken for a shadow. 'You were right.'

She didn't have to sound so surprised about it.

Katie Milne shifted on the other side of the table, setting her white oversuit rustling. 'When will I get my clothes back?'

'When our forensics lab are finished with them.' Harper gave Logan the nod.

The interview room was far too hot. Beads of sweat glistened on the forehead of Katie's lawyer – the same saggy disappointed man who'd represented her husband last time they were in here. He moved his notebook out of the way as Logan laid out the photographs from Shepherd's bedroom porn collection. One at a time. Slow and deliberate, as if he were dealing tarot cards.

'Do you recognize any of these women, Mrs Milne?'

She blinked at him, then at the images, then at her lawyer. 'Barney?'

'Superintendent Harper, are you deliberately trying to distress my client?'

'We're trying to get at the truth, Mr Nelson. Please continue, Sergeant McRae.'

More women joined the ranks on the tabletop. 'How about now?'

'Look, this has nothing to do with the unfortunate events surrounding Martin's death. Please move on.'

The very last picture was Emily Benton, looking back over her shoulder.

Katie flinched.

Harper sat forward. 'So you recognize *her*?'

'I...' She licked her lips. 'No. I've never seen her before.' But she didn't seem to be able to look away.

Logan put the other faces back in the folder, leaving Emily Benton in the middle of the table. 'Do you want to tell us about her?'

Katie wrapped her arms around herself, rocking back and forwards. 'I didn't... It... I don't know.' She stared at the photograph. 'I mean, she could—'

'One moment, please.' Her lawyer put a hand on her arm. 'I think, in the circumstances, my client and I need to have a further discussion. We—'

'He *lied* to me. When Ethan was born, Martin swore he'd never cheat on me again. He *swore*.'

'Katie, I really don't think this is a good—'

'I got a text meant for her. He sent it by mistake. There was a ... an intimate photograph.' She ground the palm of her hands into her eyes. 'He was *screwing* her.'

'Katie, please. Let's take a minute and—'

'So I did what any good mother would do: I confronted her. Told her she had to stop seeing him. He was my husband. He loved *us*, not *her*.'

Harper went to say something, but Logan nudged her with a knee under the table. She closed her mouth.

'The little bitch laughed; rubbed it in my face.' Katie bared her teeth, eyes narrowed as she glared at the woman in the photo. 'Him and her. And she *laughed*.' Katie reached out with one hand, placing it flat over the picture. Then crumpled it into her fist. 'She laughed at me and my family.'

Logan kept his voice low and neutral. 'And what did you do, Katie?'

'I made her stop.' A frown. 'I don't know how. One minute we were in the car park, and the next we were in the woods. Her head was all broken and there was a wrench in my hand. It was all … sticky.' Katie let go of the photograph. Emily Benton's face was creased and distorted. 'I left her there.'

Logan nodded. 'Is that what happened with Peter Shepherd, Katie?'

She blinked at him. 'I started going through Martin's pockets. Checking his email. Checking his phone. I needed to know he wasn't doing it again.'

The radiator growled away to itself, pumping out heat into the already oppressive room.

No one moved.

Then Katie shrugged. 'I found a receipt for three business-class tickets to Dubai. Him, Ethan, and Peter Shepherd. They were going to work for some firm building roads and bridges on the other side of the world. Martin was going to *leave* me.' She bared her teeth. 'Peter Shepherd was going to take my family away from me.'

Her solicitor sighed. 'Maybe you shouldn't say anything more, Katie?'

'You wouldn't believe how he cried. Pleading and bawling, all covered in bruises on the forest floor. And Martin begging me to stop…'

'Katie. Please.'

'Then all that stuff in the papers. The Emily bitch wasn't a one-off mistake, there were *dozens* of them. And him and Peter. The sex. The dirty filthy lying bastard. He promised me. He swore!'

Logan leaned forward. 'Whose idea was it to pretend that gangsters killed Peter Shepherd?'

She frowned at him. 'You'd have found his body sooner or later: Martin said we had to make it look like someone else did it. That he could make it look convincing. That he could lie about some Edinburgh heavy lending Peter money and you'd jump to all the wrong conclusions.'

And he'd been right.

'Where's the money now?'

'I knew GCML was in trouble, but I didn't know it was going bankrupt. Not till then.' She laughed, short and bitter. 'Two hundred and twenty-five thousand pounds embezzled from the company. They thought they could run away to Dubai and set up house before anyone noticed what they'd done. Can you believe that? Oh yes, *they'd* be fine, but what about *me*?' Katie curled her top lip. 'When the bank forecloses on the company and repossesses our home? What was *I* supposed to do?'

Katie dug her nails into the tabletop. Stared at them as the quicks went white. 'All those lies about how much he loved me. I'd be *homeless*. Poor. What kind of man does that?'

'What happened to the money, Katie?'

She turned and blinked at her solicitor. 'Barney?'

'I'm sorry,' her solicitor shook his head, 'but I don't think I can represent you any more.'

'OK, let's forget about the money for now.' Logan eased his hand across the table, until it lay next to hers. 'Do you want to tell us what happened in the house tonight?'

Outside, someone thumped along the corridor, setting the floor creaking.

The radiator pinged and gurgled.

Harper shifted in her seat.

Then Katie Milne brought her head back around and sighed.

'It's OK.' Logan took her hand. It was cool and dry. 'You can talk to us.'

'No comment.'

— Monday Lateshift —

to sink like a stone

53

'Next.' Logan pointed and Isla clicked the mouse, bringing up a picture of a little girl in a pink frock. All gaptoothed smile and pigtails. 'Isabella Cameron. They had to amputate her right arm and it'll take years to reconstruct her face.'

Tufty stuck his chin out. 'I've been doing the rounds of the pubs. Seems there's a new dog-fighting ring in the area. Mastiffs, bull terriers, Staffordshires, anything big and compact.'

'Stay on it. Whoever's responsible, I want their balls in a vice by Friday, understand? Calamity, you help him.'

'Sarge.'

'Next.'

A click and the little girl was replaced by an elderly woman with about twice as much skin as any normal human being had a right to, all folded and creased.

Isla groaned. 'I thought they gave her fourteen months?'

'That's right, campers: Mrs Wyatt's out on parole again. Make sure every shop between here and Macduff knows to keep an eye out. Isla: get a grade-one flag put on her ex-husband's flat. Last thing we need is another geriatric war. And while we're at it, when—'

There was a knock on the door and a skeletal face appeared. Inspector Gibb – Napier's sidekick, his own private

Renfield. Responsible for making the odd cup of tea, taking notes, eating bugs, and shifting coffins. 'Sergeant McRae? Chief Superintendent Napier would like a word soon as you're free.'

He checked his watch. Ten past five, the shift had barely started. Surprised Napier had waited this long. 'Constable Anderson can finish the briefing.'

Logan followed Gibb out into the corridor, back straight, arms swinging at his side. Off to meet his doom.

Through the main office, out and up the stairs.

Gibb didn't say a single word until they were standing outside the Major Incident Room on the top floor. 'You have the right to have a Federation representative present, if you wish?'

What was the point?

'Let's get this over with.'

She opened the door and ushered him inside.

Napier sat at the head of the table, with the windows behind him. A china cup in a china saucer on one side and a pad and pen on the other. He motioned to the chair diagonally opposite. 'Sergeant McRae.'

Logan lowered himself into the seat. It faced a small digital camcorder on a tripod, the little red light already on. Nothing off the record today.

OK.

Inspector Gibb closed the door then took the seat next to the camera, notepad out. A nod from Napier and she opened it to a fresh page. 'Sergeant Logan McRae, can you confirm that you've been offered Federation representation and declined it.'

'Yes.'

'Thank you. Now: where were you last night, Sergeant?'

Logan pulled his chin in and frowned. 'Last night?' OK, wasn't expecting that. 'We were on lateshift till three this morning. Why?'

'I see. And after that?'

'We went to Constable Nicholson's house to celebrate.'

'Celebrate what, Sergeant McRae?'

'Constables Quirrel and Anderson caught Wee Wullie McConnell. We've been after him for months.' He sat forward. 'Look what is this all about?'

'And when did this celebration end?'

'I don't know. Couple of hours? The baker's was open on Seafield Street, so had to be gone five. I got a chicken curry pie.'

'I see. Thank you, Sergeant.' She reached up and switched the camcorder off. 'Now, would anyone like a cup of tea?'

Napier gifted her a smile. 'Thank you, Shona. Sergeant McRae takes milk, no sugar.'

And they were back in Creepytown.

As soon as she was gone, Napier opened a folder and took out some blurry stills from a security camera. 'Reuben Kennedy went missing from Aberdeen Royal Infirmary last night, between the hours of three and four.'

A couple of indistinct figures were caught in the act of manoeuvring a wheelchair down the corridor away from the camera. The wheelchair's occupant was a big man, rounded, powerful looking.

Oh that was just great. Spectacular.

Reuben was missing.

Sodding, buggering, bastarding hell.

'Are you all right, Logan? You've gone rather pale.'

'I ... didn't know Reuben had a last name.'

'According to his doctors, he'd regained consciousness. Confused and unable to talk, but awake and alive.' Napier held up a hand. 'Don't worry, we're keeping an eye on all the ports to make sure he doesn't flee the country.'

Oh they wouldn't have to worry about that. Reuben wouldn't be going anywhere until Logan and Harper were pig food.

'Speaking of Mr Kennedy, you will be pleased to know that we've concluded our investigation into the incidents of the seventeenth. Both you and Detective Superintendent Harper have been cleared of any wrongdoing, which I'm sure will be a weight off your mind. There may even be a commendation in the offing.'

What?

He didn't move. Didn't dare. 'Thank you, sir.'

'Of course, it would have been nice if we could have persuaded Mr Jones to turn on his employers, but you know what these career criminals are like.'

Gavin Jones, AKA: Jonesy, AKA: Mr Teeth.

Oh thank God.

Maybe he wasn't going to prison after all?

Napier steepled his fingers and leaned forward. 'I have to say, Logan, that I was impressed by your handling of the investigation into DCI Steel. There were those who predicted you'd try to cover up for her. Conceal the evidence. But you didn't.'

Logan blinked at him. 'You knew all along, didn't you? You set me up.'

'As I told you when we took our bracing walk, "You're an honest man, Logan McRae."'

'You already *had* the proof, but you wanted to see if I'd find it and bring it to you.'

'A test. Yes.' He held his arms wide. 'And you passed, as I always knew you would.' He let his arms fall. 'DCI Steel arrested one Lawrence Collins a year ago for possession of indecent images of children. He had over five thousand of them on three different computers, more on an assortment of CDs and flash drives. The usual filth, where the abusers keep their faces covered.' Napier chewed on his cheek for a moment, frowning. 'Dundee University have a team who can analyse photographs for the vein patterns on the back of offenders' hands, or on their penises. Unique as a fingerprint, apparently. They were working their way through Collins's images, trying to cross-reference and identify the abusers, when they noticed something. A subset of the pictures were identical to ones they'd already processed: the images Steel "found" on Jack Wallace's laptop.'

'Wallace and this Collins were part of the same ring.'

'So Dundee passed the information to the Child Abuse Investigation Unit, and when *they* interviewed Collins about it, he wanted to cut a deal. Time off his sentence for information about the detective chief inspector he'd supplied with a flash drive full of child pornography and information on how to plant it on someone's computer.'

Logan's shoulders sagged. 'Steel.'

'Apparently she told him there were plenty of people in HMP Grampian who owed her favours. And if he didn't do what he was told, one of them would hold him down and carve "paedo scum" into his forehead.'

'You didn't need me. You already had everything you needed.'

A shrug. 'This is my last case, Logan, now I can retire. Superintendent Gray will be taking my place, but there's a role for you in the department, if you want it?'

It was a struggle to keep his face in one place, but Logan did his best. 'Professional Standards?'

Holy Mother of God.

'Oh you don't have to decide right away. I'll be here for the rest of the day, tying up loose ends. If you want to discuss things, let me know.'

The world had gone completely mad.

'All right, Lumpy, is there anything in your pockets I should know about?' Calamity snapped on a pair of blue nitrile gloves. 'Anything sharp – blades, needles, that kind of thing?'

Lumpy Patrick raised his skeletal hands over his head, letting free a groin-curdling reek of rancid sweat. 'Nah, I'm like, clean as Mr Sheen, and that...' His breath was even worse.

Logan backed off a couple of paces as Calamity patted

him down. 'Don't forget to check his turn-ups.'

The bottom edge of Lumpy's tracksuit bottoms had been rolled back to nearly mid-shin, showing off stick-thin pale hairy legs and grubby socks. His trainers squelched with water on the snowy pavements.

She grimaced, keeping her face as far away from the man she was searching as possible. 'Gah... Have you never heard of soap, Lumpy? God Almighty.'

Logan's phone launched into its anonymous ringtone. 'McRae?'

'*Mr McRae, it's Sandy Moir-Farquharson.*' As if anyone else could own that oil-slick voice. '*I wanted to appraise you of our progress on your friend's case.*'

'Right.'

Calamity finished with Lumpy's top half, took a deep breath and started on the bottom.

'*Although the evidence against Detective Chief Inspector Steel is definitely there, we have managed to spot a number of procedural cracks in the way it was gathered and presented. There's enough technical variance here to make me confident we can get this whole unfortunate incident to go away.*'

'Aaagh...' Calamity flinched back from Lumpy's tracksuit bottoms. 'Why are you not wearing any underwear? God, it's all dangly.'

'That's great news. We—'

'*However, she still has the internal Professional Standards review to worry about and, sadly, their burden of proof is much lower than that required in the criminal courts. In all likelihood, they will find her guilty.*'

Ah. 'Right.'

'*This means she could face a fine, expulsion from the force, or demotion. But she certainly won't be going to prison.*'

At least that was something. 'Thank you.'

'*My pleasure. Our invoice will be in the post.*' And Hissing Sid was gone.

* * *

'All units be on the lookout for a silver Subaru Impreza last seen heading north from New Pitsligo on the A98. Suspected drink driver.'

Logan sat in the driver's seat, tapping his fingers on the steering wheel.

Meltwater dripped from the eaves and gutters of the buildings, the pavements all shiny – gold and green in the light spilling out of the Co-op's window.

'Update on that missing eighty-two-year-old: she's been found in New Aberdour, safe and well.'

Calamity hurried out of the shop, her arms full of assorted things. She hauled open the Big Car's door and clambered up into the passenger seat. 'Bleeding heck, it's *freezing* out there.' She held out a bottle of Lucozade and a paper bag. 'Last hot sausage roll in the cabinet.'

'Ta.' He took a swig, then a bite of mouth-scalding meat and pastry.

'Anyone in the vicinity of Scotstown Road, Fraserburgh? Reports of a domestic disturbance.'

She helped herself to what looked like a chicken slice, getting crumbs all down the front of her high-viz jacket. 'What time you taking your sister and her sexy sidekick down to Keith, Sarge?'

Logan raised an eyebrow. 'Fancy Narveer, do we, Constable Nicholson?'

A shrug, then more crumbs, talking with her mouth full. 'Wouldn't say no to a Singh-along.'

'Half six, you randy little sod.'

She checked the dashboard clock. 'Twenty minutes? Might go with you; maybe help our C Division brethren with their bags.'

Inspector McGregor's voice crackled out into the car. *'Bravo India to Shire Uniform Seven, safe to talk?'*

Logan pressed the button. 'Batter on, Guv.'

'William Campbell and Alastair Simmons are at it again. Tearing lumps out of each other outside the football club. Go give them a kick up the bum, will you?'

'Will do.' He started the engine and smiled at Calamity. 'I know this'll sound weird, but it's nice everything's back to normal again.'

Logan pulled into a parking bay and killed the engine. 'Here we go: five minutes to spare.'

The car park was pretty much empty at this time of the evening – the Big Car joining a couple of muddy four-by-fours and a small dented van. The building in front of them looked more like a convenience store on an industrial estate than a train station: a long metal shed with a grey pitched roof. Glass along one wall.

'Thanks.' Narveer climbed down from the back seat, closely followed by Calamity.

'Why don't I help you with the bags, DI Singh?' All bright and cheerful.

Hussy.

Harper lowered her voice to a whisper. 'Just between you and me, I think Narveer has a thing for your Constable Nicholson.'

Good luck to him – the poor sod would need it.

'Don't forget, you've only got seven minutes to change trains in Aberdeen.'

'You're taking this whole "big brother" thing seriously, aren't you?'

'And don't talk to any strange men.'

They got out and Logan humped her suitcase from the boot. Locked the car. Checked his watch. 'You need anything?'

'We'll be fine.'

They followed Calamity and Narveer to the platform, the wheels on Harper's case making clattering growls against the lock-block and paving slabs. A bitter wind whipped along the line, setting a couple of empty crisp packets dancing.

Logan stuck his hands in his pockets and watched them whirl. 'Before I forget: we got the forensics back on Martin Milne's car. Peter Shepherd's DNA was all over the boot, and the fibres from the bag over his head match the car's carpet.'

'Katie Milne still no-commenting?'

'Changed her plea to diminished responsibility.'

'Probably for the best. No sane person bashes three people's heads in, then stuffs sleeping pills down her six-year-old's throat.' Harper shook her head. 'You know she's not asked about Ethan once? And you think your mother's bad.'

Narveer and Calamity were down the other end of the platform, sharing a joke about something. The pair of them laughing like drains.

All right for some.

'Niamh?' Logan looked off down the tracks. 'Reuben's gone missing.'

'I know.'

'He's going to come after us. Might take him a while, but he's not a forgive-and-forget sort of guy.'

She stuck her chin out. 'So, let him come.'

'Look … keep an eye out, OK? If something happens to me, you'll know he's back.'

Harper stuck her hands in her pockets and hunched her shoulders against the wind. 'You're a strange fish, Sergeant McRae. You handed your old boss to Professional Standards because she broke the law, but you're on first-name terms with gangsters. I'm not sure what to make of that.'

'Yeah, neither am I.'

High-pitched twangs sang their way along the rails, getting louder.

Logan cleared his throat. 'I'm sorry our father wasn't more on your side.'

'I'm sorry he abandoned you and your brother.'

Not much they could do about that now.

The train roared into view, slowing as it approached the station, its blue, pink, and white livery streaked with filth. A bleeping, then the doors hissed open.

'Right, well, this is us.' She stepped back. Stuck out her hand for shaking. 'It's been … different.'

He ignored the hand and hefted her case onboard instead. 'Don't leave it another thirty-four years.' Then took a deep breath and gave her a hug.

A moment passed, then she hugged him back.

Kind of awkward, but it was a start.

54

'Tufty, you in the vicinity of Portsoy? We've got another fire in a wheelie bin.' Logan took the Big Car on a slow drift through New Pitsligo.

'Can be in fifteen, Sarge.'

'Maybe this time someone will have seen something.' Rows and rows of little grey Scottish houses with dormer windows and slate roofs. 'Any luck with the dogs?'

'Work in progress: you know what these Dogmen scummers are like. Everyone hates everyone else, but they're too scared to dob each other in.'

'Friday, remember?' A few chunks of snow clung in the lee of buildings, the drifts gone from pristine white to grit-flecked piddly yellow.

'Balls in a vice, Sarge.'

'Good boy.' On the right, the houses gave way to dark fields and the bones of trees. And then it was just farmland, skulking beneath the light of a miser's moon.

'Hold on, Calamity wants a word.'

'It's not a phone, Tufty, she's...' What was the point? 'Put her on.'

'Sarge? Are we aiming for tenses?' She lowered her voice. *'Only we've still got visitors.'*

'Napier hasn't gone home?'

'Tell you, even Hector's scared to go upstairs.'

'Don't care: Bingo baked a cake. We're having tenses.'

'Sarge.'

'Now go do something productive.'

The road straightened out, the tyres hissing through the meltwater.

A badger flashed by at the side of the road, the top half of it anyway. The rest was smeared into a dark-red paste on the tarmac, glistening in the headlights then disappearing into the darkness.

How long would it be before Reuben got over his bullet in the head?

Any normal person would have had the good grace to die, but not Reuben. Not with a solid granite skull.

Three weeks? Four?

Probably be in a wheelchair for the rest of his life, but that wouldn't stop him. OK, so he might not be up to swinging the hammer *himself* any more, that didn't mean he couldn't have fun watching.

'*All units be on the lookout for a turquoise Vauxhall Astra in the Pennan area. Driver acting suspiciously.*'

'It's not fair.'

The Logan in the rear-view mirror nodded. 'We shot him in the head. In the *head*.'

'Got no business being alive.'

He drummed his fingers on the steering wheel. 'So what are we going to do about it?'

'What *can* we do?'

'Track him down and finish the job.'

'And how are we going to do that, Officer Rambo? You heard Napier: they've got all of Police Scotland hunting for him. Think you can do better?'

'*Sierra Two-Two to Control, you can tell the ambulance there's no rush on that OAP. Better get the pathologist up.*'

'And what's going to happen if you *do* manage to find Reuben? Murder him in cold blood?'

530

'I shot him in the face.'

'Yeah, to save your sister. But in cold blood? what happened last time?'

Logan's shoulders dipped. 'I am so screwed.'

'You're too much of a wimp. Couldn't sleep for da wards.'

True.

Fields and trees, as far as the eye could see.

'*Anyone seen Stinky Sammy Wilson on their travels? Sus, breaking and entering on Gellymill Street, Macduff.*'

The countryside flattened out, widening the pale-grey vi

All that heartache and soul-searching and falling off sodding cliff for nothing.

The road into Lovie's came up on the right, and Logan pulled onto the apron. Sat there with the engine running, frowning out at the night.

Of course, *one* person would know where Reuben was.

Logan pulled out his phone and called John Urquhart.

It rang, and rang, and rang, and rang...

'*Yellow?*'

'It's Logan.'

'*Mr McRae? Dude. Heard you beat the shooting rap, congrats.*'

'Reuben's missing.'

'*Yeah. Shame about that.*' There was something in the background: a snuffling grunting noise, as if a lot of people had the cold. '*Still, on the bright side, things are settling down again. And no war, which is cool.*'

'He's going to come after me.'

'*Nah, he's really not. Hand on heart, Reuben's never going to bother you, or anyone else, ever again.*' More snuffling. Then what sounded like squealing, getting louder and more excited.

'Urquhart? Why can I hear—'

'*Listen, I know you don't want to step into Mr Mowat's shoes, but you don't mind if I do, yeah? I figure it's what he would've wanted. Bit of common sense and continuity, and stuff.*'

OK, that was definitely a scream.

'Urquhart—'

'Anyway, got to go. There's an old mate I need to see off.'

ogan slotted the Big Car in between a patrol car with a flat tyre and the Postman Pat van. Both of them needed a damn good wash – could barely see the Police Scotland logo on the sides.

Banff station loomed above him, in all its ominous glory. The lights were on way up there on the top floor. That would be Napier in the Major Incident Room, tidying up loose ends. Fashioning them into nooses.

Yeah, well, maybe some people deserved to hang.

'And you're one of them.'

Mirror Logan scowled back at him. 'Shut up.'

'You sacrificed Steel for the sake of your grubby bloodstained "integrity" and here you are up to your neck in organized crime.'

'I'm not up to my neck in anything.'

'And they want to give you a job in Professional Standards?'

'I haven't done anything wrong.'

'Of course not. Other than entering into a conspiracy to commit murder. Culpable homicide. Failure to report a death. Possession of an illegal firearm. Attempted murder. And multiple counts of conspiracy to pervert the course of justice. Other than that, you're *golden*.'

He folded forward and rested his head on the steering wheel. Biting his bottom lip.

'Yes, but I got away with it.'

'That doesn't make it *better*. You're not a police officer any more, you're a...' Logan sighed. Then sat up. 'I don't know what you are.'

'Neither do I.'

A smile spread across his face. 'Why don't we go and find out?'

He climbed out of the car and let himself in through the tradesman's entrance.

The station was quiet, just the hum and buzz of the vending machines in the canteen to break the silence. He straightened his back and marched through the main office. Up the stairs to the top floor.

Took a deep breath.

And knocked on Napier's door.